THE EDGECOMBE DIARIES

NELL YOUNG

Print edition ISBN: 9781916245105
Ebook edition ISBN: 9781916245112

Produced by Throwleigh Press in Great Britain

For my lovely Mum and Dad.
In my heart always.

PART ONE

AUTUMN TERM

CHAPTER ONE

1972

WEDNESDAY 26TH JULY

My secret was finally out!

It began like any other day of the long summer holidays. Tessa and I were playing on our bikes down Mill Lane. We rode past Leslie Parker's house, the largest and newest in the lane. Tessa spent half her time telling me how snobby she thought the Parkers were. Come to think of it, she said everyone who was new to the village was a snob. As we circled round on the dirt track outside Leslie's double gates, skidding our bike wheels and kicking up clouds of dust, the front door burst open. Leslie shot out of her doorway and came tearing down the drive yelling our names. Scrambling up onto her gate she called us over.

She perched on the edge of the gate swinging her legs and started babbling away about us all starting new schools in September. I began to get an uncomfortable queasy feeling in the pit of my stomach. True to form, she flicked her hair over her shoulder, stared straight at me, drew a deep breath and landed me right in it.

"I know where you're going to school in September!" she spat.

1

My mouth went dry and Tessa glared at me.

"What's she talking about, Lara?"

I shrugged as casually as I could, pretended I didn't know what she was talking about and attempted to change the subject. Leslie clearly knew Tessa was unaware of my impending departure from the village. She revelled in my discomfort and was like a dog with a bone.

"Why don't you tell her? You're such a chicken."

I swallowed hard, praying she'd put a stop to my misery, but no such luck.

She took a long breath, pursed her lips and, drawing her eyebrows together, let the cat out of the bag.

"Why don't you just tell her you're going to BALLET SCHOOL?"

For a brief moment there was utter silence. It felt like the world had gone into slow motion. Tessa's face was a study with her chin dropped to the floor and Leslie smirked. The deed was done and now there was no going back. In my desperate need to escape, I lost my balance and fell unceremoniously into the dirt.

"Why didn't you tell me?" Tessa said with a nasty glare.

Trying to regain my dignity from ground level, I struggled to push the bike off my legs.

"I was going to," I muttered, flinching as the pedals grazed the skin off my shin, "I just hadn't had a chance."

Tessa scowled.

Leslie called Tessa over and whispered conspiratorially to her. I saw my escape route, leapt on my bike and, pedalling like a lunatic, raced home without looking back.

I then realised that at long last I would be able to get away from Tessa and have a chance to make new friends, girls who would all have something in common and wouldn't get catty and jealous like Tessa. I would finally escape being bullied, teased and sent to Coventry. It would be so great not having to hide from my friends that I wanted to do something different from everyone else and become a ballet dancer!

CHAPTER TWO

Only eighteen days to go before leaving home and starting my life at ballet school. I had no idea what it would be like, but I was sure it would be loads of fun. I had so many things I needed to get to take away with me but didn't know how I was ever going to get everything ready in time!

I was eleven years and two months old. I had to pinch myself because I still couldn't believe that I had been accepted to start training to be a ballet dancer, and at one of the best ballet schools in the country. I'd been attending weekly classes at Stavely Brookes Ballet School for almost four years. I loved going there more than anything and soon I would be living there as a full-time boarder.

For the millionth time, I flicked through the glossy photos in the school's prospectus. There was a photo of the huge main house and another of the vast studio inside, with its full length mirrors and wooden ballet barres all the way round the back and side walls.

This was where I did my ballet classes. The main building was beautiful - Mum and Dad always said it looked like a stately home. Dad knew about buildings because he was an architect. There was a large pointy tower at one end of the main house

4

and two turrets at the opposite end. The school's grounds were massive with a picturesque lake, woodland and a theatre where the school presented performances. Mum and Aunty Ellen took me to one of the school's summer shows at the theatre and the show was brilliant. The girls performed 'La Fille Mal Gardee', which was the first ballet that I ever saw at Covent Garden. Aunty Ellen showed me a newspaper cutting from a review in the Telegraph. It said that the school had put on a first class performance and even named a dancer who was leaving to join the Royal Ballet Company. I was in awe, and couldn't wait to start full-time.

THURSDAY 24TH AUGUST

I saw Tessa from my bedroom window today walking down the road with Leslie. I didn't feel upset that she wasn't my friend any more. I told Mum if I'd had the guts I would have invited them in and shown them the prospectus for my new school. Mum said it was best not to rub their noses in it and to leave it all behind. She told me to save my energy for things that were worth it. Mum was always right!

I wondered whether my regular ballet teacher, Miss Fisher, would still teach me when I became a boarder. Mum reminded me I ought to write her a thank-you letter for giving me extra coaching before my ballet school audition. After all, it was Miss Fisher who told Mum I should audition for a place when I turned eleven. She obviously thought I had some talent. My sister said that my talent was for being annoying because I was always spinning around and breaking things. I was glad I managed to get a scholarship for the school fees. I had seen the cost in the brochure and it was loads of money.

Dad asked if this was what I really wanted to do. I promised him I wanted this more than anything ever in the whole history of mankind and this made him laugh!

I hoped I wouldn't have to do any more of those horrible dancing assessments up at the Royal Academy in London. During my assessment, three women and an angry looking man made me do a lot of my Grade III Ballet exercises plus a few which were much more difficult. This was followed by another teacher who looked Spanish coming into the studio. She demonstrated some dance steps and then taught me some tricky combinations. After that she examined my 'turn-out' and then turned me sideways-on to the other four. I had to stand there for ages while they talked about me as if I wasn't there! Finally they made me do 'improvisation'. The pianist played some music, which I was allowed to listen to - once - then I had to dance. With their beady eyes fixed on me my mind went blank for a moment, but the music had started so I ended up using all the steps from the dances I'd done with Miss Fisher in ballet class. I even attempted a small 'Grande Jété' leap; this was a really bad move as when my feet hit the ground they made such a horrible thumping noise it sounded more like a crash landing! The lady with the glasses made me point my left foot very hard. She looked disappointed and asked if I could stretch it harder. I felt like saying NO, unless you want it to drop off. She tried again, asking if I could make it look as nice as my other foot. I guessed that this meant I'd have to practise extra hard with my left 'pointe' before I started school. EEEK!

SUNDAY 27TH AUGUST

Sixteen days left to go! Mum and I sorted out all my school uniform, dance kit, night clothes and bed linen. The list went on forever and included extras like clothes for the end-of-term Christmas party, wellies and plimsolls.

Granny, Grandpa and Aunty Ellen Edgecombe came down from London yesterday to see us. Aunty Ellen did ballet when she was younger and was very musical. She said she would still be able to take Mum, Lily and me to the Opera House in Covent Garden to see ballets, but now we would have to go in the school holidays. Aunty Ellen said I would probably be seeing lots of ballets anyway as part of the dance training. I would have to get used to sitting in the stalls and not in her 'special box'. We were dead lucky as Aunty Ellen had use of a box at the Opera House and once or twice a year she took us with her. This was where I had first dreamt of becoming a ballet dancer.

To get my school uniform, Mum and I made a special trip last week to a big shop in London called Bourne and Hollingsworth. It was full of very posh people and there was a ginormous department just for school uniforms. Stavely Brookes' colours were grey and maroon. Mum thought it was smart - I thought it was cringing and deadly old fashioned. We were assigned to a very snooty shop assistant who was the supervisor. She asked Mum for her school list and gave an approving snort when she saw it was Stavely Brookes. She called Mum 'Madam'.

"Of course, Madam realises that all Brookes gals are quite the young ladies, and the ballet school uniform is very refined bla-bla-bla."

I must have glazed over as I watched the various items of grey and maroon clothing forming an ever-growing mountain on the counter. Twin sets, flannel skirts, blazer, blouses, tie, raincoat, big overcoat, grey flannel knickers, vests, woolly socks, bowler hat, summer dresses, berets with a pom-pom on top, plus the obligatory tuck box and travel trunk.

"Oh, and Madam must remember that the gals," she couldn't seem to say 'girls', "must never wear their skirts more than two inches above the knee, no more and no less."

Mum looked drained and I was sure her purse was too. She politely asked if two coats were really necessary. The supervisor gave a tolerant look followed by a tight-lipped smile.

"Of course, if one can't *manage*," she placed a certain emphasis on this word, "the luxury of two coats, I suppose one can *make do*," she looked positively pained at this description, "by wearing a blazer with a raincoat worn over the top, so to speak, to withstand the draughts."

Mum held her ground and followed up with, "The Travel Trunk and Tuck Box are largely superfluous to our needs, as fortunately we already possess these from her older sister who has just left boarding school."

Supervisor's face was a picture. In one sentence my mother had flattened her. Looking flustered, the supervisor busied herself with amending the bill.

Mum and I had a fit of giggles in the lift. I asked Mum how she kept a straight face and she said, "You can't buy breeding. That 'supervisor' lady needed putting in her place."

Smiling, Mum grabbed my hand. "And our next stop is St Martins Lane and Freeds!"

Freeds sold dance kit and weren't snobby. A much nicer girl served us and fitted me with pink satin ballet shoes, leather ballet shoes, pink tights for ballet and black footless tights for modern dance, long sleeved V necked leotards, plus a short half-skirt called a 'frill'. The lady made Mum laugh, saying the frill was good because it concealed your bum-cheeks if they hung out of your leotard! The kit supply was never ending. I had to force my feet into some ugly pointed-toe red leather character shoes, black Oxford tap shoes and a swirly skirt for national dance. I was hoping I'd get pointe shoes, but the girl told me that special pointe shoe-fitters visited the school regularly and my teacher would be there to check the shoes were right for my feet. Finally I was fully kitted out and Mum breathed a sigh of relief.

While we were shopping Dad had been busy making this majorly cool tuck box for me. It came to me by way of our vicar 'Little John', who was six foot seven inches tall. Little John was close friends with Mum and Dad and godfather to my younger brothers, Benjamin and Samuel. He was visiting Mum and Dad last week and came into the hall with a blanket-covered bundle under his arm. We eyed the bundle with suspicion as Dad took Little John into the sitting room, and we all gathered round as he placed the large covered bundle on the floor and dramatically swept the blanket back to unveil what lay beneath. On the carpet lay this extraordinary trunk that I could only describe as a pirate's treasure chest. It had a huge bowed lid with black hinges and would make any theatrically inclined junior proud. Dad was going to refurbish it 'Edgecombe' style with my initials on the front. No chance of mistaken identity then and more fitting than the Bourne and Hollingsworth standard boring tuck boxes.

I was amazed that there was so much gear. I had candy-striped bed linen and two peachy blankets, which were a present from Mrs Furst, Mum's German friend from across the road. Mrs Furst was rich and always passed on brand new things which she bought and then never used. Dad gave me his favourite army blanket so I was taking a bit of history with me. I asked Grandpa Edgecombe if he'd let me take his helmet from World War One - it had a bullet hole in it which had missed his head by a fraction - but Grandpa thought it may upset the other girls. He said a family photo on my bedside locker would be nicer than an old relic from the Great War! Mum gave me a vast cuddly toy, which might take up half my bed and reminded me of a drawing of the 'March Hare' in my Alice in Wonderland book. It was quirky with huge ears, enormous hips and a harlequin covering from the waist downwards.

I made sure to get loads of writing paper, envelopes and stamps as I would have plenty to write home about. I had masses of hair elastics, pins, grips and a giant hairspray for getting my slippery long hair into a neat bun.

Last, but not least, was my trusty yellow leather 'Philco' radio with ear plug for private listening and my diddy 'Ever Ready' pocket torch. Hopefully we'll be allowed these after lights out. I was a bit worried about having non-regulation items because I didn't want to get into trouble. The grey flannel knickers that the supervisor lady conned Mum into buying were itchy and as a result Mum bought me some fakes; grey Ladybird look-alikes made out of soft cotton.

Mrs Furst had knitted me two pairs of revolutionary looking leg warmers. They were majorly long, stretching from ankle to crutch, in baby pink and deep purple. With thick ribbing, they were the business.

I hadn't thought about this much and I knew I would miss my family, but I didn't feel they would be very far away. We would get two Visiting Days each term and half term, so I didn't expect to be homesick. I was well prepared… or so I thought!

CHAPTER THREE

SUNDAY 10TH SEPTEMBER

Today I started my life as a ballet boarder!

I was now officially at ballet school, sat on my bottom bunk writing my journal. I started thinking about how much I had longed for a single bed when I got here, only to find I was back on another bottom bunk. Mum, Dad and I arrived at 2 o'clock this afternoon. I felt very excited and jittery as we drove into the school entrance and it started to dawn on me that this was finally it! Mum was nattering away to Dad and the cars in the long approach drive were stuck in a queue. We had stopped alongside a massive dark wooden sign with gold letters declaring: 'Stavely Brookes Ballet School - Victoria Spires'.

The 'Spires' were the single and double turrets at either end of the main house. Opposite this notice was a little gate house which stood guard over the main entrance like a mini watch tower. As we inched along I looked at the colourful flowering bushes lining the driveway. Our convoy moved slowly like a giant snake in a grand procession. We passed a car park with a sign saying 'Theatre Parking' on our right, and another driveway leading to the theatre on our left. As we approached the main house the cars started to disperse. Dad drove further down the winding driveway and parked near the tennis courts.

11

There were masses of girls milling around in uniform, and men lugging suitcases and dragging the hefty school trunks. All of a sudden I was standing in the junior dormitory. We seemed to have arrived without me even walking here!

As I looked around I noticed lots of anxious looking girls. The Dads were leaving and the Mums were occupied with helping girls unpack. Mum and Dad had already made my bed up and I could see my funny March Hare stuck inside the bed sheets, its ears poking up in the air. Mum asked me if I needed anything else, then they were both hugging me and saying goodbye, telling me they'd see me soon. I watched them from the dormitory window as they walked towards the car and I had an overwhelming feeling of panic and for some reason had an urge to chase after them. I was saved from myself by the girl on my top bunk. She swung her legs over the edge of the bed just as I turned away from the window and hit me square in the boobs with her feet.

By the time we'd finished giggling and apologising, we'd swapped names and Mum and Dad had long gone. Abbey Cameron was going to be my bunk-buddy and first new friend. She wanted to be a ballet dancer too. She also adored Marc Bolan as much as I did and had two older brothers. We made a pact to look out for each other.

Our huge dorm, for juniors only, was built on top of a large mirrored dance studio. This grey, ugly building reminded me of the old army camp building where I used to attend Brownies. It was an oblong shaped room with twenty-two identical beds in it. The dorm had two bunks at the far corners, two single beds between these bunks which were under the window at the bottom end, and eight more single beds up either side. The walls were covered in bright pink and purple flower-power wallpaper. Our travel rugs folded at the ends of our beds made the room feel more homely. The end nearest the entrance stairs had curtains covering a clothes-hanging space and above that were loads of pigeon-holes for us to store the rest of our school uniform and dance kit. The other side of the entrance door had a line of mirrors, with a long dressing table and wooden stools where we could sit and do our hair in ballet buns.

Just before the Junior Dorm entrance were two smaller rooms. One had two bunks in and was called little dorm, and on the opposite side of this landing was a room with a gold plaque on the door saying 'Junior Matron', who we were to call Nanny. Nanny told us she was our house mother. She was quite old and plump. She had a Yorkshire terrier called Hamish, who obediently followed her up and down the dorm like a remote control dog.

Next door to our bunk was a tall blonde girl called Millie Dwight, who came from Tobago in the West Indies. While we were unpacking I noticed twin girls enter the dorm. They were completely identical, seemed to know everybody and were very loud. One of the other girls had a mother with a scary hairdo which looked like a giant beehive. Another new girl - Gabriella Pagoni - had an argument with her Mum when they were unpacking. Her Mum, who was very large and dressed head to toe in black, went red in the face and shouted at Gabriella saying she'd forgotten to pack her dance kit. The other Mums all looked embarrassed. To make it worse, Gabriella started crying. I didn't think she would miss her Mum.

At 5-30 p.m. when everyone had finished unpacking, Nanny gathered all twenty-six juniors in a long crocodile line. We

13

marched two-by-two over to the main house where we queued for tea in a tunnel of narrow dark corridors. These corridors started at the top of some deep stone steps on the outer-side of the main house which led down in to a damp basement, which in turn snaked through an underground corridor, up more narrow stairs into a maze-like, panelled corridor and led eventually in to a neon-lit canteen. Every so often, our queuing boredom was broken by older girls coming to nose at who the new juniors were. One girl said I looked cute and they all stared at me saying they loved my fringe. Everyone was so friendly. I'd been so used to Tessa's bullying that I'd forgotten plenty of other nice girls existed. I felt too shy to tell the girls because it was my first day, but my fringe was really there to cover my birthmark which, although faded, had still not completely disappeared. Straight after my audition here Miss Brookes said I'd have to grow out my fringe, but when I showed her my birthmark she said I could keep the fringe until the birthmark disappeared. I was the only girl I'd seen so far with a fringe, so the other girls must have wondered why I had one. Back in the dorm a new girl called Dulcie Fielding introduced herself. She said she'd been told to grow out her fringe before starting school as ballet dancers don't have fringes! Oh dear…

Supper arrived sometime after 7 p.m. when older girls wearing name badges brought steaming metal jugs of cocoa into the dorm and trays of iced buns. Tonight lights out would be half-an-hour later because it was our first night. A couple of the girls started crying just before lights out. I tried to cheer Millie up, but there was no consoling her. She said it was her parents' idea she boarded and only travelled home during holidays. I must look up Tobago on a map.

CHAPTER FOUR

MONDAY 11TH SEPTEMBER

Today was crazy busy. At 7 o'clock this morning we were woken by the loudest alarm bell in the world. The bell was situated above the dorm door and sounded louder than if you were standing beside church bells in a bell tower. Everyone buried their heads under their pillows. We were all dog-tired. Not surprising really. Half the dorm spent all night crying, while the rest of us spent all night trying to cheer up the weeping masses. When the deafening alarm finally stopped I could still hear stifled sobs from beneath Millie's pillow.

When we were dressing Nanny came in with a vast laundry bag, called us into a group and told us we had to each take a new pinafore. She dug deep into the bag and held a pinny up so we could all see what they looked like. Then, with a sweep of the hand, she pulled one of the unsuspecting twins forward to demonstrate how to put it on. These 'pinnies' were revolting. According to Nanny they were made 'especially for juniors' and were unlike any apron I had ever seen before. Perhaps Alice in Wonderland might have worn one (with a gun to her head). My mother must be psychic - so this is why she got me March Hare. The pinnies had absolutely no fashion credibility and were royal blue with ghastly frills down each side. Their purpose, Nanny informed us, was to keep our school uniform spotless. I could only assume that previous juniors must have dribbled.

Nanny was a hard task-master – she breathed down our necks while we got ready as though we were on some military drill. Our morning wake-up routine was like an assault course: sinks - flannels - wash - rinse - teeth - spit - dry - next!

We arrived exhausted at the main house for an 8 a.m. breakfast with Nanny and Hamish following our every step. Why the rush I didn't know, as we still had the same long queue to wait for breakfast. In the canteen was a very old man with a large chef's hat perched on his head. He was serving cereal and his name was Burt. He told us that whatever we wanted to know about the school we should ask him. Jabbing his bony finger at his chest he leaned right over the canteen until I felt his hot breath on my face and said, "I'm your man." He looked positively ancient. The twins had warned us to watch what we said to Burt because he was the school snitch. This morning I noticed that the tea trays smelled horrible, the tea was lukewarm and the toast was soggy because the margarine had soaked into it. No wonder, when the toast was piled high like a mountain. I must remember to ask Mum to get me a jar of Bovril. I had seen some of the older girls holding jars of it in the breakfast queue. Maybe it disguised the foul tasting margarine.

At 9-30 a.m. sharp we had our first assembly in the main hall. It went on all morning. We stood up so long I felt faint - and one girl did actually faint - lucky escape! Finally at the end of assembly there was a hush, when the pianist nodded towards the teachers and everyone broke into singing the school song. I didn't yet know it and we weren't given any hymn sheets to follow. It was unlike the hymns at my primary school, and even less like the hymns I'd sung in the church choir at home. It had some funny Latin words in the main chorus. Everyone, particularly the teachers and prefects, squared their shoulders and looked proud and serious.

Lunch followed soon afterwards in the main hall. It was like a mad cattle market, full of long tables and shouting girls. There was some kind of crazy food exchange system going on throughout the meal which went something like this:

When you didn't like your food you stood, held your plate high in the air and yelled, "Quiz chips."

If you wanted to claim these chips you bellowed at the top of your voice "Eggo," meaning you wanted those chips.

The first girl to scream "Eggo" got the chips.

When you claimed your chips, the 'Quizzer' of the chips would say "Veins!"

Veins meant the chips were yours. Decide you then didn't like the look of them? Hard luck, because there were no returns. 'Veins' meant they were yours - forever - infinity and beyond!

At 3-15 p.m. all of us juniors gathered again in the main hall, this time for organising and making copies of our school and dance timetables. It became a frenzied task with girls crammed at tables, papers flying everywhere and teachers with irritated raised voices. They finally managed to coordinate two hours of dance classes a day, on top of school work, for each girl. We had at least one hour of ballet a day, two hours of modern dance a week, two hours of tap and one hour of national dance. One new girl was put in the advanced tap class called Gold Star. The rest of us were beginners.

Even with students helping us we didn't finish until after 5 o'clock. My student was called Rose. Shirley and Rowan (the

17

twins) came up to Rose when she was helping me and kept distracting her. I felt embarrassed and awkward. Hannah Greenwood, one of the older juniors who'd been there at least a year, said Rose was the best dancer in the school and told me the twins had a 'crush' on her. Hannah warned all the girls at our table not to be too friendly with Rose because the twins wouldn't like it! I didn't know what a 'crush' was, but I was going to find out, and FAST!

Back in Junior Dorm before tea, Hannah was busy organizing a 'New Girls Ceremony'. She told us we would have to take it in turns to stand on our beds and then say our name, age, where we came from and how many brothers and sisters we each had. I was in the middle of my speech when the tea bell 'siren' went off. Hannah then made me start all over again. How hateful was that? By the time we'd got through everyone we were late for tea but missed the queues.

The basement where we joined the food queue was called 'The Dive'. It had a dingy Tuck Room where the Tweenies (middle school girls living in the main house) kept their tuck boxes. There was also a boiler room which Hannah said was Burt's secret hideout, a drinks machine, an old pay telephone stuck on the wall inside a battered chipboard booth, a piano room where girls had private piano lessons, some seriously grotty toilets and a day girls' changing room which was so dark it looked like Dracula's lair. With layers of pipes running along the low ceilings, the Dive was more like dungeons. It felt damp and the pipes dripped on you as you waited in the meal queue. I noticed many girls brought books and sat on the Dive floor reading as we waited for our food.

When we grabbed our trays tonight Burt joked saying we had 'kippers and custard' for tea. It was almost as bad. Frankfurters and sauerkraut. PUKE! Sauerkraut was truly disgusting and the 'Quizzing' in the main hall was frenzied. There wasn't a single 'Eggo' to be heard!

When we walked back to Junior Dorm, a younger junior called Paula showed us the 'long-way' back. This was known as the 'Covered Way' running parallel to the drive and it had a long line of school huts on either side. The Covered Way was a pathway with a domed roof of clear corrugated plastic which ran the whole length of the pathway. It went right up to Junior Dorm. Running either side of the domed roof and straight across these arches were metal support poles, positioned at regular intervals like monkey bars. Paula said they were strong enough to swing on, but it was against school rules so to make sure no one was watching. School classrooms (wooden huts) were on either side of a path which led to the art room, staff room and headmistress's office. Hidden behind bushes close by was a wooden summerhouse which was our 'Tuck-House'. It was exclusively for junior tuck boxes, and was opened up once a day, mid-morning, for starving juniors. 'Tuck-House' held all our supplies of biscuits, chocolate, sweets, tinned fruit and cakes. Being very close to Junior Dorm Nanny guarded the keys. It reminded me of Hansel and Gretel's Cottage.

Off to the side of Tuck-House we passed a rickety hut with a battered tin roof called 'Wash House'. Paula said they nicknamed it 'Scrub House', or 'Scrubs' for short. This was where the older girls did their washing by hand. Lucky juniors have Nanny who uses the washing machine - one of the few benefits of being a junior.

When we got back to the dorm, a girl called Esme Giles had a circle of girls around her. She was telling them she lived in Kenya, East Africa, so she could only go home during holidays.

I felt sorry for Esme and Millie and was glad my parents didn't live abroad.

We had been given a bath rota and were either allowed to have a bath or a strip-wash. This happened on alternate nights. Tonight was my turn to strip-wash. I was dreading it when Maddy, Abbey and I headed off for our first strip-wash in the ancient bathroom downstairs. The bathroom had two baths which stood on curved legs. There were three sinks with old rusty mirrors above them. Nanny had us on a military timed conveyor belt, and it was too bad if you were shy. As soon as we got to the bathroom it was clothes off and scrub-up! The bathroom wasn't heated so it was freezing. As we washed I noticed that on the far side of the bathroom wall was a cracked window. Beyond this was a dark wood. Goodness knows why, but Nanny insisted on flinging open the window to 'let the steam out', letting all the moths and daddy long-legs inside. It was my idea of sheer hell - starkers, dripping wet with flapping insects swarming everywhere.

An American girl called Sydney Tyler lay submerged in a bath as we manically tried to duck the invading insects. During this chaos Nanny was summoned upstairs. Immediately she disappeared, Sydney wasted no time. Leaping out of the water, she grabbed a bottle of 'Badidas' from her dressing gown pocket and emptied the glossy green liquid into the steaming bath. We gawked. Sydney had the hugest boobs ever. She gave us a sympathetic look when Abbey asked if Nanny allowed bubble bath, and proceeded to tell us 'THE RULES'.

As we stood shivering and completely naked, she informed us in her silky American drawl that, sadly for us, new girls *were* just that, simply 'new girls'. She said we had to do our time and do as we were told. I wondered how long this would be for and she must have read my thoughts. A whole year.

Maddy bravely asked why we had to wait a whole year and Sydney's eyebrows met in the middle as she replied.

"It takes a year to earn the title of 'old' girl, idiot!"

I couldn't think of anything to answer back but could feel my face flush red. We desperately tried to speed up de-soaping ourselves before Nanny's return.

Sydney took full advantage of her naked audience. Sweeping the green bubbles over her huge boobs she had our undivided attention. Naked, shivering and caked in soap we were at a distinct disadvantage. She continued with her 'old girl' crusade.

"If you get cheeky, you can be punished."

"How?"

"A Glitto bath," she replied triumphantly. She flashed her perfect white teeth, giving us a dazzling smile. Pulling the plug from her bath she emerged from the green foam glistening.

Then fate intervened. Nanny swept in, scowled directly at the bathtub and demanded to know where the green foam had come from. She rounded on Sydney. It was grim. We saw our chance to escape and, grabbing our dressing gowns, we fled upstairs as the sounds of a terrifying argument shook the bathroom and corridor walls.

For supper we had Ovaltine and malted milk biscuits. Esme Giles had the Osmonds playing full blast on her tape recorder. I thought Donny Osmond was cheesy. He was singing 'Puppy Love'. GROAN! I wished I had my own tape recorder so I could play some decent music.

I needed to find out pretty quickly:

1) What was a Glitto bath?

2) What a 'crush' was?

Nanny gave us a five minute warning before she turned the lights out. My radio was tuned in to Radio One with the ear plug installed. I guiltily hoped it would block out the sound of Millie crying. I felt exhausted from lack of sleep. I bet Margot Fonteyn never had these problems.

CHAPTER FIVE

TUESDAY 12TH SEPTEMBER

This morning the deafening sound of the alarm bell blasted out for nearly a minute. I knew because I timed it. If you didn't get out of bed, Nanny came and prodded you. Then, on her second round of the dorm, she'd yank the bed sheets off you. Nobody waited for the third round. I was half expecting her to set Hamish onto Hannah, who wouldn't budge for ages.

Later, Hannah told me that Millie had grizzled until 3 a.m. Millie's face told the whole story; eyes all swollen and face red and blotchy. It wasn't a good look.

Today was our first day of school work. We all arrived late to our school hut, having been sent in the wrong direction by a third year girl. In the mad dive to claim the best desk positions, I ended up with the desk nearest to the door. I couldn't believe it when I turned round to see who else was in our form and I was face to face with my Saturday morning ballet buddy Kerri Legge, all dressed up in school uniform. We were both as surprised as each other and speechless. Then we both blurted out, "What are you doing here?" and burst out laughing.

At this point the teacher arrived and banged on the desk. She introduced herself as Miss Bell. Her face was as white as a sheet, with hair pulled back in a low bun and thin, pencilled-on eyebrows. She scanned round the class and gave us a tight-lipped smile, telling us she would be our form and maths teacher for the next year. When she asked if we were all happy with our seating positions, Kerri jumped up and asked if she could change her place and sit in the desk next to me! We shuffled until everyone was happy. The old-fashioned desks had deeply grooved carvings of desperate messages and slogans like 'no escape', 'I love my crush' and 'Alice Cooper is mine'. I made another mental note to put the 'crush' mystery to the top of my 'FIND OUT FAST' list. The desks had ancient inkwells at the top right hand side which looked well used. Our desks were arranged around three sides of the room, facing inwards on the two long sides, and along the back wall facing straight towards the teacher's desk. Miss Bell banged on her desk to restore order.

She told us that there had been a larger than normal intake of new girls this autumn.

"As a direct result of this, Year One has to be split in two. The new intake eleven year olds and anyone younger will become 'Prep' form."

An audible gasp erupted from the many eleven year olds, me included, who felt they had earned their Year One position simply by leaving primary school. 'Prep form' sounded more like 'mistake form' to me! Miss Bell - sensing unrest - lamely added,

"During the next year you will be assessed and eventually placed in the correct classes according to your abilities and ages". Before we had time to protest, she descended on us with printed timetables, handed out large sheets of pink blotting paper and asked Paula to pour ink into the inkwells. I was glad I'd remembered my Parker Italic fountain pen. Sydney handed out exercise books, then text books and by then the subject of forms seemed to have been all but forgotten. Not, however, by me. I was infuriated.

This morning was boring. We put our names inside books, sorted out pens and ordered basic equipment for girls who'd forgotten to bring things like compasses.

During the mid-morning break Kerri and I burst into questioning each other. Unknown to me, she'd also auditioned here on the advice of Miss Fisher but didn't need to board as she only lived a five minute drive away. Kerri was a day girl and I was so happy she was here; we'd been doing Saturday morning classes together for years and taken every single ballet exam together. I showed her the Tuck-House and she admired my pirate style box, saying it was outrageously cool! Having overheard Kerri, all the other juniors now wanted one identical. Dad was a genius.

At lunch time I decided to show Kerri the ropes, explaining the intricate system of the 'Quiz' and 'Eggo' food trading. After eating lunch Kerri said the food was vile and if I got desperate she'd bring me survival supplies from home!

Before afternoon school started she showed me inside the day girls' changing room, which was cold and damp. I told Kerri she'd have to come to the Junior Dorm with me tomorrow as it was so much nicer.

We had a real French teacher this afternoon called Madame Nuffer. She was chic in what I imagined was a French way. Speaking softly with her French accent we could barely understand her, but I was not happy with what I did understand. She explained that because nobody had studied French at primary school, we'd all begin learning together. What Madame Nuffer didn't know was that I'd studied French at primary school for four years! Not wanting to appear an egghead, I cleared my throat and cautiously put my hand up to inform her.

"I've studied French." I felt horribly conspicuous.

"Combien de temps?" She raised an eyebrow

"Four years!"

Madame Nuffer smiled kindly. It was the kind of smile you gave your pet.

"Oui, Cherie," and, moving closer to me as though she was going to pat me on the head, she said, "then it will make it much easier for you, n'est-ce pas?"

I then spent a whole afternoon period copying basic French verbs and the masculine and feminine differences. To make matters worse, having decided to tackle my dilemma after class, I was denied the opportunity when a new male teacher made a sweeping entrance which distracted me. Madame Nuffer vanished and my moment for change had gone. Zut Alors!

The geography teacher was a tall man called Mr. Mainwaring, though some of the old girls called him 'Manners'. When he stooped over (which was most of the time when he talked to us as he was so tall) I noticed he had thin strands of blondish hair scraped back to cover an almost-bald head. With his small, round glasses and large hooked nose he reminded me of a cartoon vulture, ready to swoop down on its prey. Mr. Mainwaring instantly commanded attention as he swept theatrically across the space in front of our desks. He took in everything as his beady eyes surveyed the room. He announced he was going to teach us about our world. I think he meant geography.

"Minions!" he boomed, "I welcome you to take a journey with me into the world of miracles, wonders and danger; a world which is fragile and ferocious, elemental and extreme. We are going to learn about the world around us!"

We were momentarily stunned by this direct and different approach. The twins were itching for trouble and for some reason Shirley wanted to provoke him. She stuck her hand in the air and, giving an innocent smile, asked Mr Mainwaring how Lake Titicaca got its name. Manners was no fool and, not about to fall into a trap, was quick to react. His glasses fell to the end of his nose as he drew himself up to his full height. In one fast stride he descended on Shirley and, leaning over, slammed his hands on her desk. The whole class jumped as books toppled off the desktop. He paused for effect as we all cringed. Then, with a sly smile, he launched into a long tirade about The Lakes of the World, manically scraping on the blackboard as he drew supporting sketches and diagrams. Not surprisingly, our homework for Friday was to find the names of the Great Lakes and why they'd been given their names.

Later, our first ballet lesson after school was given by a young lady called Miss Wanda. She looked younger than the other teachers here, with long brown hair pulled into a high ponytail. She had slightly bulging eyes and red cheeks, like pink apples. She seemed nice and friendly and told us she had trained at this school for eight years. Now she was a qualified junior teacher she would be teaching us modern and national dance as well. After the barre work, Miss Wanda showed us how to 'limber up'. She told us that limbering exercises would make our muscles more flexible and help improve our turn-out, but *only* if we did them every day.

As we practised, I noticed Mika Miyagi-Jones, the pretty, slightly oriental girl from our dorm doing the front-splits. It was amazing! She could also do side-splits and when she leant forwards put her tummy, boobs and forehead flat on the floor! Mika showed us how she could 'shoulder her leg'. This involved grabbing her heel and hitching her leg up to the side of her ear in a standing upright side-split. We were gobsmacked. Miss Wanda said that daily practise would help us become flexible like Mika. Most of us were joined in places Mika probably wasn't, and as I wasn't even half way down in the front-splits yet, this seemed a long way off.

Our next class was tap. Our teacher, Mrs Balmaine, was the female version of Fred Astaire. She had a bulldog called 'Biba' who drooled in big puddles and huffed every time Mrs Balmaine moved. Yukky! Our lesson was a blast. With everyone practising their tap it was noisy but loads of fun. After ballet, tap has got to be my next favourite class. Mrs. Balmaine's feet moved with the speed of a drum roll. She had very bendy legs, like 'Twangy Pearl the elastic girl' from the comic 'The Dandy'. None of the girls in our class had tapped before, and our efforts made Mrs. Balmaine shout to be heard above the deafening tapping. The music was funky and I loved it. We ended the class watching her demonstrate our tap routine to Herman's Hermits' 'I'm Into Something Good'.

After the disgusting ravioli we had at tea we walked into the dorm and found a prefect sitting at the central table. She called us all around the table and informed us it was Nanny's night off and she was on 'junior duty' till Nanny got back.

Her name was Gina Farley. She was tiny and pretty, and her skin was so translucent that with her sky-blue eyes she looked like a perfect china doll. Hannah said she was one of Miss

Brookes's favourite students. Apparently Miss Brookes had nicknamed her 'Tinkerbell'. She spent all evening telling us stories about life outside Junior Dorm and told us that once we moved up to middle school we would have more freedom. She said when we got to the fourth year we would even have visiting weekends. She told us stories about midnight feasts, fire drills, amazing shows in the school's theatre and what life was like as a student without school work. It sounded like heaven.

When she went out to Nanny's room I pretended I was going to the loo, tapped on Nanny's door and Gina called me in. I plucked up courage and asked her what a crush was! She told me a crush was like a surrogate mother. When you needed a mother figure, someone to talk to or a shoulder to cry on, you could talk to your crush. She also said older girls could have a 'honey bunch'. This was similar to the role of a crush, so she could 'look out' for a younger girl, help and advise her and even buy her presents. I thanked her. Mystery one solved! I cheekily threw in the question of the mysterious threat of the 'Glitto bath'. Gina roared with laughter and said it was a scare tactic to terrify new girls. I asked what it was. She said Glitto (a powdered bath cleaner like Vim) was rubbed all over the victim's naked body with a scrubbing brush and then she was forced to sit caked in Glitto powder in a bath full of cold water. She must have seen my shocked face because she added it had been banned. Mystery number two solved.

Sadly for me, as I wrote my journal before lights out Millie was already weeping. I was too tired to comfort her and just wanted some sleep. How could anyone cry so much?

WEDNESDAY 13TH SEPTEMBER

I was woken up before the bell this morning, but pretended to be asleep when I spotted Millie being tucked up in bed by Nanny. My travel clock said 5 a.m. I fell back to sleep and was woken up again later by the bell from hell. I noticed Millie had her head buried under the covers. I guessed she would be off sick today. Abbey reckoned she would go back to Tobago after this term and said Millie was too wussy to last out the year. Sydney said she was a cry baby and that if Millie wanted to be a dancer she had to learn to live with it and 'grow some'. Grow some what? Sydney uses really odd expressions sometimes. Well, I'm afraid I don't share Sydney's tough love attitude; after the wind-up about Glitto baths I found it hard to trust her!

A giant debate followed over breakfast, with Esme Giles trying to calm everyone down and saying in a very shrill voice that we should all be more tolerant. Esme was what Dad called an 'oracle'. She was a fountain of knowledge on every subject, and was always using heaps of big words and spouting off with quotations.

We had a new teacher today, Miss Knox. She had flame-red hair, a mad gleam in her eyes and told us she had Gaelic ancestors. *As if anyone cared!* She was wearing an impressive shocking pink skirt and jacket, her eyes were painted very blue and her lipstick was crimson. Miss Knox was as mad as a hatter. I was starting to see a link here, my cuddly toy the March Hare, 'Alice in Wonderland' junior pinafores, the Mad Hatter aka Miss Knox… She spent the whole double history lesson telling us about her own history. She had come to Stavely Brookes after ten years abroad working as a private tutor in India, West Africa and the Far East.

Her voice faded into the background and I struggled to stay awake; I was sure it was interesting, but my eyelids felt like lead weights and it was all I could do to stop my head lolling onto my desktop. I was vaguely conscious of her saying that she had to flee the country unexpectedly when the lunch bell rang out, drowning her voice just as she was getting everyone's attention.

Lunch was dismal. Burt slopped his version of shepherd's pie on our plates, full of lumpy gristle, greasy gravy and pale-green processed peas. Luckily pudding saved the day. Kerri and I queued up for second helpings of apricot crumble. No-one Quizzed their puddings because dinner was so gross.

After lunch, Kerri took me down to the Dive and into the day girls' changing room. As we sat on the benches chewing gum we heard raised voices coming from behind the hanging coats, like an argument. Kerri rolled her eyes and whispered 'Lydia Kane'. We sneaked a look through the coats. Lydia had a square shaped head, slitty eyes and black hair. Kerri said Lydia was always angry with everyone. I wanted to show Kerri around Junior Dorm, but for some reason boarders weren't allowed to take day girls into their dorms. It seemed silly and I was embarrassed for myself, as well as Kerri.

During afternoon school Millie appeared. Everyone was kind to her because if Millie was happy she wouldn't sob all night. Mr Mainwaring took us for geography and asked if anyone came from abroad. Several hands shot up, Millie, Esme and Sanchia among them. Mr Mainwaring said it would enrich our views of the world around us if we heard first hand accounts from anyone who lived abroad. He asked them to tell us about the countries they lived in and its customs, scenery, climate and lifestyle. Esme rose to the challenge in true oracle style. She talked fluently about Kenya and the capital Nairobi. Her house was near Mombasa and many expatriates lived nearby. She spoke Swahili, the National language, and said English was the official language. They had houseboys, maids and her family owned a pet dog, Jamal, meaning 'handsome one'.

Reassured by Esme's tales, Millie forgot her shyness and spoke about Tobago's sultry climate. Becoming enthusiastic she grabbed some chalk and drew sketches of islands on the blackboard, showing Tobago farthest south of the island chain. She described it as warm and humid, with ancient rainforests, crystal clear sea with coral reefs and beaches with powdery pink sand. Mr Mainwaring interrupted, asking if she could bring photos in. Not having travelled outside England it sounded like paradise. No wonder Millie felt homesick. I'd love to live on an island like Tobago.

Sanchia Salazar told us all about Spain. We were appalled by her bloody descriptions of bullfights. She spoke fluent Spanish and lived near Madrid. Mr Mainwaring had saved the day and Millie looked happier than I'd ever seen her. Hooray!

After school we had ballet, then modern. In ballet Miss Wanda said we would all need to wear elastic briefs, not only to help hold our tummies in, but to stop us continually pulling our leotards down whenever we moved. The pesky leotards constantly rode up our bum cheeks revealing our knickers. She took our sizes and placed orders at the end of ballet class, telling us the bill would be sent to our parents. My parents will be pleased…

Modern was brilliant. We learned several warm-ups to funky drum music, isolations, limbering exercises to help us become more flexible (mental note to practise these as well as splits and turn-out) and some improvisation which was scary. Miss

Wanda put on some amazing rock music and we were told to dance doing whatever came into our heads. We froze because nobody had done modern dance before. Miss Wanda groaned, got off her chair and moved into the centre of the studio, then suddenly started spinning around the room, swaying her arms and kicking her legs round her ears. After some slinky hip gyrations, several crazy jumps and freaky feet combinations, she slithered to the ground, writhed around on the floor and ended up in the splits with her head thrown back and one arm reaching to the ceiling. We were bog-eyed and applauded loudly. When she stood up she grinned and said, "Now it's your turn." She rewound the reel-to-reel tape and, as the music blared out, we danced our socks off - apart from the occasional collision. Our shyness was thrown to the wind and when the music finished we were gasping for air. The class finished on a high note because we started to learn our Grade I modern routine to Elvis Presley's 'Burning Love' (world's best male singer) and Miss Wanda's status had now been raised to 'super-cool-best-teacher-ever'!

By tea time we were famished. I demolished a Cornish pasty with baked beans then Eggo'd another pasty, narrowly escaping a face-off with Sydney who picked an 'Eggo' battle with me over the same pasty. I was too fast for Sydney who was a poor loser. She threw a vicious look in my direction, so I did what any starving girl would do and quickly scoffed the lot. Better to die with a full belly.

Whilst waiting in the long tea queue today, I noticed some girls were beating teaspoons against the insides of their mugs (we take our own mugs to breakfast and tea) and I asked what they were doing. They explained how mixing Nescafe granules, masses of sugar, a touch of water and beating it vigorously turned it into a thick, caramel paste. By adding boiling water and milk, a thick crust of foam will rise to the surface creating instant frothy coffee. How cool was that!

Back in the dorm this evening we played musical statues to Top of the Pops chart music on Karlyn Bryce's giant tape recorder. It was so loud the walls shook. Nanny had her TV on full volume to drown out our racket. I survived the game, only just, losing third to last. We collapsed on our beds to read, write letters, or just generally annoy each other. Nanny then brought us supper – staggering into the dorm with steaming jugs of cocoa and plates piled high with malted milk biscuits. Before she turned the lights out I leaned out of my bottom bunk and whispered to Millie how much we'd all enjoyed hearing about Tobago. She whispered back to me that she felt heaps better and that made me feel happy too. Just as Nanny switched the lights out, I spotted Hannah Greenwood at the far end of the dorm. She seemed to be sneaking about in the dim light and fiddling with something on Esme's end-of-bed locker. She looked very shifty.

CHAPTER SIX

THURSDAY 14TH SEPTEMBER

I was first up and in the bathroom before anyone else this morning. I stood by the row of washbasins and listened to the silence. The freezing cold made me shiver. When I turned the hot tap on there was a loud gurgling noise and all the taps shook when the hot water spluttered out, first coming in bursts, then the tap rattled again, made a weird moaning sound and suddenly hot water exploded into the basin soaking my dressing gown. As the basin slowly filled I examined the label on my bar of Imperial Leather soap. The smell reminded me of my Dad just after he's shaved. I was lost in my own thoughts about home when I heard an almighty scream echoing down the stairs from the dorm above. Moments later, Maddy and Abbey burst into the bathroom and slammed the door shut. Out of breath and giggling, they informed me that when Esme had taken her mug from her locker she'd found a massive dead spider in it! Esme had marched straight into Nanny's room, telling her that Hannah had put it there last night. We concluded it would be dorm war today. When I headed upstairs I was prepared for all eventualities. Hannah and Esme were officially not speaking; at breakfast, in school, in fact not at all.

Kerri brought me some homemade flapjacks today, which we ate after lunch while finishing our Titicaca homework that was due in on Friday. She told me Mr Deluca, a school governor, had visited the changing room early today with the school secretary, Miss Riley, and Kerri overheard them saying it had to go. A new changing room with toilets was being built for them near the new studios. The new studios would be named after the famous ballerina Alexandra Haydon, who trained at our school.

I apologised to Kerri for not being allowed to take her to my dormitory and Kerri said I could come and spend time with her instead. I made another mental note to find out why the day girls weren't allowed into the boarders' accommodation. I didn't understand these old fashioned rules.

During afternoon school we had Miss Knox again. She began ranting on about civil wars, but sensing our boredom changed tactics and launched into a full-blown lesson about the Tudors. Miss Knox's passion for the Tudors was powerful and her eyes sparkled. She was a woman with a mission.

After this intense historical lecture, dance was a welcome break. Ballet was followed by national, which was great fun because we got to learn lots of different character styles from around the world. Today we started the 'Gavotte' from Brittany in France. We learned about the origins of the dance, the costumes and even the time signature of the music we danced to. We wore our swirly coloured skirts and red leather character shoes from Freeds. The pointed shoe shape made my toes hurt when I danced.

Fish fingers were on the menu for tea, with bread and butter. Burt was obviously a top chef. Whilst I waited for a cup of tea to be served by Burt's wife Nancy (who looked much too old to be serving, as she kept missing the cups), I noticed a prefect standing by the canteen exit. She was handing out post. It was a very large pile of post and when I reached her I asked if there was anything for Edgecombe. Whilst balancing my overflowing tea cup on the tray I saw a notice board on the wall, displaying a notice with a couple of girls' names and black marks beside them. Hannah nudged me, sending my tea slopping all over my fish fingers. She leaned forward, put her mouth right against my ear and whispered, "Those girls on the notice board, they've been gated from Visiting Day in two week's time," she hissed, "they live in main house and are always in trouble."

I was interrupted again by a letter landing on my sodden fish fingers. It was Mum's handwriting. I rushed through the dining room, hoping to stop the tea soaking into my letter. The other juniors all seemed to have post and I sat down and devoured my letter. Mum said they missed me and the house seemed quiet without me. Dad had got a motorbike to ride to the station, so she could use the car for her part-time secretarial work. I couldn't wait to see Dad's bike, and wondered whether it was a Barry Sheen 125cc Suzuki, or an even bigger bike? Imagine how cool it would be to arrive back from a visiting day riding on the back of a motorbike (though not very ballerina like!). Mum told me that Benjamin had been moved up a class and Samuel had his first day at school. She asked me to let her have a list of anything I needed and to phone home on Sunday after church. Mrs Furst wanted to know if I needed any more leg warmers knitted. Everyone had signed their names on the letter and drawn pictures of our cat, Patch, and our budgie, Joey.

Back in the dorm lots of girls were making their own calendar countdown charts. These were to plot the progress of how many days there were left to go until visiting-days, half term, and then the end-of-term. The terms were roughly split into three parts. I worked out that with two visiting-days (called Vis Days) separating the four day half term, this autumn term should speed by. I joined in the artwork effort for our corner of the dorm and sketched some pin-men dancers, with very flexible legs, all around the calendar. Millie had drawn a large smiley sun on the going home day. Abbey and I both agreed we really missed home, but thought life in the dorm had been fun so far and we *loved* the dancing. It was ok for us because we really wanted to be here, but for girls like Millie it was hard, because their parents had made them come.

During my strip wash tonight I chatted to Tiffany Hardwick. She casually informed me that she thought the girls in little dorm were way more mature than the big dorm because they all had pubic hair and already had their monthly periods! As I took off my dressing gown, Tiffany very rudely stared straight at my body. I quickly realised I had more pubic hair than her (though neither of us had much anyway!) which must - as Tiffany saw it - mean I was at least nearly as mature as her. She wasted no time in pointing the hair difference out. I felt like I had been added to some elite 'body-hair' club. Maybe having pubic hair - but lack of periods - gave you certain 'club rights'. During this weird conversation, I spotted a tin of Glitto on the edge of the bath. In an effort to change the subject, I asked Tiffany if she had heard about the Glitto baths. She laughed loudly and said that new girls always fell for that rubbish. Just as she finally stopped cackling, I became aware of a scratching noise going on outside the window. Tiffany leaned towards me with a wicked glint in her eyes and whispered, "Men we call 'Prowlers' sometimes creep up from the woods and come to spy on the naked girls in the bathroom!" Clearly encouraged by my appalled reaction, she nodded knowingly.

"That's why Mr Julius patrols the grounds every night with his huge dog called Sultan who frightens all the prowlers because he's the size of a horse".

I could hardly wait to see Mr Julius and Sultan the horse dog! Tiffany said that Mr. Julius taught music and was quite dishy. Tiffany was obviously very mature, and for some strange reason I had the urge to appear her equal, so I asked as casually as I could, "Good looking in what way?"

"Well, let's see."

She furrowed her eyebrows.

"He's a bit of a hippy I s'pose, very sexy though, with loads of long, dark hair. He often wears an Afghan coat with groovy Ostrich-skin boots and ripped jeans."

I had no idea what an Afghan coat looked like.

Back upstairs supper had arrived and a massive pile of custard tarts was being decimated by the starving juniors. I grabbed one quickly and noticed a 'Bunty' magazine on Sanchia's bed. Sanchia lent it to me with a magazine called 'Diana'. I'd never read them but it would give me something to read in the evenings until I got some books from home. I found a section at the back of the 'Diana' advertising girls looking for pen pals. I chose to write to a couple of girls who had similar interests to me like dance, visiting different countries, reading, and also because they were living in parts of the world I would like to visit – in case I should be lucky enough to be invited on an exchange visit. Pen pal one was Grace Short from Auckland, New Zealand. The second was Maria Lazares from Capri. The third was Lin Wang from Hong Kong. I wrote on featherweight air mail paper Esme had given me. I was worried that Grace was thirteen and I was only eleven, but hoped she'd see I had a mature attitude for an eleven-and-a-half year old. I'd got some black and white passport photos that Lily and I had taken in a Woolworth's photobooth. I had to identify which one was me because my sister's big head had taken up most of the photo. Esme said I wasn't supposed to put anything in the envelope, but I chanced it and stuck on extra stamps for good measure.

FRIDAY 15TH SEPTEMBER

During geography we handed in our Titicaca homework. Mr Mainwaring seemed agitated today, scribbling diagrams on the blackboard like a man possessed as we struggled to take notes. I couldn't wait for end of school and for dance to begin.

Grotty lunch again, but fortunately Kerri had brought relief supplies and we gorged on peanut butter sandwiches in the cloakroom. She confided to me that she was in trouble with Lydia Kane because she'd answered her back. Just at that moment Lydia came barging in and we had to hide behind the cloakroom door. Lydia was built like Goliath! When she went to the far end of the cloakroom we scarpered outside to safety.

Ballet today was with a new, slightly older ballet teacher called Miss Olsen who used to be a ballerina. You could see this when she demonstrated because she moved so gracefully. Sometimes in the middle of an exercise, particularly barre work, she forgot to tell us to rest when she was correcting someone. Today we all had our legs held high in the air in a 'developee' (or as high as we could!) when she began correcting Hannah. Our legs started to shake because she forgot to tell us to relax and I could have sworn my leg was about to drop off.

Miss Olsen got a better pianist than Miss Wanda and the pianist we had today was fantastic. Her name was Miss Yates and she never stopped smiling, which made all of us smile. She even added extra musical phrases if you got your timing wrong so she covered your mistakes. A genius pianist. In class today, poor Gabby Pagoni was saved in the nick of time by Miss Yates when we were doing jumps called 'changement battus'. Miss Olsen made us do them one-by-one and the first person usually sets the pace. When it came to Gabby's turn, she started on the wrong beat and barely got off the floor. Miss Olsen became frustrated and said she must develop more 'ballon', then made her do it continuously until Gabby turned puce and breathless with the effort. On her final attempt, Miss Yates speeded up the tempo so Gabby's 'changements' were performed at double tempo. Kerri had a fit of giggles as we were next in line to Gabby and then we all started sniggering. Miss Olsen got irate and said that in our next class she hoped to *hear* less of us and *see* more effort.

Modern was great and we learned more of our 'Burning Love' routine. I loved the crazy, funky moves and it was amazing to see everyone moving freely after our very controlled ballet. We were presented with our elastic briefs today, which was a bit of a shock. They looked like small versions of the Playtex girdles advertised in women's magazines. I hoped we could breathe in them.

Back in the dorm at long last it was my bath night. It was also pocket money night. We queued outside Nanny's room to collect twenty pence pocket money, which we had to sign for. I wondered how everyone would manage to eke out twenty pence for a week, but as we had nothing else to spend our money on apart from our Saturday shopping trip, I guessed we didn't need any more.

SATURDAY 16ᵀᴴ SEPTEMBER

After nearly a week of hearing the rising bell it no longer made me jump. We were late leaving for breakfast as Nanny wasn't breathing down our necks and hurrying us along. When we reached the canteen there was no queue and the food had been cleared away. A prefect called Rita Warlock, who had a nose like a ski-slope and a mean, pinched up face rounded on us as we were poking around the empty canteen.

"What do you juniors think you're up to, sniffing around the canteen?" she snarled.

"We haven't had any breakfast," Abbey complained, and we nodded our heads in agreement.

Rita drew her eyebrows together until they met, looking like Pinocchio with caterpillar eyebrows. I stifled the urge to giggle as she rifled in her shoulder bag and brought out a large black book, saying, "Names, please." She was busy telling us that Nanny would get to hear about our late arrival when an amazing thing happened. The inner doors of the canteen opened and a tall, lanky boy with long ginger hair rushed towards us. He was wearing a large chef's hat. He looked at us, then at Rita and asked us if we'd missed breakfast. Before Rita could start on another tirade, he told us that he'd only cleared breakfast away because Burt hadn't told him what time to finish (saved!) but there were loads of leftovers, and if we were hungry he could get us some cereal and toast from the back. Rita narrowed her eyes, huffed loudly and then skulked away to her prefect-hiding lair to lay in wait for her next victim while we triumphantly awaited our specially prepared feast. We

nicknamed our ginger-haired saint Radical Radish; a true ally
in a school of constantly famished trainee dancers.

After we had feasted on hot buttered toast, we raced back to
the dorm to do our hair. We'd been told that a neat, secure
ballet bun was essential. High buns (according to Miss Wanda)
helped us perform better pirouettes. It had taken a lot of help
from older girls to master the art of the perfect bun. I was now
quite good at it, having very long but slippery hair. My hair
had so many metal pins holding it in place that if an alien
spaceship had chosen to hover over me and hold a magnet over
my head I would have skyrocketed headfirst towards the
magnet faster than the speed of light. When I took my hair
down in the evening my hair had a halo style ridge going right
around my head. In fact we all did, and the effect was slightly
surreal - we probably looked like brides of Dracula - or
something!

Everyone had major struggles trying to get into the spanking
new elastic briefs. They were killers. Podgy tummies and
knicker-elastic outlines riding down our bum cheeks didn't
stand a chance. These were designed by the devil to punish
girls not built like stick insects. Excruciatingly tight from the
moment we put them on, we suffered silently throughout
ballet. I asked Miss Wanda if they ever loosened up so you
couldn't feel them. She gave me an unsympathetic look and
muttered "Possibly."

At 10-30 a.m. we were done for the day and had the rest of the
weekend free. Back in Junior Dorm we prepared for our
afternoon adventure out of school. Music was blaring out from
different corners of the dorm. I could hear the sickly sweet
chorus of 'Puppy Love', and somebody had 'School's Out'
rocking deafeningly from Karlyn Bryce's tape machine,

probably to drown out the Osmond dirge. Donny was finally overpowered as we all joined in with Alice Cooper's rousing chorus. It sounded like a riot and I hoped Miss Brookes couldn't hear us caterwauling from inside her house.

Miss Brookes and her husband, Chester Stavely, had this exotic house close by called The Pavilion. It was striking, like an Indian palace. A large cage in the front archway was home to an exotic bird. I'd been told it could mimic voices, but so far I'd only heard it say "Lookout!"

Esme and Paula told us all about our afternoon shopping trip to the local village store and we planned what we could buy with twenty pence.

After lunch at 2 p.m. sharp a stout looking prefect called Cimmie Krause appeared and told us we were her responsibility today. Cimmie looked a toughie. She had black-as-coal eyes (the kind of black-black eyes you'd see on bloodsuckers in a vampire movie). Maybe she was related to Lydia Kane, or maybe they were both descendants from a long line of medieval witch-like hags who tortured hapless juniors on a whim. With a voice like a foghorn she bellowed at us to find a partner and get in line. Two of the younger juniors ran to hold her hand (creeps) as we lined up in a human crocodile. Standing in pairs our immaculate uniform was scrutinized by Cimmie, school blazers, perfectly knotted ties, polished brown leather lace ups, long wool socks held up with elastic garters and skirts 'no more than two inches above the knee'. Topping off the outfit were bowler hats. Sydney, Tiffany and the twins were at the back of the crocodile, and once Cimmie had returned to the front of the line I noticed them hitching up their skirts.

Twenty-six girls began marching out for the three mile walk to Postbridge Stores. We could barely catch our breath to talk as Cimmie hustled us along the side of the main road at breakneck speed. Postbridge Stores was a country shop selling everything, including cigarettes and alcohol. I noticed we'd lost the twins and Gabby was already bickering with Sydney. Our troop of girls was split in two. Half of us waited outside while Cimmie escorted the other half into the small shop. When we were out of Cimmie's eagle eye-line the fun began. Hannah got us all to sit on the grass forecourt in front of the shop. Although mid September it was sweltering and the fast walk and thick uniform hadn't helped. There was a commotion from behind the hedge on the far side of the forecourt. Tiffany was performing her snake-in-the-grass impersonation travelling in the direction of the hedge. She slithered down below the hedge as we gaped in her direction. Rings of smoke were rising up out of the bush. Maddy and I exchanged looks and she leaned towards me.

"They're smoking," she hissed.

I told her it hadn't escaped anyone's notice, so when Cimmie noticed, then what? Hannah assured me they'd be gated. We could see Cimmie's stout frame marching to and fro, herding the junior shoppers around inside. Sydney had now joined the war party and, with her legs poking out of the bushes, we witnessed a variety of smoke signals. Mesmerised by this audacious act of daring, it was Hannah who brought us down to earth and told us to move away from the bushes so we wouldn't be associated with the crime. A distance was rapidly established between the criminals and the eyewitnesses.

Suddenly, without a moment's warning, Cimmie emerged from the shop and with a single deft glance scanned the

forecourt. Her eyes locked instantly on the crime scene and her
feet didn't touch the ground as she swept down on the girls in
the bushes like a tornado. For a small girl, Cimmie was like
power woman (I could picture her in a comic strip as the troll-
like warrior midget that wades into dangerous situations).
Strong as an ox, she hoicked Sydney and Tiffany from the
undergrowth like puppets as they shrieked and protested.

The shop owner rushed out, words were passed between her
and Cimmie then they shook hands. A pact had been made.
The elderly shop owner then guarded the offending girls in a
sort of unofficial shop arrest. Cimmie swept her eyes over the
remaining group outside. She was like a one-woman army.
Miraculously, the twins had made their way back into our
group unnoticed. Cimmie stalked around us and barked a few
orders before firing a parting shot in the direction of Tiffany
and Sydney.

"When we get back you're going straight to Mr Deluca."

Then in a Jeckyl and Hyde transformation she turned back
into Cimmie the junior escort, ushered us into the shop and we
were able to breathe a collective sigh of relief.

I never thought twenty pence would go so far. Cimmie let us
sit outside on the grass and devour our goodies. I'd ended up
with an odd collection of smoky bacon crisps, a walnut whip, a
bag of flying saucers and a bottle of cream soda, which I'd
never tried. Nervous tension made us gorge and after glugging
back the cream soda I felt ready to explode as we were herded
back to school in a close-knit crocodile. Cimmie further
humiliated the 'criminals' by forcing them to hold her hands.
EMBARRASSING OR WHAT?

Back at school Tiffany and Sydney were given a stern lecture
by Nanny and were still under threat of a visit on Monday to

Mr Deluca. That evening the dorm was rife with rumours; would Tiffany and Sydney be gated from Visiting Day, or even expelled?

I checked our countdown chart and there were only two weeks till Vis Day. I spent the evening writing home with details of our first week (leaving out the smoking incident) and asked Mum and Dad if they could get me:

1) Basildon Bond pad of featherweight air mail paper
2) Stamps for overseas mail
3) Giant hairspray
4) Bovril
5) Mug (tin if possible so it wouldn't break)

Supper was watery orange squash and bread rolls, with piles of vile looking slices of ox tongue. When Nanny left the dorm all hell broke loose. Devilry was in the air. The twins closed the dorm door and began the vandalism by slapping two large, wet ox tongues onto the dressing table mirrors. We all collapsed in hysterics, as one-by-one we took our turns in slapping a piece of ox tongue on the line of mirrors until they were covered with gory looking tongues and it resembled a Hammer Horror scene. Twenty-six girls rolled around the dorm floor and flailed on their beds in uncontrollable fits of hysterical snorts and guffaws. Hearing the commotion, Nanny appeared in the doorway with Hamish to heel. As she was facing away from the scene of the crime, she was perplexed as to why we were collapsed in hysterical laughter.

"What's all this, girls?" she demanded, her head wobbling from side to side.

"We're telling jokes" Hannah lied. Someone then let out a huge fart which immediately set off a secondary ripple of uncontrollable laughter. Hamish was then drawn into all the excitement and piddled on the wooden floor. I could barely breathe - the tension was side-splitting. The next few seconds were a blur. Seeing Hamish pee, Nanny panicked and lunged at him. Hamish panicked and ran blindly towards the dressing table. At that exact moment a piece of ox tongue fell off one of the mirrors and dangled provocatively towards the excited Hamish who, smelling the meat, jumped up onto the dressing table and began a mirror licking feast. Nanny saw the dog, mirrors and ox tongue simultaneously, shrieked in dismay and ran out of the room clutching herself like a crazy woman. Seconds later, as we scurried over to calm Hamish and attempt to scrape chunks of the ox tongue off the mirrors, there was a thunderous noise on the stairs. Cimmie stormed the dorm like a one-woman tornado, sweeping us into formation. Before we knew it we were armed with buckets, rags and brooms. 'Glitto' and scrubbing brushes were distributed and we spent the next hour scrubbing the decks and polishing the woodwork. Abbey caught my eye and muttered, "She's like a little Hitler!"

Exhausted after our punishment we were then ordered to scrub up and sleep. We feebly crawled into bed, with no will left to fight. Cimmie's military machine had even beaten the legendary courage of the twins. We were further threatened with a possible visit to Mr Deluca on Monday *if* we created more havoc. The thought of losing a Visiting Day was instantly sobering.

CHAPTER SEVEN

SUNDAY 17TH SEPTEMBER

At 8-45 a.m. sharp we lined up for a uniform check. A student called Sian was on church walk duty. We walked two miles up the hill in crocodile formation without any incidents, terrified of more punishments. Hannah silently provoked Esme and I could vaguely hear Sydney's American drawl at the back of the line. When we arrived at the church we were briefed on good behaviour and informed that juniors sat in the front pews, with the veiled threat "where they can be seen but not heard".

St Barnabas was Church of England and seemed vast compared to my local church where I'd sung in the choir. As we filed into the front row pews I turned and glanced back. The church was a mass of grey and maroon uniforms. Whilst the hymns were being sung, I became aware of several pews of choir boys sitting on either side of the aisle leading up several steps to the altar. As communion time approached I noticed the lead choirboys leaving their places and heading towards our front pews holding some odd looking lanterns on chains. Just as I wondered what they were going to do, they started wafting the lanterns into the air and an intoxicating smoke started to fill the front pews.

The congregation began to sing and I grappled to find the order of service. This was called 'The Kyries'. I didn't know them, so I started to mime the words but was feeling slightly nauseous from the spicy smell, and we were fast disappearing under a sea of smoke. The choirboys then swung the lanterns in our direction and wafted the suffocating incense smoke all over us. We'd been standing for ages when a girl called Tamsin Barrie went and fainted. Fortunately for Tamsin our pew was so tightly packed that she remained in an upright position until she was rescued by some ladies in the congregation. They must have seen our plight and, rushing forward, they proceeded to carry Tamsin out of the pew to safety and fresh air.

After the fainting incident we were ushered into the aisle ready to queue up for communion. None of the juniors were confirmed so we had to be blessed. As we queued up, moving inch by inch towards the altar, the choir boys on either side began staring at us girls. We stared back. It was like one of those no-blinking games and my eyes filled with water. I could see Maddy's shoulders going up and down in front of me and someone in front of her snorted. I had to stifle a strong urge to giggle and ended up biting my lip till it bled. The line moved on painfully slowly. I was saved from myself when I gained the last place in the line and knelt at the altar. Esme was doing signs of the cross over her chest and I copied her because she'd been here before and knew the ropes. I made a mental note to ask Mum about this. She was an authority on 'C of E' customs and knew all about church etiquette. Father Benedict blessed us by laying his hands on each girl's head and we made more cross signs over our chests and walked (calmly this time without choirboys in their seats to stare at us) back to our pews to pray. I knelt on my hassock and, bowing my head to concentrate, thanked God for allowing me to come to ballet school. I added a special request that we wouldn't get sent to see Mr Deluca.

On the walk back Sian took us on a different route. Esme said it was the long way back. It was nice because we walked through a large park and were allowed into the play area with its swings, slides, roundabouts and swing-boats. Twenty-six juniors unleashed their energy like animals out of a cage. I think it was a reaction to last night! We eventually walked back calmly and there were no more incidents.

Sunday afternoon everyone did the prep we'd been set. I was learning a whole new vocabulary of boarding school slang and jargon.

Homework was Prep

Farts were Guffs.

Scones were Skons.

Fathers were (sometimes) Papa

Mothers (in Esme's case) were Mammaa (the second syllable 'mmaa' bit was very pronounced at the back of the throat, and spoken with a dead posh accent!)

Plimsolls were Pumps

Loos were Bogs

Elasticated Girdles were Laggy Briefs

Middle School Girls were Tweenies

The list so far was small but expanding.

I wrote to both sets of my grandparents. I told Grandpa Edgecombe that his helmet with the bullet hole would have looked impressive on my end-of-bed locker, but my March Hare had caused quite a stir with its size alone. I told Aunty Ellen about the different dance styles I was learning and so far I wasn't 'sur la pointe' but would be soon. Grandpa and Nana

Huntley got a drawing of me practising the splits so they could see what hard work it was (my pin man was smiling so it didn't look too strenuous). Then I spent the rest of Sunday afternoon practising splits and new tap exercises ready for tap class on Tuesday. We started our proper timetable this week so I wanted to be prepared. Mika and Sanchia joined in the tap practice, which made such a din that Nanny came storming in and threw a wobbly. She said that not only would the floor collapse but Mr Stavely would be woken up! Out of respect for Mr Stavely we stopped our practice and agreed we'd have to find another place to practise tap.

The tea bell rang and we raced off to the Dive and another never-ending queue. Most middle-school girls had changed back into the week-day uniform of twin-sets and some were wearing fluffy slippers. I stood behind Esme in the queue and she was talking about her Mum's perfume. We smelled her wrists and she said it was 'L'Air du Temps' by Nina Ricci, adding, "I've got the limited edition bottle in the dorm."

I wondered what some of the girls' families were like, as we all seemed to be very different. I was fascinated by the girls who lived abroad; their lives seemed to be worlds apart from mine. I hadn't been abroad yet, but hopefully that would change with all my new friends and pen pals.

Gabby started talking about her Italian father who she said had married her mother to live in this country and then deserted them. Gabby said her mother felt bitter and she felt angry with her mother. After tea there was another roll call. A couple of the Tweenies were missing when their names were called out.

This evening Nanny told us that there'd be no supper. She gave us a stern lecture and said that until we learned to respect our food, supper was withdrawn. Mika whispered to me we'd have to sing for our supper!

It was my turn to wash my hair the following day, thank goodness. Everybody thought one hair wash a week was gross, and the only good thing about greasy hair was it scraped back easily into a bun. I wished the bathroom had a shower spray. I had to ask Nanny - when she was in a good mood - if we were allowed to bring plastic shower sprays from home to put on the taps to help rinse our hair.

MONDAY 18TH SEPTEMBER

Last night I went to sleep thinking about the possible visit to Mr Deluca and dreamt we were gated from home visits and each given a Glitto bath. I woke before rising bell pouring with sweat and realised that my adventures were only just beginning.

I couldn't get back to sleep, so I decided to use the bathroom before everyone else and passed Nanny on the stairs in her hairnet and dressing gown. She smiled and asked if I was okay and I thanked her, saying I was going to wash before the early rush. She chuckled and said, "4 o'clock is a bit early to get up!" I went back to bed and continued tossing and turning until it was time to get up.

Everyone burst into chatter about the possible visit to Mr Deluca. I couldn't listen to it anymore and beat a hasty retreat to the bathroom. Whilst cleaning my teeth I peered in the mirror and realised how much better my teeth looked after a year of wearing my brace. Maddy and Abbey were fascinated with my brace. Maddy said she couldn't understand why I had to wear a brace when my teeth were perfectly straight. My dentist obviously thought otherwise. We reckoned I was the only girl in the school with a brace *and* a fringe. We placed bets on whether or not we would be given the threatened punishment and then voted unanimously that the punishment outweighed the crime.

At breakfast I overheard Sydney and Tiffany bragging about their fool proof cover story. It sounded dodgy. It ran something along the lines of finding a lit cigarette smouldering underneath the bush and beating the undergrowth in an attempt to stop a fire. I doubted this thin plot would hold up under interrogation, particularly if Cimmie had anything to do with it.

Saphi, the head girl, leaned over our long breakfast table and told Sydney and Tiffany to come to her room immediately after breakfast, adding that they could take their pinafores off. The powers that be had obviously forgotten the ox tongue incident. I could sense the general relief across the junior table.

It was the start of the full school timetable today. We began with assembly in the dance studio which had a grand piano in the corner. Squashed in like sardines we sang 'Oh Jesus I Have Promised', with a student playing the piano. She was brilliant, her curly flame-red hair bobbed up and down as she darted from one end of the keys to the other, playing her own jazzed up version of the tune I knew so well. I made a note to sneak into the Dive to listen to private piano lessons and would try to teach myself, although I was sure it would take me longer than it would for me to get into the full splits.

After a boring form period we had tuck break. I shared my Jelly Babies with Kerri and we discussed the growing threat of Lydia Kane that loomed over her.

In double English we studied great poets and read a poem by Rudyard Kipling. Homework was to learn *If* by heart, ready to recite on Friday. Kerri and I agreed to practise together in our lunch breaks.

During lunch there was still no hint of a visit to Mr Deluca. Sitting in the day girls' changing room after lunch, Kerri and I learned the first four lines of *If*. Thankfully there was no sign of Lydia, but she'd left a sinister note on Kerri's peg saying 'Watch your back, Legge'. Lydia was really hateful and must definitely have been related to Cimmie.

In boring maths after break we struggled to stay awake and then went straight into our first drama lesson. I'd never studied drama before and I was looking forward to it. On our way to the drama studio we passed the lake. Sydney told us that the ghost of the Blue Lady still haunted the lake and main house. We were all agog. Relishing her captive audience she continued her story.

"During the Second World War the school served for a short time as a convalescence home, nursing sick and wounded soldiers back to good health. A nurse in blue uniform tended the soldiers and the men adored her. One day she mysteriously fell to her death from the tower's balcony which overhangs the lake..."

She paused for effect and we urged her on. Clearing her throat she continued.

"So her death has always been veiled in mystery, but she is said to return to her duties in the small wee hours, a sad lost soul drifting from room to room so that she could continue to tend, soothe and comfort the sick soldiers."

Esme broke the trance by interrupting that we were running late for drama. We had to make a dash for the studio and arrived only just in time.

Drama was a blast. Our teacher, Miss Lazenby, had a teenie-tiny Chihuahua called Voodoo. It was a mystery as to why so many of our female teachers kept dogs at their feet all the time. Miss Lazenby was really whacky. She wore a voluminous, orange-sequinned kaftan teamed with huge gold-framed glasses which sparkled, and possessed heaving bosoms which rested on her desk. Masses of jangly copper bracelets decorated her wrists and layers of coloured rocks hung round her neck.

We had to do an 'ice-breaker'. This involved crawling across the floor pretending to be animals. We felt ridiculous, but it became fun when Miss Lazenby told us to be wild animals. Gabby took it literally, got carried away imitating a lion and bit Hannah's bum. Hannah then turned on her and Miss Lazenby had trouble separating the fight. We were then given a lecture on the different types of acting used in theatre and films. Miss Lazenby approved of method acting. She told us we had to learn to separate reality from fantasy (listen up Gabby!). I couldn't wait for double drama on Wednesday.

In ballet, after barre work when we were warmed up, Miss Wanda showed us how to improve our turn out. We had to sit with our backs against the wall, our heels together and knees dropped out to the sides. The aim was to get your knees flat on the floor in a position called a 'Frog'. Mika's frog was a 'flat-turned-out' frog and looked very different from the rest of us, who looked more like grasshoppers with our knees up in the air! I wondered if I would ever be as loose as Mika. I've added Frogs to my daily practice list, along with practising the splits and learning *If* (and teaching myself piano too).

In modern we learned the hippy bit in 'Burning Love'. Feeling cold I wore my purple-ribbed leg warmers for the first time and the girls loved them. Sydney bagged first in the queue for borrowing them if I lent them out. They made my muscles really hot. If I wore these all the time maybe I'd get into the splits more easily.

At tea we had cheese on toast and it was actually edible – so far only two out of nine teas have been fit for human consumption.

When a pile of post was brought to the junior table I was excited to receive a padded letter. Mum had sent me a sachet of beer shampoo. Perhaps this was because I told her that Esme had a French perfume. The slogan on the shampoo sachet said 'shiniest hair ever'. There was also a cassette tape which Lily had recorded for me. Yippee! She'd written on it 'Best of Top of the Pops' and sent a note saying it had got to be better than living in hell listening to the Osmonds. She wasn't a fan either.

Back in the dorm later there was still no word about the punishment. Before my hair wash I asked Nanny about bringing a plastic shower spray from home. She scowled and said no! During hair washing I shared my sachet of beer shampoo with Maddy and the foam was so rich we couldn't rinse it out. As we were stuck in waist-high bath water the situation became worse, because in an effort to rinse out the lather the masses of foam rose over the bath tops. Eventually the hot water ran out. We ended up using an old tin jug and icy water which turned my skin blue with the cold. Nanny came in to hurry us up and muttered about the huge waste of hot water.

After she'd gone, we heard scratching sounds on the outside window. It was probably only the trees creaking, but with seeds of the Blue Lady ghost planted firmly in our minds we started to doubt ourselves. Maddy bravely said that she didn't believe in ghosts and that it was probably a trick to terrorise the new girls.

Finally, with scalps gleaming from beer shampoo and icy water, we made our way back to the dorm. On the dorm door was a notice. It was a 'punishment duties' notice. Each girl had a separate punishment to do for one week. Mine was cleaning and polishing school shoes, but I was teamed up with Abbey. I noticed that the two youngest girls had been assigned to 'walking Hamish with Nanny'. What a jammy punishment! Thankfully I'd avoided bath and sink cleaning duties and sock pairing and folding. Later Nanny brought in a supper of digestive biscuits and cocoa and called a meeting. She made us sit on our beds before laying into us.

"Following your disgraceful behaviour with the ox tongue incident," here she pulled a disgusted expression, "you girls are very lucky to be given any supper at all. However, rather than gate you from your first Visiting Day," which she knew meant a lot to us, "I have decided it would be more useful if I assigned everyone with a job-duty rota to keep you all busy and out of trouble in the evenings. This rota will be in force until further notice. Perhaps with your minds on more constructive things, you may learn to be better behaved. Anyone wishing to swap their duties must ask my permission first."

Twenty-two hands flew up for dog walking duty.

Before lights were turned out, Hannah gathered us around her bed and told us tales of Blue Lady sightings in the main house.

"She's most likely to appear during the night of the full moon. The Blue Lady is a spirit in limbo. She's been heard opening dorm doors in the main house at night, followed by the creaking of floorboards as she wanders between beds nursing the sick soldiers."

I told Millie that Hannah had made it up to scare us, as I was afraid she'd start crying again. During the night it was me who was startled when Millie drifted past my bed in her long white nightdress on her way to the loos. I waited for her return with my heart thumping. After what seemed like ages she drifted noiselessly back into the dorm and sat on her bed in a trance just staring blankly into space! She looked kind of weird, so I sat up and asked her if she was okay. She just sat on the edge of her bed with a vacant smile on her face and looked straight through me. I tried waving my hand in front of her face and she moved her lips - but no sound came out! It was dead creepy. Fortunately, after persuading her to lie down she just closed her eyes and went back to sleep. This was way scarier than the Blue Lady.

TUESDAY 19TH SEPTEMBER

Last night I eventually drifted off into a troubled sleep and dreamt about floating nurses in blue gowns.

I checked my diary before breakfast and my worst fears were confirmed. Friday was a full moon! We now had punishment duties, wore baby aprons every day and I was sleeping in close proximity to a sleep-walking Tobagan. I'd also discovered, during my fitful sleep, that *someone* in our dorm snored.

With ten more months of being a new girl junior I had to toughen my resolve. On my morning foray to the bogs I discovered a notice on each of the loo doors which said:

'Anyone found putting ink in the loos will be gated'.

I was now scared to sit on the loos as they were stained with ink and I didn't want a blue bum. It was bad enough wearing a blue pinny. Rumours were rife in the bathroom. It seemed the fourth years living in the adjoining outhouses were under suspicion for the ink crimes. Apparently they sneaked in when Nanny was asleep.

At breakfast, a notice on the canteen notice board named two girls gated from Visiting Day. Guess who?

In English we practised handwriting with our Italic pens. It took forever but the end result looked beautiful. I nearly fell asleep in double maths with my thoughts drifting to sleepwalking and the as yet unidentified snorer. Kerri and I passed notes under our desks about the Lydia Kane situation. My first and best thought was that we could pay someone to kidnap her - problem resolved! For now, I suggested to Kerri that she killed Lydia with kindness and to do that, she must give her some expensive chocolates. Kerri said she'd rather give chocolates to her dog. I said she didn't have a dog and we both giggled. It was a hopeless situation.

After lunch I raced back to Junior Dorm to collect the Marc Bolan poster I'd cut from a magazine for Kerri (she's crazy about him). I hurried back so that Kerri and I could practise *If* together, but as I walked down the Dive steps I could hear a huge commotion coming from the day girls' changing room. Reaching the door I found it was blocked and screaming and yelling was coming from inside. Unexpectedly Lydia emerged looking wild, and with tears pouring down her face she forced through the gathered crowd and fled up the Dive steps. I pushed past the crowd and inside the changing room clothes and ballet shoes were strewn everywhere. Girls were huddled around Kerri who was sobbing and her hair was sticking out in all directions. I rushed to her side to console her and accompanied her to Sick Bay, where Matron dished out aspirin and a note off school.

Kerri said Lydia was hiding in the cloakroom and had attacked her for no reason, getting hold of her by her bun and dragging her across the changing room floor. It was horrific. After Kerri went home I wondered if Lydia would be expelled.

After lunch we had Art with Miss Batty, a frail, mousy lady who found it difficult to maintain class control. Some old girls were rude, chewing gum loudly with their mouths open, which she obviously hated, and made constant excuses to leave the classroom. I enjoyed learning how to draw a 'still life' with charcoal, and sketching a bucket, broom and scrubbing brush reminded me of all the shoes we had to clean later.

Mr Mainwaring was back on form today. He did a quiz game he'd invented called 'Round the World'. This involved two girls, one blindfolded and one to guide, and a large globe. Mr Mainwaring spun the globe and on his command the blindfolded girl's hand was placed on the globe, stopping it from spinning. Where the hand was placed was crucial as that would be the country we would have to answer questions on. Once a country had been identified, an egg timer was turned upside down and we had to name as many facts about that place as we could in one minute. It was a fast paced game and great fun. We had some ridiculous facts like 'the only country that has a man-eating spider' (Tiffany must have made this up), and extraordinary facts like 'Cockatoos can fly 500 miles per day in search of food', and 'In some Arabic countries it's polite to burp after meals as a sign of appreciation'. For some reason Mr Mainwaring started calling me Minimus. I wasn't short, in fact I was one of the slightly taller girls, so I didn't understand – I'd ask Dad about this unusual name. At the end of class he asked me how I knew so much about different countries. I told him about Dad's National Geographic magazines and assured him that when I left school I intended to travel the world. Most people laughed when I told them this, but not Mr Mainwaring.

He said I could get lots of good books out of the school reference library and that he would bring me some of his own books from home if I would be interested, which he said were written for people who travelled to far-away places. Of course I bit his hand off!

Ballet was with Miss Olsen today - Miss Wanda was ill. We learned to do a tricky step called 'entrechats', where we had to jump straight up, beating and changing our legs in the air beneath us, and then land back on both feet. She waffled on about the dreaded 'ballon' and about reversing the laws of gravity, then she took off into the air like she was on a trampoline ensuring we clearly understood what ballon was all about. Miss Olsen looked like springs were under her feet. When we practised pirouettes one girl fell over and Miss Olsen told her she was turning with her eyes closed. She said we must use our eyes and gave us slow quarter turn exercises to each wall to help us practise 'flicking' our heads, and get used to using our eyes. By spotting on an object and not moving your eyes from it when turning stopped dizziness. It looked easy but everyone kept falling over.

It was a relief to get into tap class. Mrs Balmaine taught us to do 'stomps' and how to clap basic rhythms. We then stood at the barre practising ankle loosening exercises. At the end of class we went through the first steps to our dance routine. I must practise loosening my ankles and relaxing my knees.

Later we stood in the long tea queue and practised *If*. I knew the first six lines off by heart and hoped I'd remember it as well when I recited it alone in front of everyone.

The sausage rolls Burt made today were yummy and we ate like gannets. This meant we were either so hungry we'd eat anything, or we were finally getting used to school grub. Either way I was eating for England. Some girls were given baskets of fresh fruit with their tea, which Abbey said her mum paid extra for. On Saturday I had to remember to get some fresh fruit with my pocket money – Granny told me you got rickets if you didn't eat fresh fruit.

After tea, walking back towards Junior Dorm with Maddy and the twins, we met Miss Brookes. I hadn't seen her since my audition. She looked so elegant and upright; during my audition she'd shown me how to improve my pointe. She'd slipped off her own shoes, pointed her toes and revealed these amazing insteps. She smiled, said good evening and then the twins dropped into a curtsy. For a moment I felt panic stricken, but the twins indicated for us to copy them. Miss Brookes asked if we were enjoying our first week of school. She seemed pleased when we nodded our heads.

When she was well out of earshot I asked the twins why they'd curtsied. Shirley said all the girls did whenever they met Miss Brookes outside the ballet class and it was a mark of respect because she was the Principal of the school. I hoped my next curtsy wouldn't be so wooden because I felt very un-ballerina-ish.

Back in the dorm I noticed some of the juniors glancing over in the direction of our bunks. As I collected my towel for my strip wash, I surreptitiously looked around for signs of lurking dead spiders.

On my return from the freezing torture of strip washing, I found masses of school shoes lined up neatly on newspaper at the far end of the table. Abbey and I set about our duty buffing up a reflective shine on each shoe. It reminded me of Sunday evening at home polishing shoes on the kitchen table.

After supper I wrote to Great Aunty Phyllis in Devon. She was nearly a hundred and talked for England. I also wrote to Mrs Furst thanking her for the leg warmers. I told her they were highly coveted and asked if she would be kind enough to knit me a crossover in soft pink for my ballet classes.

Whilst writing my diary I was still conscious of curious sidelong glances from some of the girls in the dorm. Abbey leant over from top bunk and whispered to me we were getting loads of strange looks. We agreed that Hannah must have been plotting some mischief.

CHAPTER EIGHT

WEDNESDAY 20TH SEPTEMBER

Last night I discovered the reason for the curious looks. After lights out I snuggled down into my bed and my legs suddenly hit the bottom end - but I was only half way down my bed. The dorm was unnaturally quiet. Top bunk started swaying violently and Abbey leaned over the edge of her bunk and hissed "I can't get my legs down to the bottom of my bed!"

"Me neither!" I replied.

We both crept out of bed and I grappled for my diddy torch in the darkness. Armed with the beam of light, we examined my bed. My top sheet had been folded in half and looped back to cover my top blanket so it appeared normal. As we inspected Abbey's bed, giggles erupted from the darkness and Hannah's head emerged from under Millie's bed making us jump.

"Gotcha!" she sniggered. "Every new girl's given an apple pie bed – its tradition."

We spent an uncomfortable night sleeping on the top of our beds covered over with our travel rugs, fearful of incurring Nanny's wrath again. I slept restlessly, and Dad's travel rug tickled my skin. I had Herman's Hermits song 'I'm into Something Good' repeating in my head like a stuck record. I wondered if army training was anything like this.

On my morning visit to the bathroom there was an 'Out of Order' notice sellotaped to the farthest door. At the end of the corridor a trap door lead to the fourth year annexes. The connection seemed obvious. The loo I chose had dodgy blue staining around the seat so I made sure I didn't touch the seat with my bottom cheeks.

Over breakfast I told the juniors about Lydia Kane bullying Kerri. Sydney said Lydia was 'psycho'. Hannah declared she'd like to give Lydia a taste of her own medicine and drag her by her hair to the lake and offer her up as a sacrifice to the Blue Lady ghost. We giggled nervously, because you just never knew with Hannah.

In history lesson today, Miss Knox lingered on her tales about Henry the Eighth and his six wives. She wanted to arrange a visit to Hampton Court for Prep Form and Year One. This was great news, because it would mean an out of school trip. I felt unhappy that Kerri was still not in school and I hoped she would be coming back. Lydia Kane wasn't in today's assembly, which was fortunate for her with Hannah having dangerous thoughts...

Double Drama was hilarious today. To avoid any repeats involving animal role model pranks, Miss Lazenby began class with some crazy tongue twisters, starting with:

'Slowly the sinking steamer sank' repeated in rapid succession. This was followed by;

'Unique New York' spoken continuously.

Then we formed a circle and were given the subject title 'Carry it On', where one person in the group started a story with a made up sentence. Tiffany led the way with

"I was walking down the street when I..."

Sydney joined in "bumped into my friend Errol who was..."

Esme next "wearing his slippers outside with…"
Shirley followed "gold lamé hot pants and…"
Paula chimed in "a long blond wig with…"
Soon we had a blond, cross-dressing mechanic delivering
encyclopaedias to a sex shop in Soho! Not surprisingly Miss
Lazenby called time out and changed tack. We spent the
remaining lesson playing role models (this time human) and
we all had to guess who someone was by asking questions like,
"are you an artist?" As the 'actor' you could only mime and say
'yes' or 'no' to questions asked. Some of the confident girls
gave excellent mimed demonstrations and I noticed they were
less inhibited.

Lunch was sausage and mash with pukey processed peas.
Major 'Quizzing' was going on in the dining hall, but the
strawberry shortcake pudding saved the day. I was starting to
worry about my sanity!

We had a 'Best Nature Project Prize' incentive from Miss Knox
during nature studies which was to be completed by half term.
I decided to do mine on 'The Deer of the Forest'. I could ask
Dad to get me some books and pamphlets about the forest
before Vis Day.

In ballet we practised our 'spotting' technique in preparation
for pirouettes. There was a lot of falling over when we tried to
spin. I would have to add 'spotting' to my increasing list of
things to practise and improve on. So far my list included:

Splits – improving, but a way to go.

Frog – loads better - I look less like a grasshopper.

If reciting – almost there.

Spotting – bottom of list. Needs huge improvement, have a
bruised bum.

Ankle loosening exercises – a work in progress.

In modern we learned a new kick routine. Not being the Kung Fu kind, these kicks only looked good on those with flexible legs. Mika was a 'kick genius' with legs like rubber. Fortunately this studio didn't have a mirror. Miss Wanda also demonstrated a new sequence from the corner of the studio which travelled diagonally across, called 'Drag Runs'. They looked utterly ridiculous and should have been featured in fast motion on the *Benny Hill Show*. The idea was to run continuously staying very close to the ground whilst dragging your back leg behind you. We did it badly and looked completely wacky. Maddy said we looked like Spotty Dog from *The Woodentops* which sparked off ripples of uncontrolled laughter. Gabby got her coordination muddled and performed a fair impression of a one-armed bandit which caused more amusement. Furious, Miss Wanda put her hands on her hips and marched towards us saying, "It's part of your modern syllabus so grow up and stop behaving like babies!"

It was a shock seeing her angry.

I checked my bed this evening for apple pie folds. Abbey and I set up some dastardly traps round our bunk area. Millie joined us and helped us tie a piece of cotton to the ear of my March Hare and then to the side of the bunk. I finished polishing a few shoes and went through *If* one final time in my head. It was an inspirational poem and I hoped my recital did it justice. Karlyn played my Top of the Pops cassette tonight at full blast. Jo Jo Gunne's voice singing "Run, Run, Run" reverberated around the dorm, and I had to raise my voice above the music to be heard as I said to Abbey, "This would be a great song to get us going in our drag runs."

Hannah overheard me and went charging off across the dorm floor doing manic drag runs and had everyone in stitches.

By lights out we were exhausted.

THURSDAY 21ST SEPTEMBER

I had crazy mixed up dreams last night. I dreamt Cimmie was crawling under our beds in Junior Dorm and when she came to my bed she yelled at March Hare and ordered him to do the splits. March Hare ignored her (obviously), then miraculously came to life and started tap dancing like a raving loony across the dorm floor. Nanny's dog Hamish raced into the dorm and bit March Hare on his harlequin-pants leg and all the stuffing started to fall out. I woke up karate chopping March Hare in a major sweat and was trembling. Falling back to sleep into more fitful dreams I tossed and turned with the words 'If you can keep your head when all about you' repeating in my mind.

The disturbing sound of rising bell today was actually a relief.

I was first down to the bathroom. This had its disadvantages because it was freezing cold and because no-one had used the bathroom yet, no hot water had been run and even the handles of the taps were frozen and hard to budge as I forced them to turn. I stood an arm's length from the hot water tap, waiting for water to gush out as the tap rattled violently and the pipes made strange groaning noises. Just then Mika came in. I told her the taps weren't working. She grabbed the mop handle and said, "Stand back." Raising the handle high above her head she brought it crashing down on the tap with an almighty thwack! The tap instantly burst into life and hot water came spluttering out drenching us. We both laughed and as we dried ourselves off, I told Mika about my March Hare dream and she had fits of giggles and said I'd got a really good imagination. I confided to her that before I wanted to be a dancer, I thought I'd be a Librarian because I could read every book in the library.

I asked Mika how long it had taken her to become so flexible. She was three years old when she started dancing and gymnastics. Last year she'd had an accident and her arm had gone straight through a mirror at the top of the landing. She pulled up her sleeve revealing a thin scar running up her arm, saying it nearly prevented her auditioning for Stavely Brookes. I pulled back my fringe and showed her my birthmark, and was pleased she didn't look shocked; in fact she said I looked pretty without my fringe and shouldn't worry about it. I asked her about her unusual name. Her mother was half Japanese, and the name Mika meant 'New Moon'. Her mother kept her Japanese surname because she had no brothers or sisters to carry on the family name and now she had a double-barrelled surname. I felt comfortable with Mika. It was nice to know other girls had things they were self-conscious about and I knew we'd be good friends.

At breakfast we discussed the punishments Nanny had dished out. Suddenly the doors to the main hall burst open and a tall boy with dark curly hair stumbled through the entrance. He looked embarrassed to have burst in at breakfast time and, flushing red, he rushed through the dining hall with his eyes glued to the floor. Esme said Callum Monnier was thirteen years old and the only boy in the whole school. I wondered if Callum would be in our ballet class and thought back to when I first started on Saturday mornings. I remembered a tall boy in my class but it wasn't Callum.

Kerri was in assembly today - yehhh! We flocked around her like bees to a honey pot and devoured her news. She told us Lydia Kane had been cautioned and we agreed she'd got off lightly.

During assembly Miss Bell announced the names of girls gated from the up-coming Visiting Day. Her speech was followed by a painful silence during which her spectacles dropped to the end of her nose, everyone's backs stiffened and she barked in an unpleasant manner, "Unacceptable behaviour will not be tolerated at Stavely Brookes under any circumstance." Raising her voice she added, "Mark my words girls - retribution to offenders will be swift!" It sounded horrible. I must look up what 'retribution' meant.

With Kerri back at school today lessons whizzed by. I really missed her yesterday. We had our first music lesson with the much talked about Mr Julius. The music room was beautiful, with an elegant grand piano set in the large bay window area. Mr Julius was what my Granny would call 'otherworldly'. All I knew was he was very tall and exactly as Tiffany had described him. The horse dog called Sultan sat sprawled across the floor throughout the whole lesson, also looking otherworldly. Mr Julius played us various beautiful pieces of music and we sat gazing goggle-eyed at his expertise. He brought us back down to earth by demonstrating examples of what he called 'simple chords' and asked how many of us could read music. Janice and Paula - both had private piano lessons - shot their hands up in the air. Mr Julius studied them, linked his hands behind his back, stared at the ceiling, closed his eyes, said a long "Hmmmm" and then (with his eyes still closed) said in a whisper, "You're all going to have to learn to read music, dahlings."

As we blinked at each other he glided around the class, handing us each our own individual music books. I was eager to open mine, but less interested when I opened the front cover to find a book full of blank staves. Mr Julius pulled his piano stool in front of us and then, clearing his throat, proceeded with our first music lesson. Today we learned about black keys being grouped in twos and threes, low sounds and high sounds, the names of the white keys and the important middle 'C'. After learning 'counts' and 'bars', I was positive I'd soon be able to play an easy tune and made a mental note to hang around outside the piano room in the Dive, in the hopes I might grab any moments it was free to practise what I'd learned.

Before the end of the lesson he told us to sit quietly and close our eyes. He then played such a heartrending piece of classical music we were hypnotized. I fantasised being a soloist in a ballet dressed in a stunning tutu. When he finished playing we clapped loudly. He then stood to the side of the piano and bent forwards into a mock bow. I wondered why he hadn't become a musician.

Later, Kerri and I had our final *If* rehearsal. I noticed Lydia sitting quietly in the far corner of the day girls' changing room and I hardly dared to look.

In English lesson we studied Creative Writing. Our set prep for Monday was an essay with the title 'The Secret Box'. I was looking forward to this, but needed somewhere quiet to do homework because the dorm was too noisy.

Ballet flew past today and Miss Wanda said our pirouettes were improving because we were using our eyes.

Following ballet we had national with a stand-in pianist. Miss Wanda quickly became tetchy with Miss Gildersleeve, who was obviously inexperienced and played everything at a snail's pace. Consequently we danced in slow motion which was agonising. After Miss Wanda commented on the speed making our movements laboured, she stepped it up to an impossibly fast tempo leaving us gasping for breath. Imagine twenty odd girls in a circle, linked by their arms with hands on each other's shoulders, spinning round and round with voluminous character skirts whirling round their waists – that was us! Just before the end of the dance Tiffany trod on Shirley's toe, tripped up and we then fell over each other like a stack of tumbling dominoes. To compound our hysterics, Miss Gildersleeve still had her head down and was bashing on the piano keys long after we'd stopped, blissfully unaware she was playing to an empty house. Miss Wanda went crimson and yelled.

"Miss Gildersleeve, will you STOP R-I-G-H-T N-O-W!"

Weak with laughter and terrified all at once, we pulled ourselves together. Miss Gildersleeve then stood up, her piano stool scraping noisily on the polished floor, and with a deadpan face uttered, "Is something wrong dear?"

We expected Miss Wanda to explode in frustration, but she simply stalked out of the room. No one breathed a word but there was lots of silent mouthing going on. Moments later she returned calm and composed and behaved as if nothing had happened. The rest of the lesson was spent studying French national costume and learning to recognise time signatures for each piece of music. Without further musical fiascos the lesson whizzed past.

This evening, Mika came to my aid while I was struggling doing my front-splits practice. Whilst I worked towards achieving the ultimate flat-turned-out position, she gently pressed my knees down to touch the floor. She said I was definitely getting better, reminding me that it was still early days. It was painful but I so wanted to get a better turn out.

I wrote a short letter to Nana and Grandpa Huntley and told them about our latest dance classes and the poem recital tomorrow. Grandpa Huntley drew cartoons on the back of his letters to me, so I drew a cartoon of a pin-girl in a tutu doing the front splits. My matchstick ballerina had high insteps, amazing splits and smiled radiantly like she was enjoying the whole tortuous process.

Only ten days left on the countdown calendar until Vis Day. Millie was teaching me some Caribbean patois while I shone shoes. It was amazing how much I was learning about other countries and people as well as dancing. I hoped that someday I would travel to all these places that my friends called home. How amazing would that be?

FRIDAY 22ND SEPTEMBER

Tonight was a full moon. I kept this strictly to myself but was on my guard.

Reciting *If* in front of the class turned out to be a doddle. As luck would have it I ended up reciting last. After the long wait I felt a bundle of nerves with a horrid dry mouth. One by one we had to stand by the blackboard in front of the rest of the class and recite the whole poem from memory. Miraculously, and despite all my fears, I didn't succumb to stage fright. More interesting was that I was able to detach myself in front of my classmates. Normally shy, this just went to show that constant rehearsals did pay off because I didn't even have to think!

After ballet we had a specialist come into class to fit and measure us for pointe shoes, with each girl's foot being examined closely. Miss Olsen and Miss Wanda discussed metatarsals, ankle strength, pointe shoe makers and then which shoe offered the most support for each girl. The pointe shoes looked beautiful but certainly weren't comfortable! When my turn came to try a pair I felt like Cinderella! Miss Olsen said we'd be starting pointe work soon so must learn how to darn the blocked toe area. Esme informed me that juniors asked their crushes to darn their first pair because they had more experience. This left me with two problems:

1) I didn't have a crush
2) My sewing was lousy.

During shoe-polishing duties, Abbey and I discussed the lack of available students who were not already crushed. Abbey said she didn't need a crush and so far had managed well without one. We agreed we'd help each other with darning when the shoes arrived.

Much later when I thought everyone was done with baths, I had a strip wash alone in the bathroom. As I wiped the condensation off the mirror to wash my face I thought I saw something - a shadow - passing the bathroom window. I glanced around and there was nothing. It was probably a trick of the light, but I looked out of the window just in case and as I leaned out Maddy burst into the bathroom making me jump out of my skin. I told her why I was looking out of the window and mentioned the full moon tonight. She agreed that we must be vigilant after lights out.

When Nanny turned off the lights I waited ages for something ghost-like to happen. I must have drifted off to sleep because I was woken at 11-30 p.m. by Maddy prodding me and hissing in my ear, saying she'd heard spooky noises. Hidden under my travel rug we laid in wait on my bottom bunk until well past midnight, but no Blue Lady materialised. I could only guess that a watched ghost never performs.

CHAPTER NINE

Only one week until Vis Day. After class finished Miss Wanda showed us some exercises to practise which would prepare us for pointe work. She must have read my mind because she produced a pointe shoe, a large needle and pink darning thread and demonstrated how to darn a pointe shoe. It looked easy enough. Then she produced a bottle of foul smelling liquid saying, "Girls, you have to toughen the skin on your toes before you even start pointe work. Every night you must get into the habit of wiping your toes with cotton-wool." She waved the cotton wad at us and doused it in the stinky stuff, "Soaked in surgical spirit it will toughen the skin on top of your toes and help prevent them skinning." This was followed by one of her lopsided grins. It sounded like torture!

Back in Junior Dorm the twins showed us their single trophy pointe shoes, complete with specially penned messages written across the blocked satin toe of the shoe, presents from their crush Rose. I was slightly envious of their special pointe shoes, but more so because they were personal gifts from the best dancer in the school. I made a mental note to find a suitable crush who was a brilliant dancer that I could aspire to.

Our afternoon walk was commandeered by the lesser evil prefect, Rita Warlock. After last week's disaster and subsequent gating combined with the dorm punishments, we were eager to please. Rita had an eagle eye *and* a black book. During our out-of-school excursions, Rita operated a cunning 'crocodile rotation' system. After the obligatory facial make-up check and a glance at our knees for hitched-up skirts, we hurtled down the road like an invading army. Every two minutes Rita moved the lead couple to the back. Perhaps she imagined it would deter us from plotting further mischief. Subsequently we arrived at the stores, shopped and returned to school all in less than one-and-a-half hours.

This was a victory for 'Sergeant' Warlock. My measly twenty pence pocket money bought me a Fab ice-lolly, a Barratt's Sherbet Fountain and a real pomegranate from the fresh fruit selection. I'd seen a junior called Janice buying one and she said they were tasty and lasted ages. This sounded like a good idea.

Back in the dorm Janice conducted a pomegranate eating lesson. Several of us sat at the central table with our pomegranates cut in half. Janice handed out pins and showed us how to ease out a fleshy pip, suck the juicy flesh off and spit the pip out. Although delicious, the pip-by-pip method took forever and I didn't imagine Nanny would be impressed with the discarded pips scattered over the floorboards. Janice wasn't bothered, saying Hamish would hoover up the evidence.

Before tea we all trooped round to the side of the lake. It was serene and had a slightly surreal quality about it in the early evening, but the ornamental balcony that overhung the lake looked slightly ominous as it loomed over our heads in the fading light. Esme said there was a list as long as the tea queue for a place in the dormitory nicknamed 'Doom Dorm' after the

Blue Lady legend. The atmosphere made me shudder and I suggested heading for the safety of the dining hall.

At tea Burt asked me if we'd found any ghosts in the lake? It sent a shiver down my spine and I felt my cheeks redden. Burt had to be a spy. Squinting at us with his skew-whiff chef's hat he looked a bit bonkers as he simultaneously ladled a heap of beans onto my sodden toast. I suspected Burt had shares in a baked bean company as we always had beans with something.

We had a disco dancing competition in the dorm this evening using my Top of the Pops cassette. Released from punishment duties (hurrah for Nanny) we could let our hair down. Lily had recorded the best songs on my cassette including T Rex's 'Metal Guru'. One surprise she slipped in was Benny Hill's funny song 'Ernie' which, when his comical voice blared out, everyone larked around to – even Nanny got caught up in the fun and sung along when we screamed out the chorus '…and he drove the fastest milk cart in the west.' The competition was won hands down by Abbey, dancing a funky groove to 'Telegram Sam' and stealing the show. Abbey said I could come and stay with her in the holidays and we could go to a disco together.

Before supper and the competition, three students came into our dorm carrying a tuppaware overflowing with homemade muesli and selling it for five pence a mug full - daylight robbery! Hannah told me that tuck sales weren't allowed but existed like a kind of 'black market'. Goodness knows how they sneaked past Nanny's room, but what a jammy way of earning extra pocket money.

SUNDAY 24TH SEPTEMBER

I slept like a log after the dancing competition. My good mood faded when I found out that Rita Warlock was on church duty today. The church service was uneventful to begin with. When the yucky incense was wafted over us, Tamsin Barrie rolled her eyes to the top of her head and narrowly escaped fainting head first over the pew bar. The two girls either side of her held her upright and lowered her onto the pew bench. Queuing by the choir stalls waiting to be blessed, I noticed one of the senior girls, already kneeling at the communion rail, had taken the wine goblet. She appeared to have prised it from Father Benedict's grip and, tipping her head back, she downed the lot. Father Benedict's bushy eyebrows met in the middle. He cleared his throat loudly and scowled at the top of her head which was lowered in a praying position. We stood waiting for ages while Father Benedict refilled the goblet and returned to the communion rail. I noticed Hannah - never missing an opportunity for a prank - pass a folded piece of paper to the boy in the end choir pew as she passed en route to the altar. When we returned to our pews I noticed the choir boys leering at Rita as she walked past them to take communion. I wondered what the note had said.

After church Rita 'eagle eye' Warlock frogmarched us back to school with not so much as a skip in the park. Back in the dorm, Hannah bragged that she had written a note to the choirboys saying that the girl wearing the blue skirt (Rita) had no knickers on!

My afternoon was taken up with prep in the privacy of the library. It was a very peaceful room and not many girls seemed to come in here. The floor was tiled and when no one was around I tested the floor out with a few tap moves and it made a brilliant - but deafening - noise. My 'Secret Box' essay was coming along nicely. It was about a young girl who opened her grandmother's jewellery box and found a secret compartment.

When the compartment was prised open, she experienced a woozy sensation. Unbeknown to her she had released the spirit of her late grandmother. The girl absorbed the wilful character of her grandmother, who drove her on in a relentless quest to discover the mystery surrounding her death. I got carried away and had composed the whole story by the time tea bell rang. I realised I was starving and had a niggling headache.

In the tea queue everyone was talking about next Sunday's Vis Day. I mentally went through my list of things to ask Mum to get:

1) Writing paper, featherweight airmail, envelopes and stamps
2) Bovril
3) Hairspray
4) Soap
5) Mug
6) Dad's photos of forest / deer
7) Dad's National Geographic magazines
8) Books
9) Surgical Spirit

My headache got worse over tea so I beat a hasty retreat back to the dorm and lay on my bed. Later, Hannah became really noisy, whipping up enthusiasm for a new plan she'd hatched. Always craving attention, she'd planted herself on the centre table so we couldn't avoid looking at her and clapped her hands loudly until she'd got our full attention. Her scheme involved writing complaint letters to receive freebies in return. She based this on a letter she claimed her Mum wrote about a sub-standard box of Maltesers which were stuck together. The manufacturers replied to her Mum returning two boxes as a goodwill gesture. She rounded up the dorm's waste paper baskets and fished out our sweet wrappers. I told Hannah to count me out because I didn't possess any evidence. She said it was a lame excuse, found my blazer and rummaged its pockets, rescuing an old walnut whip wrapper. I was doomed! Hannah instructed us to find the manufacturers' addresses on the wrapper labels and compose our complaints enclosing wrappers as evidence. Mine was:

Dear Nestlé

This week I purchased my favourite chocolate treat, a Walnut Whip, and on biting into the chocolate cone, discovered to my horror that the normally delicious cream tasted off. It would be unhygienic to post mouldy food.

Walnut Whips have always been a favourite of mine, and I felt it my duty to inform you as your chocolate is normally so delicious.

I am very disappointed.

Yours faithfully

Lara Edgecombe

Hannah checked not only our letters, but watched as we sealed them and then forced us to hand them over and menaced a first class stamp from each of us, knowing most of us would have chickened out.

After lights out I was in a lot of discomfort and eventually had to nip out to the loos. To my horror I discovered my period had started, so I raced back upstairs and had to wake up Nanny who was 'keeper of personal supplies'. By the time she'd found an assortment of giant pads, I was sure Little Dorm (opposite Nanny's room) had overheard. Back downstairs in the dimly lit loos as I fumbled with the ludicrously oversized towels, I heard my name being whispered. It was Tiffany. She'd overheard Nanny talking about sanitary towels and thought I'd need moral support. She said all Little Dorm had started their periods and I was obviously way more mature than the other girls and then announced I was 'one of their gang' now. I decided to go along with it for a quiet life.

Back in the safety of my bed I snuggled up to March Hare wishing I was in bed at home. I drifted into a fitful sleep wondering why, now my periods had started, that my boobs were still the size of cherries. There was simply no justice.

MONDAY 25TH SEPTEMBER

In the bathroom this morning Sydney cornered me and presented me with a bag of assorted sanitary towels and tampons. Predictably, my period had now become public property. She reassured me it was okay for a virgin to use tampons and I should come to her for advice on everything. Not too sure I'd take her up on that. I knew Sydney was only trying to help, so I thanked her anyway and beat a hasty retreat upstairs before I got involved in more embarrassing interrogations.

My 'Secret Box' essay was collected in English today. I was surprised when Miss Bell said mine was quite long – I mean - how long *is* an essay? For no reason it made me irritated.

Later in drama, Miss Lazenby taught us correct breathing technique using our diaphragms. She said all dancers had to act! Aunty Ellen maintains that the best dancers are able to portray dramatic qualities and have passion. I felt very emotional about everything today which must have meant there was hope for me.

In ballet, lucky for us, Miss Yates was back at the piano. Miss Wanda was happier and we practised jumps called 'pas de chats' - the step of a cat. One of the juniors had a very high jump. Miss Wanda called her elevation 'natural ballon', which made me think how great it would be to defy gravity. I'll remember not to stand next to her whenever possible during the centre work.

During modern class Miss Wanda demonstrated our new lyrical dance routine which had crazy head rolls, floaty arm movements and loads of body-bends. I loved the music called 'A Horse With No Name'. It was kind of rock-ish, but with a folky feel to it. I asked Miss Wanda the name of the band. It was called America. I recognised it from Top of the Pops and thought I was probably a closet rock fan disguised in a sugary pop shell.

Hurrah! In the tea queue I was presented with an air mail letter. I was so excited when I saw it was from Capri and could hardly wait to get to the dining tables to read it. Everyone had post today. I ripped open my air letter to see it was from my new pen pal, Maria Lazares. I read it with excitement.

Dear Lara

Thank you for your letter. I was interested to hear about your hobbies and ballet school. Here are some details about myself.

I am 12 years old (nearly 13) and I like reading, collecting pen-pals and pop music. I'm in love with Donny Osmond and hope to marry him soon. When are you getting married?

I think our pen-relationship ended on this last sentence. I noticed a piece of paper had fallen out of the envelope. Picking it up I realised it was a small photo. I looked at it and couldn't understand why she'd sent me a photo of a boy. I showed the photo to Abbey who grinned and said 'nice boyfriend'. I turned the photo over and read the tiny writing on the back.

'Maria Lazares. June 1972.'

I couldn't hide my disappointment but deep down felt mean and judgemental. I didn't know quite what I had expected from a random pen pal selected from a girls' magazine, but anyone thinking of getting married at twelve - particularly to Donny Osmond - was clearly not on the same wavelength as me. Mind you, if she knew I wore a blue pinafore over my school uniform and polished shoes every night I don't think I'd appear very cool either. So our paper friendship had ended before it had begun. Perhaps I would get to visit Capri when I travelled the world in a ballet company. I hoped I'd have more in common with my New Zealand pen pal, Grace Short.

Walking back to the dorm with Abbey and Esme we bumped into Mr Deluca. We stood there smiling until Esme nudged me and we all trilled "Good evening, Mr Deluca." He addressed Esme by her surname and after observing me for what seemed like ages he tapped his head.

"I remember your face from the audition. You've got a cheeky smile."

I sensed Esme eyeballing me. He asked if we were looking forward to Visiting Day and straightaway Esme went off on one about Kenya, saying how far away it was and how she only saw her parents during the holidays. Thankfully Mr Deluca cut her short and told us to hurry back to the dorm because it was getting late.

Esme went round telling everyone I was a teacher's pet because Mr Deluca said I had a 'cheeky smile'. For some extraordinary reason (probably the bad relationship she'd got with Esme), Hannah defended me, saying it was a load of rubbish when it was obvious to everyone Esme was the teacher's pet. Some of the other juniors put in their two pennies worth and instantly a gigantic dorm argument erupted. Nanny heard the raised voices and came storming in with her arms flapping and Hamish hot on her heels. She was furious and broke up the shouting and barracking, separated the yelling masses and set us all to work on menial punishment duties.

The argument seemed to be all but forgotten after we'd slaved away at our duties and later, just before lights out, as I was making my way to the bathroom, Nanny quietly called me into her room and asked kindly if my period was giving me any problems. I thanked her, telling her I was okay. She offered me some shortbread fingers which I devoured under the watchful glare of Hamish, and then I excused myself to go and wash.

In the bathroom it was steamed up and airless. I wiped the mirror with my dressing gown sleeve, removed my brace and stared at my face. I wished I could be like everyone else and outgrow my fringe, but at least my hair was dark and straight. I supposed I could look a bit like an Indian Squaw. I stood pulling faces at myself studying what changes wearing my brace had made. My moment of solitude was interrupted by some fourth years bursting into the bathroom, one holding a bottle of ink. Ink Girl looked menacing and said I wasn't to tell anyone. I obviously failed to convince her and they grabbed my arms behind my back and Ink Girl stuck her face right up next to mine and made me swear I wouldn't tell or else. Mentioning a Glitto bath helped me decide! Clutching my brace in my hand, I raced like a frightened rabbit back upstairs to the dorm. Sometimes boarding school seemed like a prison. Realising I'd nearly crushed my brace during the interrogation I replaced it and, kneeling down beside my calendar, I crossed off yet another day. Only five days left until Vis Day. Yippeeeeeeeeee!

CHAPTER TEN

WEDNESDAY 27ᵀᴴ SEPTEMBER

Yesterday evening we had an unexpected fire drill. This involved deafening alarm bells, getting out of bed, putting on dressing gowns and slippers and filing down the stairs to wait outside in the freezing cold. I told Kerri about it in break whilst we raided my tuck box. She thought my life as a boarder was a great laugh. I told her that standing outside in the middle of the night and being yelled at by a prefect was not my idea of fun. I enjoyed seeing Kerri every day, we always had loads to catch up on. She was my link to the outside world and my best-best friend. The twins overheard us talking about the fire drill and said that main house drills involved escape hatches, trap doors, climbing down never ending ladders from great heights and, if you slept in the 'Doom Dorm', you might even be dangled over the edge of the balcony, sitting in the fire escape 'sling'. Apparently most girls were too afraid to be lowered over the edge!

THURSDAY 28ᵀᴴ SEPTEMBER

In the bathroom before breakfast today Maddy and Sanchia collared me and asked what my period had been like. I felt like putting up a poster to keep everyone updated.

Maddy said we were all sisters in this, but I wished this had happened to someone else first. I put on a brave face and told them that laggy briefs were ten times more uncomfortable. I have so much to tell Lily, not least because I'd gained notoriety as being the only girl with a brace, a fringe and who started her periods in Junior Dorm aged 11 years. Notoriety for being the only new girl to do the splits would have been far cooler!

School seemed to whizz by when we had single lessons. Our 'Secret Box' essays had been returned. Miss Bell gave me an A minus and wrote on it, 'Well done! An intriguing plot held together with honest dialogue'. I wasn't sure what she meant by 'honest dialogue', but I was pleased because English was my favourite subject.

In history today Miss Knox discussed our potential school trip in October to Hampton Court, reminding us we would need extra pocket money for the trip.

During ballet we were given new regulation frills. These were small half-skirts that only just covered our bottoms but looked very elegant. Miss Wanda said we now looked more like ballerinas. I couldn't wait for our pointe shoes to arrive so we could start pointe work and *feel* like ballerinas. I'd read about one of the great romantic ballerinas, Marie Taglioni, whose Russian audience were so captivated by her farewell performance that after taking her pointe shoes they cooked and ate them. Gross!

I found an interesting ballet book in the library and brought it back to the dorm to read. I was in the middle of reading about a famous Ballerina who used to go to our school when there was a commotion at the far end of the dorm. Nanny entered looking agitated and clapped her hands for the music to be turned off. A moment of unnatural silence passed then she offloaded.

"Girls, it has come to my attention that the large laundry bag carrying the clean pinafores has gone missing."

This was followed by a heavy sigh as her gaze drifted across the dorm.

"If anyone knows of its whereabouts please return it to the wash house before the weekend."

She then added for good measure, "Of course we are due to stop the punishments this weekend as everyone has been on such good behaviour, but..."

We hung on this last word as she shrugged her shoulders and scooped up Hamish, who had just finished patrolling up and down the room, turned on her heel and closed the door behind her. The air was heavy with silence and we fidgeted uncomfortably. Nanny should have been an actress.

Hannah immediately called a meeting and demanded that the guilty party confess. No one owned up. It would be awful to cause an upset so close to Vis Day. We were put on alert and 'Operation Pinny Recovery' was set in full swing. Spies were recruited, window watch was elected and Hannah appointed herself 'Operation Controller'. We had 24 hours to find and return the wayward bibs. I suggested we called the operation A.W.A (Aprons with Attitude) and Mika piped up, "How about B.A.B - Bibs and Babies", which caused ripples of sniggers and everyone got stupid. Hannah called order in the nick of time just as Nanny burst in with the supper tray. Hurray, it was iced buns! Nanny knew how to weaken our resolve.

Before lights out I crossed off yet another day on the countdown calendar. I was really looking forward to Visiting Sunday and seeing all my family.

FRIDAY 29TH SEPTEMBER

I wanted to phone Mum and Dad tonight to ask what time they would be picking me up the next morning. The phone 'booth' in the Dive was so public you could hear everyone's conversations. Mum had said not to worry if I couldn't phone because Dad might think I was homesick. I was secretly hoping Dad would pick me up on his motorbike.

The Pinny Patrol was on red alert today. Operation Pinny Recovery was fully operational. Over breakfast Hannah galvanised us into action calling us 'spineless', saying we'd never achieve our aim if we allowed ourselves to be seduced by a tray of iced buns. I thought that was a bit rich coming from the girl who'd Eggo'd a second bun, but kept my mutinous thoughts to myself; a lot of what Hannah said didn't make sense. She just liked controlling everything. She was a control-a-thon. My task with Abbey and Mika was to search inside the Scrub House without being spotted.

In school I told Kerri about Hannah's military operation and she agreed to check the day girls' changing rooms - just in case.

After tap Abbey, Mika and I sneaked into the Scrub House. Paula, being the smallest, was going to be our watch. She hid discreetly in the cover of the bushes. It was like something out of *Dad's Army*. Inside it was dark and dank. On one side the roof was lower and had narrow slit windows beneath which were deep stone sinks. Each sink had a large, wooden slatted scrubbing board to the side. Facing the doors a couple of ancient washing machines had a large printed notice above saying 'Staff Use Only'. Behind the doors and up a concrete step was a maze of rusting pipes, covered with steaming layers of dripping ballet tights, which were coiled and wrapped round the end pipes like boa constrictors. Above the 'drying-pipes' hung a large wooden airer draped with soggy school uniforms and coat hangers suspending all sorts of dance kit. It smelt like a wet dog! An ancient mangle with a rusting enamel bowl underneath stood nearby. Abbey spurred us into action and we began scurrying around looking behind washing machines, in an old cupboard at the back of the hut and bingo! There, right at the back of the cupboard, was a large laundry sack. We dragged it out and it was covered in dust. Inside we found the missing pinnies. I cautiously poked my head out of the door to alert Paula who, much to my horror, had deserted her post and was running towards Scrub House. Fortunately no one saw her. Dragging her inside we instructed her to find Hannah and let her know of our discovery. While all was quiet we replaced the laundry bag where we found it.

Back in the dining room, we exchanged different versions of our discovery in breathless whispers. Hannah instructed us to remain tight-lipped and leave the rest to her.

By supper time I felt I was about to explode in anticipation of the pinny return. On cue Nanny burst in with a huge tray of bread rolls and corned beef. As she left the dorm Hannah silently waved her arms at us and put her fingers to her lips. We heard Nanny opening her door and after a long silence she said, "How did this get here?"

We stifled giggles and Hannah motioned us to be quiet. Nanny came back and announced that the laundry bag with the missing pinnies had miraculously appeared and asked if we knew anything about it. Her eyes rested on Hannah who looked Nanny straight in the eyes without blinking and cool as a cucumber said, "Dunno, Nanny. None of us have the faintest idea."

Eat your heart out, Pinocchio!

SATURDAY 30TH SEPTEMBER

In the bathroom this morning I remembered I hadn't phoned home, so I got ready quickly and, armed with my list, raced to the phone booth in the Dive before the rush for breakfast. The booth was a wall-to-wall chipboard Tardis and smelt sweaty. Once the door was closed and I was sealed inside, the stink was horrible.

I dialled home and Mum answered. She said they couldn't wait to see me and was making my favourite rhubarb crumble with clotted cream posted from Aunty Phyllis in Devon. I could hear my brothers shouting in the background. I read Mum my short list of essentials, sent my love to Dad and asked if he could pick me up at 9 a.m. tomorrow. Then the pips went and in mid sentence I was cut off.

I escaped the suffocating Tardis and raced up the Dive steps to the canteen, finding myself alone in the breakfast queue at a quarter to eight. A record!

Ballet and our walk to Postbridge Stores seemed to whiz by. We were so excited about tomorrow.

After the walk I lay on my bottom bunk with my ballet book and read again about Alexandra Haydon, who had originally studied at this school and later became a soloist with the Royal Ballet Company. It talked about her lifelong love for ballet, her years spent training at Stavely Brookes and her 'unfailing dedication', with photos of her dancing the lead roles in Swan Lake and Giselle. I so wanted to be as talented and beautiful as her.

Gazing at the photos I had this brilliant idea. Alexandra Haydon was my perfect role model. If I could ask her to be my 'crush' it would be the most amazing inspiration for me, and she would be that perfect dancer that I could look up too. I was now wondering how to find out her address and write to her. I decided to ask Mum first.

Abbey and I were bored this afternoon so we walked over to tea early. We stopped by the new studios near the lake to see who was inside and it started to rain. We could see some older girls inside and they were playing loud rock music. The three girls were wearing coloured jazz pants and we had to peer around the edge of the farthest window to watch. I had to stand on my tip toes and as Abbey and I craned our necks to see what the girls were doing there was a tap on my shoulder. I spun around to find one of the girls we'd just been watching was standing behind us grinning.

"Hey you two, fancy coming inside and watching us?"

We smirked like idiots, silently nodded our heads and shuffled behind her into the bright strip-lights of the Alexandra Haydon studio. The three girls introduced themselves as Tassia, Sophie and Sian, and said that they were working on some choreography ideas in preparation for next term's choreographic competition. Because we didn't say anything they must have thought we were gormless. I cleared my throat to find my voice and almost dribbled. When my voice finally emerged it sounded high and squeaky. I asked why they were starting to rehearse this term. They laughed and told us they all had major exams coming up and were trying to keep on top of things. I felt awkward but the redhead smiled and grabbed some chairs for us, saying that before tea they'd just got time for one more run through.

Tassia had this wild mass of long, curly red hair and my eyes were riveted to her as she walked into the centre of the studio and lay on the floor on her back. Her lime green jazz pants looked almost luminous under the fluorescent strip lights.

Sophie was operating the record player. I spotted the Pink Floyd album sleeve, called 'Meddle'. Tassia started the dance lying on the floor and shaking different parts of her body. The guitar music was distorted and weird. She then threw her head in half circles to either side whilst the music built up into a pulsing sound. Then Sian ran around the room in this crazy, zig-zagging run, every so often doing a head-over-heels floor roll and landing onto one shoulder, then immediately springing back up into a run. They finished the dance with Sian suspended in mid-air, face-down in a horizontal line supported by Tassia's feet, which were positioned under her tummy to hold her up. It looked painful.

Sophie turned off the music and they collapsed into a heap, gasping to catch their breath. In total awe, Abbey and I clapped like lunatics. The girls laughed and then asked us what we thought of their choreography. Abbey told them it reminded her of the music from *Doctor Who* and they agreed. Tassia was dripping with sweat and, catching her breath, she told us how they all wanted to be contemporary dancers when they left ballet school. She said that they loved the style and freedom of this kind of dance and could experiment with their bodies more than with classical ballet. I nodded my head knowingly (I hadn't got a clue, but what I did know was I liked this crazy style and wanted to see more). Tea bell interrupted us and Tassia said we could watch them practising any time. They were so cool!

CHAPTER ELEVEN

BACK TO SCHOOL

MONDAY 2ND OCTOBER

After yesterday's out-of-school Visiting Day everyone was more relaxed. Even the girls whose parents lived abroad had relatives arrive to take them out. Last night Millie showed me her photo album. Tobago looked really lush and she had some amazing photos of big leatherback turtles and scary looking caimans.

   In drama we played some interesting games based on animal images. Miss Lazenby was either very brave or suicidal; obviously the Gabby versus Hannah bum-biting incident several weeks ago had slipped her mind. Splitting us into groups of six, she told us to focus on 'bringing into play the sounds and body movements of any animal we chose'. It worked like this: each group had to decide on an animal and then one group at a time moved around the studio acting in their chosen animal character. With everyone else watching, Miss Lazenby would shout instructions like 'focus on the tail' or 'move the mouth' until we were really immersed in the animal's character. However, the situation got tricky when she instructed our group to make noises in character with our moving animal. Voodoo, Miss Lazenby's pet Chihuahua, leapt up looking alarmed when he heard Sydney in cat-mode, making a very realistic cat wail as she arched her back in a mock fight pose. Voodoo then did two laps of the room, skidded on his hind legs and careered round Miss Lazenby's chair before leaping up onto her desk with a blood curdling snarl and then launching himself like a canine missile towards the wailing 'cat'. Sydney realised her impending fate and like lightning rolled onto her back, legs and arms in the air in submissive surrender position in the nick of time. Voodoo landed unceremoniously, sniffed Sydney, then cheekily lifted his leg and left a steaming puddle. He trotted out of the studio with Miss Lazenby, a billowing mass of floaty skirt and clanking bangles, staggering after him in hot pursuit which caused mass hysteria amongst the class. It was a close call for Sydney, who received a thunderous round of applause amidst cries of 'gross dog', and slaps on the back for her quick thinking. Sydney was clearly going to be a good character actress.

Later in ballet, Miss Wanda told us that the pointe shoe fitters would be visiting school on Thursday afternoon, so national class was cancelled. I was sure my feet were getting stronger. I'd been practising an exercise called 'short foot' every evening for strengthening foot muscles. After barre work today Miss Wanda demonstrated a new exercise called 'Flippers'. She explained pointe shoes wouldn't allow our feet to work in a natural position because of their close fit, so we needed to practice relaxing and strengthening the toe muscles and ligaments with daily drills. She showed us how to spread our toes and hold this position for as long as was comfortable and imagine wearing flippers. I wasn't sure if my feet would ever look as beautiful as Mika's, but I've added Flippers to my ever-increasing list of things to practise.

Our modern routine to 'A Horse With No Name' was really groovy now. We'd all become dab hands at flick ball changes and practically the whole class could do continuous step-turns without falling over. Dancing in groups of three, everyone had to watch each other and I felt less shy dancing in front of my friends. Miss Wanda thought we'd all improved and said we'd soon begin practising improvisation in preparation for next year's modern exams.

WEDNESDAY 4TH OCTOBER

It seemed Nanny had completely forgotten our punishment schedule. Narrow escape! I spent ages yesterday after dance classes trying to sort out my nature project. I was still finding it hard to get quiet moments to myself with no one else around. When I was alone it gave me room in my head to think, plan and practise. With Mum's approval I'd been mentally composing my letter to Alexandra Haydon. Now I needed to put pen to paper and make sure I didn't sound pushy or cheesy. After all, she was famous and I didn't want to blow it. My draft copy began:

Dear Alexandra

I hope you won't mind me writing to you with an unusual request. I am 11 years and 4 months old, and have just started as a full time boarder at Stavely Brookes School. My dream is to become a professional ballet dancer and having followed your career closely, I am proud to say I am your biggest fan.

While settling into my life here as a ballet boarder, I have recently found out that all the girls have to choose a crush. I expect you know about the crush/mother figure thing from when you were at school here. All the girls - except me - have chosen someone who inspires them and is still training here, but my biggest inspiration is you and your dancing career. Therefore I would like to ask you if it would be possible for me to have a crush on you. I know it would be more like a pen-pal crush because it is going to be by mail and from a distance, but it would be the biggest honour if I could, and of course only if you think it's OK. If you were to agree to be my crush, please could you send me a signed pointe shoe (worn during one of your performances) together with a signed photo?

I hope to hear from you soon

With love from

Lara Edgecombe

I read it several times, and decided to write the final copy on my best quality Basildon Bond paper using my non-smudging fountain pen. I didn't want to make a big deal about it to the other girls so I kept the envelope, marked Personal and addressed to The Royal Opera House, Covent Garden, London, safely hidden away from curious eyes.

After modern I nipped into the main hall on my own to drop Alexandra's secret envelope safely in the post box so it was ready for the next collection. My heart missed a beat when I dropped it into the box and I realised there was no turning back now. I raced back to the dorm with my fingers and toes double-crossed.

That night Abbey, Maddy, Sanchia and I practised doing the splits, frogs, flippers and short foot. Afterwards we set to work on our nature projects. Miss Knox had brought the handing-in dates forward to just before half term (the last week in October), leaving just over three weeks to get it finished. I showed Millie Dad's photos of deer on the forest. Millie chatted to me for ages about her project and showed me sketches of humming birds and jacamars. I wrote to Dad asking if he could find anything unusual on the forest to make my project more exciting like Millie's. I suggested a deer skull would be an unusual but welcome addition...

THURSDAY 5TH OCTOBER

In the bathroom this morning there was an overpowering smell of perfume. Everyone who came in immediately sniffed and asked what the smell was. It reminded me of the French perfume Esme always wore but I didn't dare say anything. Everyone was excited about having their feet matched up with the pointe shoes we'd ordered. After ballet we headed straight to the main hall, which was crowded with queuing girls and piles of shoe boxes. Several ballet teachers were there to help us, as well as the shoe fitting specialists. While waiting, Kerri told me that during half term she was going over to Ireland to see her family. I said I'd probably be visiting my grandparents in London. We discussed our favourite ballets and agreed that if we couldn't become famous ballerinas at the Royal Opera House, then we would travel abroad together on our audition tours to gain a place in a European ballet company.

When my turn came and my foot was eased into the satin blocked-toe, I was shocked how inflexible the pointe shoe seemed. The shoe-fitting lady made us try several to find the right fit and produced shoes of various widths and shapes. She said every famous dancer had their favourite maker, and showed us how the shoe soles were embossed with the maker's stamp. Mine had Δ *and* x on the sole. After a lot of rising up and down onto our pointes on a special mat to avoid marking the shoes, Miss Olsen suggested I tried an *xx* with a long vamp. She said my shoe would only fit properly when my metatarsus didn't slide down into the shoe and was properly supported by the sides of the block. She explained that dancers had to work on their shoes which stretched a bit through heat, movement and sweat.

Eventually I left the hall, excitedly clutching my first Freeds pointe shoes and a length of satin ribbons that I had to sew on. We were told to 'break them in' by wearing them around the dorm with socks over the top to keep them clean, I couldn't think of a more uncomfortable way to spend each evening, but we had to because our first pointe work class was next Monday. Esme maintained that a ballerina must suffer for her art.

This evening we'd all been clomping around the dorm's wooden floorboards in our sock-covered pointe shoes and we sounded like a herd of elephants. On Saturday night Rose, the twin's crush, was going to show us how to darn our shoes. This was assuming everyone's crushes weren't going to be doing all the hard work. I wondered whether Alexandra Haydon darned her shoes now she was famous. Why would she bother?

My calm moment was broken when a loud wail arose from the far end of the dorm. Everyone stopped what they were doing and looked in the direction of the sound. Esme was standing in the dorm doorway with her eyes bulging, brandishing a perfume bottle in the air and exclaiming in a shrill voice, "Who's been using my perfume?"

She was holding an ornate, empty perfume bottle upside down and was waving it around looking bonkers. I suddenly remembered the smell of French perfume in the bathroom. Everything went quiet. Esme drew in her breath, her nostrils flared and she threw an accusing look around the dorm. We all stared back at her, stiff with tension. Her glare landed squarely on Hannah who, feigning innocence, just raised her eyebrows and shrugged. Esme pulled a contorted face, uttered a guttural cry and fled noisily out of the dorm, scrambling to keep her balance. She looked completely ridiculous trying to break into a run in her long-grey-sock-covered pointe shoes as she screamed her parting shot over her shoulder.

"You bitch!"

Then we heard her feet going 'clomp, clomp, clomp' as she fled down the stairway.

CHAPTER TWELVE

FRIDAY 5TH OCTOBER

When rising bell went off this morning I noticed Esme's bed was empty. I hoped she hadn't run away. When we did our hair before breakfast I was watching how Mika did her bun. Her oriental black hair was even thicker than mine. Using a big hairnet she squashed her hair from the pony tail into the hairnet, pushing it into a donut shape on top of her head with just five big pins. My hair was stubbornly slippery today and I had to enlist Mika's help to create one long plait, secured with elastics each end, so I could then jam pins into the plait and force it into a bun-like shape. It was torture.

My thoughts were interrupted as Mika elbowed me and rolled her eyes in the direction of the doorway. Esme entered and her face was unrecognisable. Nanny had her arm around her shoulder and pounced on Mika and me (everyone else had suddenly vaporised) and asked us if we would look after Esme and accompany her to breakfast, adding that she had been very homesick. We leapt to attention and I felt horrible that Esme had been so upset by the fued with Hannah. She may have been an oracle, but I couldn't help feeling sorry for her. I looked up oracle in the library dictionary; it said it was an authority who was always correct. I wondered if Esme had told Hannah something which wasn't true and Hannah was punishing her. Poor Esme.

As we raced past the Scrub House on our way to breakfast, Esme said my bun looked like a loaf of plaited bread. I laughed and she said my face would look a better shape if I made my ponytail higher, quickly adding it would also make my pirouettes better. I could see Mika pulling a funny face at me behind Esme's back.

We were late for breakfast and, arriving to an almost empty dining hall we found Radical Radish, who sneaked into the kitchen behind Burt's back and returned with some leftover soggy toast. Radish took my tin mug and filled it with tepid tea. By now we were alone in the hall. Esme eyed my jar of Oxo suspiciously, informing me that Oxo was gravy. I explained liquid Oxo tasted just like Bovril and could be made into a hot drink or spread on toast. When I tried to open it the lid was stuck, so I had to turn it upside down to get a grip on the lid. It loosened, and when I placed the jar the right way up on the table and lifted the lid an amazing thing happened. The liquid Oxo rose up in a giant bubble like an erupting volcano and hovered momentarily in a shimmering mound. Then the bubble burst and it was instantly sucked back into the jar! We all stared, gobsmacked. Esme was stunned and asked where I had learnt this trick. I had to dig Mika's knee under the table and told Esme it took skill and practice. Maybe this trick would give me some status amongst the old girls.

Being late for breakfast made us late for assembly so we had to sneak in the back. No one took much notice because two juniors were desperately trying to play the piano for the hymns. The piano was out of tune and sounded dreadful. I prayed the rest of the day would get better.

Later we had double geography with Mr Mainwaring. It was a lovely bright day and he made us get our gum boots and arm ourselves with warm woollies. We tore back to the dorm, grabbed scarves and boots and arrived back at the classroom a few minutes later excited and breathless. Mr Mainwaring clapped his hands together purposefully and cleared his throat.

"Today, ladies, we are going to learn to be self sufficient."

He paused for our reaction. We stood gawping at each other. Tiffany and Sydney started giggling as Mr Mainwaring swept across the floor and herded us like a flock of silly sheep through the doorway towards the open land in front of the 'out of bounds' wood. He purposefully strode in circles around numerous spades, forks, hoes, trowels and packets of seeds that lay on a huge plastic sheet.

"This," he gestured towards the pile of garden tools, "is our new outdoor project. To get some fresh air and as part of our 'grow your own' project, we're going to create a first year vegetable patch. Get yourselves into pairs. You will each have your own allotment. At the end of this year the best vegetables will get a prize!"

Excited chatter followed and Mr Mainwaring wiped his brow.

"It will mean getting your hands dirty and your boots muddy, but you will all learn how to live off the land."

I started having a Robinson Crusoe moment as I envisaged travelling to far-off lands and owning my own banana plantation. My romantic thoughts were brought to an abrupt halt as Mr Mainwaring bellowed, "Wake up girls, find a partner, choose a plot and get digging!"

I scanned the mass of blue pinnies, spotted Kerri and we quickly linked arms just in the nick of time because out of the corner of my eye I noticed Esme was making a beeline for me. I didn't think I was ready for her expert gardening knowledge to be thrust upon me. Armed with a spade and Kerri with a fork we marched across our rugged piece of land. It was a far cry from a banana plantation and a bit nippy. The gardening area had obviously been used for bonfires because there was a lot of ash lying around. For the next hour we sweated and toiled accompanied by the background drone of whingeing from Sydney and Tiffany. I found the only way I could get my spade into the solid clods of earth was to position the spade upright and then jump on it with both feet. It was quite effective until everyone recognised my usefulness and borrowed me to show them my fool proof clod-crumbling technique, which nearly killed my thighs. By lunch time we all had small rows of rectangular-shaped plots and were ready to begin digging-in some compost. Mr Mainwaring weaved in and out of the borders scattering his special-mix compost across our miniature allotments, his free hand holding his cloak out to the side so it caught the wind.

All seemed to be going well when there was a sudden cry from Millie. Everyone looked up to see that Paula had caught Millie's finger with the edge of her spade; the nail had split and blood was pouring from the top of her finger. At the sight of the blood Millie dissolved and began wailing. Mr Mainwaring looked alarmed and asked for a volunteer to escort the injured party immediately to Matron's sick bay. Everyone volunteered! Millie, who was crying bitterly, asked Mr Mainwaring if I could take her. I asked if Kerri could come just in case Millie fainted and we needed two pairs of hands. He gave me a dark look but agreed!

As we escorted Millie to the sick bay I realised how much mud was stuck all over our pinnies. Finally they had found a practical use. Kerri had escaped the pinny wearing torture (a day girl benefit) but now her uniform was caked in mud. Millie's finger had now ballooned and gone a yucky blue-black colour. We arrived at Matron's home, a long, old barn positioned underneath the shadow of a big weeping willow tree. The barn looked ancient with a lopsided roof, crooked walls and tiny dark windows. The sign hung above the front door said 'The Stable'. It was very different to the rest of the school buildings and the main house. I wondered who had lived there hundreds of years ago, but it was probably horses or mules. The entrance porch had a thick wooden door and a hideous, rusty knocker nailed bang in the middle in the shape of a gargoyle. I rang on the outside bell and it clanged noisily. The distant echo of a dog howling came from inside but there was no answer so I had to ring again. Instantly a louder howl answered the bell-ring, which shook the walls and made us jump out of our skins, closely followed by the clunking, scraping sounds of stiff bolts being loosened and the muttering of an agitated voice coming from behind the thick wooden door. Suddenly the door burst open and a large rounded woman dressed in a blue uniform filled the doorway. We found we were at eye level with Matron's massive boobs. When she started to talk her dog went haywire so we couldn't hear anything she said. Turning around she filled the whole doorway with her vastness, and speaking in a high voice with a funny accent said, "Max, be quiet this instant."

She shuffled round to face us, directing her gaze straight at Millie, who was still sobbing.

"Oh, I see we have an injured soldier. Well come on in my dears and I'll sort out that finger in no time. Oh, would you mind taking your muddy boots off dears, so we don't go messing up the floor now."

We followed behind her - there was only just enough room for Matron to go single-file in the tight hallway - as she squeezed her large body through a narrow door which led us into a long room with low ceilings and a neat row of six beds.

"This is the sick bay", she told us. "If you are too ill to go to classes, or infectious, you are isolated here until you are well enough to return to your dormitory." As she inhaled deeply her boobs rose in front of our eyeline and I had to bite my lip to stop myself laughing.

"And *if* you're ill for too long, you will get sent home."

Millie then came to life, eyes wild like a rabbit in headlights.

"What happens if you die in sick bay?"

Matron roared with laughter.

"That's not very likely, but if that was the case, then you would still be sent home, but in a box!"

The thought made us giggle nervously. During this unusual conversation, I noticed that all six beds were covered in identical pink candlewick bedspreads and the room was quite cosy, with pretty matching bedside lamps and old-fashioned lanterns on the walls. It was the sort of room I imagined Snow White and the Dwarfs living in. Matron ushered us into the far corner. There was a table, some wooden chairs, and a small padlocked cupboard which she unlocked, opened and got out all sorts of first aid equipment. While she was cleaning and dressing Millie's finger, she asked if we liked dogs. I only nodded because the others did, but I'm secretly nervous of most dogs – especially when they are large and snitch their teeth. Matron had a funny, rolling accent which made me wonder where she came from. Finally, Matron held Millie's hand up in the air to admire her handywork. Beaming at Millie's mummified finger and looking satisfied, she mumbled something about the surgery and we followed her along a further corridor, which then led us to a room with a large engraved brass plaque on the door. It said 'Doctor's Surgery'. Matron tapped on the plaque.

"This will be your first port-of-call if you are ill or injured, and hopefully it will be in Doctor Feer's visiting hours."

She sat us on a wooden waiting bench and then shuffled off humming to herself. We waited until she was out of earshot, then Kerri leaned towards me and whispered, "She's clearly from Ireland because she's got an Irish accent." She would know because she had lots of Irish relatives.

When Matron returned, she was accompanied by a very large Husky dog called Max, who looked like a giant wolf fluff-ball and was a bit scary looking because of his size and all that fur, but he seemed completely soppy and docile. As soon as Max saw us eyeing him, he immediately rolled over like a puppy and, as Millie rubbed his tummy, his tongue lolled out of his mouth and he made a deep purring noise like a giant cat. I knelt down and joined the tummy rubbing, no longer terrified. Watching us cooing over Max like a baby, Matron chortled, saying Max's appearance often scared people, but in fact he wouldn't harm a fly. After a while, she told us we must run along or else we'd be missing our dinner.

We arrived late, charged along the Dive corridor, threw our wellies into the day girls' changing room and rushed shoeless up to the main hall. Girls were queuing for seconds of fish and chips. Burt must have remembered I was late for breakfast and eyed me suspiciously. I told him it was my day for being

Florence Nightingale and he gave me a toothless grin saying, "It'll be kippers and custard for you next time."

Later today in ballet, Miss Olsen told me that my bun was looking much neater. I didn't dare look at Esme. I also performed a set of near-perfect pirouettes and didn't fall over once (te-he-he!). Miss Olsen was in a springing mood today. We spent forever practising 'sissonnes', named by the dancer who invented the step. We did a 'sissonne fermée en avant', which involved a spring forward into the air while taking one leg straight out behind you, then landing softly on the front foot and lowering the raised leg down to 'close' the position. Unluckily, Miss Olsen became distracted during corrections. Leaving us balanced on one leg for ages, she talked about not leaning the body forward when alighting from the spring and to keep lifted out of the hips. We struggled in vain to maintain our positions. She became agitated, then made us perform travelling sissonnes one by one from one corner of the studio to the other. Mrs Yates, our amazing pianist, valiantly tried to inspire us with her wonderful playing. Miss Olsen even stood behind Gabby and physically lifted her off the floor, attempting to show us how to 'spring effortlessly'. By the look on Miss Olsen's face I bet she wished she'd chosen someone springier!

We arrived in tap exhausted and learnt the last steps to our 'Herman's Hermits' routine. I loved tap and got a second wind because the music really got everyone going and made you want to dance. Mrs. Balmaine had so much energy and she made everything such fun. I was sure I saw her dog, Biba, tap with its paws as it sat watching from beneath the grand piano. When we were split into groups to practise, Esme sat next to me. I told her I thought Biba was cute, and she then went off on one about the dog being named after a famous 1960's fashion boutique - she was sooo annoying!

The highlight of this evening was the post. I received my long awaited letter from my pen pal in New Zealand. I thought I was going to burst with excitement. I must have frustrated Abbey and Maddy by refusing to open the letter at tea, because I wanted to read it quietly back in the dorm without half my friends reading it over my shoulder. I raced back to the dorm after tea, flung myself on my bottom bunk and excitedly tore open the big air mail envelope and read the rough, scribbly writing:

Dear Lara

Hi from Auckland! I hope you won't be too disappointed when you read that this is not Grace writing back to you, but her twin brother, Joseph. She asked me if I'd like to write to you, as she's already got two pen pals in the UK and she's not interested in ballet, travelling, pop or rock music. I'm very into heavy metal, and although I don't do ballet I want to become an actor, so I guess you could say we share some similar interests.

I am thirteen years old, five foot five, enjoy all kinds of theatre and music, taking photos and, like you, I want to travel the world - New Zealand is miles from anywhere!

I have three sisters including my twin Grace, an older sister called Annette (17 years) and a younger sister called Bonnie (10 years). I go to drama classes twice a week and am learning to play electric guitar. I have lessons every Saturday morning with my sister's boyfriend who's in a rock band. Our house is near the beach and during the holidays we go sailing in my Dad's yacht. I also like canoeing and have a dog called Napoleon.

I've read the letter you sent Grace and I hope you are not upset that I have taken her place as your pen pal. I won't be offended if you don't

*want to write to me because you may prefer to write to a girl. Please
let me know by return of post, and I'll look forward to hearing from
you.*

Best wishes from

Joseph

*P.S: Hope you like the photographs. I am better looking in real life (so
is my dog!).*

I studied the handful of photos. Joseph sounded fun and
looked like a nice guy. He'd sent photos of his house, which
had enormous palm trees all around the garden and looked
really tropical, and there was one of him and Napoleon
standing beside a purple sports car. His dog looked like Lassie.
There was also a photo of his Dad's sailing boat (it looked like
something out of a Bond film) and a picture of the whole
family. I wanted to go and visit him in New Zealand now! I
was so excited and lay back on my bed and pressed my feet up
into the mattress of Abbey's top bunk to get her attention. She
peered down, shrugged and pretended she wasn't interested,
so I told her I was writing to a boy who had a yacht and an
electric guitar. Suddenly I had the whole dorm's attention. I
was then instructed by all my friends to ask Joseph if he had
any similar friends who'd make good pen pals - for just twenty-
one other girls!

SATURDAY 7TH OCTOBER

I dreamt about New Zealand last night. I'd never been abroad,
but was sure that if I got a holiday job I could manage to save
the air fare. I read a few articles about N.Z in some of Dad's
National Geographic magazines, but I was going to look in the
library this afternoon after the walk to the shop to learn as
much as I could about the North Island and Auckland.

One of the students took us for ballet this morning. We didn't have a pianist so it was quite boring until another student came in and they used some pop records for the ballet exercises. Hannah said they weren't allowed to do this, but no-one ever checked up on them. It was outrageous practising pirouettes to rock music. Whoever said ballet was stuffy?

The rain drowned us on our walk to the local shop, where I bought one packet of crisps and saved the rest of my money in an envelope, hidden at the back of my writing folder for future travels. It was going to take me forever to save anything with our measly pocket money, but my Gran always said that if you save the pennies, the pounds take care of themselves.

After our walk I settled into the library which I had to myself. After working on my nature project, I looked for information on New Zealand. My peace was soon shattered when some of the older girls raced into the library yelling and laughing. One of them stared at me and then announced in a loud voice to her friends that I looked sweet. I hated being told I looked sweet. Luckily I was saved by the tea bell and fled.

I then had the embarrassment of having to go back into the library because I'd left my mug on the table by the newspapers. The girl who'd said I looked sweet asked me my name. I told her and she said that I reminded her of the girl on the Pears soap advert. She then caught me off guard by asking for a honey bunch on me. I had no choice because all her friends were watching me, so I agreed and mumbled that I was late for tea and tried to smile as I fled out of the door. The girl who had honey bunched me shouted out her name (it sounded like 'Batsy') as I retreated into the main hall.

I was thankful for the safety of the tea queue and could hear Esme's authoritative tones above everyone else. Following the

111

sound of her voice, I finally found Esme, Mika, Maddy and Abbey queuing up near the canteen. I told them I'd just been honey bunched. Esme told me I was lucky, adding that I'd now get spoilt rotten for no reason and receive loads of presents. She made me feel like I'd done something wrong. I could see Abbey pulling a silly face behind Esme's back, so I quickly changed the subject to talk about Rose, who was going to come to Junior Dorm tonight to demonstrate how to darn pointe shoes. Esme said we had to use 'Beau Care', a special cleaner to keep our ballet shoes looking beautiful. When I phoned home tomorrow I'd ask Mum to get me some.

Rose came round at 7 p.m. and showed us how to darn our shoes. It looked easier than it was and before long we'd all stabbed our fingers and thumbs with needles and blood stains marked our beautiful pink satin pointe shoes. Oracle informed me that if you pricked your finger when darning a pointe shoe you should mark the sole of the shoe with your blood for good luck. I ensured my shoe had a good bloodstain on the sole as I needed plenty of luck with my weedy left pointe. Rose patiently demonstrated how to darn the area around the toe block and down the sides. She had another pair which were brand new and set about showing us how to soften the pointe block by either hammering one block against the other, or by squeezing the toe block in the door hinge. My Dad would go barmy if he saw what we were doing to our expensive pointe shoes.

Nanny eventually came in to turn off the lights and I was relieved to stop darning and listen to my radio through the earphone. David Cassidy was singing 'How Can I Be Sure'. I thought about the poster Lily had of him on the wall beside her top bunk and I still think he looks like a girl.

CHAPTER THIRTEEN

SUNDAY 8 TH OCTOBER

I went to sleep last night composing a letter to Joseph, '…oh, by the way, have you got twenty-one other friends…' However, I slept like a log right through the rising bell and was woken by irritating prods from Nanny and with Hamish licking my face. Yuk! It was time someone invented a dog-breath freshener.

When we'd all gathered outside Junior Dorm, done up to the nines in hats and coats, we discovered - to our dismay - that Cimmie was to be our duty prefect walking us to church, which explained her scheming expression when hovering around us at breakfast. This would be fun.

Our walk was unusually fast and the high winds were whipping up everyone's skirts and blowing our bowler hats off. We all got a bit hysterical and Cimmie got very agitated and told us it was time we behaved like ladies and not babies, adding, with a cruel twist of her lip, "or maybe you should stick to regular nappy changes." Then she turned on her heel, purposely barged into Paula who was knocked sideways and then stomped off, muttering just loud enough for us to hear her say, "Gormless bunch of blue-bibbed midgets!"

During the service it got very hot and everyone started peeling off their layers of gloves, scarves and big overcoats.

With all us juniors stuck on the front rows we were not difficult to spot and couldn't easily get up to much mischief in church. When the choirboys did their ceremonial task of wafting the suffocating incense from the censer, the sickly sweet smelling smoke drifted immediately towards our front pew. Feeling slightly sick myself I looked up, wondering if Tamsin would faint - the warning signal was when her eye lids fluttered, eyes rolled upwards and she turned grey - but realised she was still trying to struggle out of her overcoat. Paula then grabbed her sleeves and with a lot of effort helped her to yank her coat off. To my horror and through the cloud of thickening incense smoke, I saw she was still wearing her pinny! Mass elbow digging followed, with all eyes turned to Tamsin and bursts of uncontrolled giggles erupted from our pew. The sight of Tamsin in her blue-frilly pinafore in the front pew of church was killing. To make matters worse, Cimmie had sneakily - as if by magic - appeared on her hands and knees in the side aisle. Like a woman possessed, she hissed her orders at us to make Tamsin put her coat back on. The choirboys had by this time joined in and were leaning over their pews and openly pointing at Tamsin, sniggering and snorting. By the time Tamsin had struggled back into her coat everyone's eyes were fixed on our pew. She must have been so embarrassed and hot that her eyes rolled upward and before anyone had time to react she fell into a dead faint with a loud thud as she keeled over, hitting the pew railing like a rag doll. The whole pew then descended on her as one before she had time to slide towards the floor, all of us grabbing any part of her body we could reach. Cimmie rose from her crouching tiger position and went into commando mode. Before we had time to blink she'd swept Tamsin up and thrown her over her shoulder like a sack of potatoes and carried her outside. Amazingly, not one single person batted an eyelid. The congregation simply returned to their prayer books and the service carried on as though all this kerfuffle was a normal part of Sunday service. Am I living on another planet?

Cimmie's fury continued when she made the unwise choice of walking us back to school through the park. The wind once again caught our skirts, sending them flying up round our ears. While we grappled hysterically with our hems, the boys playing football were having a proper eyeful of our knickers. They yelled some really rude things and made loud wolf whistles. Cimmie looked like a wild woman. With her mad-zombie expression and strands of black hair wrapped round her face in a tangle, she stormed across the football pitch towards them. I thought she was going to box their ears but she stood right in front of them with her legs astride in the centre of the muddy pitch. Putting her hands on her hips she yelled, "I'm calling the police, you perverted bunch of hooligans."

Unfortunately they just laughed at her. In a terrible rage she uttered a cry of fury and spun round, but her foot flew up from underneath her and she came down to earth flat on her face in the mud. We all burst out laughing. When she lifted her head up she looked like a cave woman with war paint daubed all over her face. As she staggered to her feet we all fell silent in fear of her reaction. She stuck her neck out and let rip a mad sort of scream. Caked in mud, she advanced with lightning speed towards our crocodile to vent her newfound fury on us juniors. Striding towards the front of the line she purposely kicked Millie, giving her a dead leg. Grunting, she turned on Gabby who was standing next to Millie and shoved her so hard that she nearly fell over. Luckily for Gabby we all grabbed her as she toppled backwards. Cimmie was seriously OUT-OF-

CONTROL! She then stormed forwards and returned to her leading position at the head of our crocodile, yelling, "If I catch any of you gormless nappy-pants making fun of me again, I'll gate you until next summer!"

Pausing to check how deeply we were crushed by this verbal threat, she added, "Now get your dribble-caked pinnies back to your nursery!" She then inhaled deeply before screeching at the top of her voice, "On the count of three!"

The walk back to school was an Olympic challenge. I mean, we actually did a half-hour downhill walk in ten minutes flat. We couldn't have done it faster skiing down a mountain - it should be recorded in the Guinness Book of Records.

I spent the rest of the afternoon working on my nature project and slaving away at darning my pointe shoes. It was a thankless task and my darning was useless. I remembered that I had to phone home about the Beau Care pointe shoe cleaner. I checked in my writing folder on my savings status and unfortunately had to use some of my meagre travel money savings for my phone call. At this rate I was going nowhere fast.

The Dive and phone booth were empty when I got there. Dad picked up the phone and we talked for ages. I told him about Mr Mainwaring making us all dig a vegetable patch. Dad said it was a useful skill. I mentioned travel plans and he promised me extra pocket money if, in return, I helped him dig our garden. I asked Mum about the pointe shoe cleaner and she said she'd get some posted. Mum told me Aunty Ellen was arranging for us girls to go to the Royal Opera House during half term to see a ballet. My money soon ran out and we were cut off. After leaving the phone booth I went into the piano room and tried to play a few tunes. There was a piano book already set up from the last lesson with very complicated pieces of music. Reading music was not as easy as I'd imagined. If I could learn the notes by sound, separating the notes from each hand it may help. I needed basic Grade 1 music.

That evening I got a shock when the girl who'd honey bunched me yesterday came to see me in the dorm. She'd even brought me a box of Maltesers. I confessed that I hadn't heard her name when I ran out of the library. She said she wasn't surprised I'd run off, because her parents were always telling her off for being too loud. She said everyone called her Patsy but her real name was Patricia, which she hated because it sounded ancient. She was really sweet and told me all about her family who live in Bahrain. Her older sister was at our school, but left last year and now worked for a ballet company in Austria. Patsy was 15. I told her all about my sister and brothers. When I told her about what happened in church today she fell backwards onto Millie's bed, laughed out loud, called Cimmie a dragon and said Nanny was an angel compared to Cimmie. I showed her my efforts at darning and she pulled a long face, saying she didn't like ballet as much as she used to and her favourite style of dance was tap. She stood beside my bunk bed and demonstrated some really groovy tap moves called 'wings'. My friends quickly gathered round her and she ended up teaching Abbey, Mika and I some cool moves called 'time steps'. Nanny came in with our supper and unfortunately Patsy had to leave, but not before Nanny gave her a hug goodbye.

MONDAY 9TH OCTOBER

After form period today, we had double English with Mr Mainwaring because Miss Bell was ill. Mr Mainwaring told us about the importance of literature. I could see he'd got something up his sleeve. He brought out a great stack of books by Charles Dickens. He then took up his eagle-like standing pose in the centre of the class and scanned round the room.

"Today, Lieblings, we are going to read passages from the master. 'Great Expectations' will stretch your minds and allow you a glimpse of the past."

I had no idea why he called us Lieblings, but it had to be better than him singling me out and calling me 'Minimus'.

We went round the class reading aloud, one page each, then Mr Mainwaring read aloud until the bell ended the lesson. I was going to enjoy Charles Dickens and the orphan Pip. The man who frightened Pip by coming up from behind the graves sounded terrifying (even more terrifying than Cimmie covered in mud) and I couldn't wait for our next literature lesson.

After lunch today I was still starving. Kerri and I ate her peanut butter sandwiches in the day girls' cloakroom. Between mouthfuls I told Kerri about the weekend. She wanted to see my newly darned pointe shoes, so we raced back to Junior Dorm. No one was around and Nanny was at lunch. I warily sneaked Kerri up to the dorm with my heart hammering in my chest. Just as we sat down to examine my pointe shoes we heard footsteps on the stairs. In a panic I hid Kerri behind the wardrobe curtains! Nanny came in and asked me why I was there when it was clearly time for me to be in afternoon school. My stomach started crawling. To make matters worse Hamish came in and, stupid dog, headed straight for the curtains. In a blind panic I raced towards Hamish and did the only thing I could think of and picked him up. He was not happy. Nanny looked shocked and told me to put him down immediately. I carried Hamish as far away from Kerri's hiding place as I could. Nanny frowned and said she was just about to take him for a walk and asked if I could go to her room and get his lead off the coat hook. Still carrying Hamish I staggered towards the dorm door.

"Are you alright?" she asked.

I assured her I was and asked her to open the door for me. She sighed looking puzzled, opened the door and I walked out carrying Hamish, who by then weighed a ton and was wriggling like an eel. We were followed by Nanny who opened her bedroom door and I was able to put the struggling Hamish down inside her room and effectively block his exit. I told Nanny I was late for class and had left my project back in the dorm. Without waiting for her answer, I quickly closed her door behind me shutting Nanny and Hamish inside, ran to get Kerri from behind the curtain, checked the coast was clear and we fled down the stairs giggling helplessly. During maths, Kerri and I whispered about our lucky escape and agreed it was both scary and exciting breaking the rules. I still didn't understand why day girls couldn't go into the boarders' dorms, and I hoped that things would become less strict when we left Junior Dorm.

In ballet we all arrived armed with our newly darned pointe shoes. Miss Wanda inspected the ribbons and told a few girls they were sewn on in the wrong position. She showed us again how to fold down the back of the shoe and follow the line that the edges of the outside heel made, and then to sew our ribbons on following that diagonal line. She said it made sure the ribbons laid flat and held the shoe on securely. At the end of class we put our pointe shoes on and went to the barre for our first exercises. Miss Wanda made us face the barre with our feet together, and we then spent what seemed like forever practising rolling up and down through our feet, then doing the same in turned-out first position. She said this was as important as tendus and frappés were for ankle strength.

Gabby complained that her toes were hurting, and when we took our shoes off animal wool was passed around the class to help cushion our toes. I made a note to use more surgical spirit on my toes. Pointe work was obviously not for wimpish feet!

Modern class went by in a flash because we were busy polishing off our 'Burning Love' routine. There was this really crazy bit at the end of the routine where we had to do massive shoulder shimmies right across the room. These reminded me of something I'd seen in old movies, where jungle tribesmen performed war dances and moved around shaking their shoulders (and other things) and went completely bonkers. I just know we all looked barmy! I was sure I saw Miss Wanda hide a smile when she was watching us. All she said at the end was, "That was an interesting effort. Now, let's stop marking it and *do it properly!*"

Before supper this evening our dorm was turned into a rehearsal area. With the middle table pulled to the side we had a huge space cleared for practice, and we shimmied the evening away. As usual, bossy Hannah took charge and broke the routine down so that we could practise it bit by bit. I overheard Esme muttering under her breath that Hannah danced like a 'fisi'. I asked Esme later what that meant and she told me it was a Swahili word for hyena! There were definitely bad vibes between Hannah and Esme.

When Nanny arrived to turn lights out, she was surprised to find us all in bed asleep.

I had crazy, weird dreams about jungles, monkeys and hyenas. I dreamt that I was in a swamp and Cimmie rose out of the quicksand with a blackened, muddy face and was dragging behind her an iron chain attached to her leg! I think it was all muddled up with Great Expectations, the man from the marshes who'd grabbed Pip, and Esme's sinister Swahili mutterings.

In drama Miss Lazenby tied Voodoo to the long leg of the TV stand, which was at the top of the drama studio. She told us he was 'in season' and she had to keep him away from the other dogs.

It was a double drama lesson and with us all sat on chairs in the usual circle formation with Miss Lazenby at the top end, she theatrically cleared her throat and jingled the little glass bell which she kept on her desk purely to restore order. Voodoo acknowledged the tinkling bell sound by whimpering and pulled the TV stand closer towards our group. Miss Lazenby leant forward, heaved her ample chest over the desk top, picked up a book and announced in a slightly breathless voice, "Year One. Our challenge today will be to do justice to the comic masterpiece of Richard Sheridan by reading his marvellous play 'The Rivals'."

We all stared, none the wiser. Her bosom heaved and she continued with passion.

"This is a farce - a comedy of manners - and a comic masterpiece about false identities, romantic entanglements and," she narrowed her eyes and jutted out her chin in our direction, "parental disapproval."

We were all eager to take on the challenge, not least because this was the first time us Prep formers had ever been given the title of 'Year One' by a teacher. We were given characters to share, taking our reading parts in turn. I read the part of a Mrs. Malaprop. It was great fun and nice to have the chance to read a real play. During our reading Voodoo nearly strangled himself and, despite his short lead, he still managed to perform disgusting looking movements on the curved leg of the chaise longue. We were all grossed out.

At tea the duty prefect, Julie, told me that a large parcel had been personally delivered for me by a gentleman friend of my parents. She said it was being kept safely in the head girl's room. I gobbled my tea and dragged Kerri with me to visit Saphi's room. Julie led the way. The second floor of the main house was a mass of winding staircases, long, creepy looking corridors and loads of dark wooden doors with name plaques on them. Saphi's plaque said 'Head Girl'. We knocked on her door twice but there was some very loud music playing. Then Julie banged really hard with her fist until finally someone opened the door. I noticed several prefects were lounging on the two beds inside the room and it stunk of cigarette smoke. I spotted Cimmie through the thick smog and she gave me a double dose of the evil eye. I could feel myself shrinking under her menacing glare. Fortunately Saphi came out from behind another door at the back of the room and broke the tension.

"Lara Edgecombe?" she said, looking from Kerri to me. I held up my hand and she laughed in a friendly way, saying that I wasn't in the school classroom now. She bent over beside the bed Cimmie was lounging on and lifted a large cardboard box off the floor.

"A man called Mr Mercy came to school today when he was passing through the town and he kindly delivered this parcel for you. He said it was from your father."

Mr. Mercy owned the baker's shop in my village.

I hoped the parcel contained my pointe shoe cleaner but it was too big. Kerri and I struggled down the stairs with it and she helped me carry it over to Junior Dorm before her Dad arrived at school to take her home.

Opening the parcel took forever because Mum always used loads of sellotape. Inside the box were masses of scrunched up newspapers to stop things breaking. Wrapped in a plastic bag hidden right in the centre was a bottle of Dab it Off and a notelet from Mum, explaining it was better than the Beau Care because, (a) it had a built-in applicator sponge and (b) it was much cheaper! Then I opened the shoe box which was hidden beneath the newspaper and discovered a grim, bony deer skull. How cool was that?

Everyone in the dorm came to examine the skull. Esme announced that it was, indeed, the real thing. Being an oracle she would know. Also inside the box was an assortment of tiny animal bones carefully wrapped in tissue paper. Dad had numbered each one and given me a list of the type of bone and named which animal it came from. We laid it out very carefully on the central table. Studying this animal graveyard we all agreed that it was a spooky looking assortment.

Nanny nearly jumped out of her skin when she saw the bone graveyard with the centrepiece skull. I proudly thrust the skull towards her and her eyes popped as she put up her hands in horror and demanded to know what on earth I intended to do with it. I explained all about the nature project and she said that it couldn't possibly stay in the dorm because it was unhygienic and would give us all ticks. I tried telling her that I only needed to keep it until half term, which was when Miss Knox would take the project and my bone exhibits away, but poor Nanny was not happy and kept stalking up and down the room glaring at the display like it was going to come alive.

Then Hannah had a brilliant and cunning idea. She told Nanny that it would smell if it was kept inside and, because I needed the skull for my supporting project material, during the cold weather it would come to no harm *and* be much more hygienic if I could hang it outside the dorm window. Nanny needed no convincing and produced some string. The skull was suspended on an elaborate pulley system of Hannah's dubious design outside our dorm window, which conveniently faced the woods. Millie said it was a good thing we weren't living in Tobago, as it looked like some kind of creepy black magic mascot hung out to ward off evil spirits. Maybe it would ward off Cimmie!

CHAPTER FOURTEEN

WEDNESDAY 11ᵀᴴ OCTOBER

First thing this morning I checked that my deer skull was still intact. Thankfully it was okay. I didn't like to admit this, but it did look quite evil just hanging there like some cannibal had chucked out a leftover.

Double maths was so boring that poor Gabby fell asleep and was given a detention. We were getting ever closer to revealing who the phantom snorer was. Maddy told her Mum, who's a nurse, about the girl who snores and she told Maddy that people who snored didn't sleep well. I was peeved that she failed to mention what happened to the people who were kept awake by the snorer. Maddy reckoned the noise was definitely coming from Gabby's bed. Gabby hotly denied the allegations. Hannah said she was going to borrow Karlyn's tape recorder one night and secretly record her.

We had to dance our modern routine one by one today. When it got to my turn I tried to think of something which would stop me getting so jittery in front of everyone, and I remembered Esme saying Hannah danced like a hyena! Just imagining Hannah with the head of a hyena and cackling as she danced made me laugh to myself and feel less nervous. When I finished

125

dancing my routine, Miss Wanda said my shimmies had
excellent attack. That entire practice had obviously paid off.

THURSDAY 12TH OCTOBER

It's confirmed! Gabby was definitely the phantom snorer. I'd
woken up in the night boiling hot and dripping with sweat,
because Millie insisted on closing the window before lights out.
While I lay on top of my sheets cooling off, I had become aware
of a distant purring sound, which got louder and louder until it
sounded like an old man snoring. I crept out of my bottom
bunk and wiggled like a snake on my tummy all the way over
to the far side of the dorm. This took forever as the floor boards
creaked and I didn't want to wake anyone else up. As I reached
Gabby's bed the snoring sounded deep and sure enough, as I
raised my head level with her pillow, I was confronted with her
snores. Stifling my urge to giggle, I spent the next ten minutes
creeping back to bed on my stomach and getting mouthfuls of
dust, hair and fluff. Nanny should invent a 'sweeping under
the beds' duty.

During ballet today Miss Wanda decided to spend half the
class correcting our pirouettes. No amount of rosin or spotting
was working and the whole atmosphere had become very
tense. Tiffany called Miss Wanda's bouts of anger 'hormonal
tantrums'. Miss Wanda said that none of us used our stomach
muscles despite wearing laggy briefs, then talked about
listening to our music, focussing our eyes as we turned and the
benefits of learning how to 'fake a fall' gracefully. Next came
the story of a famous dancer who fell flat on her bottom during
her grand entrance scene in front of a full house, but recovered
gracefully as though nothing had happened and did her best
ever performance.

Abbey leaned towards me and whispered something about a boob popping out, which made me laugh and Miss Wanda demanded that we shared the joke which instantly shut us up!

She then made her point by teaching us what she called a 'failsafe' step which, she claimed, allowed dancers worth their salt to fake any incorrect or badly held pose.

"It will give you a chance to recover as you fall from your pirouette," she glared at Sydney, "*and* to successfully fluff an off-balance 'arabesque penché'."

She demonstrated one perfectly with her leg almost in an arabesque splits behind her, with the foot of her raised leg pointing to the ceiling. "Above all, this will help you to recover in style. I want you to memorise this rhyme: when in doubt, coupé out."

We spent the rest of the class practising the dancer's best friend step, the coupé, until our legs were aching.

I was longing for a bath that evening and so plucked up the courage to ask Nanny if I could swap my bath night with Abbey, who was lagging seriously behind on her nature project and needed the extra time to finish it. I was surprised when she agreed and decided that she was always in a better mood the night before her day off. Sydney was hassling us all for chocolate and had been sniffing round my locker for ages before spying the box of Maltesers that Patsy had given me. It was like watching a bloodhound at work. I gave in and traded a full layer of Maltesers in exchange for some Badidas foam bath. I was becoming a dab hand at doing deals, developing skills I never knew I had. Maybe I could use these skills to make some pocket money to boost my travel savings - so far I hadn't even saved enough for a train fare to London!

Nanny was engrossed in *Z Cars* this evening, relaxing before her day off, so Mika and I took a big risk and filled the bath tubs half full and shared my Badidas. Maddy was having a strip wash and kept guard by the door to create a naked diversion if Nanny should come down the corridor. The green foam was sheer luxury and smelt divine as we lay soaking and chatting. We were having such a nice time until there was a peculiar scratching sound on the bathroom window pane. We all stopped talking but the scratching continued. We both shot out of the baths and, grabbing our towels, stood huddled together shivering. Dripping wet and covered in green foam, we edged closer towards the steamed up window. Maddy grabbed a flannel and wiped the steam off. We couldn't see anything, so I pulled down the rusty metal handle and with effort pushed the stiff old window open. Right in front of our eyes as we stood half naked, we could see the distant shape of a tall man wearing a long black coat running towards the woods then disappearing into the darkness!

Panic stricken, I banged the window shut and, shivering in our bath towels, we discussed what we should do. We had already used humungous amounts of hot water for our bubble baths, so before we could take any action we had to drain and clean the baths. We hurried through our cleaning and raced upstairs all jittery and babbled our tale of the cloaked intruder at the window to a stunned Nanny, who looked mortified and went a bit pale. She immediately grabbed the phone and told us to stay in the dorm.

Within seconds all the resident staff went out into the grounds searching for the enemy intruder, with torch lights shining in every direction. As we squashed our faces against the windows to view the unfolding drama outside, we spotted Sultan the horse dog and Max the giant wolf fluff-ball tearing across the driveway and barking like crazy. Then there was the sound of police sirens! Junior Dorm was suddenly lit up by a blaze of headlights as several police cars screamed to an abrupt halt in front of the tennis courts. Men in uniform leapt from their cars brandishing torches and spread out over the grounds. From our window they looked like toy soldiers. Mika and I giggled as we watched Max chase a lone policeman. Max was so daft he obviously thought it was a game, as he zigzagged forwards and backwards in front of the policeman. We opened the window a crack just in time to hear him yell, "Get this stupid dog out of here."

Sadly our fun was stopped abruptly when Cimmie stormed into the dorm bellowing,

"Get into your beds this instance!" She was seething and, turning off the lights, tossed a parting threat our way.

"Any more whimpering and whining from you snivelling snot-rags and you'll be gated from next Vis Day."

Cimmie had forgotten that Vis Day had been and gone. The dorm burst into conversation when she left. Hannah said she'd set a trap for the intruder, and reckoned he was capable of doing dastardly things. I wondered what sort of things. Esme called him a deranged pervert and Tamsin announced she felt all woozy and faint. Fortunately she was lying down.

FRIDAY 13TH OCTOBER

There was absolutely no way my sister would ever believe me when I tell her I discovered a prowler and how the police and dogs had swarmed all over the school.

Nanny delayed her day off because of the disturbances and was like a clucking mother hen. She fussed around us from the moment we went down to use the bathroom until we fled over to main house for breakfast. Loads of the Tweenies from main house came up to us at breakfast just to hear the prowler story first hand. Patsy rushed over to my table and asked if the prowler really had tried to get in the bathroom window. She said it was about time something sensational happened. Patsy was such a rebel.

Sifting through my tuck box in break, I found a Wagon Wheel which I took back to class and shared with Kerri. She asked me what I was doing during half term and invited me to meet up with her if I'd got nothing else on. Mr Mainwaring then arrived, sweeping across the classroom floor with his usual flourish.

"Lieblings!" he exclaimed, "The autumn days are drawing in. We need to embrace the earth while the ground is still warm."

We scuttled back to the dorm to retrieve our wellies and coats and raced out to our garden allotments. Mr Mainwaring had put large bags of odd smelling compost to one side and had stuck an assortment of forks, trowels and small spades in the soil. We paired up beside our chosen plots. He gave us all gardening gloves, reminding us "no accidents this time!" We fell eagerly on to the hard soil, got filthy as we dug and broke up the clods of earth until the soil looked like sand, ready for planting some spring cabbage plants and shallots.

By the time we were finished we'd discarded coats, and our pinnies and knees were caked in mud. Mr Mainwaring congratulated us on our allotments and declared that the best kept plots would yield the best harvest.

As Kerri and I left to go and wash before lunch, Mr Mainwaring sidled over to us and handed me a carrier bag.

Inside was a copy of *'Swallows and Amazons'*. I thanked him and he said he hoped I would enjoy the adventure.

At lunch time we were starving after all the digging and even Burt's dodgy looking Mongolian Goulash tasted nice. Is there really such a thing as Mongolian Goulash?

Everyone was tired from last night's excitement and both ballet and modern felt like hard work. During ballet Miss Olsen taught us some new adage movements. Hannah always pulled terrible faces when we were stranded with our legs stuck in mid-air during corrections, and it was hard not to laugh. Her mad mouth reminded me of Shaggy's face in *Scooby-Doo*.

Mrs Balmaine put on some different music in tap which was really funky and made us clap the beats. When we'd got the hang of it she told us to clap out the rhythm with our feet. She didn't get cross when we went wrong and told us to imagine our tap plates were like drum sticks, so our feet were tapping out the beat. I loved the sound my taps made and didn't want class to end.

As I waited in the tea queue for my mug to be filled up from the steaming canteen urn, the girl handing out letters passed me an envelope. It had a London address and a red-wax seal stamped into the back. I trembled when I held it as I thought it could have been from Alexandra Haydon! I could barely eat my tea I was so excited. I ended up putting the envelope into my pinny pocket as I knew if Hannah saw me reading it she would stick her nose in. I bolted down my food and tore back to the classroom for some privacy. My heart was thumping as I opened the letter. Inside were two sheets of thick, ivory coloured paper embossed with a London address and written in black ink with elegant writing.

Dear Lara

I was pleased to receive your letter. It brought back so many happy memories of my days spent at your school. I would be delighted to be your 'crush', and I will try to help with advice from a distance.
I hope by now you are feeling settled. There are many things to adjust to, but you will find the school becomes like a second family. I loved every minute of my time at Stavely Brookes and I hope you will too.
I am now married so my London address is different from the one you posted your letter to.
Please give my regards to Miss Brookes who you will soon be having ballet classes with.
I have enclosed a signed photograph of my favourite role in Romeo and Juliet. The pointe shoe is being posted separately. It has trodden the boards of the Opera House and I hope it will bring you luck!
With best wishes
Alexandra

WOW! My hands were trembling. This had to be the biggest honour ever, having such an amazing ballerina find the time to write to me and to be my crush. I re-read the letter and immediately wanted to share my excitement with someone.

As I walked back under the covered walkway I felt like my insides wanted to burst and I jumped up and swung on the over-head bars, nearly pulling my arms from their sockets. Back in the dorm, I hid my letter in the back of my writing folder.

CHAPTER FIFTEEN

SATURDAY 14TH OCTOBER

After ballet this morning I went to the day girls' changing room with Kerri. When I told her about my letter she gasped, "That's amazing Lara, you must put her signed photo beside your bed!"

"I don't want to show off."

She pursed her lips, weighing up the odds.

"It could cause ill feeling with Esme," Kerri sighed, "she likes being queen bee in our group."

I waited in front of main house with Kerri for her Dad to collect her and got to meet Callum - aka the only boy at the school. Like Kerri he was a day pupil, but only attended ballet classes. Kerri introduced us and Callum said he was happy to meet me. When he left, Kerri told me that he was really shy and the boarders didn't talk to him which must make him feel invisible. If my brothers wanted to dance I would be furious if all the girls ignored them. Then Kerri's Dad arrived and she got in the car to go home, waving like crazy until her car disappeared along the drive. As I stood alone in front of the main house a wave of homesickness rushed over me and I wanted to be going home too. I felt a knot forming in my stomach which the laggy briefs were pressing uncomfortably against and remembered that I still had to change, have lunch and walk to the shop. I wandered the long way back to the dorm close by the lake. There was no doubt that I was becoming quite obsessed with the lake and the very real possibility of the Blue Lady's ghost.

It had been a warmer day than usual and as I approached the water the sun was casting dazzling reflections on the lake's surface. I raised my arms overhead to see my shadow reflected and stuck my leg into the air behind me in an arabesque, which made my reflected leg look at least ten feet long! I checked to make sure no one else was around and picked my way through the reedy grass, walked around to the far side of the lake and stood under the frame of the huge willow. The branches were gently swaying in the light breeze and I could hear distant piano music from the dance studios. Looking around I noticed what looked like the end of a small boat, but it was concealed by reeds. Clambering through straw-like hummocks and long spiky grass, I spotted a jetty close by the boat and attempted to walk on it, but discovered that the jetty planks were rotten. I abandoned the dodgy jetty and forced my way through prickly brambles, dead branches and matted grass. I grazed my legs and got soggy and just as I got within touching distance of the boat, a bird burst out of the undergrowth which made me jump out of my skin! With my stomach crawling from fright and my heart hammering in my ears, I leaned over the boat attempting to inspect it. The thought of taking a real rowing boat out onto the lake was thrilling. It seemed to be very solid and there were no obvious holes. Moving away from the boat I checked my cover. I was still breathing hard after my 'bird' fright. Creeping as low down as I could get in the long grass, which was tickling my face, I could see Doom Dorm from the cover of the tree. I glanced up at the balcony which wrapped around the outside of the tower and loomed eerily over the water, imagining a young nurse in flowing gowns, beside herself and in a tortured and wretched state, throwing herself over the edge of the balcony. As I lowered my gaze I noticed a movement out of the corner of my eye. Looking in that direction I spotted a short figure striding out on the far side of the lake. It was Burt! I remembered him seeing us here before and Hannah saying he was a proper grass. I ducked down and waited. Fortunately he hadn't spotted me and it was only when he was completely out of sight that I raced back to the dorm.

Inside the dorm there was an overpowering smell. The twins were sitting at the table painting inside their old pointe shoes with shellac. Nanny was getting in a lather, marching around the room and throwing all the windows open. She said it had "a toxic and unwholesome smell" and that she couldn't allow us to breathe in the unsavoury fumes. We queued for our pocket money ready for the walk to the local store, shivering because Nanny refused to close the windows.

Later we joined another queue for lunch. Life here was one long queue. Waiting in the snaking line I noticed the older girls were wearing make-up. I couldn't wait until I was older and didn't have to wear a frilled apron. They were the cause of many humiliating jokes. Oracle said pinnies signified servitude and wearing them was insufferable.

Lunch - anaemic chicken stew - looked like dog food and giant slabs of pastry which tasted like crusts of burned toast. I Quizzed mine and Eggo'd two lemon sponges and custard. I was so famished even that didn't fill me up.

On my way out of the hall I passed a crowd of girls reading something pinned on the notice board. I nudged through the crowd to get close enough to read. It was a newspaper cutting from the Daily Express, featuring an ex-student working in a dance group on television. She looked pretty in the photo with clouds of wavy blonde hair and wore a sparkly catsuit. The article said she'd got a part in a new Bond movie. Everybody was saying how talented she was. Listening to all these comments made me think about what it must be like to leave school and then become famous, dance in front of an audience and hear everyone clapping after your performance. I couldn't wait to dance on a real stage in a theatre.

When we walked back to the dorm Abbey, Maddy, Mika and I talked about the different types of jobs students got when they left ballet school. We placed bets, deciding that Mika would get into a top ballet company, not least because she had the loosest legs in the school. We agreed Abbey had the best funky disco steps, so she'd probably finish up in a modern dance company. Maddy would make a great teacher because she was always helping other girls with their practice exercises. The girls reckoned my taps had the best sound in our class, so I might become the new Ginger Rogers! Thankfully I was good at something because I was still nowhere near getting into the side splits. Abbey said I spent so long writing my diary every night I could end up writing a film script! As we approached Junior Dorm my heart sank and our dreams came crashing back to earth. Cimmie was standing outside the dorm entrance. Her eyes narrowed when she spotted us. It wasn't my imagination but everything went silent and the sky clouded over when she appeared. Cimmie could suck laughter from life. She sneered as we walked past and we cringed, preparing for the onslaught.

"Hurry up, I haven't got all day!" she snapped. Breathing down our necks like a dragon in pursuit of its prey she hissed, "And this time don't leave your pinnies on!"

We tore up the dorm steps, falling over each other in an effort to escape her glare of death, but Millie's arrival saved us and provided Cimmie with her next unsuspecting victim to torment. We could hear Cimmie barking like a mad dog at the bottom of the stairs and Millie's wretched, squeaky response. When we reached the safety of the dorm we saw that a large box had been placed right in the centre of the table. It was labelled in bold black marker pen 'Junior heads'. I had to resist the urge to ask if we were going to be executed.

Nanny arrived and warned us not to keep Cimmie waiting. I noticed a small smile at the corner of her mouth as she stood on tiptoe, reached into the box and handed us each a maroon coloured velvet ribbon headband, joined at either end with a thick band of elastic. Sydney and Hannah tried them on and complained loudly, closely followed by the rest of us. The dorm was soon a mass of whining and whinging. These new instruments of torture really hurt our ears and were obviously made to stay put. Nanny said they were now a part of our regulation school uniform, designed to keep our hair neat. I checked out my new look in the mirrors and thought that everyone looked like melon faces, although with my fringe I looked like a half-melon! After lots of moaning we were herded downstairs and Cimmie conducted her army style check. Tiffany, Sydney and Hannah were, as usual, sent to wipe off their make up while we suffered Cimmie's insulting tirade of drivel.

The whole performance meant that by the time everyone had been double checked it was raining. The walk to the shop was miserable. Esme collared me as a partner, which was okay until she spent the whole walk bending my ear about living in Kenya and I was subjected to the same stories again. Then she dropped the bombshell.

"Lara, this half term I'm forced to stay with my Aunt and Uncle in Wales. They never go out and hate children." She spun the whole Cinderella story and I did feel sorry for her. I would hate to spend my holidays with relations who didn't like me. I would ask Mum and Dad if she could stay with me next half term, just not this time.

No one had a chance to stray or create mischief because Cimmie timed our shopping with military precision. In less than ten minutes we were done. I bought a Milky Way because I was saving for my travelling. By the time we got back to school we looked like drowned rats with soggy velvet ribbons round our heads!

Back in the dorm Hannah declared that Cimmie must have been trained by the SAS, and Sydney complained that she was desperate for a smoke. I'd saved some change so I went over to main house early to use the phone before the tea queue started.

I told Mum about my letter from Alexandra and she sounded more excited than me! She told me that Dad was outside making a bonfire and Benjamin was on a cub-scout camp. I gave Mum my supply list and mentioned the outside heel on my school shoe was wearing down badly. She said Samuel was rehearsing to be a recorder-playing snake charmer in the nativity play. I talked to Lily and told her about the prowlers, police cars and dogs - and she didn't believe me. Mum said Dad would pick me up on the Thursday evening in twelve days time. The pips then did that annoying beep-beep-beep and I got cut off. I was already excited about half term and went to wait in the library for the tea bell to ring.

Tonight Millie was homesick. I tried to think of a game to take her mind off it. Abbey, Maddy and I started a three-legged race across the dorm with our scarves around our legs. Millie joined Mika and Esme and soon the whole dorm joined in. Gabby paired up with Hannah and ran so fast Hannah was dragged along on her bottom. We rolled on the floor laughing and Millie *seemed* happy.

Not long after lights out I could hear a muffled crying. I leaned out of my bottom bunk and whispered, "Shall we go to Nanny?" Millie nodded, so we crept through the darkness of the dorm to Nanny's room. Nanny told us to sit down and she made us both a mug of hot milk. She asked Millie if she had a favourite Saturday night TV show. Millie said *The Persuaders* and Nanny raised an eyebrow, asking if my parents let me stay up 'till 10 p.m! I told her only on a Saturday night, so she agreed. We snuggled under a blanket with Hamish at our feet and watched the whole episode. When we finally crept back to bed I thought that there really was some justice in Junior Dorm, and how very kind and like a Mum our Nanny was. Life wasn't always unfair.

CHAPTER SIXTEEN

SUNDAY 15TH OCTOBER

Rita took us to church today. The service was running smoothly until a new turn of events took place. As we demurely filed up to the communion rail, hands clasped in front of us with our heads bowed, one of the choirboys leaned forward looking a bit shifty. Just as Hannah walked past him his hand shot over the pew edge and he thrust a note into her hand. Abbey and I both saw it because we were standing behind Hannah. Standing in the other queue beside us were Maddy, Mika and Sanchia who had also noticed. After kneeling at the altar, we filed back to our front pew and Hannah was playing it really cool. We all waited in suspense. Sitting on the end I could only just see her. She was sneakily trying to read the note on her lap when suddenly Rita leaned forward from the pew behind us and tried to snatch it from Hannah's hand. Hannah's reactions were lightning fast as she clenched the note in her fist and a fight broke out. During the struggle for the note between Rita and Hannah, the rest of us squished up to the far end of our pew so we didn't get involved in the conflict. The congregation queuing up for communion had stopped in their tracks and the eyes of the church were, once again, focussed on our pew. This time no one was pretending nothing was happening and even the organ fell silent. It reminded me of Saturday afternoon wrestling, except it wasn't Big Daddy and Giant Haystacks but Hannah and Rita. In the middle of Rita grappling Hannah into a Japanese stranglehold, Hannah's face went green and she threw up all over Rita, missing us by inches. It was gross. In seconds Rita had turned blood red. Her hair was sticking out like a bog-brush from her cat fight with Hannah and now she actually did look like Giant Haystacks! There was a moment of agonising quiet and then Rita sniffed, cleared her throat, got up, smoothed down her haystack of hair and, with her nose stuck in the air, marched out of the church with her heels clicking like castanets on the stone floor. The service then continued as though nothing had happened.

The congregation of Saint Barnabus seemed to accept everything our school threw at it - however gross or bizarre - and I came to the conclusion that Mr Deluca must have secretly made donations to the church so that they put up with this madness. Or maybe it was simply that the churchgoers had previously seen the prefects in action and didn't bat an eyelid as they'd seen all the fighting before. Abbey whispered to me that the congregation probably only attended Sunday service for weekly entertainment from Stavely Brookes' girls.

Trying to keep my distance from the puke, I mouthed to Hannah, "What's happened to the note?" I was sure Rita would be waiting to pounce once Hannah was outside at the end of the service. Hannah looked me straight in the eye, pointed at her mouth (for a horrible moment I thought she was going to be sick again) and said, "I've eaten it." What an enormous porky pie.

After church we queued up outside and Sergeant Rita appeared. She looked clean, composed and oddly calm - a worrying sign. She walked down the crocodile line eyeing us up and down with a gleam in her eyes.

"Walk in pairs and walk quietly all the way back to school, girls" she said in an even tone, all the time eyeballing Hannah. Hannah lowered her chin and eyeballed her back. The tension was so thick you could cut it with a knife. We walked back to school in stony silence and I could almost feel the wrath of Rita bearing down on us like a thunder cloud. I sorely wished that she would just walk us quicker but she stayed at the front simply prolonging the agony, setting such a slow pace it was enough to send a snail into a coma. One small consolation was that it was downhill. It was a huge relief to finally reach the school gates. Back in the safety of Junior Dorm and away from Rita's manic clutches, everyone descended on Hannah wanting to know what was in the note. Hannah snapped at us, saying she only had half of the note as Rita had torn off the other half. We all descended on Hannah to read the crumpled scrap of paper she was waving in front of us. Hannah jumped up onto her bed and, with the note held in front of her as though she was making a public announcement, she read:

"It says, 'Is your'," she paused for more effect as we hung on her words, "then right underneath on the next line it says, 'any under'. So how, exactly, am I supposed to know what the stupid note says?"

Eyeing us all defiantly, her lip curled slightly into a half-smile, she methodically started tearing the note up into tiny bits, announcing that any evidence was harmful. She then gave one of her smug and irritating smiles like she knew something we all didn't. Sydney told me later that if all this note passing with choir boys in church business got out we would all be taken to Mr Deluca.

"We'll be like lambs to the slaughter," she told me and then lowered her voice, adding in a sinister tone that Rita would unleash a 'punishment of the innocents' upon us. It sounded like something from the Bible. I didn't understand half of Sydney's ramblings. All I knew was we were innocent.

The rest of the day was uneventful. I got stuck into my *Great Expectations* essay for English homework, and then spent the rest of the afternoon writing letters.

I told Granny and Grandpa Edgecombe that my flexibility was much improved, complete with a drawing of a very bendy looking pin-man. I told them about my amazing letter from Alexandra, and how much I was looking forward to seeing the ballet in half term with Aunty Ellen. I wrote a similar letter to Grandpa and Nana Huntley. Grandpa loved cats so I drew a cat on the back of the envelope. Then I wrote my long overdue letter to Joseph:

Dear Joseph

So pleased to get your letter and I'd be delighted for you to be my pen pal instead of Grace! I was really interested that you're training to become an actor, and think we have a lot in common.

Your guitar lessons sound AMAZING – I am hoping to teach myself piano but at the moment have no free time. I would love to try canoeing and sailing too. So far I'm really enjoying ballet school, every day is exciting and it's nothing like I expected.

I share a room called Junior Dorm with 21 other girls. It's fun, but a few prefects often make it feel like we've joined the army. Every morning we wake up to a really loud bell, have breakfast and then school all morning. Then lunch. Then more school. Each day we do one hour of ballet, followed by a class in either tap, modern or national dance. Then we have tea, later supper then bed. We don't have TV which is really boring! We do normal subjects in school, including drama and music and have homework. The school is like nothing else ever, and it has a ghost (which I haven't yet seen but I'm on the lookout - it's a full moon next week so I'm hopeful). There are many prefects who are always lurking around corners to keep an eye on us. Two of them are like the Gestapo! We have lots of rules and spend a lot of time breaking them and then avoiding the trouble that follows. Food here is truly awful. We spend ages waiting in tortuously long queues for (mostly) inedible stodgy food, cooked by an ancient chef-cum-spy. He is the eyes and ears of the ballet school.

The teachers are female for our dance classes. They all have dogs with crazy names like Voodoo, Sultan, Max, and Biba. Sultan is like a horse and is the tallest dog I've ever seen. No cats have surfaced - yet! We spent this morning in church where some drama always unfolds and one of my friends usually faints! My dorm is mostly new girls and they have a vile system here which involves loads of scary, old fashioned punishments to terrify new girls and make them submissive.

We get to go home three times a term. So far this term we've had one visiting Sunday, and in 12 days time have a 3 day half term, then get another visiting Sunday at the end of November and break up for a one month Christmas holiday in mid-December.

My friends live all over England and some overseas, with one from Kenya, another from Tobago, one from Spain and also one from America. I'm trying to save money to put towards travelling the world.

We have an enormous theatre next to the school which we use for productions. Every spring term we put on a choreographic show and have a regular production at the end of the summer term, running for the whole week and is open to the public. I haven't had a chance to perform on a professional stage yet, so I can't wait. Have you performed live on stage?

*I will send you a photo of myself and my family when I get some from
home on my half term visit.*
Looking forward to hearing from you.
Best wishes
Lara
*PS: You don't happen to have 21 other friends who would be
interested in having girl pen pals? Just a thought!*

I made sure to seal the letter with blood red sealing wax,
which Esme kindly let me borrow to ensure security. I thought
it looked impressive and top-secret.

Tea was frankfurters and slimy sauerkraut. Gabby could eat
for England and before long she'd Eggo'd six frankfurters and
made a giant butty with two doorstep sized bread crusts. I
wondered if I'd got worms because I was constantly ravenous,
and straight after tea I lived in the hope that supper would be
better otherwise I was sure I'd waste away from starvation.

MONDAY 16TH OCTOBER

First thing this morning I retrieved my deer skull from its
precarious hanging perch. Nanny wouldn't allow it inside the
dorm, so I took it inside the class room to dry off, placing it on
the floor near the gas heater. Miss Knox came in during the
early form period to collect our nature projects and recoiled in
horror when I presented the dreaded deer skull. She put a lace
hanky over the eye sockets, as if it could look at her or
something! After everyone had handed in their projects she
counted them and said she was missing one. Tiffany put her
hand up, and said she was waiting for some paintings that
she'd done for her project to finish drying off. Miss Knox got
very agitated and advanced towards Tiffany with a menacing
look in her eyes,

"What do you mean - drying off?" she snapped, closing in on Tiffany's desk.

Tiffany shrunk so far into her chair that her neck disappeared and her eyes popped so she looked like an owl. In a small squeaky voice she repeated her excuse. Miss Knox became even more agitated.

"Do you expect me to believe that?" she barked, going all pink in the face, waving her arms around and stamping her feet. There was an uncomfortable silence as we all fidgeted. Tiffany was looking scared because Miss Knox looked crazy. Gaping at her orange lipstick and electric blue eyeshadow I stifled the nervous snort I could feel surfacing, as I started having a vision of Miss Knox in *Whacky Races*, brandishing her fist over her head as she drove manically in an old banger in hot pursuit of the Anthill Mob's enemy car. At the same time I felt nervous at this unpredictable turn of mood. Shirley, one of the twins, saved the day by creating a much-needed diversion. Standing up, she said she felt very unwell and then neatly fell into a dead faint flat on the floor and landed with a resounding thwack! Her acting was nothing short of miraculous.

Pandemonium instantly broke out, cutting through the tension as we all rushed to her aid. Miss Knox was thrown completely off balance by the sudden change of events. Matron was summoned. I only just spotted Shirley as she fluttered her eyes then flopped her head to one side and gave a sneaky wink to Tiffany moments before she was carried by several girls outside the classroom to recover in the fresh air.

By the time Matron arrived our form period was over and Miss Bell had, thankfully, arrived for English. She entered our hut and nodded at our recently gone mad teacher. As they exchanged greetings, Miss Bell said, "Good morning, Agatha".

It was like something had been unplugged in Miss Knox's expression, because her face returned to the calm, normally friendly teacher we knew. For now, normality was restored. But for how long?

Queuing for lunch later, we all sat on the Dive stairs and discussed this morning's events. If it wasn't bad enough having a couple of unpredictable prefects, we had now gained another time bomb waiting to go off in the shape of our school teacher. Hannah said now we knew her name was Agatha that we should nickname her 'Aggie'. We decided that all the enemy teachers and prefects should have nicknames. Cimmie had such an odd surname it didn't need changing so was remaining Krause because we couldn't find anything more suitable. We nicknamed Rita 'Prickly' because she always was, though I thought her surname - Warlock - sounded more sinister.

WEDNESDAY 18TH OCTOBER

I got a reply letter from Nestlés today. It said,

Dear Miss Edgecombe

Thank you very much for your letter of the 24th September regarding the inferior quality Walnut Whip.

We apologize for any inconvenience this has caused you. Nestlé aim to produce only the highest quality products and we hope all our confectionary reaches you in excellent condition. Rest assured this matter is being investigated.

I trust this will not affect the continued enjoyment of your favourite confectionery, and as a gesture of goodwill we are sending under separate cover some replacement products for you to enjoy.

Yours faithfully

Simon Parfit

Customer Complaints

This letter was a huge surprise as I had forgotten all about the letters of complaint which Hannah had menaced us to write. I wondered what would be in the parcel when it finally arrived.

Tiffany handed in her project today and Miss Knox had now morphed back into her normal self and showed no signs of her loopy behaviour from the other day. She was wearing bright green eye shadow and kept playing with the front of her hair when talking to us. By the end of the lesson the strand of hair had been twisted into a curved spike which was poking out at a sideways angle from her temple, reminding me of a devil's horn.

I had to remember Sunday night would be a full moon.

Tonight, Abbey and I made Mika and Maddy stand on our knees to improve our 'frogs'. It killed my legs more than usual and I had to keep reminding myself that to achieve flat turn out would take time. And pain! To take my mind off the discomfort I talked to the girls about the Blue Lady mystery. Whilst we were all deep in our conversation, Hannah came over to earwig and put forward her opinion. She told us that if the theory about the nurse in blue uniform haunting the main house dorms in the small hours was true, then we wouldn't stand a chance in hell of visitations in Junior Dorm. I wasn't too sure what hell had to do with it, but I didn't think I was going to stay up to find out on Sunday night.

I also started reading '*Swallows and Amazons*'. I was sure I'd enjoy it.

Only one week to go until half term. Yippee!

CHAPTER SEVENTEEN

Miss Knox was as sweet as pie in our last lesson today. Maybe she'd had her period on Monday, which explained why she acted all crazy. She talked to us about the Hampton Court trip after half term. I was so excited with it being our first trip and I couldn't wait. I loved the thought of our past Kings and Queens living out lavish and dangerous lifestyles in this palace. I was also really curious about the ghosts which were supposed to haunt the palace. I had read about one of Henry's beheaded Queens, whose ghost was supposed to run screaming through one of the corridors, obviously headless. How gruesome.

  During ballet today we learned a fast moving step called 'chaines deboules'. Miss Wanda demonstrated masses of continuous small turns and we all stared dumbfounded by her brilliance. She said it was the easiest turning step to do because it was "simply a succession of half turns." What could be easier? After all, we were now turning on two feet, unlike the pirouette performed on just one leg. So with our now (perfectly rehearsed) spotting technique in place, we all set about practising our 'demi-tours' on half pointe. From the corner - when done slowly - they looked nice and controlled, but when we danced one by one the music seemed to pick up pace.

149

Maybe it was my imagination. With Miss Yates playing the little cygnets' music from Swan Lake to inspire us, we all lined up against the back bar awaiting our turn.

Starting in the corner Shirley led the way, her turns performed in a perfect diagonal line. Everyone took their turn and all was going well until Gabby followed too close behind Hannah. Noticing the dustbowl of rosin pursuing her, Hannah realised 'Gabby the Tornado' was advancing toward her like a spinning top and hastily changed direction. We watched dumbstruck as Gabby, using Hannah's head to spot on, followed Hannah and the pair of them quickly spun out of control. It was madness! Hannah fell flat on her face and Gabby, following closely, landed ungracefully under the piano. The remaining spinning girls parted like skittles in a bowling alley, colliding with each other. It was clearly a disaster. Miss Wanda muttered under her breath about a herd of stampeding elephants, said we'd a long way to go and that the transition from one leg turns to two leg turns was hardly a leap across the Grand Canyon. So, I guessed this meant back to more spotting practice.

Kerri and I were practising whipping our heads around in the tea queue when an argument suddenly erupted further down the queue. It was Hannah arguing with Gabby for following her and making her fall over in ballet. The bickering continued right up to the canteen until somehow everyone was involved in the quarrel. The canteen queues were legendary and reminded me of animals meeting at a watering hole with occasional fights breaking out. I always longed for a cup of tea and missed being able to just go and put the kettle on. Tonight three girls were serving food. It was macaroni cheese and tinned tomatoes. Sydney told me that it was Burt's night off and because Radish was on his own in the kitchen, occasionally the Tweenies (middle school girls) had to help.

As we left the dining room I noticed a crowd of girls huddled around the notice board. They were very excited about some new audition. Kerri and I waited until a gap appeared and then pushed our way to the front. The notice announced an audition for a new television commercial! My heart missed a beat. How exciting was that! It had a long list of names that were to attend the audition next Monday. It mentioned that a camera crew and casting director would be holding the audition and wanted to cast suitable girls for a new television commercial for a fabric softener. I wasn't sure what this had to do with dancing, but Esme told me that television and film companies sometimes visited our school to search for girls to cast in commercials, TV programmes and films. She said many dancers branched out into acting careers and we had to be good all-rounders.

My name was on the list, but so was every other junior including Kerri, which I was really pleased about. We spent the whole evening discussing what they would ask us to do in the audition. No-one knew and we all kept guessing, but it did say that we had to go dressed in school uniform *without* our pinnies (otherwise they might have thought we were auditioning for parts in *Upstairs Downstairs*) and that our hair should be worn loose and without headbands. I could now see a battle for the bathroom approaching. Twenty-six girls all wanting baths and hair washes on the Sunday evening - there would never be enough hot water!

FRIDAY 20TH OCTOBER

This morning I was first down in the bathroom and, after cleaning my teeth, spent the time alone practising for the audition by smiling at myself in the mirror. The smiley face beaming back at me looked tired around the eyes, so I decided that I had to put these worries to the back of my mind. If I had dark circles under my eyes I wouldn't stand any chance of getting a part, especially when there were twenty-five other girls to choose from.

I reached the main house early for breakfast and chanced my arm going into the piano room because no-one ever practised piano scales that early. The room reeked of French cigarettes and the many water pipes that ran the length of the basement were rattling and gurgling loudly as the main house stirred itself awake. I lifted up the piano lid and tried out a few chords - they sounded awful. I'd have to listen at the window a bit more.

Last week in geography Mr Mainwaring asked me if I was enjoying reading '*Swallows and Amazons*'. I said I was and that the plans they made in their log book reminded me a bit of me writing my journal.

During ballet class, Miss Olsen set the record for giving the longest description of a 'developpé' in the whole history of ballet. We now held the record for keeping one leg in the air - in the same position - for the longest period of time. We will undoubtedly all grow up with thunder thighs and superhuman strength!

Luckily for us Mrs Balmaine always made tap fun, even with aching legs. She made us mark through our Herman's Hermits routine, and then set us a freestyle combination of canons. She split us up into groups and each group learned a separate step, then all the groups performed their separate group steps at the same time to the same music. It sounded fantastic and I had my first real feeling of what dancing in a company must be like. We were then made to swap steps and do it all again. Tap was definitely ultra cool. If I didn't become a ballet dancer I'd love to be a tap dancer.

We finished tap late and had to race towards main house under the covered way to escape the torrential rain. It was very dark and as Abbey and I passed the Tuck House a strange and oriental looking creature shot out from under the building and stood blocking our pathway. Illuminated in the canopy lights it looked like an Egyptian sphinx with its large, pointed ears and eyes that glowed amber-yellow in the half-light. It stood staring at us without blinking and there was utter silence. I felt a shiver run down my spine. It suddenly shrank into a crouching position and, with its eyes glowing eerily, omitted a chilling, ghostly moan from deep in its throat. As quickly as it had appeared it suddenly propelled itself sideways into the air and shot off into the darkness with otherworldly grace and vanished. It was kind of spooky. Abbey and I clutched each other and ran like loonies to get to tea. When we reached the tea queue we collapsed in a heap, gasping for breath. Sydney demanded to know what we were running from, so we told her about the sphinx-cat we thought we'd seen. She said it was not only very real, but was indeed a rare cat from a mystical far-off land. It belonged to Mr Julius. Now why hadn't I thought of that? Sydney continued with her knowledgeable account of otherworldly cats, pulling us closely towards her in that slightly sinister, secretive way that only Sydney could, and whispered, "This is a rare and exotic feline, seldom seen in the day time and," here she drew a deep breath, narrowed her eyes, and continued, "only surfaces to appear before **the chosen ones** at night…"

She then pulled me so close to her face we were literally eyeball-to-eyeball, and dug her fingernails so hard into my arm I gasped when she added, "…and to HUNT!"

I shrunk towards Abbey and as we cowered away from her she gave me her peculiar lop-sided smile.

"Her name is Roxanna."

When I'd recovered from Sydney's onslaught, we reached the canteen entrance and the smell of fish wafting towards me made my stomach heave. I was about to make a quick exit when a brown parcel landed on my tea tray. This was followed by two letters. I then had to negotiate adding a plate of fishcakes and tinned tomatoes to the tray, but at least it changed my thoughts and I stopped feeling sick. By the time I'd squeezed a cup of tea onto my tray it took a supreme balancing act for me to reach the junior dining table at the far end of the hall.

I hurriedly placed the brown parcel at the end of the table, well away from food. Everyone at the table eyed it suspiciously. The twins tried to guess what it was. Oracle snorted, saying it was probably another pair of amazing legwarmers from my German friend. I ignored Oracle, who was sucking up to me because she wanted to be first in my 'lend a friend legwarmers queue' and prodded my soggy fishcakes. Eventually I gave up and Quizzed the fishcake. Yuk. I couldn't wait for some home cooked food. Roll on half term.

Back in the safety of our dorm corner Abbey and I cut open the mystery brown parcel. OH MY WORD! I couldn't believe it! It was full to the brim with Walnut Whips and other Nestlé sweets. It was a feast for hungry eyes and before I knew it the whole dorm had smelled the chocolate hoard and, like hungry vultures, had surrounded our corner bunk. I looked up to see

Hannah, who had the self-satisfied grin of 'I told you so' written all over her face. Without asking who the parcel was addressed to, she suggested that we had a mini feast and in a few seconds my parcel load of goodies was devoured by twenty-two hungry mouths. After all this evening's excitement neither Abbey nor I had the energy to argue with Hannah, who always got her own way in the dorm. Anyway, I was quite glad the chocolates were gone because they had been obtained illegally!

Once we'd persuaded Hannah that we had not hidden any chocolate from her, I settled down to read my letters in peace. One was from Granny and Grandpa, saying that they were looking forward to seeing me during my half term, and that Aunty Ellen was looking forward to taking me to the ballet. Yay! I could hardly wait.

The other letter was from my Aunty Phyllis, Grandpa Edgecombe's sister. She had written me four long pages in very scrawly, looped handwriting, telling me all about the difficulties she had endured with her ageing lodger Miss Carp, who had a liking for stuffed animals! These, Aunty Phyllis claimed, were responsible for giving her the vapours. I didn't know what the vapours were. I looked it up in my dictionary and it said 'a fit of faintness, nervousness or depression'. I reckoned all of these could probably describe my great Aunty Phyllis's different moods. Dad often called Aunty Phyllis 'contrary'. Contrary or not, she was a real character. I could imagine that she had driven my Grandpa bonkers when they were growing up together. During our last summer holidays to Devon, Mum and Dad took us to Aunty's big old house on the edge of Dartmoor. What I remembered most about her house were the glass display cases. One case in particular held a stuffed fox which had really given me the creeps. Another contained a stuffed snake which Aunty Phyllis told us was a boa constrictor, given to her as a gift from a fearless explorer she met on her travels. Benjamin and I had spent hours daring each other to touch the case, terrified for fear of the snake springing back to life, exploding out of the cage and crushing the life out of us in a death squeeze! I didn't know why Aunty never got married. Mum once told me that a whole generation of women lost out on marriage because of the Great War. I often thought how lucky it was for my Grandpa to have survived the trenches and a bullet through his helmet.

Before lights out I could see Millie peering at our countdown chart. I was trying not to think about the audition looming towards us this coming Monday morning.

SATURDAY 21ST OCTOBER

I woke up ages before the rising bell this morning and managed to get a small crack of light to shine through the edge of the curtains and light up my pillow so I could read 'Swallows and Amazons'. It was gripping.

I was deeply engrossed in my book when rising bell went off making me jump. I raced to get to the bathroom before the morning rush began. As I was cleaning my teeth and examining them in the mirror, I was startled by Oracle who burst in saying, "You're so vain."

I confessed to her that I was worried about whether I should keep my brace in or take it out for the audition on Monday. I hoped I hadn't made a mistake confiding in her, but she reassured me, saying that it didn't make a bit of difference because I had a nice smile anyway. That was the first time she had said anything really nice to me and I was lost for words.

She then spoilt it by moaning on about how boring it would be for her in half term. She was very sneaky dropping these unsubtle hints. I told her that maybe next term I could take her home, because this half term we had already made some family plans with my grandparents. She then told me to remember to ask my parents anyway.

After mid-morning ballet Nanny suggested that some of us should share our bathwater that evening, so we could get half of the dorm's hair washed then and the other half tomorrow, before the auditions on Monday. Sydney shrieked and said that it was gross and unhygienic! I agreed. It didn't change Nanny's mind and she told Sydney that she was a proper fusspot and should stop behaving like a spoilt madam. It set Nanny off on one of her 'when I was a poor wee child' rants. We had to listen to her much-told tale about the tin baths that she'd had as a child, which were placed in front of the fire in the kitchen and eleven children had to use the same water. Good one, Sydney.

We had the nice prefect called Judith on afternoon shop duty. I managed to worm my way to the front of the crocodile today and Abbey and I got her talking about the Blue Lady. Judith said that no-one she knew had actually seen her, but when she lived in the main house she definitely heard odd noises and footsteps in the night and doors were mysteriously held open. I was thrilled to hear first-hand confirmation of the possibility of a ghost existing (and why would Judith lie?) but was also secretly terrified. She assured us that the Blue Lady would not harm us and that only people who were very perceptive and in touch with the spiritual world had heard these things. It made me think about the full moon the following night. Abbey said that only wussies believed in ghosts, so I had to be a wussy, and she also let the cat out of the bag that it was her birthday tomorrow.

I had a frustrating search for a last minute present with my 20p pocket money. I confided in Judith and she came to the rescue, saying that she would buy me a box of choccys to give to Abbey and I could pay her back after half term. She disappeared into the shop and bought me a box of Black Magic. The irony didn't escape me. I gave her my measly 20p as a security down payment. She also bought me a lemon sherbert fountain which was kind of her. Judith told us about her audition tour in the spring travelling through the European capitals. It sounded amazing.

This was the first time we'd had a pleasant walk to the stores and chatted to the prefect. I wondered who chose the prefects. Judith was kind and treated us like real people, whereas Cimmie was a woman possessed.

Patsy came round to Junior Dorm and we talked about Monday's audition. She said that television commercials often featured girls from our school. I told her about my brace. She said that if I was worried, no-one would notice if I took my brace out. I didn't tell her that my dentist had told me that I could only take it out when I cleaned my teeth otherwise I would undo all the good work that had been done. I would worry about that on Monday. My stomach was rumbling loudly and it made Patsy laugh. She pulled me over to my bunk and whispered in my ear that she'd had an idea. Placing one perfectly painted red fingernail up towards her lips to silence me she indicated towards the door. When we got to the bottom of the dorm steps, she told me to get Abbey and she would meet us by the Scrub House.

She raced off and I rushed back up to the dorm and asked Abbey to come to the library with me to do some homework. I gave Abbey a look, one which I hoped said 'don't ask why'. For once she didn't and when we got to the bottom of the stairs I told Abbey about the meeting with Patsy. As we walked towards the Scrub House we could see her hanging around outside. She beckoned us over and, glancing over her shoulder, she drew us inside the Scrub House door. It was very dark and no lights were on. She told us to come to the back of the hut and led us up some steps and behind the pipes and wash racks, to where an old ironing board stood. She said juniors were not allowed in here and she'd get shot if we were found. Fearing the fatal consequences we nodded our heads vigorously, moving stealthily to the shelter of the shadows cast from the hanging bed sheets which were strung up on lines behind the ironing board. My heart was thumping and I could see Abbey looking anxious too.

Patsy then plugged in the big old iron. I wondered what on earth she was doing, because there was nothing to be ironed. She kept testing the temperature of the iron plate. Then from out of her school bag she produced two gigantic crusts of bread, placed them crust side down on the ironing board, picked up the hot iron and started to iron the bread. Abbey and I started to giggle. She shushed us and continued to iron the crusts. The smell of 'ironed' bread as it was toasting under the hot iron plate made my mouth water. We watched in disbelief until finally the crusts turned a golden brown, reduced in thickness by half. She then produced from her Aladdin's bag several mini butters, unfolded the silver wrapping, smothered the hot crusts in the fast-melting butter and handed us each an 'ironed' crust dripping with butter! We gorged on our crusts while Patsy gazed at us with a huge grin spread across her face. When we'd finished she swore us to secrecy then went outside to check that the coast was all clear. Abbey and I promised her we wouldn't tell a soul.

During the evening the bathroom rota was in full swing until the hot water ran out. Nanny said hair washing would be done tomorrow using the sinks, and she would boil up extra water using her kettle. Now I was starting to get nervous.

SUNDAY 22ND OCTOBER

It was Abbey's birthday today. I had to gift wrap the chocolates in pages torn from my Bunty magazine. Abbey said it was the coolest paper she'd ever had, as on the front wrapping was a picture of Marc Bolan. This was a complete surprise to me too but one of the many coincidences which had started to happen to me since I had been here, so I didn't let on and wallowed in my super cool status of present wrapper extraordinaire. At least I was good at that!

In church today, Father Benedict came out of his pulpit during the sermon. He normally stays put for the duration and at least half the congregation would nod off by the end of his sermon. However, today was different and he was a minister on the move. There seemed to have been some kind of drama in the local town and Father Benedict was attempting to draw the congregation into a united front. Our front pews were easy targets and with every new sentence he looked directly at one of us. His voice got very loud when he stared straight at our pew and said, "The community must draw together in times of trouble." I sneaked a sideways glance along our pew and noticed that Hannah had shrunk. I could also see Oracle further along the row, doing exaggerated wise nods when Father

Benedict walked past her. He then drew the sermon to a close and looked straight at me when he told us to bow our heads in prayer. I also shrunk under his gaze and didn't dare lift my head for the duration of prayers for fear I'd be caught with my eyes open.

 It was a relief when prayers ended and having Father Benedict eyeballing us so close up was an uncomfortable experience. During our procession towards the altar and communion rail, I saw Hannah smirk at the choirboy on the end and then he smirked and did something weird with his tongue back to Hannah. Urgh. It made me cringe and looked gross. She was definitely up to something, but no-one ever knew what. It was so annoying. During the final prayers and after I had prayed for all people in the world who were sick and suffering and less fortunate than me, I added a quick final prayer asking God if he would bless me by helping me to shine in my very first audition tomorrow.

 We had our first dorm party this afternoon. Nanny brought in a huge chocolate cake which she said had arrived yesterday. The long central table was pulled back and we played musical chairs using pillows on the floor to substitute for chairs. We used Karlyn's big tape machine and hurtled around the room to the sounds of Slade's 'Mama Weer All Crazee Now'. Maddy won and Nanny produced a Nestle's Milky Bar for a prize. Tiffany and Sydney then struggled in with a vast cardboard box for a game of 'pass the parcel'. Twenty-six of us pushed the giant box round in a circle as 10cc's 'Donna' erupted from the background. Hamish barked and ran round and round our circle in a frenzied state. 10cc obviously drove him crazy! The prizes hidden between each layer of wrapping paper consisted of dares and forfeits. Towards the end I landed a forfeit and had to tell a joke. I could never remember any jokes so I chose my usual stand by joke which was impossible to forget: 'When is a lion not a lion'? There was a quick pause for answers with none forthcoming so I gave them the solution, 'When it's a dandy lion'. Everyone groaned. I was relieved my go was over and done with and 10cc started up again. The final prize was a light-up yoyo, which Janice won.

   The party was great fun. Sydney did some brilliant impressions of some of the teachers during her dare which made us cry with laughter and even Nanny wiped her eyes. By tea time we were exhausted. During tea Abbey was given twelve bumps and an extra one for luck. On the last throw in the air she nearly hit the main hall ceiling and she went as white as a sheet. My birthday will remain a secret!

CHAPTER EIGHTEEN

MONDAY 23RD OCTOBER

The last thing I could remember about last night before I fell asleep was reading '*Swallows and Amazons*'. I couldn't even remember Nanny turning the lights out.

When I woke up I instantly remembered our audition and could feel my stomach crawling. I then looked at the countdown chart and saw the full moon symbol by yesterday's date. Blow! With all the party excitement it went clean out of my head. I would have to be more vigilant next month if I was going to even hear a rustle from the elusive Blue Lady.

After breakfast I spent ages brushing my teeth to make them sparkle. As I brushed my hair I wondered how many people would be auditioning us.

Paula broke my chain of thoughts when she yelled at the top of her voice, "They're here!"

We all flocked to the windows overlooking the drive. I could see two large vans parked up. Several men were at the back of one van taking out long poles, boxes and large cameras…oh help! I felt my stomach fluttering at the thought. Tiffany and Sydney had already spotted the best looking cameraman and were frantically waving from the window. How cringing. As I watched the crew milling around with their equipment a slim dark-haired woman appeared clutching a large clipboard under her arm. She started to talk to a tall bald man and he pointed towards the studio under our dormitory. Mr Deluca appeared and there was lots of hand shaking, hugging and cheek kissing (where they didn't actually kiss each other but kissed into the air). Then the men with their film equipment headed towards our studio.

Saphi arrived in our dorm carrying a pile of postcard-sized papers with safety pins through the top. Large black numbers were printed on them. She told us the camera crew were busy setting up downstairs and wouldn't take long. Checking our hair and faces she huffed and ordered the twins to take their lipstick and eye shadow off, saying the director wanted to see fresh, natural faces. As usual Sydney complained bitterly. Saphi tutted.

"They know exactly what they are looking for and that's fresh-faced teenagers, not made up tarts."

Sydney stared back at her, curled her lip and looked disgusted. She was sooo cheeky.

Mika, Abbey, Maddy and I decided we would stick together. When we pinned our audition numbers on each other I ended up with number 13. I hoped it would be lucky.

Saphi lined us all up and, after lots of hanging around, we were escorted into the studio. My stomach did a flutter and I practised breathing deeply like we did in drama lessons. We then stood around for what seemed like ages feeling a bit uncomfortable. No one had told us what to do. Finally the tall bald man clapped his hands and introduced himself as Wesley Price. Wesley took off his rimmed glasses to address us and had piercing blue eyes beneath his heavy black eyebrows, black stubble round his chin and a shiny head. He had a constant smile playing on his lips which made me want to giggle. He told us they were looking for young dancers for a television commercial they were filming soon.

We were split into groups by the dark-haired lady I'd seen from the dorm window. Standing close I noticed she wore stacks of make up and spider-like false eyelashes. I was separated from my chosen group and placed with Paula, Janice and Tamsin, who looked as white as a sheet and I prayed that she didn't faint. After being told to 'act naturally' I felt about as natural as a wax dummy. We stood like zombies staring at each other. Janice fidgeted and said we should do the 'rhubarb and custard' thing. I didn't know what the 'rhubarb and custard' thing was. Paula and Janice had obviously done this before, and were smiling and nodding their heads like they were in deep conversation saying 'rhubarb and custard' over and over.

While this was going on, two of the crew approached our group. The one with the large camera balanced on his shoulder had long, dark curly hair and looked a bit like a gypsy. His face lit up when he smiled and said, "Hey girls, how are y'all?"

Everyone laughed self-consciously. He said that the camera wasn't rolling yet so we could chat and get to know each other. His name was Tom and he introduced us to the other man called Jake. He asked us our names and ages, and Jake jotted notes on a clipboard. He asked us what it was like at ballet school and we told him it was fun but sometimes a bit like Colditz. He told us he used to be at a boys' boarding school and the prefects were hellish and gave all the younger boys a bad time. Before long we were all laughing and chatting like old friends. He then said he was going to film us and he moved around our group with a big camera on his shoulder as we were busy talking to Jake. Jake stared at me as I smiled and I realised to my complete horror that I still had my brace in. Too late! He moved closer with a questioning look and asked, "Can you take your brace out?"

Feeling butterflies in my stomach I drew a deep breath and, trying to sound calm, answered, "Yes." Aware the camera was honed in on my brace-face I continued, "You mean - right now?"

Jake nodded encouragingly. I awkwardly turned my head away and slipped the brace out, feeling very self-conscious with the camera bang in front of me. My top lip felt stuck to my teeth, my mouth had gone bone dry and my stomach started to crawl. Jake told us a joke and I felt myself laughing, but my laughter sounded hollow and didn't belong to me. By now Janice and Paula were in full swing, having fits of hysterics from their 'rhubarb and custarding' and the camera had now turned towards them. I realised with a sinking feeling I had lost my moment. Tom and Jake were saying, "See you later, girls" and as they moved away I saw my chances of fame slipping from my grasp. I was suddenly aware of holding something in my hand and looked down to see my pink, wire-framed brace. I felt like stamping on it but saved myself by quickly popping it back in my mouth.

Saphi came over to our group and told us that now we'd been seen we could go back to our dorm and change into our pinnies ready for school lessons. As we walked out of the studio, Wesley was stood by the door and raised his hand saying, "Thanks girls".

I felt defeated as I trudged up the stairs towards the dorm, like I'd let myself down. Saphi came in and sat down next to me as I brushed my hair and yanked the itchy velvet headband over my head. She told us we were great and that Wesley was impressed with our group. Apparently he thought they'd be using blonde girls for this commercial. With my hopes of being a fabric conditioner starlet dashed, today was simply groundwork for a tough life in show business.

TUESDAY 24TH OCTOBER

Only two more days left to half term. Yippee! I was so excited and had so much to tell everyone. I hoped Lily hadn't taken over our bedroom with her David Cassidy posters.

Kerri and I discussed yesterday's audition during our lunch break. Kerri reckoned that child stars usually fell by the wayside when they got older, suffered from over exposure and eventually burned themselves out. We both thought it was good experience anyway, helping to toughen our resolve. I nodded with all the wisdom of an eleven and a half year old rejected brunette whose brace wearing would hopefully make her teeth a stunning asset in the future. We once again agreed that life was only fair if you were blonde.

Our pointe work practice seemed to be moving at an agonisingly slow pace. Miss Wanda, sensing our impatience, constantly reminded us young feet needed to be trained carefully to gain strength in the right areas. I often watched the twins strut around the dorm 'wearing-in' their pointe shoes and doubted my insteps would ever be as good as theirs. I remembered the promised pointe shoe from Alexandra and thought maybe she'd forgotten.

I practised my limbering and foot strengthening tonight before soaking my toes in surgical spirit, then relaxed reading 'Swallows and Amazons'. Mr Mainwaring was right - this book was great.

Nell Young

WEDNESDAY 25ᵀᴴ OCTOBER

WEDNESDAY 25TH OCTOBER

Miss Knox handed us all notes for our parents about our forthcoming Hampton Court trip. We still had to wear uniform (groan) but got the whole day out of school. I couldn't wait.

We had an oral test in French and Madame Nuffer asked us questions about the adventures of Brigette Dupont, Xavier and their dog Neron. As I'd previously done all this when I was eight at primary school I knew the answers inside out and backwards. She gave me 20/20 and Oracle called me teacher's pet. I've decided I won't take her home yet, particularly since she advised me to wear my brace for the TV audition.

Nanny made us clean and tidy the dorm, strip our beds and put on fresh sheets as we were going home tomorrow. Hip-Hip-Hurray!

CHAPTER NINETEEN

BACK TO SCHOOL

SUNDAY 29TH OCTOBER

Watching Dad drive off tonight, I was thinking how this half term had flown past when I heard a voice calling me. I looked up towards Junior Dorm to see Maddy hanging out of the window.

"Hey Lara, come upstairs!"

I raced up the staircase to see my friends and we excitedly told each other our stories from half term. I glanced down at my bedside calendar and noticed that this Tuesday was the 31st... Halloween!

MONDAY 30TH OCTOBER

The rising bell frightened the life out of me this morning. Nanny appeared moments later and swung into her Gestapo style bed-stripping action. I fled to the bathroom before she reached my bunk, thinking how quickly we'd all slipped back into our army style regime.

In Form period today Miss Knox discussed our Hampton Court trip next Monday. She handed out copies of the Itinerary and told us to read the information carefully.

'OUTING RULES:

Hampton Court Trip: Prep Form/Year One

Teacher in charge: Miss Knox

Assistant teachers: Mr Mainwaring and Madame Nuffer

Meeting point and departure time: Outside Main House at 8-30 a.m.

Coach Journey: Approx. $1\frac{1}{2}$ hours

Expected return departure time: 4-30 p.m.

Dress code: Full uniform with shirts and ties (no twin sets). Velvet head bands are to be worn at all times.

No make-up or jewellery.

A packed lunch and soft drinks will be provided. Please bring some pocket money for souvenirs. Maximum allowance: £5-00 per person. Hobnobbing with boys will not be tolerated. Please remember you are carrying the good reputation of the school with you every time you leave the school gates. Anyone found flouting the rules will be gated or expelled.

We hope you enjoy your trip!

I prayed that I would be placed in Mr Mainwaring's group for the outing; after all, who knew what might happen with Miss Knox being so unpredictable. Madame Nuffer was just plain annoying with her whiney voice and I didn't know what, as a French teacher, she could possibly teach us about our English Monarchy.

Our drama practice today was entitled 'A short scene with a fight'. I teamed up with Mika, Kerri and Sydney. During what Miss Lazenby called our 'idea storming', I suggested that we acted out an old-fashioned, silent movie style drama with a Charlie Chaplin/Buster Keaton type theme. I had watched so many silent movies at home I could easily imagine this. After negotiations for parts, I was voted to play the servant with the pistols who marks out the paces. Sydney said I was a great ideas girl, which was her polite way of saying I wasn't great at acting (YET). Kerri was voted the perfect damsel, and it was her two lovers who would be fighting to the death. Sydney and Mika would play the two lovers, brandishing pistols and better known as the 'duelling, love-torn aristocrats'. We planned it carefully with a final twist to the tale: the aristocrats walked their paces and dramatically turned, aiming to kill, but their pistols didn't fire. I (the servant of one of the aristocrats) checked my master's pistol and it accidentally fired, instantly killing the other dueller. The damsel, seeing one of her lovers had fallen, grabbed my pistol and cried out in grief as she shot me in the chest. The remaining dueller, seeking to avenge the death of his servant, wrestled the pistol from her shaking hands and shot the damsel, cursing her under his breath.

"Dammit woman, you have cost me a loyal servant."

Then he gaped in horror at her lifeless, blood soaked body as realisation dawned that he had just shot his beloved. In a dramatic gesture he aimed the revolver at his own head and shot himself.

After our performance everyone clapped and cheered for ages. Voodoo got over-excited, barking like a hyena. I came to the conclusion that until I gained more acting experience maybe I would make a better silent actress. I decided this was positive as all ballets are mimed.

In the evening as I practised my frogs with Maddy, I told her that tomorrow was Halloween and I had the Blue Lady very much on my mind.

"We need to take action."

She kneaded her temples, deep in thought.

"I've got it - we'll have to stake out the lake".

"How?"

171

I doubted this was possible with Burt always roaming around.

Looking over her shoulder in Hannah's direction she lowered her voice and leant forwards, bringing her lips close to my ear.

"I'm working on a plan and I'll fill you in tomorrow.'

TUESDAY 31ˢᵀ OCTOBER

Halloween! I collared Maddy as we raced over to breakfast and asked her what the plan was. She reassured me she was still perfecting it but it was all completely under control. So as not to arouse Hannah's suspicions I was to meet her with Abbey and Mika in the library after tap class when everyone was at tea. She told us to avoid wearing anything that may glow in the dark.

The day dragged on painfully, with double maths never ending. Ballet went by in a haze and immediately after tap Abbey, Mika and I raced up to the empty dorm to find that Nanny was, fortunately, out. We grabbed our scarves and coats and headed the long way round to the lake to avoid bumping into anyone. Everything seemed to make us jump. The evening was dark and windy and I felt in my bones that tonight was the night.

As we sneaked around the grounds towards the glass walls of the library, Maddy emerged from the darkness, raced towards us and told us all to dash for cover in the trees. We moved fast and noiselessly through the long grass and I could feel the wet reeds brush my legs as we scrambled for cover. Reaching the large trunk of the willow we crouched, well hidden in its huge protective shadow. Maddy pulled our heads together and quietly hissed our plan.

"First of all, we've got to remain quiet as mice so that no one catches us out here, otherwise it's death! We've got the best part of an hour, hour and a half tops as we..."

A loud, rustling sound from the far side of the lake interrupted Maddy and we all froze like frightened rabbits. My heart was hammering so loud it sounded like helicopter blades in my ears. More rustling came and we crouched even closer to the ground, then silence. The whites of everyone's eyes made them look wild and ghoulish, which freaked me out a bit as we silently stared at each other, eyes popping in the barely visible evening light. Mika then mouthed the words we all feared most…

"The Blue Lady?"

Suddenly we were aware of a strange and ragged breathing sound, which seemed to be getting closer, accompanied by the sounds of snapping twigs, which only increased our tension. Gripping each other in fear, we couldn't see what was fast approaching us as we peered out from behind the giant tree trunk. In the gloomy half-light we could only just make out a figure moving slowly around the far side of the lake. The figure was large and seemed to be covered with a dark, hooded cloak. It was moving straight towards our hiding place! Abbey leant on me and I could feel her heavy breath down my neck as she clutched me, digging her fingernails into my hand. Just as I felt my eardrums might explode there was a loud ripping noise, sounding just like a fart! We all gaped at each other in disbelief. It was a silence-shattering, resonating fart which reverberated right around the ghostly lake. The tension exploded. We sunk to our knees barely stifling our hysterical giggles and gasped for breath. Maddy pointed theatrically to her bum and mouthed, "Who farted?" as we clutched our mouths to deaden the snorts of laughter.

Then a different noise broke the silence; this was a muffled, grunting sound. Weak from laughter we dropped onto our hands and knees, craning our necks around the shield of the tree trunk as we peered out into the inky darkness. Suddenly - to our horror – out of the misty undergrowth shot a giant hound which looked just like a werewolf. We all gasped and shrunk back behind the tree as the snarling beast stalked towards us, its yellow eyes and pointed teeth glistening. As it closed in on us my heart flew into my mouth and just as I was ready to scream and make a run for it, the crazed hound flopped on its back in front of us with its tongue lolling out of the side of its mouth. Immediately I recognised it was the giant wolf fluff-ball!

"It's Max, Matron's dog!" I hissed to the others, as I crawled over to him and nervously rubbed his tummy. "Good boy, Max, now go home, good boy," I urged.

Fat chance. Despite my persuasion, Max had other ideas. He panted excitedly and to our utter dismay started barking. GROAN. I leaped back to the tree trunk as a shrill, trembling voice wavered across the lake's surface.

"Who's there?"

The voice was definitely a woman. I glanced up to see Maddy's eyes look wild and once again fought the urge to giggle. Abbey took the situation in hand and indicated us to crawl closer to her. She was mouthing something. I strained my ears, craning my head sideways towards her moving lips to hear.

"MATRON."

"Are you sure?" I mouthed

"One hundred percent," she nodded vigorously, "and if we don't get out of here now we're more than dead - follow me!"

Realisation slowly dawned on us. Mimicking Abbey's 'all-fours' pose we crouched like tigers. Stalking through the long reedy grass we never once looked back over our shoulders until we ran out of cover. We were breathing hard as we looked to our new leader for instructions. Abbey hissed out her orders under her breath.

"When I say run - run for your lives!" and seconds later, before I had time to think, she issued the breathless command, "RUN!"

My legs pumped into flight. We hurtled past the studios, thundered like stampeding cattle along the covered-way and fled towards the safety of our Junior Dorm. It was insane and I had never felt so scared and excited. When we reached Junior Dorm Abbey paused to fling open the heavy outside door. She herded us towards the ground floor corridor in the direction of the bathroom. There we collapsed over the sinks, laughing and gasping to catch our breath.

Upstairs only a few girls were back from tea. Fortunately Nanny wasn't back either. We hurried to change into our nighties, and I could still feel the thrill of our adventure pumping through my body. I tried to involve myself with normal dorm things and began practising my ritual of evening exercises. Whilst practising my frog I realised Millie was watching me with increasing interest. Without warning she pointed her finger in the direction of my knee and asked why my knee was so bloody. I quickly invented a cover story.

Since being in Junior Dorm I'd become capable of being quite devious - maybe it was part of survival in the jungle.

CHAPTER TWENTY

I was asleep on my feet today. Whilst distributing Hampton Court study guides Miss Knox eyed me suspiciously announcing I looked peaky. I didn't dare look at Mika and Abbey sitting opposite me.

I could barely contain myself from telling Kerri about our ghostly adventure. We discussed our Hampton Court trip over dinner. Esme got involved and declared Henry a vile monster who, despite being King of England, had syphilis. Gabby asked what syphilis was and Sydney yelled "VD"! Hannah added her two pennies worth saying those infected got covered in scabs oozing pus and eventually died from madness. It put me right off dinner - gross!

During our last lesson Miss Knox arrived for nature studies clutching a paper bag. Placing it on her desk, she stood in front of the blackboard fiddling nervously with her odd strand of hair and gazed outside through the classroom windows. Moments later she shook her head as if remembering something, clapped her hands wildly and stamped her foot which indicated silence.

"Girls, I have spent considerable time reading your nature projects. Overall they are imaginative and some show considerable attention to detail. However," she paused for a rapid hair fiddle until the strand stuck out like a devil's horn, "there are three projects which deserve special recognition for outstanding research and supporting materials. For unique photography I award first prize to 'The Birds of Tobago' by Millie Dwight."

Everyone clapped when Millie was presented with a book. Millie went beetroot red and grinned like a Cheshire cat. Miss Knox cleared her throat and continued.

"For extremely unusual supporting material and detailed descriptions, I award second prize to 'Forest Life' by Lara Edgecombe."

I felt my face burning as yet more cheers erupted. My prize was also a book, 'The Anatomy of British Mammals'. She raised her voice several octaves to be heard above the din of applause.

"And finally, third prize for the most inventive use of subject matter goes to 'Bats in my Loft' by Mika Myagi-Jones".

The class erupted again and a lot of loud desk banging ensued as Mika was handed her prize. Unusually, Miss Knox didn't get agitated with our uncontrolled behaviour.

FRIDAY 3ʳᵈ NOVEMBER

Mr Mainwaring asked me how '*Swallows and Amazons*' was progressing. I informed him I had just finished it and as a result of this book I was hoping to go camping or learn to sail. He slapped me on the back which made me splutter and said, "Well done Minimus!"

I ducked sideways as his arm rose to give me another back slap. "Camping and sailing are quite an adventure. Keep up the good work." I caught Esme smirking at me and wished Mr Mainwaring wouldn't call me that name.

I'd asked Dad in half term what it meant and he told me that the word minimus was Latin, meaning small. How insulting. Perhaps he really meant slim, not small as in short. I was certainly taller than most of my friends (particularly Esme, who must have found out what it meant which explained the smirking). I hoped I would grow more now, especially since I started my periods. I'd soon know because we were 'weighed and measured' at the beginning and end of each term. Imagine if you shrunk. Can you shrink? They did in that TV programme *Land of the Giants.*

At tea two interesting things happened.

1) I had a letter from Mum and Dad with some exciting news for the Christmas Holidays. Mum said that a foreign exchange student would be staying with us for three weeks. Her name was Marie-Helene and she would live with us like part of the family. Mum was already planning cultural trips to London, saying Marie-Helene was very attractive and from a good family.

2) The long awaited appearance of the TV commercial audition results were displayed on the notice board for all to see. The notice said that after careful consideration, the successful candidates had been chosen and would be required for filming in a week's time, commencing next Friday 10th November in Studio One.

I was surprised it was being filmed at our ballet school. It said the successful girls must report to the Secretary's Office at 12-30 p.m. on Tuesday for further briefing.

Having made a complete mess of my audition with my brace episode I wasn't expecting to see my name - Saphi had led us to believe the casting director was looking for blonde girls. The girls chosen were Janice and Paula (both blonde) and Esme (black hair!). I made sure to congratulate them and they were really excited, but there had been a lot of dorm mutterings about casting. I was sure the director knew what he was looking for and they only chose girls who were confident in front of cameras.

Unfortunately, when I left the bathroom that evening with Esme, we both overheard Hannah's loud voice talking to Janice.

"It's obvious Esme only landed that part because she's small and someone took pity on her."

We both heard this and I had to physically restrain Esme from rushing back in and attacking Hannah. She looked like she could kill her. Then she nagged at me non-stop, all the way up to the dorm. There was no escape.

SATURDAY 4TH NOVEMBER

The rising bell might as well have been stuffed in my ear this morning for all the good it did. Gabby's snoring had kept Abbey and I awake again. Gabby hotly denied it. We had no other choice but to take extreme measures and record her in full-blown action. We enlisted the help of Karlyn and the use of her trusty tape recorder. Tonight we would frame the offender.

Rita led our crocodile procession to the shops in the afternoon. Caught unawares, I was collared by Esme to be her partner and once again she prattled on about her favourite subject - Esme.

Brain-drained from Esmeville, I escaped to the library for some peace and quiet. After composing a letter to Alexandra, I noticed through the glass doors some movement over by the lake. Fascinated, I went to the doorway for a better look and

179

saw Sultan the horse dog emerging from the undergrowth and loping across the lawn in the direction of the library. Following him was the tall, reedy shape of Mr Julius. His luscious, long hair had caught in a sudden gust of wind and, with his afghan coat floating behind him on the breeze, he looked like a heavenly vision. Too late, I realised he was approaching the library. As I watched in the open doorway I had no time to retreat. Sultan appeared and leaped up at the open library doors on his hind legs. Pinning me to the door with his full weight he slobbered all over my face. I tried in vain to fend off his affections, frantically saying "get off" and "down dog" which made no difference. Mr Julius then appeared and said firmly in his deep, silky voice, "Down, Sultan". Horse dog instantly dropped to the floor and lay on his back, tongue lolling out in submission. I was a vision for sore eyes in my frilly pinny, covered in smelly dog saliva with my fringe glued to my face. Mr Julius chuckled gently.

"You're not afraid of him, are you? He's really quite soppy and apparently seems to have taken a liking to you. He's normally very reserved - most unusual for him."

He flashed me a winning smile.

I managed to splutter, "I've never had a dog at home, and not one the size of a horse!"

He then threw his head back and laughed for ages, followed by a lot of coughing and told me I was very funny. During his laughing attack, I desperately tried to rearrange my hair and wipe some of the dog gunge off my face with my cardigan sleeve. Before I'd had time to regain my composure, he bent over Sultan's head and digging around his drooling, gummy jaws, extracted my barely recognizable headband from his mouth. Holding it between his thumb and forefingers like it was something disgusting, he wrinkled his nose and asked my name. He said he'd ask Nanny to get me a new one. Slapping his hand against his long leg, Sultan leaped up to attention beside him and they glided off together as if nothing had happened.

After the embarrassing incident with horse dog, I finally got to talk to Abbey without anyone else earwigging. She found me in the bathroom frantically trying to shampoo dog-gunge off my fringe. I told her what had happened and she thought it was hilarious. We then discussed the lake episode. She agreed we would have to remain secretive otherwise the whole dorm would get involved, then we'd be found out and punished. Abbey raced off to round up Mika and Maddy. Once together, we jammed the mop handle under the bathroom door handle for privacy and decided on a code name for our ghost busting episodes. So far it had just been us four girls - code name BLAP aka Blue Lady Army Patrol. It was my idea after watching the TV series M*A*S*H aka Mobile Army Surgical Hospital. The girls thought it was great. We had agreed to communicate about our BLAP meetings, or anything BLAP related, out of the other juniors' earshot, and to sign-off paper messages with the code name. After receiving any information relating to our BLAP activities we all agreed to destroy any evidence about our covert operations.

That evening, with Abbey's help, we borrowed Karlyn's tape recorder (nicknamed The Beast) and when Gabby went downstairs to the bathroom we set it up, complete with a blank tape cassette inside so it was all ready to start recording. Then we hid the The Beast under Gabby's bed. The trap was set.

181

SUNDAY 5ᵀᴴ NOVEMBER

After lights out we had waited until, one by one, everyone fell asleep. Unfortunately, even Abbey fell asleep. Despite pushing my feet up into her mattress and bouncing her bed around she refused to budge. Then the snoring started. Left to complete the crime alone, I cautiously crept out of bed. Reassured by the total silence that no-one was watching, I lowered myself onto my belly and dragged my body along the floorboards, underneath all the beds in our long row in the dust, slithering like a snake. The journey was hindered because everything my fingers or toes brushed against made me recoil. After what seemed like ages I reached Gabby's bed, which was vibrating reassuringly from her snores. Satisfied I'd reached my target, I fumbled around in the darkness for the pocket where my trusty torch was hidden and pressed the on switch. The miniscule beam gave just enough light to illuminate the controls on the tape player. From the top left I counted three buttons along, then held my breath, crossed my fingers and toes and pressed the record button. There was a small noise as the cassette clicked and started to operate. Then, without warning, the speakers screamed into action and at ear-splitting volume boomed out 'Breaking up is hard to do'…. Eeeagh! I recoiled to the deafening sound of the Partridge Family blasting out from the speakers. Rolling sideways with my arms overhead I moved faster than the speed of light, rolling underneath the whole line of beds until I reached my bottom bunk. With my world spinning I dragged myself up from the floor and swiftly buried myself deep under my bed sheets. And just in the nick of time. Literally, seconds later, pandemonium broke out with girls sitting up and moaning with cries of, "What's that noise?" and "What's going on?"

Then Nanny entered the room.

Her lethal-beam searchlight swept the room once before she cruelly switched the main lights on. I peeked out as Nanny thundered round the room, her billowing nightdress wafting in her wake. It was sheer madness. There she stood in the centre of the room, bosoms heaving as she clenched her fists and then, with great effort, somehow managed to retrieve the offending Beast, which was still blasting out the Partridge Family at a deafening volume. She hauled the booming machine up to waist level for us all to see. Everyone blinked, trying to adjust their eyes to the shock of the blinding light. I desperately eyeballed Abbey in a plea for help.

"Whoever's responsible for this," she paused to find the right word and spat out "idiotic prank, please step forward."

She was greeted with silence. Placing The Beast on the floor she found the stop button. Everyone sat rubbing their eyes, when suddenly a voice piped up behind her.

"I am, Nanny."

Nanny's back straightened and she looked dumbstruck. She shook herself and turned around to face Hannah, who had now got out of bed and was walking towards the door.

"I think I can explain," she mumbled, and as she walked out of the dorm Nanny followed her, huffing and breathing heavily, berating her and muttering as she flicked off the lights.

"Get back to sleep, girls," and then to Hannah, "this had better be good."

What seemed like hours later, Hannah returned and told us it was "all sorted" and she "had it under control." She was so infuriating but I was really glad she was able to think on her feet. I felt shattered this morning.

I also realised that it was Bonfire Night tonight, then our Hampton Court outing the next day. There was still some mystery surrounding the 'midnight musical explosion' and Hannah's abrupt confession to Nanny. We all harassed Hannah on our walk to church and made Gina, our duty prefect, cross because we wouldn't leave Hannah alone.

Church was a very solemn affair because we could hardly stay awake! During his speeches Father Benedict kept saying, "Repent all ye sinners." He looked straight at us when he said this but I was so tired I could feel myself drifting into a sleep-deprived trance.

On my way back to Junior Dorm I had the opportunity to talk to Hannah on her own. She confided that she had told Nanny about Gabby's snoring, and said that Gabby didn't believe she was the snorer. Hannah said she told Nanny she'd set up the tape recorder to record Gabby, simply to let her know exactly how loud her snoring was. She said Nanny was as sweet as pie and had told Hannah that she'd sort it out.

Why didn't I think of that?

After tea we were allowed to put on our wellies and big coats to see the school bonfire being lit before supper. I was disappointed we weren't allowed to stay up later. Mum would say I was feeling hard-done by, but that sums up how little freedom we had. We shared some sparklers then watched Mr Deluca setting the Guy alight. As we were herded back to Junior Dorm I saw something moving beyond the bonfire and realised it was BURT THE SPY lurking in the shadows…

CHAPTER TWENTY-ONE

Today was our Hampton Court trip.

I was now writing my diary after our trip and, to be perfectly honest, today might also have marked the sad day that juniors would be banned forever from school trips. And here was why: I will refer to Sydney as 'S' and Tiffany as 'T'.

8-30 a.m: Coach left on time

8-35 a.m: S and T took over the back row of coach. Applied illegal make up and started to paint nails red.

8-40 a.m: Manners smelt the nail varnish – approached back seat – spotted culprits in action. Told S and T to remove nail varnish and they protested. Manners grabbed their hands and tried to wipe it off with tissues. Tissues stuck to wet varnish. Only a man would make this idiot mistake. Manners exploded and, in a fit of pique, ordered the coach driver to drive back to school.

8-50 a.m: Coach returned to school. S and T sent back up to the dorm to clean up their tissue-hands and to remove tarty make-up. Honestly - where did they store their brains?

9-00 a.m: Coach left again - half an hour late. S and T were given a warning.

11-00 a.m: Arrived at Hampton Court Palace late, due to extended departure and two long roadside stops because

  a) Tamsin fainted from the heat in the coach and...

  b) She threw up over Karlyn. The coach smelt like vomit for the rest of the journey.

11-15 a.m: Exited coach en masse and were each given a lunch bag. Year One/Prep Form were split into three groups and allotted a leader/ teacher. Kerri and I were put in Miss Knox's group. Henry VIII is Miss Knox's favourite King, so we were in for a treat. S and T somehow managed to weave their way into Madame Nuffer's group. Madame Nuffer is 'pathetique'. I sensed trouble brewing.

11-30 a.m: Our group started a grand tour. Miss Knox supplied nonstop historical facts and figures. She was overjoyed and positively drooling with excitement. I glazed over but came back to reality when she was standing in front of me, asking me to share what was obviously far more interesting than her descriptions. I gazed up towards the Astronomical Clock, praying she wouldn't shout at me in public, and remembered reading in our guidebook about the clock showing the time of high tide at London Bridge! I told Miss Knox I'd read about this being useful for members of the court travelling by barge and she said, "Correct! That was not what I was saying but a salient point. Well remembered."

12-00 p.m: Walked past Madame Nuffer's group and noticed S and T were MISSING.

12-30 p.m: We passed through a hall and caught a glimpse of S and T talking to a group of BOYS! Our group stopped near them. I stared at S. She looked like she was staring back at me as she flicked her hair over her shoulder, smiling widely. She looked loopy so I pulled a face at her and she advanced towards me flashing her eyes dangerously.

"I'm not smiling at you, you moron!"

As I smarted from this missile of verbal abuse, Miss Knox herded us into a group and moved us on, leaving the boy-vultures in peace.

1-00 p.m: Miss Knox had blitzed us with nonstop information and yet seemed surprised that we were mentally exhausted. After clucking like a mother hen about our permanent lack of sleep, she suggested we paused for lunch to wake us up a bit. We sat outside grappling stale sandwiches filled with spam and drank warm lemonade. The food felt like lead in my stomach. Sitting outside was also bitterly cold. It was then that I spotted T in the distance, heading in the direction of the North Gardens and The Maze.

2-00 p.m: We were released to spend our pocket money. I bought a key ring for my Dad, spiral notebook for Mum and pencils for Lily, Benjamin and Samuel. I spent the rest on a book called 'Famous Ghosts of the Palace'.

2-30 p.m: The second leg of the Palace tour. Miss Knox showed us around the apartments and staircases, and pointed out where Catherine Howard's poor tortured ghost was said to haunt. She said Catherine was placed under house arrest after committing adultery. When she tried to escape to find her husband Henry and attempt to plea for her life, she was caught and her agonising shrieks were said to haunt the very Gallery we were standing in. I closed my eyes thinking about how awful she must have felt. I was feeling chilled to the bone when I heard a loud thump and opened my eyes not to find a ghost, but to see Tamsin had fainted - again.

3-30 p.m: Kerri and I were assigned to look after Tamsin (lucky escape). Outside - and alone - Tamsin slyly confessed to faking her faint! She said she feared that if she had to listen to any more historical facts from Miss Knox she would scream. Clever Tamsin. We spent our last hour alone, away from Miss Knox and her historical tirade, peacefully exploring the Great Fountain Garden, and admiring the world's oldest vine. I wondered how, exactly, did they know all these facts? I mean, did they go round recording the age of every single vine in the world? That was a huge amount of vines. We walked past The Maze and Tamsin said that she might get claustrophobic if we ventured into it. I wondered if S and T were hiding somewhere inside with kidnapped boys!

4-15 p.m: We decided to head back to the coach.

4-30 p.m: Departure time and S and T were missing.

4-40 p.m: Manners blew his top and went on the warpath. He was seething and stormed off to search for them saying they were 'foolish floozies'. I would have to look up what floozie meant.

5-15 p.m: Manners returned holding the protesting girls by their coat sleeves and chastising them.

5-45 pm: During the journey back rumours flew around the coach like Chinese whispers that S and T were caught in the act snogging boys.

7-00 p.m: Arrived back at school in time for some cold Cornish pasties and baked beans. Everyone had stomach aches afterwards.

8-00 p.m: S and T seen visiting Nanny's room. They were there for a long time.

WEDNESDAY 8TH NOVEMBER

Yesterday seemed very dull after Monday's school outing. Today marked the first ever Junior Gating from a Visiting Day. The notice said that girls were caught smoking in The Maze on the Hampton Court school outing. Guess Who?

Now we'd have to be ultra-careful with any future BLAP activities. I consulted Team BLAP and it was decided that all further ghost-busting activities would have to be suspended until after Visiting Day on the 26th November.

Now for the good news – Gabby had miraculously stopped snoring! I don't know how but perhaps we'd finally start to get some sleep.

THURSDAY 9TH NOVEMBER

The dorm absolutely stunk last night. I mean really reeked. Esme declared the smell putrid. Everyone was going round sniffing everything and everyone, accusing each other of using something which smelt like toilet cleaner or medicine. It was worse than the surgical spirits we had to rub on our toes every night and worse smelling than Burt's gungy sauerkraut. Now that *was* saying something.

FRIDAY 10TH NOVEMBER

I was now ashamed of myself, and learnt an important lesson in life - never jump to conclusions. Granny always said 'don't judge a book by its cover'. She was so right. Last night, en-route to the bathroom, I passed Nanny's room. The door was ajar. I noticed Gabby sitting with her head stuck over a steaming tin bowl covered in a towel. Nanny beckoned me in and shut the door. She said Gabby had a sinus infection. She was trying to cure this with a nightly steam inhale mixed with pungent 'Friars Balsam' to help clear her congested sinuses. I felt it was mine and Abbey's fault for getting worked up about the snoring. Life can get so complicated.

The TV crew came down to school mid-morning in our tuck break and the girls had to get made up. Then we all watched them in our lunch break, filming a short sequence of some exercises at the ballet barre. I could see Esme at the far end doing the same 'grand battements' over and over again, with a man I didn't recognise yelling something which sounded like 'cut' every few minutes. Such a big crowd had gathered in the studio doorway that eventually we were asked to go away.

Janice had started telling us about it this evening when Esme stepped in and demonstrated what they had to do. Then she told us the same story all over again. She would be a nightmare to live with for the next few days.

MONDAY 13TH NOVEMBER

With such a lot happening recently I really enjoyed a normal school day.

During modern Miss Wanda made us sit down and launched into a long explanation about next year's spring Choreographic Competition.

Everyone chatted excitedly then Miss W clapped her hands.

"However, juniors are not allowed to enter because it has not been deemed practical."

She looked around at us, gesturing her palms dramatically upwards towards the sky. "But the junior dance teachers feel you are showing such good progress that you *should* be given the opportunity to practice choreography in class."

The record she chose was the theme from *The Persuaders*. I LOVED this music, but how would I make up a dance to this? Before I had time to worry about it we were put into groups of four and my group was picked to go first. I was with Kerri, Hannah and Gabby. We shuffled into the centre of the studio as the music started blaring out. Kerri leaped into action doing amazing spins around the studio. Hannah stood dead in the centre and with legs straddled, dropped dramatically to her knees and flung her hair from side to side like a rock musician. Gabby then launched into her loony drag-runs complete with windmill arms. I felt a rush of panic as I watched my friends. My mind went blank as my legs went off on their own, doing some kind of flick ball-change movement. I had no idea why my legs were doing this but I was relieved I wasn't just standing still looking stupid. We were all going crazy when the music was suddenly turned off. *Thank goodness*. Miss W didn't look impressed. She said she'd seen stick insects with more rhythm than us. How insulting. Lucky for us the other groups were just as bad. When the last group finished and Miss W had uttered her final crushing comment, she smiled wickedly as she strolled towards the record player to stop it. She said if we had any intention of entering the competition in the future we would need counselling or body doubles...

FRIDAY 17TH NOVEMBER

Everyone in Junior Dorm is practising choreography. Patsy had given me a tape recording of Tchaikovsky's 'The Nutcracker Suite'. I knew this well as I had loads of ballet LPs at home. There was a short piece called the 'Chinese Dance' and as I'd used it to practise to at home, I could remember simple steps to this music. I had pretended to be a Chinese Doll with a fan.

SATURDAY 18ᵀᴴ NOVEMBER

After our walk to the shop today I braved it and asked Esme if I could borrow her tape recorder. She agreed - but only if she could choreograph a dance with me. Being an oracle she added, "It's all about compromise."

That evening I suffered a real ear bending session from Esme. She came over to my bottom bunk directly after tea, armed with a notepad and tape recorder to discuss 'our' dance. I told her my idea about Chinese dolls that dance like little puppets whilst holding fans and she loved it. We listened to my music and I said it reminded me of fluttering wings, suggesting we fluttered the fans in our hands like butterflies. Esme was very excited.

SUNDAY 19ᵀᴴ NOVEMBER

Burt and Nancy were serving Sunday Dinner together at the canteen today. Nancy was dishing out huge slabs of Yorkshire pudding. It was so delicious that everyone queued for seconds and the queue went on for miles. It ran out before I got there. I was permanently starving. I mean, it wasn't like we don't eat; it just never felt there was enough.

On my way through the Dive, I noticed the phone booth was empty so I phoned home. I told Mum how much I was looking forward to next Sunday. Then I explained about the juniors being too young to enter the choreographic competition, but we were practising anyway. Mum told me Dad was decorating our bedroom ready for Marie-Helene's visit. Maybe he would make Lily take down her David Cassidy picture. She also asked if my Tuck Box was empty. I said I had plenty otherwise she would worry they didn't feed us enough.

After my call home I ran back to the dorm, my mind fixed on food. No wonder the students profited from our weakness by selling illegal tuck.

Here is an example: only that very evening Esme and I had been discussing the dance. A student I didn't know came into the dorm selling a mass of tuck. She had a giant Tupperware box full of assorted biscuits, selling each one at outrageous prices:

1 Bourbon = 5 pence

1 Custard Cream = 5 pence

1 Chocolate Digestive = 6 pence

Special Discount = 3 for 12 pence

Chocolate was the favourite and therefore more expensive.

A Mars Bar = 20 pence (cost in shops 4 pence!)

A slice of Mars bar/divided between five of us = 5 pence

1 square of Cadburys Dairy Milk = 7 pence (buy 3 squares and get one free). I had no idea how much a giant bar was but I thought it was a big fat swizz. They must have been making a billion pounds in profit.

The tuck sales were secretive and strictly forbidden, and therefore mostly took place in the evening, where sellers could lurk around in the dark and travel from dorm to dorm under cover of night. The tuck seller always had another girl to keep watch and warn them of approaching prefects or staff in the nearby area.

When I talked to Esme about it she told me not to be so naïve, because it was actually a brilliant way of making money and that the person who originally thought of it was a genius. Then she blew it by swiftly eating the finger of fudge I'd bought with my remaining pocket money, smiling sweetly and saying 'I owe you.'

Grrrrr. She was sooo annoying.

MONDAY 20TH NOVEMBER

Only five days to go until Vis Day. Millie showed me a photo of her house which arrived with a letter today. It was beautiful and the surrounding garden was like a burst of colour. I imagined living there was paradise. She said I could stay with her in Tobago in the summer holidays, but I would have to ask Mum and Dad first. I hadn't got anywhere near enough money saved up yet for the air fare, even including my post-office savings.

When I ticked off the calendar days on our chart, Millie asked if I realised it was a full moon tonight. She understood my obsession with the Blue Lady. As I was writing I could hear Nanny's voice outside our dorm. It suddenly dawned on me that BLAP had absolutely no idea and it was now too close to lights out to tell the team without arousing suspicion amongst the others. I wondered what would happen after lights out.

TUESDAY 21ST NOVEMBER

I kept a tense and solitary watch last night, lying awake for ages in anticipation of some sign of other life, but there was nothing at all, not even a rustle of ghostly skirts or a glow in the dark. I must have fallen asleep at some stage and I was hugely disappointed. I would make a dismal Sherlock Holmes.

I eventually caught up with team BLAP today. All concerned seemed bitterly disappointed at the lost opportunity. We would be home on our Christmas hols for the next full moon (when the Blue Lady would, no doubt, rise out of the Lake in her full glory for a Christmas reunion with her dying soldiers, and be visible for everyone - who was not here - to see).

Perhaps she'd fallen in love with one of the men she'd nursed; or maybe it was more sinister and she was pushed to her death?

Esme and I practised more steps that I'd choreographed for our Chinese Dance. I hoped my choreographic skills were improving.

SATURDAY 25TH NOVEMBER

It was Vis Day the following day and I couldn't wait to see everyone. I phoned home before breakfast today, telling Mum I needed some oriental fans. Mum said she'd see what she could find in the loft and mentioned she'd got toiletries for me and extra tuck!

After breakfast I'd left my mug in the main hall, so I had to race back to collect it. I heard a lot of noise coming from the drama room and, walking past the door, noticed the big television was on and several Tweenies were sprawled out on the chaise longue watching 'Banana Splits'. I felt a twinge of homesickness. Life was so busy here I barely got time to think about home. Maybe that was why Millie stopped being homesick. I wanted to invite some of the girls who lived abroad home with me for Vis Days - I would have to remember to talk to Mum and Dad about that tomorrow.

This afternoon it was so cold before the walk to the shop that I had to put on two layers, my blazer and my raincoat. At the shop I wanted to buy something nice for Lily's birthday, but with little money I settled on a large Cadburys flake. With the pennies left over I bought a small Fry's Turkish Delight because it was all I could afford. It smelt like perfume so I gave it to Millie who said it reminded her of Christmas.

Before tea I checked on the library shelves for information relating to ghosts, particularly school ghosts. Some Tweenies came in and started practising their choreographic dance. Pretending to read I watched out of the corner of my eye. I realised it would take years of practice to choreograph that well.

CHAPTER TWENTY-TWO

VIS DAY CATCH-UP

SUNDAY 26TH NOVEMBER

When Dad dropped me back at school, I couldn't wait to show Esme the black lace fans Mum had given us. Esme was ecstatic and said "Your Mum's a star!"

After supper, we all swapped Vis Day news:

Mika: Went to a pub for Sunday lunch with her family. She drank some of her Dad's wine when her parents were in the toilets, which made her feel giggly then slightly sick.

Abbey: Said her brothers took her to a motorbike race and she had a ride on a Harley Davidson.

Maddy: Visited her Nan in a nursing home and said her Nan was losing the plot.

Millie: Went to Brighton with her Aunty. They visited the Pavilion, ate fish and chips out of newspaper and got dive-bombed by chip-stealing sea gulls.

Gabby: Had the most boring day ever and said she would be happy if she lived at school forever. This was the voice of despair.

Esme: Ghastly relatives from the North took her out and she hated them. She wanted to know if she could get a divorce from her relatives. Everyone kept quiet.

Hannah: Visited her older sister in London. She said after a day of culture, she realised how sophisticated the city was and she longed to be independent.

Me: I said I was lucky to go home and see all my family. I showed the girls our fans and Hannah said they looked very authentic.

Tonight, as I read my Bunty before lights out, I said a silent prayer, thanking God for my lovely family and for letting me come to this amazing school (even if it does have weird dogs, shy ghosts and scary prefects).

I wondered what the last few weeks of term would have in store for us all.

CHAPTER TWENTY-THREE

MONDAY 27ᵀᴴ NOVEMBER

Esme and I practised our Chinese dance after lunch today. We used one of the empty studios before the afternoon school bell rang. Kerri came to watch and said it was good but we looked a bit like dolls. Esme said that was a job well done as we were supposed to be dolls. I knew what Kerri meant and when the bell went and Esme raced off, Kerri and I agreed that we needed someone who had done this whole choreographing thing before to watch our dance and give us some constructive criticism. Patsy was nominated by a majority vote.

After modern today I found Patsy queuing for tea in the Dive corridor. She was sitting on the stairway with her friends and they were making a real racket as they frantically beat up some frothy coffee in their mugs with teaspoons. I had to shout above all the spoon clanging and told her about our dance. Tonight she had coaching for her ballet exam, so agreed to see us tomorrow. She pulled a long face. Poor Patsy, she really hated ballet.

Esme got a parcel in the post at tea today and passed the contents around the tea table. She had been sent a new tape cassette of The Osmonds' latest album called 'Crazy Horses' - Uh-oh!

199

TUESDAY 28TH NOVEMBER

Patsy got Nanny's permission and took us into the studio under our dorm to practise tonight. She sat right in front of us, so I made sure I didn't make eye contact with her, remembering I had to look towards the audience at the back of the theatre. I shuffled around with miniature steps and peeked out from behind my fan. On the final chord of music we dropped demurely to a kneeling position and covered our faces with our fans. I hardly dared breathe as I waited for Patsy's reaction.

Patsy walked towards us looking solemn. I thought maybe she'd hated it until she spoke.

"You little angels!" she yelled, grabbing us both close to her in a big bear hug and squeezing so hard it hurt. "It's absolutely amazing!"

"Really?" I gasped breathlessly.

Her face lit up.

"If the dance was rubbish, I'd help you re-choreograph it."

Her eyebrows met in the centre like caterpillars.

"But here's a few tips; make your movements crisper. You're Chinese dolls and I get the miniature steps, but the music is so short that with only two of you on stage you've got to create some light and shade by travelling."

She demonstrated speeding across the studio, her feet travelling in fast bourrées and I was startled by the difference.

"See?"

We nodded. I found what she said really helpful. Patsy then watched us put her suggestions into practice until Nanny arrived.

"Patsy, dear, you've got five minutes left until lights out."

Patsy said she was proud of our efforts, even if we couldn't enter the competition.

FRIDAY 1ST DECEMBER

Everyone swarmed round the notice board at breakfast to look at the running order of the competition preliminaries being held the next day. It was being held in the studio near the lake. I wondered if the Blue Lady would have a spooky influence. The judges included Miss Brookes, Mr Deluca and Mr Julius. I hoped we'd be able to watch from the studio windows.

SUNDAY 3RD DECEMBER

Today Junior Dorm went into shock. After church, Nanny announced that we were going for a walk this afternoon 'OUT OF BOUNDS'!

We got our wellies and, led by Nanny and Hamish, we headed off into the great wilderness. For once, we didn't have to be in a crocodile but Nanny warned us if we ran off this would be the first and last walk. As we left the school grounds I wondered what we might meet. I always imagined there was some evil beast lurking behind the thick bushes, or that the beast was kept at bay by the high wire fences marking the school boundaries.

Narrow paths led us through dense undergrowth. Emerging into a clearing my eyes squinted against the dazzling sunlight. In front of us was a little bridge over a stream. We crossed the bridge and Nanny and Hamish led us towards a wide road. Here the scenery changed completely. We'd entered a beautiful tree lined avenue with vast houses dotted on either side. Some of the gardens had lakes, others had pavilions with statues in the gardens like the ones you saw in museums. The sun shone so brightly we had to take off our coats. Nanny let us hold Hamish's lead. Even Sydney and Tiffany behaved.

Whilst we walked we got chatting to Nanny. Sanchia asked her if she had grown-up children. Nanny said that her husband died in the last war so they never had children, but being a Nanny she now had more than twenty children! As we walked and talked, Nanny told us how much the school had changed in the time she'd worked there, but said she would never leave as the school was her family. Everyone cooed and said "Oh Nanny!" She laughed.

"You silly lassies, now don't go filling your heads with soppy maudlin thoughts about me being left all alone. I have Hamish, my bonnie wee dog," she patted Hamish whose tail wagged like crazy at the mention of his name, "who keeps me more than occupied and is grand company, particularly during the school holidays."

The walk was lovely, and I felt really glad knowing that Nanny had found a happy home at Stavely Brookes.

That evening, just before lights out, Millie leant over to my bunk and reminded me to tick off another day on the calendar, whispering, "We've only got twelve days left until end of term!"

MONDAY 4TH DECEMBER

I was given a large padded envelope at tea which had a London postmark on the label.

Guess what it turned out to be? I now had a proper signed pointe shoe, with a message written across the toe block satin from Alexandra Haydon! I couldn't believe it when I opened the envelope and it was all wrapped up in tissue paper. It was

the most beautiful pointe shoe ever. The message written across
the top of the toe block in very beautiful writing said:

For Lara

Work hard and one day you will achieve all your dreams.

Alexandra

She had written another small letter on thick cream coloured
paper, embossed with her address.

Dear Lara

*Thank you very much for your last letter and I apologise for not
replying sooner. I have been busy rehearsing for a new role and time
has flown past, so please forgive me.*

*I am sure that by now you have probably reached the end of your first
term. I hope you have enjoyed it and had fun learning, amongst other
things, all the different dance styles. I have enclosed the pointe shoe as
promised from one of my favourite ballet roles, dancing Juliet. I hope
this will bring you lots of luck.*

With very best wishes

Love

Alexandra

I couldn't believe I'd actually got a signed pointe shoe from a
real-life, famous prima ballerina. Everyone in the dorm wanted
to see it. No one seemed to mind that I had done something
different. In fact I thought I had just started a new trend,
because now everyone wanted to have a crush on a famous
ballerina. The pointe shoe now sat proudly on display on my
bed, parked right next to March Hare.

TUESDAY 5TH DECEMBER

I brought my pointe shoe out of the dorm to show Kerri today
and she said I was sooo lucky. I hoped I was. I crossed March

Hare's chubby harlequin legs together for extra luck, but he now looked like he was stuck in a plié!

THURSDAY 7TH DECEMBER

THURSDAY 7TH DECEMBER

The notice board was surrounded with people at tea time. The preliminary choreographic results were displayed for all to check. I could hear cries of pleasure and sobs of dismay. I would have to practise hard before the competition next year.

FRIDAY 8TH DECEMBER

In geography today, Karlyn had to leave class and visit sick bay. She had obviously felt ill all morning, complaining she was burning up and asking to go to the San. Mr Mainwaring sensibly made Hannah take her there, as she looked dead pale with big black circles under her eyes. Karlyn had white blond hair and this ghostly colouring made her look a bit like an albino vampire. I've never seen one but I'm sure that's what it would look like.

  During ballet later this afternoon Paula said she felt faint and kept doing mini-swoons over the barre. Everyone thought she was faking, especially after she'd seen Karlyn going all wobbly and nearly falling over her desk, but she did look peaky. Eventually she had to be taken to the dorm to lie down. By the evening several other girls were saying they felt ill. All had headaches and complained of body aches, sore armpits and feeling like they were 'on fire', so they too were sent to bed. I hoped this wasn't catching.

CHAPTER TWENTY-FOUR

SATURDAY 9TH DECEMBER

Last night Nanny had to visit several girls who were feverish.
She looked like Florence Nightingale with her lantern and
apron, going from bed to bed, dabbing girls' foreheads with a
wet cloth and propping them up against pillows to sip water.
She must be tired this morning.

After ballet more girls were queuing outside Nanny's room
waiting for sick notes. I had modern routines to practise this
weekend and couldn't afford to be ill.

The Christmas party was on the 14th and I couldn't wait.
Hannah told me all about the end-of-term party when older
girls put on shows for the younger girls. Hannah said you
never knew what students - or teachers - might do.

Tired after the walk to the shop I lay on my bed. I must have
fallen asleep because Abbey woke me saying tea bell was
ringing. As I got up my head spun. Abbey told me to lie down
and went to get Nanny.

When Nanny arrived she checked my pulse and said, "BED"!
I couldn't believe I was ill when the end of term fun was about
to begin. Reduced to 'nil by mouth' I felt like a wet rag. Even
writing my journal was a mammoth effort. Nanny isolated all
the ill girls to one side of the room. Luckily it was my side and I

lay quietly, feeling limp and useless. She'd given us strict orders to rest and mentioned that we might be sent home. I was too feeble to grip my pen and too weedy to care...

SUNDAY 10TH DECEMBER

Nanny told us that we had a nasty type of flu, and unfortunately we had to go home to prevent the virus spreading.

I felt gutted missing my first end of term at ballet school.

Later on the bell rang, summoning 'the well' to lunch. I was gob-smacked when Nanny announced that our parents would be picking us up that afternoon. I couldn't believe it. She told us not to worry about getting up and dressed. As we lay in our sick beds, Nanny gathered our belongings together, placing them in neat piles on our end-of-bed lockers. We looked like the living dead. March Hare - complete with knotted legs - and my lucky pointe shoe, lay like fallen pillars at the end of my bed. It was a pathetic scene. What was to become of us?

As I watched Nanny glide noiselessly around the room I thought of the Blue Lady, wondering if her ghostly spirit was protecting us.

I fell asleep for a while. Returning from her lunch, Abbey had sneaked through the invisible barrier officially designated a NO-GO-ZONE to stop the spread of germs. I was woken up by something scratching my ear and nearly screamed in fright when I realised it was Abbey crouching beside my bed. Flapping her hands and mouthing 'shhh' to avoid trouble, she gave me her phone number on a scrap of paper and made me promise to ring her in the holidays. Despite feeling grim, I smiled as I watched her crawl away from my bed on her hands and knees.

Soon parents began arriving through the dorm door. Gathering listless girls from their beds they departed with long faces. Gabby's Mum wasn't sympathetic when Gabby collapsed on the floor when she got out of bed. Her Mum grumbled, "Pull yourself together, I can't carry you!"

Mum and Dad were the last to arrive. I made a supreme effort to get up and pretend I was better then went light-headed. Mum and Dad rushed over and held my arms, then decided to talk to Nanny so I had to lie down again. I watched from my bed. Dad and Mum were talking to Nanny in the entrance and looked serious. Maybe there was something they hadn't told us, and we were all going to die and the school didn't want to be left with our dead bodies.

Mum helped me to sit up and put on my dressing gown. I left in style, carried in my Dad's arms dressed in my flower-power dressing gown and fluffy slippers.

I slept the whole journey home and Dad had to carry me up to bed. I signed out of my diary as a sickly soul who was glad to be home.

PART TWO

SPRING TERM

CHAPTER TWENTY-FIVE

1973

THURSDAY IITH JANUARY

Back to school today! I couldn't believe the holidays were over and felt guilty that I'd been so preoccupied with our exchange student Marie-Helene that I hadn't made a single entry in my diary. Dad came home from London early to take me back to school.

Standing outside Junior Dorm as I hugged Dad goodbye, I wondered what excitement the spring term would hold for us.

FRIDAY 12TH JANUARY

Rising bell made me jump out of my skin this morning. That and March Hare's ear stuck in my face. The dorm felt very cold and I'd gone to sleep with March Hare cuddled against me. I read somewhere that if you were freezing to death another person's body warmth could save you - but March Hare did a great job. After home it was a shock to wake up army style.

When everyone was back in the dorm last night, we sat on Millie's bed and exchanged news from our first holiday from ballet school. Everyone's news was very different.

Millie: Spent Christmas day on the beach. Swum with turtles, went diving off a reef and spent days at sea, sailing with her Uncle. Her London Aunty arrived in Tobago accompanied by her toyboy, a Hollywood actor. Millie said no one had heard of him.

Abbey: Hated her holidays - her parents had a massive argument and her father had now run off with a younger woman. In private she revealed that her brother had punched her Dad in the eye!

Mika: Said she spent Christmas with her grandparents in Scotland. They saw the New Year in at a party in a castle where they stayed for the night. The men all wore kilts. She also attended local karate lessons with her brother and has promised to teach us some self-defence moves.

Maddy: Her Nan came out of the nursing home to spend Christmas with her family. They had a call from the home the week after she'd returned, saying her Nan was causing havoc amongst all the male residents trying to enter their rooms at night.

Gabby: Announced that she'd had the best holidays ever. Over the Christmas week her Italian relatives came to stay with them. Gabby visited local pubs with her eighteen-year-old cousin Alfonso and was allowed to drink alcohol. I didn't believe her.

Sanchia: Spent Christmas in Madrid with her family. She asked Abbey if she'd like to stay with her in Spain this summer holidays. I had to think of ways to make Abbey feel better.

Hannah: Stayed most of the holidays with her older sister in London. Her sister took her to see some creepy Dracula film which she said was terrifying. I couldn't imagine Hannah scared of anything.

Esme: Spent Christmas in Kenya. Their house was burgled by poachers who fed their dog poisoned meat to stop it barking, then the dog got sick and had to be put down. They acquired four guard dogs which barked all night, extra security bars on their windows and an indestructible security gate. She said all the men had licences to keep weapons. Hannah demanded to know what sort of weapons. Esme said it wasn't bows and arrows.

Me: I was excited to tell everyone about our lovely French guest, Marie-Helene, and about our visits to London. I said my French had improved and I was the proud owner of a bottle of Chanel No.19. I showed everyone and Esme was impressed, declaring it fresher than her Mum's Nina Ricci. She brought me a pretty beaded necklace from Kenya made with millions of multi-coloured beads.

We all dreaded our first dance class. It sounded like no one had done much practising because we'd all barely recovered from flu, but next holidays I would definitely practise. School timetables were the same as last term, but at breakfast this morning we checked the notice board and discovered names of entrants for the spring term's dance exams. We'd been entered for our Grade One modern exam! Over breakfast we discussed practising our routines before Monday's class. Miss Wanda would go crazy if we'd forgotten everything.

The start-of-term assembly, held in the main hall, lasted forever. I was dying to talk to Kerri but couldn't because Miss Bell made us sit right under her nose in the front row.

She droned on for ages about the flu epidemic and the large quantities of work we'd missed. It was baking hot in the hall and so airless it made me drowsy.

Assembly finally drew to a close with the school song and the staff got so teary eyed you'd have thought it was a funeral.

With just one hour form period in the afternoon we got plenty of time to practise our modern routines. We spent an hour in the library marking through our 'Burning Love' routine and then practised 'A Horse with No Name'. Bang in the middle of us dancing Mr Julius walked past the library with Sultan who bounded in when he saw me. I tried to run but he pinned me to the wall and started licking my face.

EUGH!

Kerri had hysterics and Mr Julius walked in laughing.

"He's taken a fancy to you!"

Covered in dog slobber I politely said, "He likes me because I run away!"

Mr Julius beamed, wearing a black silk shirt over frayed jeans and looking like a cross between a rock star and one of Jesus' disciples. He suddenly became serious and snapped his finger, horse dog leapt to his side and they headed towards the music room.

When he was out of sight we burst into giggles, then realised ballet started in ten minutes and ran like mad things.

Our first class was a disaster. I couldn't believe how unfit we'd become over Christmas. Miss Olsen did her usual snail-pace corrections, and during pirouettes Paula's leading arm whacked Janice across the mouth giving her a split-lip. Blood went flying, Tamsin fainted and Janice was sent to Matron.

The final blow came from a new, elderly pianist named Eunice, who wore a hairnet and spectacles that magnified her eyes. Eunice was accompanied by her dog called Asterix. It adopted the usual dog-watching-dance-class position, panting and drooling all over the floor until a large puddle formed beneath the piano. Asterix also farted. Eunice - being closest to the offensive smell - made a real performance of opening the windows, saying we needed fresh air. The 'fresh-air' blew in like a hurricane, then Miss Olsen got all huffy and closed the offending window. When she turned her back, Eunice got up and re-opened the closed window. This opening and closing charade carried on for some while until Miss Olsen lost it.

"Stop opening that window Eunice, for heaven's sake. The girls will catch pneumonia!"

Eunice pouted and played the 'Grande Allegro' jumps like a death march. With central heating bouncing off the studio walls and Asterix's poisonous farts we nearly suffocated.

Finally, whilst performing our curtsies, Eunice gave a smug little smile and played a long drawn out ripple up the piano keys, adding a final high 'PING' at the end, like she was saying 'SO THERE!'

As we rushed towards the studio door Miss Olsen came hurrying after us.

"Girls, before you race off, I must say I'm disappointed none of you practiced in the holidays."

She let out a large sigh and continued her tirade.

"Ballerinas of the future are those who dedicate time to practising *every single day*." We all cringed.

"S-L-O-T-H," she drew breath and cast her eyes up and down our leotard-clad bodies, "does not a dancer make, and I can see," she eyed Gabby as she moved even closer to her, raising one eyebrow and patting Gabby's relaxed belly, "that Christmas has been a little too generous."

Gabby flushed beetroot.

"Quite right, Miss Olsen" Eunice butted in.

215

Miss Olsen glared at Eunice, cutting her short with an icy look.

"What I am trying to say is this, girls. Just imagine you have a beautiful flower bud. To make the young bud bloom into a beautiful flower, you must water it daily. You are like that small bud, needing daily care and attention to reach your true ability. Lack of care and ignoring your practice is like forgetting to water your flower, and you will never achieve your future ambitions. Do you understand?"

None of us spoke. She smiled, raised her hands in front of her mouth then clapped her hands together like a small child. It gradually dawned on us that she was looking for some kind of acknowledgement, so we solemnly nodded until our heads formed one giant nod. I avoided meeting anyone else's eyes, terrified she might pick on my stomach next.

In the tea queue whilst everyone chatted about their holidays, I could hear Esme nearby yakking away about life in Kenya. I started wondering if I really would 'have what it took' to be the next Margot Fonteyn. I must, once again, firm my resolve and stop cracking under the slightest criticism. My thoughts were disturbed when I was grabbed from behind and lifted from under the armpits high off the canteen floor. A laughing voice in my ear said a loud, "Guess who?"

"Patsy," I gasped with effort. She put me down and gave me a huge bear hug. When she released me I had to shake myself. I hardly recognised her. Grabbing a fistful of her newly chopped, bright red hair she pulled the most ridiculous face, making me crack up with laughter.

"Crazy or what!" she grinned. "This will cause trouble with the headband army."

Her hair was cut all shaggy with a fringe - she was my hero! We arranged for her to visit Junior Dorm before supper that night. Patsy was such fun.

Burt was in a better mood that evening and cracked a toothless smile when he served me food. 'The Spy With No Teeth' didn't sound very 007. I must have felt less sorry for myself because I scoffed two whole beef burgers. There were no letters for me. It seemed like everyone else had post when you didn't get any. I would have to write to Joseph again.

Patsy arrived before supper. I told her about Miss Olsen's flower lecture. Patsy said Miss Olsen gave them the same flower lecture just after their first holiday break, when none of them had practised. She said I could be a weed - which I definitely wasn't - or show the old bat just how good I really was. After Patsy left the dorm I felt so much better. I would show Miss Olsen - no more shrinking violet for me.

SATURDAY 13TH JANUARY

In ballet today Miss Wanda said my elevation had improved. How amazing was that?

Whilst waiting with Kerri for her Dad to pick her up, Callum came to chat with us. When Kerri's Dad arrived he offered Callum a lift home. As I watched them drive off together I was startled by the unexpected appearance of a short figure in the distance, dressed in white and emerging from behind the bushes. I blinked and realised it was Burt sneaking around - AGAIN. I wondered whether our cook-cum-spy reported all he saw. If so, I bet Mr Deluca knew everything BLAP had been up to, thanks to Burt's sneaky undercover work. The crafty old dog.

This afternoon Janice was my partner to the shop. Esme had decided to ask Tamsin, so Janice asked if she could partner me. It was nice getting to know her. Because the dorm was so big I had only really got close to the girls on my side of the dorm. Nanny had actually swapped Janice and Hannah over this term, I supposed to stop the Esme/Hannah feud. Good move on Nanny's part, maybe there will be fewer cat fights between them.

Janice talked about her home and family. She started ballet at just three year's old and she said her Mum always entered her for talent competitions. Janice started at Stavely Brookes a term before me, at the same time as Esme. She confided to me that Esme had a habit of trying to take over everything.

After our shop trip Cimmie took the Roll Call. We hadn't seen much of her recently because of choreographic rehearsals. Today she looked weird, wearing red lipstick and heavy black eyeliner rimmed right around her tiny eyes, which made her look like some kind of psycho-goth witch.

I stayed well clear of Little Dorm tonight. In the tea queue Sydney had declared in a loud stage whisper that she was going to be holding a séance in Little Dorm before lights out. She said that if anyone dared tell Nanny they would be dead. She was obsessed with death. Oracle was disgusted and, having decided I was interesting to talk to again, sat on my bottom bunk lecturing me about Sydney's obsession with attracting unwanted spirits. It was a bit hypocritical really, as we did have the BLAP team and went in active search of the elusive Blue Lady. The difference was, we were looking for a known resident spirit, a kind of Florence Nightingale and therefore she qualified as a good ghost. Sydney, on the other hand, would actually be trying to call up the unknown dead.

All I'm saying is this: you never know who might answer your call.

Just before lights out, after soaking my toes in surgical spirits, I went down to the bathroom to clean my teeth, stopping en-route in the loos. Ever since the 'ink on the seat' episode, I always chose to go in the middle cubicle. I sat on the wobbly seat examining the loo paper. At home we had soft loo paper, and a box of hard paper which only Mum and Dad used. It was a throwback to war days and having to make things go further. The loo paper we had here was the wartime variety and brutal. I had to spend ages rubbing two pieces together just to soften it. As I was sitting minding my own business I heard a rustling in the loo next door. It went on for ages and I wondered who else rubbed loo paper together to soften it. I quickly flushed the loo and burst out of my cubicle, only to find an empty loo on both sides. The hairs on the back of my neck stood on end, my mouth went dry and I was frozen with fear. Then panic set in and I bolted back upstairs. I flew into the dorm and nearly knocked Nanny off her feet, then stumbled and fell over poor Hamish. Nanny brushed her skirt down and scolded me.

"Goodness, lass, you're racing around like a mad woman. Whatever's got into you?"

I wanted to scream GHOST at the top of my voice, then remembered Sydney's threat.

"I thought I was late for lights out," I muttered, separating Hamish's jaw from my dressing gown cord. Nanny eyed me suspiciously and narrowed her eyes.

"Get into bed. Goodness, you're as pale as a ghost. You need a good night's sleep."

FAT CHANCE.

SUNDAY 14TH JANUARY

Last night I was restless. In my mind I kept going over that ghostly rustling noise in the loos. I told Abbey about it after lights out. She said it was probably students from nearby annexes up to their old tricks. Just in case, I told all of team BLAP to be on red-alert. The prefects were busy rehearsing so our church crocodile was led by two students who I'd never seen before. Seraphina lived in Argentina and Mercedes came from Liverpool in the north and had this odd accent which was hard to understand. She told me she was a scouser. I told Mercedes she had the same name as a car and she said it was her Dad's fault because he was a "proper car salesman, like." Nobody was naughty at church when Cimmie and Rita weren't around. Oracle reckoned they looked for trouble.

Quite the opposite of our experiences with the terrible two, Seraphina and Mercedes were great fun, feeding us chocolate raisins during our walk back to give us energy. Seraphina was tall, regal looking and even spoke Spanish. She was going back to Argentina in three years after she had become a qualified teacher.

Back in the dorm we all practiced our modern routines.

I also phoned home before tea. Mum said the house was really quiet without me. She said Aunty Phyllis was gallivanting and had threatened to visit. Dad was dreading it, saying Aunty Phyllis was garrulous.

Before lights out team BLAP searched the loos and bathroom. I made them stay while I used the loo, just in case. They probably thought I was imagining it, but I knew what I'd heard. Blimmin' Sydney calling up spirits!

CHAPTER TWENTY-SIX

MONDAY 15TH JANUARY

In form period today Miss Knox made an announcement.

"I visited Rome over Christmas," she paused while we absorbed this morsel of information, "and my inspiration for this term's study has come from Rome itself, with its fabulous history."

Perhaps this meant a school trip to Rome!

During drama, Miss Lazenby had two versions of Voodoo at her feet. She gave a throaty laugh when we came in.

"Guess who's who, hahaha?"

I couldn't guess. One version of Voodoo was more than enough. She carried on,

"They're like brother and sister." She waved her hands theatrically towards the dogs announcing, "Voodoo and Venus."

I was no genius, but judging by Voodoo's indelicate behaviour, Venus wasn't his sister. I was too embarrassed to watch their undignified performance. With everyone sniggering the dogs caused a riot. Cats were *way* more sophisticated…

After that the day went downhill. According to Miss Wanda, on a scale of one to ten, our modern solos were currently level two! She strode forward yanking down the trouser legs of her woollen jazz-flares.

"Your exams are in eight weeks time and you are NOWHERE near exam standard. I WILL withdraw you if you aren't ready, and don't think I don't mean it." Turning on her heel she stormed back to the tape recorder yelling, "Again, and this time, I want to see some ATTACK!"

We danced like demons and for once Tamsin didn't faint.

Millie and I completed our countdown chart tonight, highlighting the dates of the full moon. I'd almost forgotten about them and realised that the next one was this coming Thursday. I mustn't forget to alert BLAP.

WEDNESDAY 17TH JANUARY

Yesterday was crazy busy and I got no time to myself. With the modern exam looming, another notice had gone up announcing extra modern exam coaching. My coaching was with Kerri, Tamsin and Esme every Thursday evening, starting next week. We had special permission for early tea.

We had an introduction to the Romans in history today. Miss Knox said if it wasn't for the Romans, civilization as we knew it would not exist. She had organized a quiz to find out how much we knew - or didn't!

When my question came up Miss Knox had a wicked gleam in her eye.

"Which British Queen did the Romans defeat? Was it (a) Sophie Magdalene, (b) Mona Lisa, or (c) Boudicca"?

I knew there was no such Queen as Mona Lisa and Magdalene was from the Bible ('Sophie' was clearly a red herring), so it had to be (c).

"Boudicca!" I yelled her name excitedly and nearly fell off my chair. Unfortunately, only Esme and I got our answers right. This led Miss Knox to believe I had some knowledge about Romans and kept looking at me to supply the answers to her questions. Fortunately, due to Oracle's annoying habit of knowing everything and (less annoyingly) generously sharing these facts with me, I was able to supply information in the Shout the Answer game that followed.

At tea I received a letter post-card. It had lots of pictures which opened up like a concertina and miles more room to write in. I recognised the handwriting; it was from my Aunty Phyllis. She'd filled up the length of the card, even writing down the sides in every available inch of space. She must have been the oldest Aunty in the history of the universe to have done so much travelling by herself. Most women of her age had a travelling companion for safety. Her writing was unimaginably microscopic and I struggled to decipher its contents.

Dear Lara

I am once again back on my travels. This time a cruise of the Eastern Mediterranean. Today we stopped at Haifa. As all of the passengers disembarked down the gangplank, a vicious looking red-eyed rodent the size of a skunk shot straight out in front of us. I had a touch of the vapours, but my new American friend Ivy plied me with some smelling salts. The handsome Captain had to carry me to where our coach was waiting and I was given the best front seat for the trip. We have visited the Dead Sea where we covered ourselves in black mud and then floated in the waters. I cannot swim, but here I floated for the very first time in my life and our ship photographer recorded the moment! I have extracted and reserved a jar of this Dead Sea mud for you. It is reputed to have many benefits for general ailments. Ivy covered herself in it (and looked very fetching) in the hopes her rheumatic pains would vanish.

You will notice, looking at the pictures on the front, all the different photos of places we have been or will be visiting shortly. I am going to see Bethlehem where our Lord was born and later hope to visit the Sea of Galilee. These places are so different to our villages on Dartmoor and the rolling Devon countryside.

My dear, I am very much looking forward to seeing you soon when I pay a visit to your good parents. I so enjoy seeing them as we always have so much to talk about. I hope you are still working hard and enjoying your ballet dancing.

With fondest love

Aunty Phyllis xx

One of the post-card pictures on the front was a black and white photo, showing old-fashioned looking people. The men had huge handlebar moustaches and the women wore bloomers on their legs. They were plastered from head to toe in black mud. Maybe they were rheumatic like her friend Ivy. It must have been very good mud!

Before lights out, Millie reminded me about the full moon tomorrow night. BLAP met up in the bathroom on loo patrol and we agreed that the loo I heard the rustling noise coming from was much colder than the others. For some unexplained reason there was always a mass of loo roll stuffed down the pan so it never flushed.

THURSDAY 18TH JANUARY

Tonight was a full moon. BLAP got together after lunch. We agreed to let Kerri in on our activities but she was sworn to secrecy. Abbey said Kerri could act as a decoy and throw Esme and Hannah off our scent if questions were asked. It made me feel excited when we all ganged together - it was like a secret society!

We met up by the wash-hut after tea, wrapping scarves round our heads to protect our ears from the bitter cold. As we arrived at the library the distant lake looked ghostly. We must have all had the same thoughts but Abbey spoke first.

"How the hell are we going to be invisible under this moon?"

She threw her hand up towards the luminescent orb.

"Rub some dirt on your faces like they do in films."

We grovelled on the ground, groping in the mud, and smudged it over our cheeks in an attempt to darken our glowing, pasty skin.

"Any better?" Mika spluttered, peering at Abbey. We laughed hysterically.

Finally we got ourselves under control and headed for the lake under cover of the surrounding trees. By the time we got to the willow we were all frozen and the biting wind made us shiver. We huddled together under the giant willow trunk. I bought out my diddy torch and checked the time, hoping no-one would notice our absence. As I shone my torch towards my watch there was another flash on the far side of the lake. Fear rushed through my body as we simultaneously dropped like stones to the ground.

"What was that?" hissed Abbey.

"A flash" I said.

Mika chimed in "A flash of what?"

"The Blue Lady?"

We laughed uneasily. Abbey took charge.

"Listen. We've got to go and investigate - it's now or never. Follow me."

My heart started to pound as we crawled on our hands and knees through the deep grass. Under the moonlit sky our shadows cast creepy shapes along the ground. We must have crawled for ages but travelled in the wrong direction. Everything seemed different from ground level. Suddenly there was icy water oozing from the undergrowth beneath our hands and knees.

"Oh crikey, we're in the lake!" Abbey sniggered.

"Idiot," said Maddy, "you led us here."

We fell about laughing. I don't know how long we laughed for but we got a bit hyper and couldn't stop. My face felt like it would fall off.

Maddy suggested we retrace our footsteps, which we did and it took ages. Back in the shelter of our large willow trunk we clutched our aching stomachs and gazed feebly at our surroundings. The lake was still, the moon shone bright and the old rowing boat cast a shadow where it lay abandoned. Just as everything looked hopeless there was a different noise, coming from the far side of the lake over in the direction of the main house. Squatting up on our haunches and peering out from the tree trunk, we could see several figures approaching with torches. Moving closer they were unmistakable under the moonlight. It was Burt, Nancy and Radical!

"That's blown it," I muttered, "Burt's organised a search party - someone must have grassed on us."

"Don't be silly," whispered Abbey, "he's always spying everywhere."

Maddy motioned for us to gather close and pulling us into a tight huddle whispered, "If we move now Burt will catch us. But if we sit it out we may have a chance".

She was right. Shivering and squashed up against the giant trunk, I imagined Burt hauling us into Mr Deluca's office like criminals. My thoughts were interrupted by a loud rustling noise which got louder and closer until I could feel my stomach clenching. Then a figure emerged from behind a tree and we gasped in astonishment.

Radical! He was grinning from ear to ear. He put a finger to his lips and his other hand motioned us to stay low. He then strode forwards boldly and out into the clearing and, taking us all by surprise, started running like a mad man in the opposite direction, away from our hiding place, waving his torch beam and yelling at the top of his voice,

"There they go. Burt, over there - follow me - they're getting away."

It was plenty to divert Burt's attention. As we peered from our hideout we could just make out the distant figures of Radical, Burt and Nancy moving swiftly away from the unfolding drama by the moonlit lake. They were quickly swallowed up into the darkness.

"Let's get out of here while we've got a chance" said Abbey and we bolted, running all the way back to hide behind tuck house. Looking round at the others I noticed how filthy we were and, glancing at my watch, realised it was getting near to lights out. Moments later, with the coast clear outside the dorm block, we sneaked indoors to wash and clean up, and guess who was hiding in the bathroom? Esme! She took one look at our filthy uniforms, scowled and demanded to know where we'd been. With very little choice in the matter we made her swear to secrecy, which she did under protest, though I suspect it was more because of what Abbey said she would do to her if she didn't! She promised faithfully she wouldn't blow our cover and then added - in true Oracle style - a condition to her promise, which was only if she could join our BLAP team. So BLAP was now a group of five (six including Kerri).

Before lights out Esme played her new 'Crazy Horses' album. I hate to admit this in writing, but it was much better than the usual Osmond's stuff. The whole dorm joined in the chorus, singing along with the guitar screeching 'waaaaa-waaaaaa' bit. AGHHH! It must have echoed right around the school and finally, at her wits end after the fourth rewind, Nanny barged in with her hands over her ears, yelling to get herself heard.

"Lights out, girls, and quieten down or you'll awaken the dead."

If only she knew what we'd been up to…

CHAPTER TWENTY-SEVEN

FRIDAY 19TH JANUARY

Burt was a picture of discontent at breakfast. He scowled whilst slopping milk over my Shredded Wheat. I smiled sweetly back and his top lip curled back like a dog snitching. He must hate us. I glanced at Radical, who completely ignored me and was aiming the tin teapot at the steaming water spluttering from the geyser. Thank goodness - an ally in the enemy camp.

SATURDAY 20TH JANUARY

Tonight I finally achieved a flat turn out when practising a Frog, even though Mika had to stand on my knees. I was now pretty good at Flippers and Short Foot. My front splits were better, but my side splits were stubbornly slow in making progress. Patience is supposed to be a virtue, but I'll need the patience of a saint at this rate.

   After walking to the shop with Oracle bending my ear, I decided to write an overdue letter to Joseph in Auckland. I felt guilty I hadn't sent him a Christmas card because I had been preoccupied with Marie-Helene.

Dear Joseph

I'm now back at school and I think it's going to be really busy. Sorry I didn't write over Christmas but we had a French student staying with our family. It was good fun until she went missing on New Year's Eve. My Dad went crazy and decided she needed round the clock supervision to keep her safe. Mum and Dad became city tour guides and so the whole family had to join in. I now know London better than I know my home town. I've even considered a second career as a London Tour Guide should my dancing career not work out!

Already, in one week an awful lot has happened. The students are busy rehearsing the choreographic competition which I hope to enter next year. It's held in the theatre close to the school.

We haven't tracked down the resident school ghost yet BUT, our toilets are definitely haunted! It all started when one of the girls held a secret séance. They claim they never saw a ghost and didn't even hear anything. Unfortunately I was downstairs in the loos when they were messing around with the Ouija board, and I heard spine-chilling noises, alerting me to an unnatural presence in the cubicle next-door to the one I was in. It was horrible! I would like to tell you I wasn't scared but if I am truthful it slightly unnerved me. By the way, do you believe in ESP?

My closest friends and I went on a moonlit hunt round the lake two days ago. It was a full moon and a perfect opportunity to see the ghost of the Blue Lady of the Lake (which is where she is said to have killed herself). During this moonlit adventure we almost got caught by the ancient cook-cum-spy who, when not trying to poison us with his inedible food, stalks us whenever we step outside the school grounds. In fact, I think the lake is in school grounds. It was a good job he didn't catch us, because we would have been gated - or worse!

All the girls in my dorm like different music and I've been forced to listen to bands I normally hate, like the Osmonds! I recently heard their latest album 'Crazy Horses' and - I can't believe I'm saying this - it's really cool! Have you heard it? Some of the older girls are choreographing a dance to Pink Floyd music - it is really way out and has some amazing guitar music.

What sort of heavy metal music are you in to? I wondered if you are still practicing guitar with your sister's boyfriend. My resolution to regularly practise piano hasn't progressed far, but I still want to learn.

What is the weather like in Auckland? It's freezing here! Can you still go sailing at this time of year?

I read that the North Island is tropical. I can't imagine it being tropical and hot in January.

How is your dog, Napoleon? I am waiting for some recent photos to come back from the developer to send over to you. If you have any more photos of your family, or your boat, or even some of you and your friends I would love to see them.

Looking forward to hearing all your news

Love from

Lara

Just as I wrote this Esme came over to my bunk and I caught her peering down at my letter. She said that ending a letter in 'love' or 'lots of love' meant that you loved them! She also said that a boy might get the wrong idea. I told her Joseph had sisters and wouldn't think anything of it. She talked such rubbish.

At tea Burt dished up something he called 'chargrilled burgers'. I made a big mistake when I saw them.

"Just baked beans please."

Burt took offence.

"And what's wrong with my beef burgers?"

I then made my next mistake.

"They look burnt, Burt".

Burt brought his head up sharply making a snorting sound, his glasses dropped to the end of his nose and plunged straight into the vat of steaming baked beans. He swore so loudly that Nancy dropped the cup she was holding. Burt plunged his hand into the steaming bean pot, groped around until a surge of beans spilled over the side of the vat like lava, then triumphantly pulled out his glasses, wiped them with a dishcloth and stuck them back on his nose. The glasses were all smeary and we tried not to snigger as several crushed beans - stuck on the glasses frames - threatened to drop down onto the plate he was dishing up. He then slopped such a ginormous pile of beans onto my plate, that when I lifted my tray they spilled over the edge of my plate until my tray was awash with beans. Abbey was laughing helplessly until Burt glared at her and threatened to report us for being cheeky. We shunted to the end of the serving canteen. Radical, who had witnessed the whole scene, handed me a slice of bread and butter on a saucer, perhaps to stop the bread drowning in the beans. It was a pointless act of kindness, because when we reached the end of the canteen, Nancy got her own back by filling my mug so full of tea, by the time I'd carried the overflowing tray into the dining hall it was swimming in tea-bean soup. YUK. To cap it all my wretched pinny was filthy. Abbey said it looked like baby vomit. Now Nanny would remind us why we needed bibs!

After tea I sought refuge in the cosy corner of the dorm on my bottom bunk. Cuddled up under my travel blanket with March Hare I started to read the book Esme had given me, *Gone with the Wind*. It was described as an 'epic'. It was certainly a large volume. Dad would have called this book a 'tome'. The woman pictured on the front cover was very striking and beside her was a handsome man who was dark and mysterious looking. Esme told me it was a romantic story. It was also an extremely heavy book to hold upright, so I eventually used March Hare to prop it up when I lay down reading.

SUNDAY 21ST JANUARY

After church I discovered one of Nanny's slave duty rotas stuck on the dorm door. Last term I was lucky to be allotted my favourite task - shoe cleaning. I anxiously scanned down the long list of duties. 'Dog walking' was taken. So was 'sock folding' and 'mirror cleaning'. I found my name second from the bottom and, to my disgust, I had been assigned the shared/alternate Sundays duty of BATH CLEANING. This, very unfortunately, meant more possible encounters with the spirit of the loos. I begged and pleaded with Nanny and even stooped to bribery, offering to do practically any other duty twice but, incredibly, she wouldn't alter the rota. All she kept saying was "Someone's got to do it." How stubborn was that? Mika and I agreed to share rather than alternate - after all there was safety in numbers - and we made a pact to stand guard and watch each other's backs. Part of our BLAP motto is 'Stay Alert'.

Ghosts are mean - but BLAP is keen
Spirits are invisible - BLAP is invincible!

This evening Mika and I trundled downstairs for our slave duty. Mika said she'd keep watch for the loo spirit while I got busy with Glitto on the stained old bath tubs. Then a *really* weird thing happened. Mika came into the bathroom saying she could hear a rustling noise. We hid behind the bathroom door, leaving it slightly ajar. Everything went dead quiet. Then there was a gust of air. It went freezing cold and the end loo door banged shut. We clutched each other and then heard a hollow scraping noise. Mika dug her nails into my arm so hard I nearly screamed. Another sudden gust of icy air made the hairs on the back of my neck stand on end. Then, deadly silence. Mika spoke first.

"Oh blimey, let's get out of here!"

We fled out of the bathroom and charged up the stairs like we'd actually seen the ghost and went crashing headlong into Nanny who, having heard us thumping up the stairs had just appeared in the doorway to find out what all the commotion was about. She nearly toppled over and had to steady herself against the door as she drew a breath.

"You two girls, how many times have I told you not to run and to LOOK?" Before we had time to react she took us by surprise, pulled up our arms by our dressing gown sleeves and muttered angrily, "Your dressing gowns are soaked".

"Please Nanny," I whimpered, "Please can we swap our duties?"

"Why" she demanded.

"Be-because the loos are..." I wasn't sure I wanted to say it but then it just came out of my mouth "haunted!" I blurted out.

"What nonsense," Nanny replied, her eyes now boggling out of their sockets in disbelief. Grabbing us each by the hand she dragged us - protesting - back down the stairs to stand outside the offending toilet cubicles.

"Exactly where is this ghost?"

She prodded my shoulder.

"Tell me now, before I lose my patience."

She glared at me accusingly.

Fear made me reckless and I stupidly blurted out, "You can't *see* ghosts, Nanny."

I shrunk two inches as I was met by her furious scowl.

"Don't be impertinent, Miss. This is clearly a matter of gross exaggeration, caused by some extremely over imaginative tittle-tattle and it will stop right now. Do you hear me?" We nodded but she hadn't finished.

"I will not tolerate one iota more of this trussed-up, mumbo-jumbo paranormal talk."

Unfortunately for us, Hamish decided to make an appearance. He was sneaking into the end cubicle, snuffling and whining. Whilst I was cringing behind Nanny, I wondered if dogs could sense spirits. After all, there could be a whole new world out there just waiting for the right person to discover it. Maybe if we just went with it, who knows what might happen. And what if I discovered something I didn't want to know?

I was brought back to earth by Hamish, who was scrabbling behind the toilet pan, his tail wagging furiously.

"What are you doing in there, you silly dog?"

Nanny forced her way through the toilet door, completely blocking our view. All we could hear was mumbling and Nanny's heavy breathing. Moments later she emerged from the cubicle clutching a small pack of Golden Virginia tobacco and a red packet with the word 'Rizla' on it. Grunting and with a self-satisfied smirk on her face she muttered, "Your ghost theory has just gone up in smoke, girls. Your haunting seems to be nothing more than the illicit activities of someone rolling their own cigarettes."

She sniffed and without further talk hustled us back up to the dorm where she promptly turned the lights out before we created more mischief.

CHAPTER TWENTY-EIGHT

FRIDAY 26TH JANUARY

During double geography I asked Mr Mainwaring about Aunty Phyllis's Dead Sea mud. He raised his chin from his desk to look up at me.

"Dead in name only, my dear, because it's really one of the most fascinating geographical areas…" and he was off! An hour later not only had we learned about the therapeutic qualities of the high mineral salts in the sea, but how it was so dense it enabled people to float with ease and read a book at the same time. The mud was used to help cure skin and rheumatic ailments and apparently Cleopatra used the mud for its youthful qualities. No wonder Aunty Phyllis had so much energy. I will add the Dead Sea to my growing list of places to visit.

SATURDAY 27TH JANUARY

Our walk to the shop was cancelled today because no one was free to walk the juniors - what a pity - so I spent the rest of the day snuggled under my rug reading *Gone with the Wind*. Rhett Butler sounded very dashing! If I ever married, it would be to a man who was tall, dark and mysterious. Rhett was a loveable rogue. Esme said that Ashley Wilkes was the better character but to me he seemed wishy-washy.

SUNDAY 28TH JANUARY

The student called Mercedes walked us to church today, immediately after breakfast. I could hear her talking and tried, without luck, to understand her accent. I didn't know so many different accents existed in England. I'd never travelled further north than Finchley where our cousins owned a sweet shop. I was glad to get to church today because it was absolutely freezing, and even wearing my blazer under my raincoat wasn't enough to help me stay warm.

Church was uneventful until the end of the service. Just after 'The Creed' and following 'The Prayers of the People', the congregation got up off their knees, stood up and started to shake hands, then hugged the people standing either side of them. None of us knew what to do. Mercedes came up to our aisle and muttered something which none of us could understand and then got snarky. She repeated herself twice and, because we couldn't understand her, she raised her voice louder than she should have done and bellowed, "Just hug each other, you muppets!"

Unfortunately the whole church heard. It was horrible. Cringing with embarrassment we awkwardly hugged whoever happened to be standing beside us. Poor Gabby got bear-hugged by a fat, sweaty man who'd squashed into the end of our pew. Eurgh!

After the service Mercedes made us apologise to Father Benedict and all the choirboys heard. It was sooo embarrassing. Mercedes would probably become a prefect soon. Today she showed her true colours. Resembling Cimmie, I nicknamed her

'Motor Mouth' because she was named after a car and had a mouth like a motor!

THURSDAY 1ST FEBRUARY

Kerri and I practised our modern routines today in the day girls' cloakroom. During our practice, two other day girls came in and sat down on the benches. One girl had hair longer than mine that she wore in a single thick plait. I'd seen her in Form One and in a couple of ballet classes. She was smiling at us as she watched us practise, then she turned to the girl she came in with and they started talking in a foreign language! It wasn't English or French and they spoke really fast. Kerri asked what language they were speaking.

"It's not a proper language" said the girl with the plait.

"Then what is it?"

"It's Egg language!" said the girl with the plait.

"Oh, come on, Naomie," Kerri pleaded, "don't tease - tell us what language you're talking in."

Naomie burst out laughing "It's Egg language. That's what it's called!"

Kerri and I giggled as once again they started yakkering away, only this time super-fast. It sounded bonkers.

Then Naomie turned towards Kerri and said, "Listen, Kerri, let's do a deal. I'll teach you how to talk Egg if you bring us some of your Mum's homemade flapjacks tomorrow."

Kerri and I looked at each other, and Kerri opened her hands out towards the two girls and asked, "How about two Mars bars and a Flake? Mum's working overtime this week and won't have time to bake."

Naomie spoke first "Deal."

She jumped up and they shook hands! We spent the remaining lunch hour learning the basic skills of a unique language called 'Egg'. Utter madness. I couldn't wait to talk Egg to my brothers, they would be completely fooled!

So that I didn't forget it, I scribbled an aide-memoire: *Take a word like ballet. Every time there's a vowel, place the word 'EGG' in front of each vowel in that word. The word ballet becomes 'beggallegget'. My name, Lara, becomes 'Leggaregga'.*

It seemed easy until you tried to speak it fast.

What an outrageously cool language. I loved the idea of a secret language which sounded realistic. I was surprised they hadn't used it in the war. All that Egging would have been a great disguise. Naomie said it was a day-girl invention, so I was to keep it under my hat. It made me feel empowered. Just think of it, a secret language that swiftly translated from your own language with minimum effort and no boring double French lessons. Genius!

Before I came here eggs were simply eggs. Now I had not only embarked on my first shaky steps in Egg language, but I was constantly Eggoing school food. No-one at home would believe this - there were just too many eggs!

I spent most of afternoon school silently practising Egg words in my head. In history I nearly had a fit of giggles while thinking about my family's names in Egg language: Meggummy! Deggaddy! Beggenjeggameggin!

I got no further because Miss Knox had spotted me smirking and asked me if I'd like to share my private joke with the class. Uh-oh! Terrified of retribution, I mumbled the first thoughts that came into my head, based on today's topic about 'Roman Achievements' and blurted out "I was thinking about something my Mum said about Rome not being built in a day."

Miss Knox's face froze and the class froze with her. No-one knew at that moment which way this would go.

"Has this got any bearing on our lesson?" she said, scowling, and twizzling her hair into the familiar devil's horn shape. Feeling flustered, I went into survival mode.

"Well," I stuttered, "only that I thought about the funny side of it. If it wasn't built in a day, it must have been built at night."

I swallowed hard and waited. Seconds, then minutes, until the silence was finally shattered by Miss Knox laughing.

It was a deafening laugh but we all joined in with hysterical cackles, slapping our hands on our desks like it was the funniest thing we'd ever heard. It was the laugh of the scared! Fortunately, the ice was well and truly broken by the end-of-school bell ringing out. We rose as one, like a tidal wave surging towards a beach, and flooded out of the classroom door en-masse.

Back in the dorm, whilst we struggled to squeeze into the incredibly shrinking laggy briefs (Nanny must have put them through the mangle or something), Abbey and I discussed Miss Knox and her erratic moods. Abbey reckoned Knox needed a man in her life. Hannah was also struggling with her laggy briefs and asked Abbey and me to help her stretch the waistline. As we held on to either side and tugged, Hannah demanded to know how I'd thought so quickly on my feet. I said 'fear makes you think fast!' She slapped me hard on the back and said, "Cool, Daddy-O!"

I was secretly chuffed at Hannah's approval. I thought she was very smart and sassy. I was definitely not the shy, weedy girl who started here last September. I must have got carried away on Hannah's praise because we pulled so hard on her laggy briefs that the elastic in one leg snapped. Hannah went off all huffy, with one cheek of her bottom hanging down lower than the other!

In ballet Hannah got told off because her knickers were hanging down below her leotard. She glared pointedly at Abbey and me. Miss Wanda said that she hoped by next year the wearing of R.A.D frills would become compulsory, as bum cheeks hanging out of leotards were deeply unflattering.

FRIDAY 2ND FEBRUARY

With the whole school immersed in the choreographic competition heats, I'd almost forgotten it was Vis Day this Sunday. Esme lost no time reminding me that she was going to be left at school. All alone. It was a big fat hint, but I didn't blame her.

Whilst treating my skinned toe with surgical spirit after today's pointe work, the broken skin was so raw that I nearly hit the roof with the stinging and knocked the bottle over, sending the foul smelling surgical spirits all over the end of my bedclothes and floorboards. Our corner smelled like a hospital. Abbey opened the window so wide the curtains blew horizontal and the icy draught made everyone whinge. Millie protested and closed the window, saying that she would rather die in her sleep from deadly fumes than freeze. What a drama queen.

SATURDAY 3RD FEBRUARY

I survived the night but had strange dreams. They involved running for my life along narrow corridors, which had loads of small doors leading to more narrow corridors. As fast as I ran I didn't get anywhere. Weird.

After ballet I phoned home and asked Mum about Esme coming home for Vis Day. She said they'd love her to come, but to make sure that Esme brought some walking shoes. I hoped she liked walking because Dad was well known for his long treks. Esme was excited when I told her!

CHAPTER TWENTY-NINE

MONDAY 5TH FEBRUARY

As usual our day at home flew by. When Esme and I said goodbye to Dad yesterday evening, she told Dad my family were just like hers, but more fun. Success!

In form period this morning, Kerri and I overheard the twins talking about how they had spent Visiting Day with their boyfriends. They told Tiffany the boys were seventeen. Kerri and I discussed this and decided they were telling porkies. Shirley had a red mark on her neck which looked sore and I wondered if she'd burned her neck with curling tongs.

When Sydney saw it she said, "What's the cat been up to?"

Shirley sniggered and looked very proud as she told Sydney it was a 'love bite'. How gross. Kerri whispered that her next door neighbour had one on his neck and when she asked what it was, he said his girlfriend had bitten him! Kerri said he even demonstrated how to make a love bite on his own his arm and it left a bright red mark. We came to the conclusion that Shirley's love bite was created by her twin to trick us. What did a mark on your neck have to do with anything anyway? I mean, who would want to look like they had been attacked by Dracula?

TUESDAY 6TH FEBRUARY

Mrs Balmaine taught us some new tap for our Herman's Hermits routine. We practised our routines in twos today. She said Kerri and I had excellent clear beats and would be ready for our exam in the autumn. We must be improving.

When Abbey and I walked under the covered way tonight, Abbey laughed when she heard my Blakey's clicking as I walked. Dad had put them on my school shoe heels and soles to make them last longer. Abbey said they sounded just like taps, so I started mucking around, jumping into the air and clicking my heels together like Gene Kelly. Abbey clapped and laughed. Suddenly, Mr Deluca appeared around the corner and stared at us. He must have seen me horsing around and looking directly at me demanded, "Who was making all that noise?"

I surrendered.

"Me." He frowned, so I babbled on "I mean it was me practising tap, Mr Deluca."

"Then how did you make all that noise with *those shoes?*" he said, pointing at my chunky school lace-ups.

"It's my Blakey's, Mr Deluca, which make a sound like taps."

"Show me."

He smiled and, as he exhaled, a cloud of cigarette smoke poured out of his nose. Feeling anxious, I raised my leg so that he could see the bottom of my shoe. The small, crescent shaped metal studs dotted across the heels and soles of my shoes shone in the dusk like small stars sprinkled on my feet. Mr Deluca looked fascinated as he inspected my shoe sole.

"What a brilliant idea - I do wish I'd thought of that. Jolly good thinking. What's your name?"

"Lara, Mr Deluca."

"Well done, Lara. Great fun. I wouldn't mind some of those myself. Good night girls." Without another word he sauntered off puffing away on his cigarette, leaving a trail of little red sparks drifting behind him in the night air.

Once he was out of earshot we exploded with laughter. Back in the dorm Abbey told the other girls what had happened and now everyone wanted Blakey's on their shoes.

FRIDAY 9TH FEBRUARY

I got a letter from Aunty Ellen today, enclosing a newspaper cutting. She said I might be interested in reading the reviews about up-and-coming contemporary dance companies. The cutting showed a photo of one female and two male dancers, all coiled up around each other in what looked like cling film! Their faces were covered with masks and it looked surreal. Aunty knew exactly who-was-who in the arts world. She also knew which dance companies had the best backing. She said I should keep an open mind with my dance career because contemporary dance had a big future.

I had watched contemporary classes from outside dance studio's windows. They looked athletic and the teacher continuously yelled 'contract' or 'release'. My problem was we didn't start contemporary classes until the Fourth Year. That was a long wait.

SATURDAY 10TH FEBRUARY

I escaped the shop walk today by sheer luck. Sydney had several gross verrucas and Nanny was supposed to accompany her to the hospital to get them removed. However, after ballet, Nanny came into the dorm and said she had to look after someone in sickbay and asked for a volunteer to accompany Sydney. As the only volunteer I got the job.

Nanny gave us a set of strict instructions. A school hospital visit note, which had to be signed by the car hire driver, a card with several phone numbers to ring and a handful of 10p and 2p coins for phoning the car hire company to transport us back to school. Sydney seemed pleased I was accompanying her, although she couldn't understand why Nanny hadn't allowed Tiffany to go with her. Duh!

It was good fun travelling by taxi to the local town, which I had never visited. Sydney, when separated from her partners in crime, was really fun. Stuck in Saturday traffic we talked for ages. She told me all about her family in America. Her parents were both actors. She said they were never home so she and her brother had both been sent to boarding schools in the UK. She said ballet school was her Mum's idea because she wanted Sydney to star in musicals. Sydney said she'd inherited her Mum's acting skills, but if she was honest she couldn't stand any kind of dancing. I could hardly believe it and asked her what she wanted to do after she'd finished ballet school. She replied without a moment's hesitation.

"Marry Clark Gable and have his babies."

Fortunately I knew the actor Clark Gable played Rhett Butler in the film version of *Gone with the Wind*, because there was a picture of him and Vivien Leigh on the front of my book.

"I know Clark Gable is good looking and charming, but that's only because he's playing the dark, dashing hero and he's far too old for you."

Sydney pursed her lips and tossed her lustrous hair over her shoulder.

"I don't care," she sighed, "besides, we are perfectly matched, so he would just have to tame the beast in me!"

We arrived at the hospital and the driver escorted us into the outpatients department, checking we signed in at reception before he left. During a long wait, several young men in biker jackets came into the waiting room. The one with his arm in a sling came and sat on the bench right next to Sydney and tried to chat her up. I couldn't believe it because we were in school uniform, although Sydney had her skirt hitched up. Sling man spoke first.

"Hi, girls, I'm Dino. I'd recognise that uniform anywhere - stands out like a sore thumb with them funny hats - you're from that posh ballet school near the theatre?"

"Maybe," Sydney answered in her silky American drawl and then stared right at him accusingly. "We don't wear this uniform for fun."

"Hahaha."

Sling man Dino got into his stride. Staring at Sydney's legs he gave her a slimy, lop-sided smile.

"So, babes, fancy coming to the Wimpy for coffee and stuff?"

I was wondering what kind of stuff anyone would want to do with someone like Dino when Sydney replied.

"We've got better things to do with our time," she said, nudging me for approval. I nodded vigorously to defend Sydney but felt frozen with awkwardness and prayed that Dino would just go away.

Unlucky for us, he didn't.

"So we've got some stuck up little ballet school girlies, putting on fake American accents," he mocked, lifting his feet off the floor in front of him and criss-crossing his ankles. Mimicking

247

Sydney in an American accent, he said, "better things to do with our time."

Super creepsville! Sydney's back straightened and she leaned towards his face until she was practically nose-to-nose with him.

"Don't be such a philistine!" she snapped, raising her voice an octave.

"I'm American, and for your information that means from the UNITED STATES OF AMERICA, and why would we want to be seen in a Wimpy bar with a moron like you?"

Dino glowered at Sydney and she stared back at him. Thankfully we were saved by a nurse coming towards us calling out Sydney's surname. Sydney leapt up to follow the nurse, grabbed me by my sleeve and pulled me along with her.

As we followed the nurse to a private room at the far end of the corridor, Sydney pulled me close and giggled, whispering under her breath "Moron!"

"A total blockhead!" I agreed, feeling braver now there was a corridor's distance between us and the bikers.

If I'd thought the biker boys were scary, we had a surprise in store. The hospital room had a name plate across the door which read, 'Doctor Feer'. I didn't have time to wonder what Doctor Feer was like, because the door was flung open by the nurse and there he was, sat behind his desk dressed in a white surgical coat. His hands were folded one across the other on the desk in front of him and he was wearing creepy surgical gloves. He had the most enormous black eyebrows I had ever seen. We hovered nervously at the door until the nurse lost patience and pushed us inside. She vanished, slamming the door behind her. Doctor Feer asked which one of us was Sydney and told her to

"Sit", jabbing his finger at the chair. He stared at her for ages before standing up and clearing his throat.

"Well, Miss Sydney, your verrucas need to be taken out, yes?"

I recoiled and made a brief attempt to escape by edging towards the door, asking Sydney if she really needed me to stay. Sydney grabbed my hand and looked panic stricken, saying she might faint if she didn't have some moral support. At this point a different nurse came into the room, and Doctor Feer smiled at her as she walked over to a trolley and started busying herself with surgical weapons. He had the smile of someone who knew something you didn't, and when he opened his mouth he revealed a row of gold front teeth! With gold tombstones he looked even scarier. An antiseptic smell filled the room and I felt all hot and clammy as I realised there wasn't any escape. I noticed Doctor Feer glancing towards a steel tray full of gory looking instruments, and assumed he was about to perform his verruca-mining operation.

Sidney asked to hold my hand and I stood beside her but had to close my eyes so I didn't throw up. Every few seconds I could hear the sound of Sydney sucking her breath in and was sure that the sickly smell was blood. When Doctor Feer had finished he pronounced the words I'd been waiting for.

"All done!"

Sydney looked grey, poor thing. Her foot bled and I was glad when the nurse returned to put on dressings. She then took us to another area, pulled some curtains around us and brought us a cup of tea. I didn't know who needed the tea more, but it was hot and sweet. She gave Sydney a note and told her to give it to the school nurse, and asked us for the taxi phone number so she could arrange our transport back to school. Fortunately there was no sign of Dino and his beastly biker gang when we left.

During the drive back, Sydney dug into her purse and pulled out some photos of her Mum and Dad. They looked very young and glamorous. "You can come and stay with me in the holidays if you've got nothing better to do," she blurted out.

I was taken aback and thrilled at the same time. Me! Visiting America! Staying with Sydney - oh my goodness!

"Thanks Sydney, that sounds great."

I tried to sound cool, as if I did this sort of thing every day. I had now gone from never having travelled further than Devon to being invited to stay in Africa *and* America! If Joseph invited me to New Zealand, I would have been invited to travel all round the world.

Back at school I spent the rest of the day catching up on homework. I swotted up on Romans but struggled with maths homework, which was beyond difficult.

I noticed Millie putting a ring around next Saturday on our calendar. I frowned.

"It's the full moon Lara, remember?"

I'd completely forgotten and made a mental note to alert team BLAP that next Saturday, with most girls rehearsing in the theatre, would be the perfect time for a bit of ghost-spotting, particularly with the lake en-route to the theatre.

Tonight I doused my feet in surgical spirits, hoping not only to prevent skinned toes but discourage verrucas. Let's face it, we all used the same baths and Doctor Feer said verrucas were highly contagious. Eugh. I'd rather hold a hairy spider than have Doctor Feer bore holes in my feet.

Okay, maybe not actually 'hold' a spider.

Last night I was kept awake by the constant squawking of Miss Brookes's parrot. Something must have disturbed the stupid bird for it to squawk through the night.

At breakfast rumours were rife that prowlers had been seen lurking about the school grounds. Hannah told us she'd heard that a student called Fatima Pava had caused uproar. She was seen chasing the unsuspecting prowlers across the front lawn in her baby-doll pyjamas. With her hair wound-up in spongy rollers and screaming at them in a foreign language, she'd aimed a fire extinguisher at them and drowned them in fire-foam as they retreated into the woods. We giggled at the thought.

As our perfectly formed junior crocodile marched past the main house and front lawns en-route to church, I was mesmerised by the trail of dried foam zigzagging across the rose bushes and lawn. What a hoot!

Sunday lunch was inedible. Even pudding was foul - nothing to Quiz or Eggo. Fortunately, our helpless plight was short lived. As we laid on our beds whinging about our rumbling bellies, some 5th year girls came to our rescue with illegal tuck. Huge sacks of it. Nanny was nowhere to be seen and they sold masses. One of the treats on sale was a cream egg nicknamed a 'Googly Egg'. I had no idea what the 'googly' stood for. Fortunately, and only because I didn't visit the shop yesterday, I had enough money to buy three of these treats. It was like a food fest. Juniors swarmed like gannets on the tuck sellers. Suddenly, amidst all the frenzied snatching, grabbing and chocolate trading a cry of alarm rang out as Hannah burst through the dorm doors. She screeched the dreaded words "Prefects are coming!" to make herself heard above the din, followed by a gabbled, "Krause is on her way. Hurry! Everyone scarper - she's been on a dorm raid in the main house and is heading here - RIGHT NOW!"

Everyone moved like lightning. Millie grabbed her teddy-cum-night-dress-holder. Teddy had a large, concealed zip panel running all the way down his back. Millie unzipped him, threw out her nighty and whispered, "Look. Let's stuff masses of googly-eggs inside its hidden tummy," and deftly scooping up a pile of eggs and other tuck in her arms, loaded Teddy's belly with chocolate contraband. She expertly arranged her flannel nighty around the goodies, zipped up the now bulging Teddy and turned him face up.

Teddy was the perfect hiding place, although his eyes did look a bit bulgy. While this skulduggery was taking place the tuck sellers had miraculously evaporated into thin air, leaving us juniors to face the music alone. The thunderous echoing sounds on the dorm stairs indicated the ominous arrival of Warrior Troll Midget with her equally brutal back-up support, Sergeant Warlock. They stormed the dorm like an invading army of Daleks. Hands on hips and legs astride, Warrior Troll narrowed her eyes and surveyed the terrified masses as we sat cringing on our beds. Taking one side of the dorm each they rummaged through bed lockers, shaking pillows, pulling back blankets, turning ballet-shoe bags upside down and spilling their contents across the floor. They were an unstoppable force.

Eventually, realising their search had been in vain, they lurched towards the dorm door and then swung round with a sinister parting shot.

"Did you know," Warrior Troll snarled, curling her top lip, "that buying tuck is not only prohibited to snivelling cockroaches like you, but selling tuck is also STRICTLY

ILLEGAL?" She snorted in frustration. "You've been warned, you whinging little maggots!" She then turned on her heel and marched down the stairs, closely followed by Sergeant Warlock, who released several alien grunts and waved her fist at us in a defiant gesture. We waited until the door finally banged shut and then rushed to watch them from the safety of the dorm windows, wondering who their next unfortunate victims would be. Hannah broke the tension by jumping onto her bed and clearing her throat.

"Know thine enemy," she shouted in a commanding voice. Then she slumped down onto her bed reading a magazine as though she'd never spoken. Hannah was extremely complicated.

CHAPTER THIRTY

I received a lovely letter from Mum and Dad today. Mum had started up a community magazine and was the Editor. I didn't know how she found the time to do so much. She said they missed me and Patch was lost without my lap to curl-up on in the evenings. Dad had been offered the opportunity to transfer his job to the Channel Islands. Mum said they were thinking about it. Mrs Furst had knitted me more legwarmers, this time a purple pair with lilac stripes and an orange pair with sparkly wool. Whilst reading I had an idea - maybe I could sell the legwarmers and make a profit - the proceeds could go towards my future travels.

I was deep in thought about a possible move abroad, when I looked up and saw Esme staring at my letter. I asked what was wrong and she complained bitterly she never received post. I tried to reassure her, saying her letters from home took longer to get to England, but she still pouted and parked her bottom right on the end of my bed making no attempt to move. Eventually I shared my letter with her and she said I was a true-true friend. I didn't want this to become a habit and I thought letters should be private, but Esme had this uncanny way of making me feel guilty.

Later I noticed that Millie had added hearts to our calendar. It was Valentine's Day tomorrow.

None of us had boyfriends so it would be just another day.

THURSDAY 15TH FEBRUARY

Spent much of today trying to catch up on homework - it was so easy to fall behind with all the dancing after school and no parents reminding you. Now it was all down to me. During our modern coaching tonight Miss Wanda must have been in a good mood (maybe she received a Valentine's card), because after we had danced both the lyrical and jazz routines one by one, she said we had not only improved, but if we kept up this standard we should pass with good grades.

Top marks were Honours, then Highly Commended, Commended, Pass Plus, then Pass. With all those grades, you'd have to be pretty dire to fail. During the exam we would be allowed to take off our black leather ballet shoes to dance our routines barefoot. When I saw myself in the mirror wearing black ballet shoes, black footless tights and long sleeved leotard I looked like a bad imitation of catwoman.

SATURDAY 17TH FEBRUARY

This afternoon Nanny let us off the shop walk so we could watch choreographic rehearsals. It was one of the very few chances we'd get, as the actual competition tickets were for parents only. Janice took us round the back entrance of the theatre and showed us the stage doors, which we'd use to get in and out when we performed the summer show. I felt goose bumps on my arms as we slid out from behind the exit curtains on either side of the stage. We easily found some stall seats at the front of the stage and the rest of the seats soon filled up with girls. Saphi came on stage, clapped her hands and called for quiet. We sat as quiet as mice in case she changed her mind.

The first dance we watched was a student dancing a solo to haunting jazz music. It was called 'Summertime'. The student danced barefoot, moving like liquid, and everyone clapped and cheered when she finished. Then a couple of groups came on. Problems with the sound meant the last group had to re-start five times. Then three girls I immediately recognised came on stage. They were the girls Abbey and I had watched practising in the studio last term, Tassia, Sophie and Sian. Tassia's red hair looked wilder than usual. Sophie was wearing luminous lime, thigh-high legwarmers and Sian had a gold shirt knotted at the waist and purple lurex jazz pants. I loved their crazy style. They stood on stage in a tight huddle as Tassia shouted for someone to turn the music on.

The theatre shook as the sound of distorted guitar filled the auditorium. The lights swirled and twisted around the dancers as they writhed and contorted their bodies into strange positions, leaping and somersaulting, with hair flying in a breeze coming from somewhere offstage. Even though we'd seen the end before, it looked amazing on stage. On the final wail of guitar music the audience exploded with applause and Sydney said, "Those guys rock!"

We watched at least eight more dances. One large group did a tap number wearing bows on their shoes and mimed to the song 'In the Mood'. Suddenly my eyes locked on a red-head and I realised that it was Patsy. She looked stunning. They did masses of fantastically fast foot work and I was dumbfounded at the speed they tapped.

After this Saphi appeared, clapped her hands and I was brought back to earth with a bump.

"Time out girls. Sadly, that's all we've got time for. Please return to main house for tea, taking all your belongings with you."

We raced backstage again and I paused, taking in the atmosphere and gazing at the massive wings on either side of the stage.

"People have to operate those lights standing up there. Imagine if you were afraid of heights," Abbey said, pointing upwards.

"Actually they're called 'flies'," Esme butted in. "It's the area above the stage where scenery and lighting and other pieces of equipment are kept".

"I thought that was called the gods," Mika chimed in.

"That's the highest area of seats you can get in a theatre auditorium," Esme retorted, "so when you're on stage, if you look up at the gods it's towards the uppermost level of seats."

Then she went off on an Oracle rampage but no one was listening.

Janice sneaked us into a dressing room. It had tall hanging rails down the centre and lots of individual mirrors, each with light bulbs surrounding them. I was fascinated and wanted to stay longer, but Janice said we'd get in trouble if we were caught snooping.

As we left the stage door, the crisp early evening air hit our faces and my cheeks burned. Huddling together to keep warm, we made our way back towards school, chatting excitedly. I cast a glance sideways and noticed the vast, glistening orb illuminating the inky sky.

"It's a full moon," I gasped and pinched Abbey.

Janice heard.

"So what?"

Esme had caught us up and covered for me.

"Jeepers," she exclaimed, looking at her watch, "We're late for tea. Quick, last one back gets spooked by the Blue Lady!"

We all screamed and broke into a manic run. As we dashed past the lake I looked back towards the willow tree and imagined I saw a shadow lurking.

I ran extra fast to avoid being the 'spooked one', wondering to myself if the Blue Lady had been standing there watching us, listening, with a smile on her face…

MONDAY 19TH FEBRUARY

After church yesterday I read more *Gone with the Wind*. Scarlett had a fixation with Ashley Wilkes and was becoming calculating and very unlikeable, marrying Charles just to get her own back on Ashley. I adored Rhett Butler because he was charming, a feminist supporter, and a man who thought women should be encouraged in business. In those times women mostly stayed at home, had children and weren't asked their opinions. Few had careers. It seemed all women did was dress pretty and produce families. Sydney and I would be in competition over Mr Rhett Butler!

When I looked at our calendar this afternoon I realised that half term was at the end of this week. I couldn't wait to see everyone. I phoned home after tea and chatted with Lily because Mum was out with the boys. Being away from home has really made me appreciate my family.

TUESDAY 20TH FEBRUARY

There was a rumour Mercedes was next in line to become a prefect. Patsy told me a prefect from main house had just left and a replacement was needed.

Millie said Mercedes was a cross between Cimmie and Rita and I agreed. Mercedes' demonstration of swift retribution in church had revealed that she spoke with a forked tongue. All I was saying was this: we may soon have a new foe to cross swords with in the enemy camp. My antennae were alert...

THURSDAY 22ND FEBRUARY

Mr Mainwaring took us out to our vegetable plots today. It felt more like Siberia than Sussex. We moaned so much he made us jog on the spot for ten minutes. Fortunately, a vicious hailstorm sent us running back to the classroom and we ended up doing one of his famous quizzes instead.

We still had modern coaching before our parents were allowed to pick us up. All the other girls had escaped after tea. Dad had arranged to pick me up later than normal, and I could see his car through a patch I'd cleared on the steamed-up studio window. Miss Wanda got lairy when she saw Kerri and me looking through the windows and made me wait until last to do my routines, letting the other three go before me. I thought I'd be there until midnight.

When Wanda finally let me go, I raced back to the dorm and found Dad talking to Nanny. Everyone else had gone home! Luckily I'd already packed my weekend bag which Hamish was now using as a dog-bed. Dad gave me a bear hug when I came into the dorm. He joked with Nanny.

"Do these girls let you have any peace?"

Nanny put her hands to her head and laughed.

"They keep me busy alright, but it gives an old lady something to do with herself and keeps me fit."

I'd grown really fond of Nanny - and Hamish. They were like a second family now and I felt sad leaving her. She gave me a hug and said, "Have a nice break, dear". I asked her if she was going away and a smile spread across her face.

"Now who do you think would be keeping all those ghosts away if the dorm was left unoccupied?" she said with a crafty wink.

She definitely knew about BLAP!

On the journey home I was so exhausted from class that I fell asleep. When Dad woke me up it was nearly 10pm and we were back home. The best part was that all my family were waiting up for me in their dressing gowns. Benjamin and Samuel bombarded me with a zillion questions, and Lily proudly showed me the latest single by David Cassidy and the Partridge Family called 'Looking Through the Eyes of Love'. She'd bought me Stevie Wonder's new single 'Superstition', which I couldn't wait to play because I loved his music. When the boys went to bed, Mum and Dad asked me what I wanted to do this weekend.

"Sleep without being woken up by rising bell, eat some proper food, and watch TV."

Dad laughed. "I thought you came home to see us!"

When I was finally tucked up under my eiderdown, my cosy bed had never felt so nice. I snuggled down and felt the warmth of the stone hot water bottle against my feet. Home was sheer luxury. My last thoughts before I fell into a deep sleep were that training to be a dancer was really toughening me up. At long last, the shrinking violet had - almost – disappeared.

CHAPTER THIRTY-ONE

SPRING HALF TERM

FRIDAY 23RD FEBRUARY

Mum woke me with a cup of tea this morning at 10 o'clock. She had to go out and I had the house to myself, so I decided to play my Stevie Wonder single on Dad's new stereo. The funky sounds of guitar and Stevie Wonder ricocheted round the house until the walls shuddered!

I couldn't resist trying my modern dance moves. The radiator made a great ballet barre and with the lounge light on I could see my reflection in the glass doors of the drinks cabinet, perfect for corrections. After limbering up I felt energetic, and by taking a run and leaping into a grande jeté across the room, I could see my airborne reflection flying past. My excitement was heady and short lived though. In my enthusiasm, I leapt in the air, hit the ceiling lampshade and brought it crashing down with me! I landed in a heap with the broken lampshade scattered around me.

I then sweated over what I'd tell my parents. Sifting through Dad's jazz LP's I found some great old skiffle style music, and practised some tap moves that didn't involve catastrophic jumps. Tapping around on the woodblock floor made a great sound with my hard-soled mules. Suddenly I became aware of a shadow against the front window of the sitting room. The face had its nose stuck against the window and had been watching me! I recoiled in horror as I recognised the face belonged to Gilbert Glover, the local hooligan. In a panic I dropped to the floor and hid by the sofa. After what seemed like forever, I raised my head, only to find he was still there, watching. Patches of steam had formed around his mouth and nose, which looked misshapen pressed against the glass. Probably thinking I was dead, he began frantically waving his hands. The thought of Gilbert Glover seeing me dancing was too terrible. I might as well be dead! The idea of him attempting to rescue me was even worse. What if he tried to break a window? I would *literally* die. After breathing deeply to calm myself, I did the only sensible thing I could think of doing when stuck face down on the carpet. With enormous effort to appear as though I wasn't actually moving I pressed my hands hard into the floor, slowly raised my bottom in the air and, feeling a bit like a caterpillar, slunk out of the room on my stomach. I noticed his shadow still lurking around behind the net curtains. How hideously embarrassing. I crept upstairs and ran a hot bath, wishing I'd gone out with Mum - then the lampshade wouldn't be broken and Gilbert would never have seen me practicing.

I had a lot of explaining to do when Mum came home and she suggested I saved jetés for school.

SATURDAY 24TH FEBRUARY

We visited Granny and Grandpa today in London. I wanted Grandpa to tell me about the countries he'd visited during the Great War, but he wouldn't. Later I asked Granny why he wouldn't talk about it and she said, "Because the young men wanted to forget the awful things they'd seen."

Aunty Ellen asked how my dancing was going and I demonstrated some tap springs on the tiled scullery floor. Grandpa walked in and said I sounded like Fred Astaire.

Aunty let me go up to her bedroom after lunch. She always let me try on her jewellery and make-up. With everyone downstairs I made-up my face, puffing powder on my nose, rouge on my lips and wore her gold 'snake' necklace. I looked just like Cleopatra.

I went to the loo and reached up high to pull the long chain handle, but as I released my hand I felt the necklace catch come undone and in a second it had slid from my throat and plunged like a writhing snake into the flushing loo. Panic stricken, I watched the water froth up, with the loo paper and the coil of glistening gold-snake chain spinning in a circle right before my eyes. I stood frozen as the contents were sucked down the pan and vanished. I had to think fast.

Rolling up my sleeves, I plunged my hand into the toilet. After much reaching around the back pipes, twisting my neck and stifling involuntary gags, I found the necklace at the back of the U bend. I locked myself in the bathroom and scrubbed my hands and the snake necklace with Camay soap. Yesterday I broke the lampshade and today nearly lost Aunty's necklace. Something must have jinxed me.

Before we went home, Granny gave me five pounds for holiday money, hugged me and said I looked tired. The stress had obviously aged me and I didn't feel I deserved anything. It would go into my travel fund - that was if I could stay out of trouble long enough to begin travelling.

Mum gave me a tight squeeze when I left today, saying she was glad I was enjoying school and that they were very proud of me.

After dropping off my weekend bag in the dorm, Dad hugged me and wished me luck in my exam. As I watched his car drive off, a hand rested on my shoulder making me jump out of my skin.

"Welcome back, kiddo."

It was Patsy. We sat on my bottom bunk, exchanging half term news. Everyone seemed very happy and relaxed apart from Abbey.

Half term went like this:

Mika: She had no peace at home because the local television station and camera crews were camped at her house, making a nature film about the rare bats living in her loft. She was glad to be back at school for a rest.

Maddy: Spent half term moving her Nan into a new nursing home. Maddy said her Nan was like a child and was banned from the last home because she kept instigating escapes. Her late Grandpa once escaped from a prisoner of war camp and she thought her Nan was reliving his stories.

Millie: Stayed with her London Aunty, who took her on a pottery course and they learned how to 'throw' pots. Millie loved it, saying if she couldn't be a dancer she'd become a potter.

Gabby: Nearly died of boredom and said her mother ate uncontrollably. Gabby had tried to run away but got so hungry she had to return for dinner.

Esme: Stayed with her ghastly Aunt and Uncle from the North. She had no contact with the outside world for three whole days and hadn't talked to anyone under seventy since last Thursday. She said it was like living in a mortuary.

Hannah: Went to a London pub with her sister to see a local band. She got chatted up by a 'hot' musician who was taking her out next visiting Sunday. Nobody believed her.

Me: Told everyone I broke the lampshade practising grand jetés and was spied on by a repulsive local hooligan. Hannah demanded I told the whole story and had fits of hysterics when hearing he had pushed his face against the window and I'd been forced to crawl out of the lounge like a caterpillar.

Abbey: Abbey avoided conversation, complaining of a headache. After lights out I could hear her crying and went straight up to top bunk to cheer her up. She said she'd had the worst half term ever. Her Dad returned home, talked with her Mum and then they argued. I felt horribly sad for Abbey.

CHAPTER THIRTY-TWO

RETURN TO REALITY

MONDAY 26TH FEBRUARY

The dates for our Modern exam had been brought forward to the 12th March.

Miss Wanda finished class early to show us how to wear our hair for the exam, explaining high ponytails were best. She said we must listen carefully to everything the examiner said, because she may only want to see each exercise once. Gabby said, "What happens if I go wrong in the routine?"

Miss Wanda laughed.

"Just carry on. The examiner might not have noticed."

"What if I want to go to the toilet?" said Paula.

"Really girls, please ask me sensible questions. The examiner is looking at your technique and performance. All you all need to do is smile, use more expression and try to look like you actually enjoy dancing".

Walking over to tea I noticed everyone now had Blakey's on their shoes! Kerri and I quietly practised refining our Egg language in the tea queue, but Esme was a terrible eavesdropper and somehow overheard and now wouldn't stop going on about Kerri's and my 'little secret'. Fortunately we both got letters at tea which distracted her for a while. Mine was postmarked Switzerland from a girl called Elsa. She said my Grandpa Huntley had passed my name on to her because I loved making new pen pals.

She explained that after Christmas her family were touring in England and their car had broken down right outside my Grandpa's house. Her father had knocked on Grandpa's door to ask directions to a local garage. Grandpa not only helped them find a garage but invited the family to stay overnight. Elsa said he showed them photos of my family and Grandpa told her I was the same age as her. She liked music and ballet, spoke German, French and fluent English. I was very excited. I now had Joseph *and* Elsa to write to.

Esme asked if she could read my letter and without thinking I let her, then she wouldn't share hers. What a cheek. Oracle or no oracle, she had to give as well as take!

Millie had now coloured dots all over the countdown calendar marking future events and occasions. The last half of term was going to be very busy. Nanny had also swapped our slave duty rota. Hurrah, I was on Hamish-Walking duty with Mika. There was some justice for juniors.

Before supper Nanny called Mika and I for our walk, telling us to wrap up. We'd got dressing gowns over jumpers over pyjamas, double-legwarmers, scarves around our ears and gloves. The sky was inky-black and clear as we walked around the school grounds, taking it in turns holding Hamish's lead. The too-wit-too-woo of an owl made us all jump because the darkness was so still. I told Nanny I enjoyed walking outside at night but she frowned, saying we couldn't walk Hamish alone because of prowler attacks! Nanny said that a prowler had broken into the student block a couple of years ago and was caught and sent to prison. We gasped in astonishment. It sounded like something from television.

Later on, I was in the bathroom when Hannah came in to wash. I asked her about the prowler who got sent to prison. Hannah said no one knew what had happened, only that the story went round so much that everyone believed it to be true. Hannah checked the door to make sure no one was listening and, looking very secretive, she lowered her voice.

"I know for sure a girl was expelled around this time because she was caught out-of-bounds after dark meeting a prowler."

"How do you know that?"

"Because the girl they expelled is my cousin."

I gasped, dropped my bar of Imperial Leather and watched the golden tablet slip straight under the bath tub. I was forced to scrabble around the filthy floor to rescue it as Hannah continued.

"You must NEVER tell anyone."

"I swear," I promised, staggering to my feet clutching my dented soap, and silently cursing Hannah for sharing the burden of secrecy with me.

"You know far too much already, but you're pretty cool so I don't mind you knowing."

I nodded. I'd got secrets I'd rather not have and was relieved when Hannah became bored with my company. Letting out an exaggerated yawn, she sighed, "I'm going back to the dorm to find something vaguely interesting to do in this prison block."

THURSDAY 1ST MARCH

At breakfast there was a notice on the school board with details of the upcoming Brayfield College 6th Form Dance. I imagined the girls dressing up in gorgeous gowns.

During our music lesson Mr Julius was called out, and everyone sat around talking about the Brayfield College visit. Hannah told us that last year the Brayfield boys got into big trouble for sneaking alcohol onto our school premises. According to Hannah, two of the boys were sent home by taxi for 'inappropriate conduct'. Sydney and Tiffany sniggered. Sydney said that when they visited we could spy on them from Prep Form's class hut, which was next door to where they held the annual dance. Everyone was messing around when Sydney started doing her impressions of prefects, and had us all in stitches when she did Cimmie's G.O.D (glare of death) expression. She was utterly brilliant and did hilarious things with her mouth, which was very mobile. She said if she ever needed money, she would make the perfect mouth model.

SATURDAY 3ᴿᴰ MARCH

Nanny came into the dorm before ballet with good news.

"After lunch, Mr Deluca has agreed to let juniors go to the theatre to watch dress rehearsals. Misbehave and you're straight back to school."

Noticing Sydney and Tiffany roll their eyes she added, "Is that clear?"

"Yes Nanny."

"Good, then it's settled."

I loved being in the theatre, it was like a magical world. With front row seats we watched all the choreographic entries practise.

The Pink Floyd girls wore psychedelic wigs and whirled their heads round so fast one of their wigs flew off, landing on Abbey's lap!

The afternoon whizzed past and at 5-30 p.m. I waited in the dingy theatre car park with Kerri until her Dad picked her up. It was dark and there were creepy rustles coming from the bushes making me feel uneasy. Kerri said she was glad I'd waited with her. I was relieved when car headlights flooded the darkness. Kerri's Dad waved as he drove up and, as soon as Kerri got in her car, her Dad's head popped out of the window.

"Are you okay walking back in the dark?"

"No problem, I love the dark."

"Unlike Kerri here," he joked and I could hear Kerri muttering in the back seat.

Kerri waved from the back window until the car pulled out of the car park and I was plunged into pitch darkness. I tore back to the dorm and when I passed the lake I heard noises but was too scared to stop.

SUNDAY 4TH MARCH

Life had dealt us another cruel blow! Mercedes has been elected to become a prefect and she's now wearing a badge to show her status. Esme embarrassed me by sucking-up to Mercedes all the way to church talking to her about Liverpool. With relations from the North she must have felt they had a connection. Nonetheless, I deserted Esme as a sign of solidarity with the other juniors and walked with Abbey, who told me more about her parents breaking up.

She then told me a secret: Because her birthday was in the autumn, Abbey and several of the oldest girls in our dorm would be moving to the main house this summer term. She must have meant Sydney, Tiffany and the twins, but then what about Hannah?

I didn't want Abbey to move dorms so soon. She was my bunk buddy and my first boarder friend here. We'd been through all our BLAP adventures side by side and shared ironed bread together in the mystical world of the Scrub House. She also told me more new girls would be starting in the summer term.

Feeling a bit down in the dumps this afternoon I phoned home. Dad told me Aunty Phyllis was staying and she'd like a chat, then she talked my ear off. I was sad I hadn't talked to Mum because I'd wanted to tell her about Abbey and next term. It seemed everyone ended up sharing dorms with girls closest to their own age, with no choice of who you shared with. I imagined this could go several ways for me. It all depended on whether my friends had birthdays close to mine or not. There hadn't been many spring birthdays, which meant my closest friends had all got their birthdays to come. I couldn't change the system, but I could be prepared.

SUNDAY 11TH MARCH

This week has flown past with students rehearsing choreography, modern exam practice and awful meals. I'd sent off two more letters; one to my new pen pal Elsa and one to Joseph. I couldn't wait to hear back from them. I was nervous about our modern exam tomorrow and for some reason I kept forgetting the steps. Abbey said we were over practising, but I thought that practice made perfect? Whatever the reason, I wasn't practising today as I had definitely got a mental block. I phoned Benjamin wishing him a Happy Birthday. How was he nine already? Benjamin told me all about yesterday's wrestling match and a wrestler who was a ballet dancer! I couldn't imagine a ballet dancer-wrestler, but Dad said it was true. I suppose being stretchy could help you wriggle free from a Full Nelson or a Japanese Stranglehold. Mum and Dad wished me luck and Lily said 'break a leg'. I've since found out from Mika that saying break a leg to performers means good luck.

Abbey seemed happier tonight. She told me she had an amazing plan and swore me to secrecy. Naturally I agreed. After lights out, I lay in bed cuddling March Hare, pondering over the oath I'd just sworn my life to.

MONDAY 12TH MARCH

Our modern exam was at 10-30 a.m. this morning. I felt jittery inside and couldn't eat breakfast. Patsy had left a card on my bed. She was a brilliant artist and had drawn a picture of a ballet girl dancing in front of a desk with EXAMINER written on it. The dancer was doing split runs with a huge smile on her face. It made me laugh as Patsy knew I loathed split runs with a vengeance. I showed Abbey and Mika, who said, "If only we looked that good."

At 10 o'clock we were ready in our exam uniform - black long sleeved 'V' neck leotard and black footless tights, with our hair scraped back into high ponytails. Loose wisps of hair were cemented to our heads with gallons of super-strength hairspray. I gave everyone a dab of my Chanel for good luck. I felt bad Kerri couldn't get ready in the dorm with us, so we agreed to go to the day girls' cloakroom early so that we could walk to the exam studio together.

When we got to the cloakroom, Kerri said she was glad we'd come to get her as she was starting to feel nervous.

Clutching our black ballet shoes, we ran to the studio where the exams were being held. Outside was a big notice saying 'Silence! Exams in Progress'. Miss Wanda checked our dance kit and reminded us not to forget the examiner's name, Miss Grommit. I didn't dare look at the other girls in case I giggled and made Miss Wanda lairy. She fussed around aiming more hairspray onto our sculpted scalps. We looked like proper eggheads, with ponytail fountains sticking out of the top of our heads. Plastic laminated number plates were pinned to our leotards - I was number 2 and relieved I wasn't the first one to lead us into our exam. Miss Wanda tied blue velvet ribbon around our ponytails and declared we all looked very nice when the examiner's bell rang and my stomach flipped.

"In you go girls, you first Abbey." She jumped in front of us doing one of her enormous cheesy smiles and added, "Don't forget to smile, curtsy and say Good morning, Miss Grommit".

We pinched each other for luck, saying, "Break a Leg", and I took a deep breath. The door opened and we went in. Miss Grommit looked Amazonian. In fact she was a giant and made the desk in front of her look miniature. Her white-blonde hair was swept back into a multi-coloured bandana that emphasised her tanned skin. As we filed in and curtsied, chiming in unison "Good morning, Miss Grommit", she clapped her hands together and an enormous sunny smile lit up her glowing face.

"Good morning girls. Now, please don't look so nervous."

She took a deep breath, put her hands under her ribs and breathed out loudly. We all noticed her shoulders drop and I felt myself relax.

"I want you to try and imagine this is a regular class and that I'm your teacher. Just be yourselves and let's have fun!"

We giggled as only the nervous can giggle. Even though I'd remembered to take my brace out, my top lip still stuck to my teeth. I glanced towards our pianist, Miss Yates, who had such a reassuring smile I could almost have forgotten we were in an exam.

I needn't have worried. Miss Grommit was lovely and looked like she was having as much fun as us. Her head bobbed from one side to the other as she watched us perform our set exercises. The minutes whizzed past and in no time we'd reached the end section and the dance routines.

Afterwards I couldn't remember how I'd danced, but I loved every minute of it and managed not only to kick my leg fairly high in the 'Horse with no Name' routine, but did turns without falling over. Finally we took our bows, thanking Miss Grommit and bowing, then the same to Miss Yates. Miss Grommit held up her hands just before we walked towards the door saying, "I hope the other girls smile as much as you have. Absolutely charming!"

I felt boiling hot and my throat was bone-dry with thirst when we left the studio. We jabbered non-stop when the door closed behind us and Miss Wanda overheard.

"Well done girls. It sounds like you've enjoyed yourselves - let's hope the marks are as good".

So did we.

CHAPTER THIRTY-THREE

TUESDAY 13TH MARCH

Abbey finally revealed her plan today. It was genius. This Saturday 17th, the Brayfield College boys would arrive by coach at 7-30 p.m. for the 6th Form dance. All staff would be over the other side of the school, where the largest studio accommodated the dance. While staff and prefects supervised the boys, Abbey said we could sneak round to the Junior Dorm bathroom window and pretend to be prowlers.

"How?" I gasped in disbelief.

"I want one more adventure with you before end of term and moving up to main house. I've got it all worked out. Are you in?"

I felt happy and sad as I knew it was true. Our BLAP team and all our adventures as we knew them would change forever when Abbey moved up to main house, because she always worked out all the moves and kept us out of trouble.

"Deal", I agreed, slapping her on the back. In the bathroom we were both on hair wash tonight and discussed the finer points of her plan. She told me she'd found a broom handle under the classroom hut.

"We'll smuggle the broom handle round the outside of the building and hide it below the bathroom window. I've nicked one of Nanny's yellow rubber gloves. If we stuff the glove with socks, it will look like a man's hand. Then, we fix the stuffed yellow hand onto the end of the broom handle, hide beneath the bathroom window and, when enough juniors are in the bathroom we bang the hand on the window!"

"That's so mean," I said laughing my head off, "Are you sure we won't get caught?"

"UH-HUH. We're the BLAP team remember," and she winked. Nanny appeared at the door interrupting our conversation.

"You two look like your plotting something. Your skin will turn soggy if you soak too long."

We squealed in protest as she leaned over our tubs and pulled the plugs out.

Roll on Saturday!

FRIDAY 16TH MARCH

We finally had a Fire Drill and it went on forever. We got soaked as we huddled together in our dressing gowns, shivering with cold as we tried to find shelter under the covered way. Cimmie marched round the outhouses like a demon, slamming doors and screaming in her foghorn voice, "Move it or fry in your sleep!" She was hateful. Miss Brookes's parrot squawked relentlessly - probably driven to distraction by Cimmie's frenzied yelling. Lights out was late because it took ages for everyone to settle, but I got to read twenty pages of *Gone with the Wind*. Mental note to ask Mum if Esme can come home again.

SATURDAY 17TH MARCH

Tonight was the night. The Brayfield Dance…

Abbey took me down to the loos and showed me 'the glove'. It looked horribly gruesome when Abbey waved it in the air. She said we'd have to wait in the dorm until enough girls were in the baths and strip-washing at the basins. I sat pretending to read as girls collected their towels from the ends of their beds and went downstairs to the bathroom.

By amazing luck, Gabby, Hannah, Janice and Paula were all downstairs at the same time. Abbey and I went out separately so as not to arouse suspicion and met up round the back of the dorm. It was freezing and the wind was howling so no one else was about. It was way too cold to be creeping around outside in our dressing gowns.

"Get on your hands and knees so we can't be seen by anyone walking on the path," hissed Abbey.

We dropped to the ground and crouching low, stalked round to the far side of the basement until we were nearly alongside the bathroom window. Abbey groped around in the undergrowth and found her hidden broom pole. I got out my diddy torch and watched in fascination as she forced some tissues down the rubber fingers, stuffed a sock inside the rubber glove and then secured it on the end of the pole. "Creepy or what?" Abbey whispered, brandishing the glove towards me in a menacing way. We sniggered helplessly, clasping our hands over our mouths for fear of being heard. Abbey regained self control and took charge.

"OK. When I say go, we'll sneak below the bathroom window, raise the pole so that the hand reaches the window, bang on the window several times and say 'Oi' - or grunt. Just make sure you do it in a deep voice."

After we'd controlled another bout of hysterics we hovered nervously beneath the window, clutching our one-armed prop, waiting for the right moment.

"NOW!" whispered Abbey. Crouching low so our heads couldn't be seen, we raised the armless-hand up to the window and banged several times against the glass.

There was no reaction from the girls inside, so we did it again, banging a bit harder as I added a curt "Oi!"

Then all hell let loose. Blood curdling screams were followed by cries of "Prowlers!" and "Help!" emanating from inside the bathroom. Abbey shot me her wild-eyed, crazy dog look and spat out, "RUUUN!"

Grabbing the glove from its stick, Abbey deftly stuffed it inside her dressing gown pocket and we bolted back to the dorm. As we entered the outside door we saw the rear end of Nanny's white apron disappear into the bathroom amidst anguished cries and wails. We hurtled up the stairs like lunatics and tried our hardest to saunter calmly into the dorm. We needn't have worried because everyone's attention was focussed on the area outside, with all the girls hanging out of the windows.

We grabbed each other conspiratorially and joined the audience of gawping juniors staring at the commotion. Everyone was jabbering about prowlers trying to get into the bathroom window. I glanced at Abbey who gave me a 'say nothing' look. Within five minutes the dogs of the school were leaping into the dense undergrowth, with Max and Sultan skulking around like there was an enemy attack advancing from the woods. Matron and Mr Julius were patrolling through the undergrowth, flashing their torch beams into the darkest corners of the surrounding woods. Prefects in tracksuits, stripy scarves and woolly hats were swarming everywhere. The only thing missing was the police! By now Nanny had brought the girls who were in the bathroom back upstairs. She had them sitting in her room, wrapped up in travel rugs and was feeding them her emergency shortbread biccies and steaming mugs of Milo. Loitering outside the room, I overheard Hannah vowing she was never going to bathe in the junior bathroom again.

After lights out Abbey handed a note down to me. I read it under my blankets by torchlight. It said: 'Dumped glove. Don't tell anyone - EVER. Great fun! We're the best team - even fooled Hannah. Now eat this note.'

I didn't fancy eating the note so I tore it into a zillion bits.

SUNDAY 18TH MARCH

The breakfast queue was buzzing with gossip about 'The Prowlers.' I overheard one of the students saying the Brayfield Dance was a disaster because all the girls were distracted by the excitement caused by the 'intruders'. Our playful prank had created more fuss than we imagined was possible. I mean, for heaven's sakes, it was only a hand.

On the way to church, team BLAP walked in a group, but this was only because two students were in charge. It was great not having Cimmie or her henchmen breathing down our necks.

Abbey finally told the others about changing dorms. She said because of her age she might be moved into main house before the autumn. We all agreed that the best part of leaving Junior Dorm would be not wearing pinnys.

This afternoon I finished *Gone with the Wind*. It was very sad because Rhett ended up leaving Scarlett. I didn't feel sorry for her, but I did feel sorry for Rhett, and even sorrier for myself because I had finished my new favourite book.

I phoned home before tea and asked Mum if Esme could come home again. Mum said she was always welcome.

WEDNESDAY 21ST MARCH

Still no exam results. Hannah had been whinging constantly that she's scared of the bathroom. It was most un-Hannah like because she wasn't afraid of anything. In fact, if the intruder came face to face with Hannah *he* would be the one running! Gabby was full of fake bravery claiming if the prowlers knocked on the window again she'd give them a taste of their own medicine. I knew it was done so that Nanny would rush to their rescue and let them sit in her room, eating biscuits and watching TV.

FRIDAY 23RD MARCH

Dad's birthday today. I said a special prayer for him in assembly service and thanked God for giving me such a lovely Dad. I'd drawn him a special card and sent it first class.

In modern this evening we learned some new steps from the Grade Two modern syllabus. It was nice doing different movements and the music was much funkier than Grade One. However, Miss Wanda wouldn't start teaching the routines, saying we would have enough to learn soon for the summer show.

SATURDAY 24TH MARCH

When I came back from ballet this morning, I found workmen putting up reinforced bars across the junior bathroom window. The bathroom looked like a prison cell. Nanny let us use her toilet while the workmen were downstairs. The queue made it seem like all we ever did was go to the loo. I wondered how people got on before we had toilets. I was glad I hadn't lived in the last century. My Gran told me that when she was young they only had one outside toilet which was freezing cold. She said in the war they didn't have toilet paper and used newspaper instead. I wondered if the print came off. How grim!

I couldn't wait to see my family again and Esme seemed almost as excited as me.

CHAPTER THIRTY-FOUR

Esme and I spent a great Vis Day at home with my family. When Dad dropped us back at school tonight, he said he wouldn't come up to the dorm. Then he looked like he'd remembered something and asked to see the security bars on the bathroom window (I suspect because Esme kept mentioning the prowler drama today).

When I waved goodbye I felt massively guilty that our silly prank had brought on this whole rash of security paranoia. As if dodging prefects round every corner wasn't enough...

CHAPTER THIRTY-FIVE

MONDAY 26ᵀᴴ MARCH

I slept so heavily last night that I woke up in the same position that I went to sleep in. Over breakfast we exchanged Vis Day updates.

Abbey: Said her Mum had got a gentleman friend who was kinder to her Mum than her Dad.

Maddy: Told us her Nan was back home again because she tried to escape from the nursing home. When she saw Maddy dressed in school uniform, her Nan got agitated and accused Maddy's Dad of forcing Maddy to join the army. Maddy explained the bowler hat wasn't a helmet, but her Nan wasn't buying it and hid the car keys. Eventually a double whisky bribed her into submission.

Mika: Visited the posh hotel where her parents stayed. After Sunday lunch they swam in the hotel's indoor pool and afterwards wore fluffy towelling robes.

Hannah: Went to see an X certificate movie with her sister in London but couldn't remember the name of the film. Hannah was worse than Pinocchio.

Gabby: Said her Mum ate non-stop all day. They went to Brighton and had coffee and cakes, then for lunch ate fish and chips followed by a Knickerbocker Glory, and later stopped

again for pie and mash before returning to school. She said
Stavely Brookes stood between her and obesity.

Millie: Met an actor friend of her London Aunt. He was in the
hit play *The Mousetrap*.

Esme: Said we played a fantastic game called *Mousetrap*
(nothing to do with the play.) and we even got lost in the
woods where we found some caves called the Witches Coven.
She said she wished my family were her family and I think this
meant she had enjoyed her day.

Me: I said it was fun having Esme home with me, adding that
the witches Esme mentioned were reputed to have boiled
children alive in their cauldrons... it sounded more interesting
and made Hannah gasp.

THURSDAY 29TH MARCH

Miss Wanda was ill today so Miss Olsen took ballet and
national. We were in for double torture.

After adagio, she announced that she wanted to spend more
time practising our pointe work. Shirley broke the 'back' of one
pointe shoe and had to sit out the pointe work and Gabby kept
stopping, complaining her shoes were pinching her toes which
made Olsen stressy. The final straw came when Tiffany
stopped during 'bourrée en couru', moaning about cramp in
her calves. Miss Olsen had had enough and made us sit down
for a 'talk'.

Apparently we needed further fittings from Freeds. She said
growing feet called for the right fit, maker and shape of shoe
for our individual requirements. I hoped mine were still okay.

In national Miss Olsen was all fired up and said we were
going to learn some Russian character steps. Leaning
backwards and bending our knees we waddled from corner to

corner with our hands on our hips imagining we were plump peasant women. It wasn't graceful and I could hear Gabby's sniggers.

Later in the tea queue, everyone was charging up and down the Dive corridor taking the micky out of the Russian Peasant step. Hannah and Gabby kept pushing their stomachs out like Big Daddy (the wrestler) and belly bumping!

FRIDAY 30TH MARCH

I received three letters today and finally got my modern results.

I got Honours. I couldn't believe it! Looking at the main notice board I was astonished everyone's results were displayed for all to see. I'd already prepared myself for the worst, but we all got Honours. I couldn't wait to tell Mum and Dad. I could hardly eat I was so excited. I saved my letters to read in the dorm because I was way too distracted to concentrate.

The dorm was freezing, so I snuggled up under my travel rug to enjoy my bumper crop of letters.

Grandpa Huntley had sent me a drawing of a clock he'd made in the shape of a cat. It had moving eyes and a tail which swished from side to side as the clock ticked. Nana had had a fall and been bedridden for weeks. I didn't see them often because they lived in Dorset, and hoped she would get better soon. Grandpa rode on his bike every day to the shops as it kept him fit. I made Nana a get well card to cheer her up, with a black cat drawing on it and a smiley sun shining on the cat.

Granny Edgecombe said their fingers were crossed for my dance exam and to let them know when I had my results.

Finally I tore open the stripy edged airmail envelope and read Joseph's letter. He'd sent me more photos. One showed his Dad's sailing boat with Joseph climbing up the rigging. He was deeply tanned. I tried to imagine what it would be like owning a sailing boat. It seemed a world away from life at ballet school. There were pictures of his dog and one of Joseph playing electric guitar. How cool was that! He said he now played in a jamming session every Saturday night with a band.

Tonight the whole dorm was excited about the exam results. When I got my results I was unaware that one person had been left out of the top marks - Gabby got a Pass Plus. She looked so miserable and downhearted that I went over to her bed and showed her the photos Joseph had sent me. While looking at the photos she went quiet, and I had a horrible feeling she was about to burst into tears so I asked her what was up? She looked me straight in the eyes and said,

"Do you think I'm fat?"

Although I was surprised by the question it suddenly dawned on me what was going through her mind.

"No way, Gabby," I said under my breath so the whole dorm didn't hear, and I meant it. Looking startled she shook her head violently.

"It's all very well for you because you'll never look fat - and you're pretty." Her mouth turned down and I waited for her to cry, but she simply said, "I hate myself."

I felt a knot form in my stomach and put my arm round her shoulder because I couldn't think of what else to say to make her feel better. Then it all came pouring out.

"I hate myself for billions of reasons, not only because I'm hopeless at modern and a completely useless dancer," she sucked in the deepest breath and her eyes brimmed with tears as she let out the next burst of frustrations, "but because I know, deep down in my heart," she sat bolt upright stabbing her finger violently towards her heart, "that one day, I'm going to end up looking just like my Mum."

"No chance!"

I didn't think anything I said would make any difference because she was so upset.

"I've inherited her fatness. It's all there – in my blood," she said, louder than she meant to.

At that moment everybody in the dorm looked up towards us. There was a gaping silence and everyone averted their eyes when they saw how upset Gabby was.

I wasn't sure that if something was 'in your blood' there was much you could do about it. I mean, can you change your blood? I didn't think it was humanly possible - unless you were a vampire.

At that precise moment it seemed like the whole world had shrunk down to just Gabby and me, sitting on her bed in our nighties in a solitary moment of deep thought and, for Gabby, despair.

"This is rubbish, Gabby. It will never happen because first, you're too attractive. Second, you're a great dancer."

She tried to interrupt but I talked over her. "And thirdly..." I paused, and we both giggled because I'd invented a word, then I continued, "you exercise loads."

"Really?"

"Really!"

Gabby beamed and put her arm around my shoulder and clasped me towards her saying, "You're even loopier than me, if that's possible, but you're a great friend!"

We returned to discussing Joseph's photos. Later, back in my own bed, I had the distinct feeling someone was watching me.

However, when I looked towards Esme's bed, she immediately turned her head in the opposite direction.

SATURDAY 31ST MARCH

I phoned home with the news about my exam results. Mum and Dad were really excited, and Dad said if I carried on working this hard he would raise my pocket money. Mum asked when they could buy tickets for the choreographic show, reminding me how close to end of term we were.

Kerri had arranged to come to the local shop with us because her parents were away for the afternoon. She told me every time her parents left her home alone the boy next door sat on his balcony and serenaded her with his guitar. I said I'd like to be serenaded by Rhett Butler but Kerri assured me there was nothing Rhett Butler-ish about him. If he was anything like creepy Gilbert I sympathised.

During the walk to the shop, Kerri told loads of funny stories about the boy next door, saying he looked like an ugly version of Alice Cooper. I couldn't help laughing. We talked about the choreographic show and agreed our parents would enjoy seeing the different dance styles. I shared my pocket money with Kerri and we bought some Flying Saucers, a Curly Wurley and shared a bottle of cream soda. I promised her that when I eventually got out of Junior Dorm, she could come and visit me. She said it wasn't my fault and rules were rules. It was like your parents not letting your best friend inside your house. I would have to be like those suffragette women who fought for reform, although they didn't have to battle against prefects like Cimmie Krause and Rita Warlock.

When I got back to the dorm it was cold and dark outside and I felt chilled. I changed for bed early hoping nightclothes would warm me up. As I pulled my nightdress out from under my pillow a folded note dropped out and fell onto the floor. I grabbed it, thinking it was a message from Abbey about BLAP. Unfolding it I felt excited about the prospect of a new adventure, but the handwriting wasn't Abbey's. I began reading.

Dear Lara

Thank you for spending the afternoon with me. You know how homesick I get and you didn't even ask me if it was okay if you could walk with Kerri. Thanks a lot for all the thought you give to me.

Your lonely friend

Esme

I glanced around the dorm but couldn't see Esme anywhere. What a load of rubbish. Kerri had been my friend forever - why should I ask Esme's permission? Stuffing the note in my dressing gown pocket, I grabbed my towel and went downstairs to wash and guess who was in the bathroom...

My stomach knotted into a hard ball, but I disguised my feelings and pretended I hadn't found the note. Hannah and Gabby were strip-washing whilst Paula and Janice soaked in the bath tubs gossiping. I began washing and joined in their conversation. Esme looked at me strangely so I smiled sweetly back. Inside I was fuming.

SUNDAY 1ST APRIL

After church I went to main house with Abbey to enquire about theatre tickets for the competition. When we approached Saphi's room and knocked on the door, Cimmie answered. We took a step back but she narrowed the gap and glowered at us. After ages of eye-to-eye combat and, satisfied that fear was oozing from our pores, her lips moved and an ugly noise emitted from her mouth.

"What are you dribbling baby-bibs doing in main house without permission?" she spat out, studying us with a look of disgust. The skin on the back of my neck crawled and as I tried to unscramble my thoughts, I noticed some spittle at the corner of her mouth and fought the urge to giggle. Fortunately Saphi emerged and, putting her hand on Cimmie's shoulder, she drew her back into the room.

"I'll deal with this, Cimmie, thank you!"

She smiled at Cimmie and raised her eyebrows as she looked towards us.

"Girls, how can I help you?"

Stunned into speechlessness by Warrior Troll's outburst, Abbey gathered her wits.

"Sorry to bother you, Saphi, but our parents asked us to reserve them theatre seats for the choreographic competition and we thought you'd know who we can buy them from?"

Saphi asked our names and said as we were the first to ask, we were top of the list. Unfortunately, it was only two tickets per girl.

"First come, first served" she told us, with instructions that our parents must send a cheque poste-haste made payable to Stavely Brookes School. We thanked Saphi and then scarpered back to Junior Dorm where Millie was colouring our countdown calendar.

"Guess what?" she said.

"What?"

"Only fifteen days until the Easter holidays."

"Can't wait" I grinned, adding, "for the choreographic show" in case Esme was ear wigging and got any funny ideas.

Patsy came round this afternoon and took Abbey and me on a toast ironing mission. Whilst the whiff of hot toast drifted up from the iron, I showed Patsy the crumpled note from Esme. She read it and screwed up her nose.

"Don't you remember what I said to you ages ago?" she chided. "Just watch out - she's possessive - and you're too nice. You've got to stand up to her."

"What can I do?" I wailed, complaining Esme was a control freak.

"Listen to me," Patsy said, recklessly smearing several individual butter portions over a browned crust and, as I watched the butter dripping over the ironing board, she continued.

"We're at an all-girls school, right? Some girls can get really funny when they're growing up and become kind of jealous. My Dad calls it the green monster."

"Jealous of what?" I said, through a mouthful of hot buttered crust.

"Oh, Lord. I don't know exactly, but anything and everything. So you just ignore it. She's childish and if you don't rise to the bait she'll get over it."

Patsy gave me a big hug and handed Abbey her toasted crust to devour. I took my turn guarding the entrance and was amazed no one had come into the Scrub House, especially as the smell of toast was so appetizing. I felt loads better after talking to Patsy.

After tea I played Scrabble with Hannah and Karlyn and listened to the Top Twenty. Nanny produced supper that looked suspiciously like Ox Tongue with stacks of bread rolls. No one touched the tongue, particularly after last term's episode of the tongue getting stuck on the mirrors. Nanny got the measure of the situation and tackled us.

"Well if you're too fussy to eat the tongue, then you can jolly well go without the roll," she said in her sternest voice, "You ought to think about all those starving children in Biafra and know which side your bread's buttered." She finished her scolding with a huff, folded her hands across her chest and shook her head.

I noticed the corners of Hannah's mouth twitching and thought she'd make some comment about the bread being a roll, or that it wasn't buttered. Thankfully she didn't. Nanny was in no mood for sarcasm and stared us down until, one by one, we slunk towards the supper tray and reluctantly took a slice. It was slimy and made me feel queasy.

When Nanny left the room Hamish had a rare feast. For his sake I hoped he wasn't fed later!

CHAPTER THIRTY-SIX

MONDAY 2ND APRIL

I glanced at Millie's countdown chart before breakfast today and wondered if the juniors would be allowed to watch the choreographic competition when our parents came to see it. Esme was still behaving as if nothing had happened, which Patsy had predicted. What a relief.

THURSDAY 5TH APRIL

Mr Mainwaring followed Miss Knox into class before the last lesson, carrying a small wooden box full of Roman figures, pillars and columns. They acted really strangely when together and Miss Knox went all giggly when she got near him. Sydney said she was sure Mr Mainwaring had twanged Miss Knox's bra strap as he put the box down on the desk behind her. She'd jumped out of her skin, gone bright red and had fits of giggles!

During the history lesson that followed, I could hear music blaring out from a nearby open studio window, making our classroom vibrate and it was impossible to concentrate. I was glad for Miss Knox's sake when the bell went.

FRIDAY 6 TH APRIL

A running order notice for full dress rehearsal had gone up on the main notice board and half the school was gathered around it, a mass of heads with perfect buns all craning their necks to see what time they had been allotted. And the best thing was juniors were all allowed to watch. With the choreographic competition only one week away there was lots of practice needed by all girls taking part. Juniors were allowed to sit in the front seats tomorrow. The run-through started immediately after lunch at 1-30 p.m. After tea Mika, Abbey and I checked the notice board again. The technical rehearsals ran throughout the morning. The final run through in the afternoon said girls must arrive in 'full make up and costume'. It made me realise how much there was to prepare in a show and I couldn't wait!

SATURDAY 7 TH APRIL

It rained hard last night with thunder loud enough to wake the dead. I didn't see the Blue Lady but I was sure she was floating around somewhere, because all the best ghosts like a violent storm (well, they did in *Scooby-Doo*).

The thunder woke me before rising bell and I lay awake listening to everyone's breathing, watching the sleeping bodies huddled under their counterpanes like giant pink blancmanges.

Two students taught ballet class this morning. Because it was non-syllabus we practised ballet exercises to pop music which was great fun. Doing pliés to 'Nights in White Satin' and battement tendus to 'Jean Genie', it was hard to be serious - especially pirouetting to Chelsea football club's 'Blue is the Colour'! We gave the students a round of applause at the end of class then scrambled back to the dorm to change and watch the dress rehearsals.

When we got to the theatre everyone quietened down. I glanced around to see the auditorium full of girls in costumes. The middle row of seats was occupied by dance teachers, clutching clipboards and preparing to make notes. A yell from Miss Wanda was answered by a man's voice coming from the lighting box behind us, and as the lights dimmed the theatre gradually went dark.

I shivered with anticipation, clutching Kerri's arm. The curtain went up to the sounds of jazz music, a whistle blew and a single spotlight focussed on a student in a sparkly costume standing right at the back of the stage. She did some amazing tap, with her feet sounding like drumsticks rolling, and then there was an explosive trumpet blast. About fifteen girls in sequinned costumes came onto stage, tapping fast and energetically.

The dance went on for several minutes and was dazzling. When they finished the audience went wild and I clapped so much I thought my hands would explode!

We watched the rest of rehearsals mesmerised. Different dancers came and went, appearing on stage in all sorts of fantastic costumes, looking unrecognisable in their stage make-up. They performed all styles of dance. One number had a student singing, and in another dance there was a bit of acting and dialogue half-way through. Finally Miss Wanda called for a twenty-minute break, so we sprinted back to school and shared a cup of tea from Kerri's thermos. I wouldn't survive if it wasn't for Kerri's supplies.

We arrived back at the theatre just in time for the second half. I loved the barefoot ballet solo, performed by an oriental student who appeared to cast a spell on the audience. I hoped one day I might dance like her.

The last performance was the Pink Floyd contemporary. Tassia, Sophie and Sian came onto stage in really crazy make up and danced with such energy it seemed more out-of-this-world than ever. When it ended the applause was deafening. All three girls ran to the front of the stage and then travelled backwards, whilst linking their hands together and raising their arms into a high 'V', then bringing their arms to their sides and bowing. They were soaked with sweat and glistening. Finally the curtain came down and remained.

Some of the girls in the audience were stamping their feet, clapping and shouting 'Encore'.

When we eventually made our way back to school, I had a single thought in my mind. I had never wanted to dance so much in my entire life as I did at that moment, and I knew without a doubt that dancing made me feel happier than anything else. This was where I belonged!

SUNDAY 8TH APRIL

On the way to church today, Esme whispered she had some confidential information to tell me!

"I've heard a rumour that some dances from the competition are going to be used in the summer show."

"Which ones?" I thought it sounded a bit odd.

"How should I know, stupid. I was, um, ear-wigging yesterday on the Tweenies sitting behind us in the theatre, and just for your information it was actually a private conversation."

She had a cheek calling me stupid, but I didn't want to start getting into an argument for fear the note business might surface.

That afternoon I wrote a long letter to Joseph about the competition, and drew pictures of the girls in different dance costumes. I told him about Abbey moving up to the main house and becoming a Tweenie. I wondered if there were schools in New Zealand like this.

Later, I wrote to Nana and Grandpa Huntley, also including sketches for Nana of the costumes. I hoped the drawings would cheer her up after her nasty fall.

In my letter to Granny and Grandpa Edgecombe, I told Aunty Ellen that I thought she would enjoy the choreographic show, but unfortunately I could only get two tickets. I said how pleased I was with my modern results, mentioning my limbering practise because Aunty knew how important it was to practise daily. I sealed the envelopes realising these were the last letters I'd post this term. I'd never known school terms go so fast.

Pinned on the notice board beside the post box was a new notice, asking girls to collect pre-ordered theatre tickets from Saphi's room after 6 p.m. today. Mika, Abbey, Maddy and I joined a long queue up the windy staircase leading to Saphi's room and waited half an hour. I think the seat numbers were good, but I asked Esme to check them because she knew the theatre better. She said they were somewhere near the middle, reminding me the judges always claimed the centre row. It was rumoured that Alexandra Haydon may be asked to judge. When I heard this my heart skipped a beat. I hoped it would be Alexandra, so I might get a chance to meet her in person!

I phoned home to tell Mum I'd got her tickets. Mum said Dad wanted Aunty Ellen to go in his place because she was far more interested in dance than him and would be thrilled to go.

Nobody seemed to be concentrating in school this week. In double drama we did mime and Voodoo and Venus kept howling, which was very off-putting. In the end Miss Lazenby threw her hands in the air saying it was hopeless. Making her way to the props cupboard she announced we would be learning how to apply stage make-up. She produced foil wrapped tubes, black compacts, make-up brushes, several blue tins of 'Crowes Cremine', baby-powder, 'Simple' soap, wads of cotton wool, tissues and unlabelled medicine bottles containing clear liquid.

Everyone's hands shot up when she asked for a volunteer and Sydney was chosen. We all watched as Miss Lazenby scraped Sydney's hair off her face and placed a wide head band over her hairline. Next she made Sydney's eyebrows disappear by sweeping a moistened bar of Simple soap across each brow until she resembled an alien. Then she applied different coloured greasepaints, 'Brick Red' and 'Ivory', blending them until Sydney's face looked smooth. Miss Lazenby admired her handywork.

"There," she said, peering through her diamond studded spectacles "is your perfect blank canvas to begin work on your classical ballet face."

The colour on Sydney's face was a mixture of Red Indian and Baked Bean. Sydney eventually complained, saying her face felt stiff, and Miss Lazenby sighed, saying we'd continue next week. She'd forgotten we'd be on holiday then. She grabbed the Crowes Cremine tin, scooped her fingers into the crème and unceremoniously slapped a massive dollop of goo straight onto Sydney's painted face. Sniggers ran through the captivated audience as Sydney attempted to open her eyes, looking scarily like a clown as the gloop parted around her eyelids. Miss Lazenby set about rubbing the goo vigorously into Sydney's skin and she whinged throughout as tissues were dragged across her face which became red and irritated. Miss Lazenby brandished an opened medicine bottle under our noses.

"Smell the perfume! This is your theatrical skin-saviour. Witch Hazel and Rose Water applied after cold crème refreshes the skin."

She cleared her throat and shoved the bottle under Tamsin's nose. There was an ominous silence as Tamsin sniffed the bottle. Her nose twitched and her eyes rolled upwards and for a split-second the whole class froze, anticipating an approaching swoon. She swayed back and forth, opened her eyes wide, looked towards Miss Lazenby and beamed.

"Smells exactly like a rose-garden, Miss Lazenby."

"Quite, quite. Excellent. Girls, on your next trip home I want you to visit the chemists with a clean bottle and ask the pharmacist to fill it with equal parts Witch Hazel and Rose Water. Witch Hazel discourages spots and Rose Water calms skin. 'Leichner' greasepaints can clog your pores and you don't want blemishes."

Everyone pulled long faces.

In the lunch queue Sydney looked very blotchy and predicted instant acne. This got me wondering how skin breathes under all that pore-blocking stuff. I asked Sydney why it was applied so heavily.

"If you think this is bad, Lara, wait until you try false eyelashes."

Groan.

THURSDAY 12TH APRIL

Two days until the choreographic show! I was gutted that we couldn't watch the show because there were only enough tickets for parents and guests. It was only a small theatre without dress circles and balconies, not Covent Garden Opera House. Hannah had already told us there weren't enough seats for all the girls. I thought it was unfair because the rest of the school - apart from juniors - were in the competition. They would all get to be part of it. Hannah asked Nanny if she would talk to Mr Deluca, to see if it would be possible for juniors to sit at the front of the stalls, on the floor near the exits. Nanny said she'd see.

FRIDAY 13TH APRIL

I couldn't believe we were going home in less than a day. Everything always happened at the same time. I felt sad watching Abbey take down her Marc Bolan poster and emptying her bedside locker. I sensed that my group of friends would change forever when Abbey moved up to main house. BLAP wouldn't seem right either because Abbey was the unspoken leader. Millie looked like she might cry and said she couldn't go home until Sunday, when she'd be escorted to the airport by chaperone. I gave her my phone number and said if there were any problems to phone me which cheered her up. I also reminded Abbey to phone me so we could visit each other over Easter. Abbey swore solemnly to visit me in Junior Dorm when she moved to main house and to let me visit her new dorm next term. I kept wondering which dorm she'd be in. I really hoped that my new bunk mate was as nice as Abbey and I thought about what the new juniors would be like, too.

Nanny came into the dorm during supper and inspected our bags, checking all our belongings were packed, apart from uniform and ballet kit to wear tomorrow. Then she told us to sit down. She looked serious and I thought she had bad news.

"Girls, in view of the fact that the choreographic competition is part of school tradition, I have talked with Mr Deluca. Unfortunately, juniors end up missing out on the whole experience."

She sighed in resignation, shaking her head from side to side, her silver curls bouncing as she moved her head. Raising her shoulders she pressed her lips together.

"It's so not fair," Esme trilled with her most disapproving face and we all joined in. Without warning Nanny stood up and shooed her hands at us, raising her voice.

"No 'buts' girls; stop this nonsense. It's been decided. You can't have luxury all the time. You will just have to sit quietly *on your bottoms* by the front stage exits for the whole show, and not a squeak out of any of you. Am I clear?"

Slowly the penny dropped and Esme jumped up and squealed.

"YEEESSS!" We all leaped up and hugged Nanny until she had to pull us off. I couldn't believe our luck. We were given strict instructions on good behaviour, including a warning that if one of us stepped out of line we would *all* be taken straight back to school, regardless of who was to blame. She looked directly at Tiffany and Sydney.

CHAPTER THIRTY-SEVEN

The whole dorm was a frenzy of excitement about watching the choreographic competition.

After ballet we raced to get changed because the show started bang on 2-00 p.m. Nanny made us wear Sunday uniform, saying we should set a good impression *even* when sitting on the floor.

"You never know who might see you. You may be spotted by a director and look the part for a film he is casting. Start off as you mean to carry on in life and BE PREPARED."

Sydney yawned, which made Nanny scowl.

"This is a professional performance with highly influential people present, not amateur dramatics. Now hurry along to lunch."

At 1-15 p.m. we lined up while Nanny checked our uniform and hair and endured the usual make-up removal squabble from the twins and Sydney. Honestly, it was so tedious. Fortunately they didn't give Nanny any further grief and we finally marched over to the theatre in a giant crocodile. I spotted Dad's red car parked at the far side of the car park with Mum and Aunty sitting inside. I waved and Nanny did her 'hand shooing' at me. I could barely contain myself. Kerri joined our crocodile as we flooded into the theatre, with Nanny marching us to the bottom of the auditorium steps until we were bang under the edge of the stage and the glowing footlights. Our group was split into two halves and I grabbed Kerri in case we got separated.

Sitting cross-legged on the floor was uncomfortable but better than missing the competition.

When the theatre door opened at the top of the auditorium, daylight lit up the entrance and I noticed Mum and Aunty Ellen coming down the steps. The lighting was dim and we were hidden from view under the shadow of the stage, but I could see their top halves and noticed their posh dresses. Their seats were fifth row from the back just behind the judges.

The theatre filled up quickly with no sign of Alexandra. Several dancing teachers made their entrance carrying clipboards, closely followed by Mr Deluca, who was arm-in-arm with a tall older lady with black hair piled high on her head. My heart sunk - it wasn't Alexandra. The auditorium doors opened again, and everyone stared as two men walked in. One of them was Wesley Price who'd auditioned us for the television commercial last October. He was smiling as he talked to the other man, who kept flicking his floppy blonde hair off his face.

When the audience settled Mr Deluca gave a speech welcoming all the parents, and said we were fortunate that this year's budding talent was going to be under the auspices of three very experienced judges. He then introduced them. First off was the tall lady with the big hair, Ruth Jennings. Mr Deluca said she was a journalist and RAD examiner. She stood up and everyone clapped. Then he introduced Wesley, who made everyone laugh because when he stood up he did an exaggerated bow. Last was the man with floppy blond hair, introduced as Charles Chipper, a "familiar face of stage and screen". I'd never heard of him. Finally everyone settled down and I shivered with excitement as the lights dimmed and we sat in a black silence for a few seconds.

Then a blast of music came from the speakers above us, which made us jump out of our skins. I hadn't realised the speakers were so close whilst sitting in the theatre seats during rehearsals. We clutched each other as the curtain started to rise. My stomach tightened. The oriental girl was alone on stage. She began to dance slowly, swaying her body rhythmically and the audience seemed held in a trance. When she finished the lights were cut and the spell was broken. The deafening applause reassured me that what I had watched was real!

The rest of the dances flew past. The audience loved the tap number which Patsy was in, clapping for ages after it had finished. I liked the comedy routine 'Wit or Less' performed by two students, one tall and the other short. Dressed like Laurel and Hardy, they acted just like them and made the audience roar with laughter. Their act got a standing ovation, which was good as my bottom had gone numb.

Once the applause finished and the curtain lowered, the lights came up and the judges put their heads together – they had an impossible choice. Mr Deluca stood up and announced a fifteen-minute break while the judges conferred.

Nanny made us stay put and after what seemed like forever waiting, Mr Deluca walked towards the side exits followed by the judges. After a minute the curtain went up and the judges were standing on stage behind a semi-circular table, on which glistened several silver trophies. Mr Deluca cleared his throat and spoke into the microphone.

"Ladies and Gentlemen. We hope you've enjoyed watching the talented and creative demonstrations of the students' choreographic work. The standard this year has been so high that the judges found it difficult choosing one overall winner. However, before we announce winners, a couple of groups deserve a special mention."

Wesley smiled and leaned towards the microphone.

"Congratulations to the best comedy entertainment, with their duo 'Wit and Less'. Let's give them a well deserved round of applause."

The two girls ran on stage holding hands and took a bow. Wesley called them over to the table where the judges shook their hands. He said to the audience, "If I want to make any funny TV commercials in future, I know who to use", and everyone cheered. Then Ruth Jennings moved to the microphone to begin her announcement.

"Another special mention has to go to the audacious 'Tap Fever'." Masses of sparkly clad girls tripped out from the wings, to another deafening round of clapping. I saw Patsy grinning from ear to ear and was very proud of her and yelled out "Bravo".

Finally, Charles Chipper leaned towards the microphone and cleared his throat.

"I have pleasure in announcing the three winning entries. In reverse order, third place goes to … 'Nightclubbing', choreographed by Angelina Fysh."

The girls ran onto stage to a round of applause and Angelina stepped forward to be presented with a silver trophy. The dancers moved to the sides of the stage and Charles leaned towards the microphone, flicking his annoying, floppy blond hair again.

"Second place," followed by a dramatic pause, "goes to 'Summertime', choreographed and performed by Maetai Wang."

The applause was thunderous. A happy but tearful Maetai came on stage and the audience cheered her. When she received her trophy Charles Chipper had to shout into the microphone to be heard above the audience.

"Finally, first prize goes to…'Fracas', choreographed by Tassia Dales." A scream burst forth from backstage as the audience exploded into clapping and cheering. The trio ran onto stage holding hands and after they had bowed five times, Tassia was presented with a large trophy by Charles Chipper, who planted a whopping kiss on her cheek (gross). The clapping continued and I was relieved the curtain went down as my hands were stinging.

Nanny then herded us into a crocodile towards the exits to keep us out of the way, telling us we'd meet our parents in the dorm. I saw Mum's head bobbing up and down in the crowd as she tried to see where I was going, and hoped she knew where to take the car. When we walked through the side exits, I could hear all sorts of squealing and girls sobbing. Kerri hugged me then raced back to the day girls' changing room to find her Dad, saying she'd ring me in the holidays.

Back in the dorm Mum and Aunty Ellen were standing by my bunk. It was lovely to see them and they both gave me a big hug, saying the show was brilliant. Aunty Ellen said she was really pleased I was at Stavely Brookes because the quality of training was exceptional.

By the time we'd got my kit together it suddenly dawned on me that I wouldn't see my friends for four weeks. We all hugged and wished each other happy holidays. Esme even promised to phone me from Kenya. As everyone picked up their bags and queued to leave, Millie began sobbing. I felt gutted, but Nanny was there comforting her.

I got into the car and looked towards the dorm entrance only to see Abbey and Mika bursting through the door yelling and waving at me. I waved back as our car slowly pulled away. Passing through the school grounds, I was aware of torches and car-headlamps illuminating parents as they rushed to and fro, fathers loaded-up like pack-horses heaving trunks and Mums dragging suitcases. Girls in uniform were running everywhere waving frantic farewells. The car started to gather speed and as I gazed through the car window, the school grounds were swallowed in darkness as we headed for HOME.

CHAPTER THIRTY-EIGHT

SPRING HOLIDAYS

SUNDAY 15TH APRIL

This morning I woke up at 10-30 a.m. I'd slept for ages and found a note on the kitchen table downstairs.

"Lara, I hope you slept well. Aunty and I are at church, Samuel's at Sunday school and Benjamin's doing football practice. Lily's got final dress rehearsals for *Oliver* and didn't want to disturb you. Dad's in the garden. See you later. Love Mum xx."

A shadow flicked past the window and Dad walked through the back door. He crossed the floor in two strides and lifted me up in a bear hug. He smelt of smoke.

"What's that smell?"

"Bonfire. Fancy helping me stoke up the fire?"

Dad knew I loved helping him build a bonfire.

"Eat your breakfast and see you in five minutes. Bring us both a mug of tea and you can tell me all about yesterday."

I devoured three Weetabix then charged upstairs, threw on my oldest clothes, made two teas and took them down the garden. Dad had put two deckchairs close to the crackling fire and we sat sipping steaming tea, prodding the bonfire with long sticks. It felt good to be home.

He wanted to know all about the show, and then asked if I was still enjoying ballet school. I told him more than ever! He said he was glad because there might be some assessors visiting the school next term. My stomach flipped and Dad smiled.

"Don't look so alarmed. Most children awarded scholarships have to have progress reports."

I gasped.

"Does that mean if my progress isn't good enough I'll be thrown out?"

Dad laughed and put his arm around me.

"Of course they wouldn't just throw you out. A scholarship involves funding, and the people paying for your training like to monitor your progress. Rest assured they keep tabs on anyone with awards like yours throughout most of your school life, because they are investing pots of money in you. Miss Brookes thinks you're worth it otherwise you wouldn't be there."

"But she doesn't see me much at the moment" I wailed, "and what if the assessors come to watch and I dance badly?"

"Don't go so far away," he laughed. "Just carry on doing your best like you always do, and I'll let you into a secret. Your mother has already been in touch with the school to check as we know how much this means to you. Miss Brookes assured us that she has no concerns regarding your abilities, *and* she told Mum she's received excellent feedback from your dance teachers."

I felt my confidence grow when he mentioned Miss Brookes and pulled my shoulders back.

"Well, I did get my highest mark ever…and I'm working so hard in ballet that my toes sometimes bleed."

Dad laughed and called me a 'poor old soldier'.

During Sunday lunch Aunty Ellen and Mum discussed the choreographic show. Aunty said she would keep an eye out for any press coverage, as no doubt The Telegraph would do a review. She promised us another trip to Covent Garden and I wondered what we would see this time.

Later, we took Aunty to the station to travel back to London. Whilst we were waiting on the platform for her train she gave us some coins to spend in the chocolate machine. Benjamin's coin got stuck and when Samuel kicked the machine it released about fifteen bars of Dairy Milk. The boys went bananas! Dad was busy talking to Aunty and, with no one else on the platform, Benjamin and Samuel stuffed the lot under their parkas. Lily got really hissy, saying they'd be arrested. I told her it couldn't be as bad as selling illegal tuck at ballet school. She looked irritated and snapped back at me.

"Well you're not at ballet school now, Lara, so SHUT-UP!"

Talk about stress. Maybe I should teach her Miss Lazenby's deep breathing exercises.

During the drive home Lily wouldn't talk to anyone and stared out of the car window with her arms folded across her chest for the whole journey. Dad tried talking to her.

"Lily, what's up, love?"

"Nothing!" she snapped. "I'm tired and I've got a splitting headache."

She gave me a withering stare and we drove back in silence. Later, alone in our bedroom, she started talking to me again.

"I've had a really bad monthly," she told me.

"Horrid" I sympathised. "That's why we call it the curse."

"Who's we?"

"Girls at school."

"Whatever," then she added, "Anyway, you haven't started yet so how would you know?"

"I have, actually, had one, and it was horrible. And I haven't had one since."

"That's so weird!"

"Thanks! But I'll show you what's really weird is the elastic briefs we have to wear to hold our tights up and tummies in."

I demonstrated pulling in my tummy and she laughed.

"Sounds like an old lady's girdle to me."

I rummaged in my drawer and showed her my elastic briefs.

"They're so tight," she said, tugging at the waistband. "Can I try them on?"

"Go on."

She tried them on and we had fits of hysterics. She said they were so tight she couldn't breathe. We had another burst of hysterics when she collapsed on the bed struggling to get them off.

That evening, when Lily was in the bathroom, Mum came into our bedroom and said how proud she was of me and my exam results. She asked if I had any plans for after Easter because she had to work. I asked if I could stay with either Abbey or Kerri and Mum agreed.

MONDAY 16TH APRIL

I phoned Kerri early but she already had relations staying so I phoned Abbey, arranging to stay at her house next week. Abbey lived near Chichester. She said there was a disco at her brother's old youth club we could go to. I couldn't wait!

WEDNESDAY 18TH APRIL

I went to Lily's school with her today to see *Oliver*. She left me in the main hall where I bagged a middle front row seat. I sat by myself for ages until Lily came to check I was okay, bringing three boys with her who she said wanted to meet me. I was *so* embarrassed. I wondered if my brace showed when I smiled. One of the boys said they'd heard all about me from Lily. I wanted the ground to swallow me up. The worst part was I couldn't think of anything to say and stood like a gormless dummy. I said 'break a leg' - twice - to the boy with the nice smile (he was playing the Artful Dodger) and I could feel my neck and face burning. How embarrassing.

Fortunately other people started to arrive and Lily and the boys left. Lots of teenagers joined me on the front bench and the hall was noisy with chatter.

I loved the show and the Artful Dodger was amazing.

The second half was even better - Oliver had the voice of an angel and Fagin was so evil he made me shiver. At the end everyone stood up cheering. Boys in the audience wolf-whistled and one girl kept screaming 'O-l-i-v-e-r!' Oliver, Fagin, Nancy and the Artful Dodger got the most curtain calls and Dodger smiled at me when he came to the front to take his bow (or maybe I imagined it).

THURSDAY 19TH APRIL

We took Lily to Dover today for her French trip and waved goodbye, watching from the dockside as the ferry disappeared out to sea. Dad squeezed Mum's hand as he said, "Don't worry, love, she's quite grown up really." Mum gave a sad little smile, nodding.

Later when I was in bed reading, Dad tapped on my door and told me that Lily had arrived in France. I was so excited for her.

SUNDAY 22ND APRIL

We went to the Easter service at church today. Sitting in our usual pew behind the Buchanan boys, Angus (the oldest, best looking one) turned round and spoke to me.

"So where's your pretty friend today?" he said, eyes searching my pew.

He was referring to Marie-Helene, our French exchange student.

"I don't know who you're talking about," I fibbed.

"You remember, the dark haired girl with you at Christmas."

I could feel my face getting warm, so I took a deep breath and leaned forward.

"Actually, she's in France now."

"Oh."

He looked bitterly disappointed.

"Will she be visiting again?"

"How do I know?" Then, as an afterthought added, "My sister's in France now."

All the Buchanan boys then turned around and a whole row of dark eyes bored into me. I shifted in my seat and sat up tall, wondering how to carry this conversation on. Taking a deep breath I leaned towards Angus.

"She's French" I whispered.

"Your sister?"

"No. Marie-Helene, the girl with us at Christmas."

Angus turned back to his brothers and I saw him grin and wink with a knowing look. I felt crushed.

After church, Dad went to the station to pick up Granny, Grandpa, Aunty Ellen and Uncle Noah, who gave us Easter Eggs and Belgian chocolates. Aunty Ellen gave us each holiday spending money, which I put straight into my travel-fund. New Zealand here I come.

After lunch we went out for a long walk. Grandpa and Uncle Noah must have led armies in the Great War, because they set out at such a stride none of us could keep up. Granny didn't share Grandpa's enthusiasm for marathon walks and sitting on a log said, "If you don't slow down you will have to carry me home."

It did the trick!

MONDAY 23RD APRIL

Mum woke me up early today to go shopping. She said I could choose a pattern and material for my end of term dress.

The haberdashery shop was crammed with large pattern catalogues displaying hundreds of designs. After scouring through every catalogue in the shop, a long dress pattern with a frilled hem, ruched bodice and off-the-shoulder sleeves caught my eye. Mum said it looked easy enough, so I chose a pale green material with random flowers which looked pretty. I hoped it would look even better when made up as a dress.

TUESDAY 24TH APRIL

I was all set to go to Abbey's today when we had a phone call from Lily in Paris and by the time I got off the phone we were super late. I decided to leave my journal at home. If Abbey's brother accidentally found it he might read it.

TUESDAY 1ST MAY

I had such fun with Abbey. We spent a lot of time at the youth centre playing table tennis, swimming at the local pool and looking round shops in Chichester.

I also went to my first disco. Abbey and I had made up a dance which fitted most music, but the disco floor was so small that we ended up bashing into everyone. Some of the girls tried to copy our funky moves and asked us to teach them our dance. We added some head spins, but I kept my mouth tightly shut because I was scared my brace might fly out.

Abbey's brother came to collect us at 9-30 p.m. He had a girl with him who kept putting her tongue in his ear. Gross. She was dressed from head to toe in leather and had black spiky hair with a fringe cut straight across her eyebrows. Her name was Marlene and she said our dancing rocked.

Abbey gave me her favourite cassette with songs we'd danced to at the disco which her brother had recorded. She said he would be a DJ when he grew up. I thought he *was* grown up, but I never saw him doing anything apart from hanging out at the youth club and scorching up and down Abbey's road on his Harley with Marlene hanging onto his back.

THURSDAY 3RD MAY

Lily arrived home from Paris late this afternoon. She gave me a little framed painting from the Paris flea market of a cute little street urchin looking over his shoulder, holding what looked like a potty. She said this style of painting was very popular and the flea market was very bohemian. Long after the boys were in bed Lily and I were still talking. She'd learnt lots of swear words but wouldn't tell me because they were too disgusting!

SATURDAY 5TH MAY

Lily started a new Saturday job today as a waitress and this evening said she'd never worked so hard in her life. I couldn't wait to start earning. My twenty pence pocket money wasn't stretching far, although Aunty Ellen's Easter money boosted my savings up to £12-00.

After packing this afternoon, Mum gave me my first dress fitting, showing me how I could pull the sleeves down to be off-the-shoulder. Now I just needed platform sandals.

This evening Dad told me to close my eyes and put out my hands. When I opened my eyes I saw these dinky mini pointe shoes, which he suggested I tied to the iron rail of my bed-head to bring me good luck.

PART THREE

SUMMER TERM

CHAPTER THIRTY-NINE

SUNDAY 6TH MAY

Back to school today! Mum had got me loads of tuck, a year's supply of hair spray, pins and enough cotton wool for an army. She'd also got me a medicine bottle full of witch-hazel and rose water and some Dab-it-Off to clean my point shoes. I had remembered my mini-pointe shoes Dad had given me for good luck.

Dad took me up to the dorm and I noticed that there were parents who I hadn't seen before, who must have been there with the new girls. Dad left my case inside the dorm and hugged me at the entrance door.

"What's up?" he asked.

I gave him one of my biggest smiles.

"Sorry Dad - I hate saying goodbye. I'm fine, really."

Just at that moment someone yelled my name, making us jump. Dad looked up and glanced back into the dorm, then back at me.

"Hey, you've got to get ready for a big school show this term. I'm coming to see a ballet for the first time in my life and only because you're in it, so I'll be expecting a good performance." He gave me a gentle nudge and I nudged him back.

He kissed me on the cheek and turned to leave.

Tearing back up to the dorm, I pushed past the crowd of parents and ran to the far end towards my bottom bunk. As I reached my corner I stopped dead in my tracks. *It had all changed!* No candy striped bed sheets or army travel blanket and worst of all, no March Hare! I felt a wave of panic then realised that Millie was standing the other side of her bed.

"Millie" I gabbled, trying not to sound hysterical, "where's my bed stuff?"

She widened her eyes at me and beckoned me closer to her.

"Nanny's decided the youngest new girl's having your bed and I've got to look after her!"

I was flabbergasted.

"But that's my bed. She can't just move my things."

Then someone yelled from the far end of the dorm.

"Lara, over here. We've been moved together!"

I looked up and saw Janice waving and grinning. I marched towards the beds where Janice was sitting. There was a bed made up with my candy striped sheets and my army blanket folded across the end. March Hare was perched upright against the bed-head rails, looking startled. I took a deep breath and forced a smile towards Janice, but my stomach was knotted and I felt agitated. Janice chattered away as we toured the dorm checking out everyone's new bed positions. Fortunately Mika and Maddy were directly opposite me beside the mirrors and when they arrived I relaxed as we chatted about the new dorm arrangements, and soon it felt like we'd never been away.

When everyone was gossiping I noticed Gabby was one bed down from mine beside Janice. Esme revealed Hannah had been moved into Little Dorm with Karlyn to share with Sydney and Tiffany, so hopefully no more Hannah/Esme arguments. Abbey, the twins and two older juniors had been moved up to the main house. When the new girls' parents left Nanny came into the dorm and clapped her hands to get our attention.

"Welcome back, Girls!" She walked into the centre of the dorm, folding her arms as she prepared for an announcement.

Hamish whimpered and he let out a small 'yelp' before beginning his own patrol of trotting up and down the dorm, sniffing all the beds and their new owners. Nanny cleared her throat before continuing.

"I hope you've enjoyed your holiday and feel refreshed for the summer term. We have some new faces to welcome to our Junior Dorm family." She cast her eyes towards the new girls.

"So let me introduce you."

The five new girls looked nervous when Nanny said their names and gestured towards them, particularly the small girl standing next to Millie who now had my old bed. Nanny said she hoped we'd make them feel at home, particularly nine-year-old Tija. She had clouds of golden hair and looked so timid I wondered if, like Millie, she'd get homesick being so young. Secretly I was grateful I wasn't sharing her bunk - I'd spent half of my first term with sleepless nights consoling Millie.

After supper I went over to Mika's bed and our old crowd - minus Abbey and Hannah - gathered to catch up on our holidays.

Millie: Said Tobago was hot. She was officially a member of her Dad's dive team, showing us a certificate to prove it. How cool was that! She spent Easter cruising round Tobago on her Dad's boat, taking photographs and helping him study marine wildlife and was thinking of becoming a marine biologist.

Mika: Spent most of the holidays at her local karate club with her brother and took her first karate exam. I was deeply impressed - this might be useful for future BLAP expeditions. Mika reminded me you couldn't karate chop ghosts as it would go straight through them.

Maddy: Had her first holiday at home with her Nan in residence. Her Nan was enjoying a close friendship with an imaginary gardener. Every morning her Nan wandered down the garden with a pot of tea and a glass of whiskey, which she said she shared with him.

Gabby: Confessed she knew about BLAP, but hadn't told us because she thought we didn't want her to join us. No wonder she felt awful. She'd spent all holiday wondering how to tell us. Gabby also told us she was so scared she'd turn into her mother that she'd given up chocolate for Lent, and no more cakes, biscuits, crisps and fizzy drinks for the summer. This would be challenging with Burt's stodgy food and constant tuck sales to tempt her.

Sanchia: Said she was glad Gabby had confessed to knowing about BLAP, because she knew as well! Spain was scorching and she'd missed her friends.

Esme: Said she'd tried to phone me but my Mum had told her I was staying at Abbey's house. After her dig at me, she rattled on about spending most of her time with the boy next door, Stephan, who was fourteen. She said he fancied her but she wasn't interested. She'd been on a real safari and watched some lions kill a zebra and learned to drive her father's jeep. I was very envious - about the jeep - not the dead zebra.

Me: I said I'd enjoyed staying at Abbey's and been to a disco. Esme pulled a face of disapproval so I changed tack and talked about the musical *Oliver*. I showed them the painting Lily had bought me in the Paris flea market, adding "it's very bohemian". Esme frowned when I said this.

At that moment Nanny saved the day as she breezed in to turn lights out and we had to get into bed. Although it felt strange without Abbey, I told Janice I was glad I was sleeping next to her. Janice agreed and said she'd also been dreading Nanny putting someone like Hannah next to her. Not many girls liked Hannah, but I would miss her and the fun she created. She was raving bonkers, but somehow made life in Junior Dorm more exciting and unpredictable.

CHAPTER FORTY

Nanny was on top form today, hustling the new girls into action. The best part of this morning, apart from seeing Kerri, was watching the new girls' faces when Nanny came into the dorm armed with a laundry basket of freshly laundered pinnies. I could barely contain my giggles when she showed them the blue bibs, and couldn't believe it when Gloria marched into the middle of the dorm and, pointing at the pinnies, said, "Nanny, I don't understand why we have to wear aprons?"

Nanny hesitated. New girls didn't usually have opinions, but she quickly recovered and raised an eyebrow.

"Why do *you* think, young madam?"

Gloria went red and shrugged.

With a wicked gleam in her eye Nanny distributed the bibs.

"Juniors have been wearing aprons for as long as there have been juniors at this school. They save having to wash your uniforms every day."

Finally the mass of pinny-clad juniors were released and raced towards the main house for breakfast. Hannah had crept up on me from behind and without warning jumped onto me for a piggyback. Unprepared, my legs buckled and I nearly fell face downwards. She gabbled in my ear about how cool it was sharing Little Dorm with Sydney and Tiffany and I was the only girl in Junior Dorm she'd miss. I wasn't sure if this was good news, when out of the corner of my eye I spotted Esme hanging around in the background ear-wigging and for a millisecond I wished Hannah would find someone else to miss.

Our first breakfast felt like we'd never been away. Burt was as miserable as ever and one side of his glasses was covered with a big strip of plaster. Mika asked him what had happened and he got *really* tetchy saying he'd got a cata-something in his eye. This cata-thingy was bad news and I imagined what might end up in our food with his limited vision.

Abbey came over to see us at our junior breakfast table. She said Tweenies couldn't sit with juniors so she'd catch up with us in school break. She was in a dorm called 'Archway', and wanted us to visit later but warned they were surrounded by prefects' rooms.

On the way back to the dorm, I saw Kerri getting out of her Dad's car and raced to catch her up. She gave me a cool T-Rex poster which I intended to pin on my bedside locker. My new bed was right under a window so I didn't have any wall to stick posters on.

Assembly was really exciting today. All the dance teachers attended and there were announcements about events during the summer term. There was more talk about the lead-up to the summer show, the rehearsals and hard work involved, and lectures about dedication and integrity being the motto of our school. Mr Deluca stood up and announced a zero tolerance policy for girls caught flouting school rules. The school had also decided everyone had to take an IQ Test and our parents would be informed.

During this announcement I made the mistake of turning around to sneak a look at the prefects standing at the back. I instantly recognised Mercedes and Cimmie who caught my eye, giving me her Glare of Death. A chill ran along my spine and I swiftly turned my back to her, feeling her eyes burning into the back of my head.

Before assembly finished everyone sung the school song and some teachers wept. Awkward! I noticed Mr Mainwaring pass Miss Knox his large white handkerchief. Then our line seemed to sway to one side and there was a loud thump. I looked down our line and saw that Tamsin had fainted. Some things never change.

After lunch we had a Form period and guess what? Mr Mainwaring was now our English teacher. Yippee! He told us we would be studying English Grammar, and have the opportunity to enrol for Latin lessons.

He recommended we concentrated hard on school work this term, because the teachers were making final decisions about the new streaming system next term. Prep Form girls (us) would be assessed on this year's work and in the autumn would be placed in 'A' or 'B' stream. Sydney asked what that meant. Mainwairing glanced at Tiffany and said that the 'A' stream was for girls who consistently performed with good grades, showed aptitude and were above average intelligence. HELP! The only person fitting this description was Oracle. Goodbye to daydreams in double maths - I didn't want to be in 2B next term!

Getting ready for ballet this afternoon, I decided I was going to wear my new ankle-length calf warmers. Knitted in hot-pink wool, they had millions of black sparkly flecks running through the ribbing. Now the whole dorm wanted a pair.

I had a genius idea to make some money to fund my future travels. I'd ask Mum if she or Mrs Furst could knit me some ankle warmers in assorted cool colours, we'd decide a selling price (to pay for the wool and labour) and I could take a cut of the profits for selling them. Mainwaring would call this 'showing initiative'. I was working on the 'aptitude' bit.

Before ballet today Miss Wanda flattened my genius business idea, informing me I couldn't possibly wear non-regulation leg warmers for R.A.D ballet. I could wear them *to* class but not *during* class because they were far too distracting.

Ballet was a killer today. So were the laggy briefs after not wearing them for ages. Miss Wanda was a slave driver and gave us so many jumps we dripped with sweat. We were pathetically unfit.

Miss Wanda got all hot under the collar and, slamming her hand down on the top of the piano, demanded we confess who *had* actually practised. Everyone put up their hands. I didn't think it was the right answer. She gave us her 'that does it' look and set us non-stop jumping steps until the windows were completely steamed up.

Fortunately she was calmer for our modern and we learned the new Grade Two set warm-up exercise. She showed us the new Jazz routine, set to music from the TV series *Hawaii Five-O*, and flew around leaping, shimmying and shaking. At the end she jumped high into the air, split her legs sideways and, with multiple shoulder shimmys, landed in a lunging position with her head on her knees. We all cheered and clapped.

That night in the bathroom Hannah collared me and told me Little Dorm was great because she wasn't subjected to constant Osmonds' music. She was backstabbing Esme, but I'd gain nothing becoming her enemy. I told her I liked T-Rex and she babbled on about the London pubs she'd visited with her sister.

"Ever heard of Thin Lizzy?"

"I like their recent single".

"What's it called?"

"I think it's 'Whiskey in a Jar'."

Hannah looked astonished and said my musical tastes were radical!

WEDNESDAY 9TH MAY

It was Janice's twelfth birthday today. Last night I made a card with a big yellow smiley face on the front, with a pin-man body wearing a tutu and doing an ultra-high kick. Gloria had drawn a brilliant card using special colouring pencils. I watched her drawing it last night. She had a tin of crayons with 'Caran D'Ache' written across the front. Gloria called them water colour crayons which, when dipped in water, painted like watercolours. She was the best artist I'd ever seen.

Kerri brought Janice's present into class during first lesson. Just as we were handing over Janice's present Miss Knox arrived for history with Mr Mainwaring hot on her heels heaving a heavy box. He leaned over to rest the box on Miss Knox's desk. At the same moment she leaned forward to put down her pile of books and Mainwaring's nose hit Miss Knox's cleavage. She gasped and they both collapsed into laughter. Mainwaring had to remove his spectacles as tears streamed down his face! It was sooo embarrassing.

During this commotion, Janice tried to hide her present, but it caught Miss Knox's attention. She stopped laughing and asked Janice what she was hiding underneath her desk. I had a horrid feeling she was going to flip. Instead, she smiled when Janice said it was her birthday and told her birthdays were special occasions and should be celebrated in style. Mainwaring was still dabbing his eyes with his handkerchief and looked completely exhausted. Miss Knox asked Janice to unwrap her present and suggested we sung Happy Birthday. She was in a *very* good mood. She walked behind Janice and started singing 'Happy Birthday', the sound of her high soprano voice filling the classroom. Mainwaring squared his shoulders and joined in, his deep bass voice booming out. There was something rousing about the teachers singing in our tiny classroom, and we all joined them, singing like it was the last song we would ever sing.

Kerri and I were talking to Abbey after lunch today. She said their lights weren't turned out until 9pm, but if they were caught talking or out of bed after that they were given punishments.

Abbey could now take the bus into town every Saturday. I couldn't wait until I was a Tweenie.

That night, playing monopoly with Maddy, Mika and Esme, Dulcie Fielding started crying. I didn't know her well, even though she'd started last autumn because she'd slept on the far side of the dorm. I sat next to her and asked what was wrong, which made her cry even more. It turned out she'd just received a letter from her Dad, saying they might be moving to Long Island in America soon. She'd lived in their London house all her life. We got out an Atlas and pinpointed Long Island. I called the girls over and Dulcie produced photos of her Dad beside an amazing aircraft and he looked at least six feet tall. She joined us playing Monopoly and it was nice getting to know the other girls in the dorm. Dulcie did box splits and had unbelievable insteps. Some girls have all the luck.

THURSDAY 10TH MAY

I slept like a log and dreamt the Blue Lady threw herself off the balcony and plunged to her death in the lake. I wondered what *really* happened to her.

Earlier Esme had presented me with an unusual bookmark from Kenya, hand made by a local tribeswoman especially for me. She said she'd missed me loads and I was her best-best friend EVER! She made me feel uncomfortable about doing anything that didn't involve her, but she didn't exactly live down the road. She couldn't have been that lonely with Stephan's company and going on safaris. I knew which one sounded more exciting to me.

CHAPTER FORTY-ONE

FRIDAY 11TH MAY

Kerri had a genius idea today, solving the 'waking before midnight' dilemma without an alarm. Her brother had told her if you banged your head on the pillow before you went to sleep for the same number of times as the hour you wished to wake up at, then you would automatically wake up at that time. Something to do with the messages you sent your brain.

During ballet Miss Wanda made us practise these weird 'step-ball-changes' from corner to corner, travelling in circles and leaning backwards, hijacking our tap class to teach us even more steps. She informed us we had several 'potential' dances to learn before deciding which was best, producing photos of well-built dancers wearing red costumes and head-dresses like donuts. How depressing.

"Time is ticking girls. We're learning a Ukrainian dance and this weekend I want you to practise these steps and develop a broad, strong style. Imagine your body is rolling as you move."

She demonstrated and it looked hilarious, but no one dared laugh.

"Next week, we'll practise floor patterns. With character dances the style and feel of the movements are vital."

She demonstrated how we should look 'in character', capturing the 'leaning back' and 'keeping the steps low into the ground'. Making us copy her she declared some of us had "captured the spirit of the Ukrainian peasant." I nearly died when she picked on me to demonstrate and said "Bravo!" Out of the corner of my eye I caught Esme giving me a really sour look. I'd be in for it later.

SATURDAY 12TH MAY

My prediction was correct. I got the silent treatment from Esme last night, so I ignored her today and wrote to Joseph so she could see I had better things to do than get sucked into her petty games.

I walked to the shop with Dulcie today and discovered she was great fun. She told me all about her home in London where they had a butler and a cook. She was dreading moving to America because home would be far away. I said she could come home with me anytime and mentioned that my parents might end up living in Jersey. I wondered why Mum and Dad hadn't mentioned it for a while.

At 5 p.m. I made my way over to main house and waited in the library for Abbey, who arrived at 5-15 p.m. having only just got the bus back from town. Heading up to her dorm she said there were way more rules in main house, and every Saturday they had roll call at 8 p.m. to ensure no-one stayed late in town. She jabbered away as we climbed the steep spiral stairs. Looking back down made me dizzy and I grabbed the hand rail, fighting an urge to launch myself over the edge. Abbey then led me along a dark corridor and past several prefects' rooms.

Inside Abbey's dorm were three bunks, with one single bed squashed into the far corner of the room under a tiny round window. The walls had posters of rock bands and Marc Bolan. Abbey saw me sniffing and said they burned joss sticks after lights out because the room smelled mouldy. Her bunk had this amazing leopard print blanket covering the bed, and the ceiling beams were carved with graffiti like 'Escape from Colditz' and 'I hate prefects.'

We shared a Curly Wurly and Abbey showed me a trap door beside the single bed. When opened there was a gap between the top rung and the first step of the fire-escape ladder. Abbey said they'd tried it and counted eighteen steps. I couldn't make out what was below. Abbey shone her torch down saying it was the kitchen pantry, but before we'd got a better look we heard a loud clattering and Abbey quickly closed the trap door.

"It's Burt's office. Inside there's a hidden supply larder."

"Amazing. Does that mean you can raid the larder?"

Abbey looked at me with a 'don't be daft' look.

"It's Burt's turf, remember, the eyes and ears of the school? Duh!"

She bashed her hand against her forehead as she said this and we both laughed at the ridiculous thought. Abbey glanced at her watch.

"Oh crikey, I must get you out of here before tea bell goes off."

We crept past the prefects' doors and down the long staircase.

As we neared the bottom stairs the tea bell vibrated and girls sprinted towards us from all directions. A narrow escape!

CHAPTER FORTY-TWO

At breakfast a crowd had gathered around the notice board and I was shocked when I read the notice that Vis Day was cancelled. The notice simply said:

Following a late Easter, the decision has been made to cancel the normal Visiting Day this month. A letter has been sent to all parents. The summer show commences in nine weeks and therefore we have limited time available for theatre rehearsals.

Half Term Dates:

Start: Friday 25th May after 6 p.m.

Return: Monday 28th May between 6-7 p.m.

I was disappointed but couldn't wait to start learning all the show dances.

Before Sunday lunch today, I made Esme a paper crane, wrapping it in coloured tissue paper. Patsy visited me while I was doing this, hobbling into our dorm and exposing the worst skinned toes I'd ever seen. She said Miss Brookes went crazy with her posé turns, making her stay behind after class until she got them perfect. Now her toes were too raw for surgical spirits. I asked Esme if Patsy could use her Zambak. Esme said in Kenya they used it for everything from cuts to snake bites.

I felt sorry for Patsy not enjoying ballet and wondered how many dancing jobs there actually were for girls who eventually decided ballet wasn't for them.

That evening after dorm duty, Hannah bulldozed into our dorm with Tiffany and Sydney and pulled the tables back, instructing us to practise the Russian Dance. It was Nanny's night off and Ginnifer helped us practise the steps. Ginnifer was a new prefect who Sydney confirmed was American and 'a real pussy cat'. I wasn't convinced. During practice everyone looked really absurd, staggering around imitating plump peasants. Hannah and Sydney stuffed pillows down their pyjama bottoms and soon created a riot. Ginnifer watched but was clearly not amused. Bored by our juvenile behaviour she rolled her eyes, turned her back on us and shut herself in Nanny's room, turning the telly up to full volume. Left to our own devices everyone went crazy and we ended up in a mass pillow fight! No one noticed Ginnifer leave Nanny's room. Concealed behind the door she watched disapprovingly as the dorm filled with feathers. Suddenly a loud whistle blew and everyone dropped their pillows, the air thick with feathers. Someone spluttered as Ginnifer strode through the dorm entrance sending more feathers into the air. Placing her hands on her hips (classic prefect intimidation), she drew an elongated breath and we waited.

"Whoooo started... THIS?" She waved towards the airborne feathers. Silence. A solitary feather landed on her nose and her eyes widened like a crazed horse as she puffed to dislodge it, spluttering, "I'm giving you one minute."

More silence. She tapped her foot. Finally she couldn't contain herself.

"Okay then - have it your way. Clean this mess up RIGHT NOW, and I'm giving you until next Saturday to write me a list of TEN GOOD REASONS why you shouldn't upset me when I'm on duty. If anyone forgets, just remember Mr Deluca would love to hear about this behaviour."

Warming to her tirade, she continued.

"You pip-squeaks better get real busy. I want your best handwriting, no biros - proper pen and ink - on your best writing paper without spelling mistakes, understood?"

She strode out barking, "Clean this garbage up," but not before skidding through the doorway, dislodging feathers upward as she hurtled through the entrance. The door to Nanny's room banged behind her.

Sydney cautiously checked Nanny's door was shut and returned looking peeved. "Ginnifer's no pussy cat."

We began picking up feathers - what Mum would call a 'thankless task'. Ginnifer eventually stomped back in and made us go to bed without supper. It was past ten o'clock, but we were starving. I bet she kept our supper so the greedy prefects could gorge it later.

MONDAY 14TH MAY

I gave Esme her birthday gift before breakfast. She loved my paper crane, saying it reminded her of pelicans on Lake Naivasha. At last I'd got something right.

During breakfast Burt brought the prettiest cake ever to our table. It had 'Happy Birthday Esme' written on the cake in gold icing and an edible ballerina in a gold tutu balanced on top. Esme asked Burt to keep it in the fridge until tea time and Burt said only if he could eat the ballerina. Creepy.

We had Mr Mainwaring all morning. He informed us he'd had such a poor response to his Latin classes that he was abandoning the idea. I will practise Egg instead.

At tea, just before Esme was lifted into the air to be given twelve bumps she yelled her knee was injured. Pulling down a leg-warmer she revealed a knee support and warned the girls not to throw her too high. What a crafty one. She escaped with a few gentle lifts and then fed the whole school with her cake - it was ginormous.

Esme won Monopoly tonight and Nanny gave her a box of Jelly Fruits. We had five days left to invent 'ten reasons' for Ginnifer.

I thought of my first stupid reason to start my list.

I must not upset Ginnifer while she is on duty by joining in pillow fights: she might be allergic to feathers.

This was going to be fun.

WEDNESDAY 16TH MAY

I got a letter today from my Swiss pen-pal Elsa. Her parents were hoping to visit Grandpa in Dorset and she wanted to meet me if they visited London. She wrote such brilliant English I felt ashamed I didn't speak better French. My spoken French had been reduced to basic baby words like "Je m'appelle Lara, j'ai onze ans" by Madame Nuffer, who treated prep-former's like five year olds. Unfortunately I *had* started learning these words when I was five. I will ask Esme to practise with me - at least she speaks French like an adult. With all the travelling I will be doing in the future I must speak at least one other language.

This evening, Millie reminded me that the following day was a *full moon*. I'd almost forgotten. That gave me number two reason on Ginnifer's list.

I must not upset Ginnifer while she is on duty because it might give her bad dreams.

Fat chance.

I was talking to the girls about our stupid punishment earlier. We agreed the prefects must have a really good laugh at our expense. Janice said her brother went to a boys' boarding school, and a prefect made him warm the toilet seat for him on winter mornings. Gross!

THURSDAY 17TH MAY

Full Moon. I reminded all BLAP members, including newbies Gabby and Sanchia, to keep their eyes and ears open for apparitions.

After tea we walked via the lake but it didn't seem spooky. In fact, without a chill in the air it was hard to imagine the shrouded cloak of our resident ghost rising eerily out of the calm water. However, we caught a rare glimpse of the glowing eyes of Roxanna, Mr Julius's otherworldly cat, as she crouched hidden in the undergrowth, watching us walk past.

When Nanny came to turn our lights out, Hamish was ferreting around our beds and sniffing anything he could stick his nose into. Nanny shouted at him and eventually shut him in her room. I wondered if animals could sense a supernatural presence.

I decided to bang my head on my pillow eleven times before I went to sleep. If Kerri's brother had his facts right, I'd wake up at 11 p.m! I was determined to see the Blue Lady. Surely after all my efforts to connect with her - not to mention lakeside vigils - she would feel she could trust me and at the very least show herself in some shape or form.

FRIDAY 18TH MAY

I was furious with myself this morning. I'd missed the full moon and to add insult to injury, Nanny had to shake me awake from my coma-like sleep. Infuriating! Perhaps banging my head eleven times on the pillow produced a knock-out effect instead.

I managed to swap notes with team BLAP and no one heard so much as a squeak last night. I laid the blame squarely on Sydney and Tiffany's wretched séance upsetting the natural rhythm of paranormal appearances.

SATURDAY 19TH MAY

During ballet this morning all the teachers watched our Ukrainian dance. I secretly hoped it would be thrown out so that we might learn something less embarrassing for the summer show.

Our walk to the shop this afternoon was cancelled because all the prefects were in rehearsals. Nanny offered to take us for a walk, which would have been fun but it started raining, so we were stuck inside the dorm but I did manage to finish my ten reasons punishment list - the deadline was tea-time. Hannah collected them and announced we ought to read them out loud, 'we' meaning Hannah, of course! The reasons everyone had conjured up ranged from the ridiculous to the totally insane. Gabby's was best:

"I must not upset Ginnifer while she's on duty because she might want to return to America and we'd be very sad".

We fell about laughing! Hannah press-ganged her into writing out fresh reasons, saying if Ginnifer read these we'd be writing punishment lists for the rest of the term. Under pressure Gabby caved in and I realised Hannah had gained her reputation by being outrageously bossy.

Before queuing for tea I phoned home and Mum seemed excited because she'd almost finished my garden party dress, saying she'd need me for one final fitting. I told her about the cancelled Vis Day and the earlier Half Term, but Mum seemed pleased because Aunty Ellen wanted to take us girls to the Royal Ballet again. Mum said she and Mrs Furst had knitted me five more pairs of calf-warmers. Help - I'd forgotten to tell her we couldn't wear jazzy ones for syllabus classes. I didn't say anything, still hoping I'd sell them. If I wanted to travel I'd have to boost my savings and start thinking with an 'A' stream mind.

MONDAY 21ST MAY

At breakfast there was another notice on the board.

'Juniors to attend Miss Brookes' studio: 4 p.m. sharp. Please bring character shoes and skirts'.

GRIM! Even though I didn't like the Russian Dance, I wanted to perform well. I prayed I wouldn't forget the steps in front of Miss Brookes.

Just before 4 p.m. we waited outside Miss Brookes's studio, eager to be called in for her to judge our Russian Dance.

After a boring wait, we eventually got to perform and all through the dance she drummed her long, red fingernails on the arms of her wooden chair. She was popeyed when we finished, as though she couldn't believe what she'd seen. She turned towards Miss Wanda.

"Meredith, daahling, what exactly *are* the girls supposed to be doing?"

"They're Russian peasants, Miss Brookes, performing a traditional dance in the village square."

"What's wrong with their backs?" She pointed to Gabby. "She looks like she's about to fall backwards. It looks awkward."

Miss Wanda looked aghast and began defending herself whilst we stifled titters.

"This is the accurate dance style for that region and the locals are meant to look stout."

Neither spoke for ages and we stared at our feet until Miss Brookes lit a cigarette and took several puffs.

"I'm afraid I don't like it," she said, shaking her head vigorously.

"Perhaps watching it again will help!" Miss Wanda pleaded with her.

"Meredith, we need to talk."

So off they went for a chat and ten minutes later Miss Wanda returned alone with a face like thunder. "That's it for now, girls, you can go."

She stormed out and slammed the door, then opened it again, her head peering round the corner.

"By the way, the Russian Dance has been cancelled."

The door slammed again. Miss Brookes obviously wasn't happy with the dance but I liked to think we'd done our best.

At tea we had Ravioli. These were inedible parcels of tomato coloured cement floating in salty tomato sauce. The dining room was out of control. I could just about see over the ceiling of dinner plates which were held in the air and shrieks from girls quizzing food were so loud I couldn't hear myself think. During the commotion I spotted Mrs Balmaine hover around the entrance notice board and pin something up, so I began to weave my way through the crowd. Unfortunately someone else had the same idea and, before I'd made it halfway across the hall, there was a stampede towards the notice board. I'd read about Lemmings doing this, except they stampede en masse then fall over the edge of a cliff to their deaths.

After being half-squashed, I spied Hannah. True to form she was slyly elbowing her way forwards, so I joined forces and grabbed the back of her apron, quickly reaching the notice board. There were several casting lists for new dances in the show. With my heart thumping I was relieved to see my name on at least one of them for a dance called 'Blue Suede Shoes'. Scanning the other names it included all of our Grade Two modern class. I was thrilled. Sydney said it was definitely a Rock and Roll number. We'd soon find out - our first rehearsal was after school tomorrow. Yippee!

CHAPTER FORTY-THREE

TUESDAY 22ND MAY

Today was our first rehearsal for 'Blue Suede Shoes'. Mrs Balmaine was choreographing the dance and I loved it! She wanted us to practise over the half term break so I wrote down all the new dance moves so I didn't forget them. These were:

Leap Frogs in a circle. I'm a 'leaper'.

Backward Hitch-Kicks. Back to back with partner, link elbows and partner pulls you over their back as you scissor your legs towards the ceiling.

Jump Lift and Swing-Slide-Through. Face partner, who holds either side of your waist and helps lift you as you jump upwards. As you come down partner swings you straight through their legs.

Cartwheel Legs. Leaning backwards (like hitch-kicks) roll across your partner's back with stretched legs kicking outwards in a half-circle, cartwheel action, hitting a side split mid-movement.

Hitch-Kicks were terrifying. Tiffany was my partner for one practise lift and had to bend her knees before we locked elbows. When she bent forwards Tiffany pulled me over with such force I narrowly escaped crashing onto the floor on my back! Then Hannah partnered me and I did land flat on my back. Rehearsal ended in chaos.

FRIDAY 25TH MAY

I had a restless night's sleep. The dorm was airless, sticky and hot. I was sure I could hear the sound of men's voices drifting up to the dorm from the open windows at around 1 a.m. this morning. The window behind my bed was wide open and the voices were calling out girls' names. I got up quietly to look out of the window, but in my drowsy state nearly overbalanced on top of Tamsin's bed. If I'd collapsed on top of her she'd have woken up - fainted with fright - and Nanny would have come in and thought I was trying to talk to prowlers. I wished Abbey was here - she always knew what to do. In desperation I woke Janice and, straining our ears, we heard a car engine revving. Janice crawled to the window at the far end of the dorm and peered beneath the curtain. She returned gabbling about an old banger filled with men, which was stopping and starting as it travelled down the main drive. I wondered why none of our male staff or man-eating dogs had come to chase them away. What was the matter with them? And, more to the point, where were all the prefects? If we had a major prowler invasion we'd all be doomed, with no one to save us as we slept in our beds.

Janice and I decided that after half term we'd take evasive action in order to prevent this happening. Our male staff, guard dogs and prefects were hopeless and suffering from severe early deafness! All I'm saying is this: how can a car load of prowlers lurk around our grounds in the dead of night and remain unnoticed? Clearly school security was non-existent and we'd have to take matters into our own hands - I already had an idea.

I couldn't wait for the long weekend and to see my family. After half term it was going to get crazy here for more than one reason, I could feel it in my bones...

Meanwhile more lists went up on the notice board. I had to attend a new rehearsal for 'The Magical Toyshop'. Six juniors had to attend: me, Janice, Kerri, Esme, Tamsin and Gloria the new girl.

As I walked back to the dorm after tea, I spotted Dad reading a newspaper in the car outside Junior Dorm. I was so pleased to see him. When he got out of the car and hugged me I could smell his Old Spice, and I thought how much I missed my parents. I raced up to the dorm to say goodbye to my friends. Esme was just leaving with 'THE AUNT AND UNCLE'. I went over to give her a hug and she grabbed my arm, took me to one side and whispered, "I really wish I was coming home with you today."

Feeling horrible, I promised her faithfully she could come home on the next Vis Day, and she made me swear I wouldn't break my promise.

I slumped into the car beside Dad and relaxed my head back. I was going home at last.

CHAPTER FORTY-FOUR

SUMMER HALF TERM

SATURDAY 26 TH MAY

Mum had to wake Lily and me up early, reminding us we were driving to London this morning. I'd forgotten we were going to see Giselle with Aunty Ellen.

Mum gave me a final fitting for my Open Day dress for the summer garden party. I put it on and felt very elegant. She'd also bought me some cool platform sandals which made me look taller.

The drive to Granny's house was clammy and when we got to Aunty's we had a rush to catch the train. During our journey Aunty Ellen told us the story of Giselle.

"Giselle is a demanding role not only because it requires a strong technique, but the ballerina must possess strong dramatic abilities. The ballet is based on the title..."

"Giselle!" I blurted out enthusiastically. Everyone sitting in the carriage stared at me and I felt my face redden.

"That's right, dear," Aunty continued, "and Giselle is a young German peasant who's madly in love with Loys, the local peasant boy who happens to live in the cottage opposite. The story revolves around a love which cannot be."

"Like Romeo and Juliet?" Lily chimed in.

"Not quite. You see, Loys is not who he says he is and, unknown to Giselle, is already betrothed to another. Poor Giselle's life ends tragically when she loses her mind and dies of a broken heart."

"Is that it?"

I imagined it was more complicated. Aunty smiled.

"No. Loys had concealed his identity to Giselle but is really a Duke called Albrecht. After Giselle dies, he keeps a vigil by her grave at night. There is an evil ghost who is Queen of the Wilis (female ghosts) called Myrtha. Myrtha compels ghosts of young girls to drive young men to their deaths in the lake. She orders the Wilis to capture Albrecht and force him to dance to his death. However, the ghost of Giselle protects Albrecht and she dances with him until dawn. When the sun rises, the Queen's power is gone and Albrecht is saved by Giselle"

I spent the rest of the journey thinking what a coincidence we were about to see a ballet with ghosts *and* a lake. Perhaps it was an omen. By the time we got off the train I was *convinced* there *had* to be a Blue Lady at our school.

Inside the Opera House I got butterflies walking up the red-carpeted stairway towards our box. Aunty Ellen let me sit right at the front of the box so no-one's head blocked my view and I watched the stalls filling up below. Finally the lights went down.

The ballet was beautiful and in Act II the ballerinas seemed to simply float and it felt quite spooky. Wearing brilliant white, long romantic tutus, the Wilis were so convincing I felt the hairs on my arms stand up on end. Hopefully our lake didn't have a Myrtha for Burt's sake.

When the curtain went down the audience stood and there was deafening applause. Someone in the balconies shouted "encore" and Giselle was presented with a massive bouquet. I clapped until my palms stung. People in the stalls hurled single roses and I wondered if Giselle's face ached from smiling, like mine did in my modern exam.

Back on the train I told Lily about the Wilis reminding me of our lady ghost at school. Mum and Aunty raised their eyebrows. Lily said ghosts didn't exist, so I didn't bother to tell her about the spirit in the loo.

We arrived home after midnight and just before I got into bed, my evening was ruined when I spotted the largest spider in the world on my eiderdown. Lily was in the loo and I couldn't yell because my brothers were asleep, and if I took my eyes off it it might hide. Trembling, I spotted my Princess Tina magazine, rolled it into a tube and lunged towards the spider, swiping it hard. I missed and spent the next hour trying to find it. Exhausting!

MONDAY 28TH MAY

It was roasting hot again. Lily and I sat outside in the shade.

I'd started reading *The Adventures of Tom Sawyer*, because I knew Mr Mainwaring would ask me about it. Tom was clever and resourceful like Hannah with her devious tricks and thinking on her feet. She managed to persuade us to get involved with things we'd never have dreamt of doing.

Sitting reading I hadn't realised my legs had got sunburnt. Mum smothered me in calamine, reminding me ballerinas couldn't have suntans.

Lily recorded most of her singles onto cassettes so I'd have some different music to take back to school. Sadly, Esme was the sole owner of the only tape recorder in the whole dorm, Karlyn and her ghetto blaster having moved into little dorm. We'd been tortured with non-stop Osmond music on a daily basis. It was the biggest source of dorm arguments.

All my school stuff was packed. Mum had also filled a crate with fifteen giant-size, empty Maxwell House jars with lids for my school 'project'.

The coffee jars were part of our master plan to bring down the pesky intruders.

My plan so far was that we ran a cobweb of 'trip wires' across the tangled undergrowth close by our dorm. We would thread string through holes pierced in the metal lids of the coffee jars, and then create a cobweb network of lethal trip wires. The bottom of the coffee jars would be filled with small stones and pebbles, and then the suspended jars would dangle from the strings, concealed from view by the long grass. When the prowlers emerged from the woods they'd make their way towards the dorms tripping on the network of wires, which would make the coffee jars rattle, alerting us to the presence of intruders. At which point the intruder alarms could be raised and the lethargic staff might swing into action.

CHAPTER FORTY- FIVE

BACK TO SCHOOL

TUESDAY 29TH MAY

This afternoon I told Lily about OPA (Operation Prowler Attack) and her face lit up.

"It's a genius plan with one exception. The trip wires must be positioned at head height."

I ran this through my mind and visualised headless victims. URGH!

"Too messy! We want them left alive."

"Good point! Better alive with their heads left on!"

Later on, Mum drove me back to school because Dad was working late in London. She agreed to Esme coming home next visiting weekend so that's good news for me to tell Esme. I thanked Mum for making my gorgeous dress and for the platform sandals.

Mum asked if I'd like a cake for my birthday in June and said Dad would arrange the delivery. I couldn't believe my twelfth birthday was coming up soon, and I had to find a way of avoiding the bumps from hell.

When we arrived at school it looked deserted. For a second Mum thought we'd arrived a day early. As we approached

Junior Dorm we spotted one solitary black car parked close by, which looked like an American stretch limousine. Mum raised an eyebrow at me.

"I think some important people are visiting.

A tall man in a dark suit got out of the car. He opened the passenger door and out jumped Dulcie Fielding. The man reminded me of Clark Gable. Dulcie waved frantically in my direction and ran towards us. The man followed, introduced himself to Mum (he was Dulcie's Dad) and asked if he could carry my suitcase to help her. He told Mum this would be the last time he'd be driving Dulcie back to school, because his job was taking his family over to Long Island in New York. He ruffled Dulcie's hair as she leaned against him. Mum was so kind and said if Dulcie wanted to she could come home with us on visiting weekends. Dulcie's face lit up and she nodded in agreement. Yippee, I now had two friends to take home. Dulcie and I raced up to the dorm, leaving Mum and Dulcie's Dad to follow.

Before Mum left I gave her a big hug and told her I loved her.

"Enjoy yourself and work hard, because we're all coming to see the summer show." She leant out of the window just before driving off and pressed something into my hand. "Keep it safe and be careful with those coffee jars."

As she drove off I waved. Suddenly tears welled up and I grappled to maintain control. Bringing my hand towards my mouth I discovered a five pound note clenched in my hand. A loud yell interrupted my thoughts.

"Hey, Lara, tea bells just gone, come on."

Dulcie was sprinting towards me.

"I'll race you there!"

Later, back in the dorm, Nanny took a roll call. When she returned to her room we gathered round Mika's bed to compare news.

Millie: Spent three days with her Aunty and was making decisions about her career. Training in marine biology would mean leaving ballet school. I didn't want Millie to leave - we'd been through a lot together, and who else would keep an eye on the lunar charts *and* remind me about the Blue Lady appearing - or not.

Mika: Had passed her first karate exam and demonstrated some blows called knee and elbow strikes, and crazy looking moves called 'Knife Hands'. I was fascinated.

Maddy: Wanted to spend the summer holidays abroad and asked if Sanchia or Millie wanted a paying guest for eight weeks. Her Nan was driving her parents' nuts and she needed a break from home.

Gabby: Spent three days in a state of paranoia. On the night before we broke up for half term, she'd overheard Janice and I plotting and men's voices. The stress made her overeat and she'd put on weight again. She asked that anyone catching her scoffing tuck made her pay a penny into the fine box. I donated a Maxwell house fine jar, punching a hole in the lid. Gabby had zero willpower.

Sanchia: Agreed Maddy could stay with her in Spain for the summer. She said she got bored in the holidays and would love company.

Esme: Said she hated her Aunt and Uncle, and staying three days with them was the equivalent of a life sentence. Her Uncle snored, constantly farted and belched. Maddy and Mika started giggling and Esme got stroppy.

"This isn't a laughing matter!"

She ran her hand across her forehead dramatically.

"My only glimmer of hope whilst I endured this hell," she paused, "was receiving daily phone calls from my boyfriend Stephan in Kenya."

We were gobsmacked and Esme looked triumphant.

"He has finally declared he's madly in love with me."

"Where does he live?" Maddy asked.

"Nearby. He says that he lives only to hear my voice."

No one believed her, but no-one was stupid enough to tell her, otherwise we would have been in for a night of ear-bashing.

Me: I told everyone about Giselle and the spooky similarities between the Lake and the Wilis, who I explained were the ghosts of dead girls compelled to dance young men to their deaths.

Esme declared that the link with our ghost was undeniable, revealing a deeply disturbing connection between the Blue Lady's downfall and the hospital turning into a ballet school. Everyone agreed and nodded seriously. Only a fool would cross the Oracle on such matters.

Last but not least, I discussed Operation Prowler Attack. Everyone wanted to play a part. It was code named OPA.

Janice: Was now one of our gang and it made sense, because she was at least half responsible for the prowler attack plan. She'd even volunteered to do the undercover dirty work. I suspected Janice was more cunning than Hannah.

I told Nanny that my unusual cargo of empty coffee jars was for collecting insects. At the mention of insects she forbade them in the dormitory forcing me to store the jar-filled box by the boot-rack downstairs. How convenient!

It was Dulcie's birthday today. Fortunately I was well prepared, having remembered to keep a box of Maltesers hidden inside my tuck box in the event of surprise birthdays. As usual everyone had forgotten and I ended up letting them share my present and card. The bonus was I made a small profit by suggesting that everyone contributed 25 pence. I was actively practising 'A' stream thinking: 22 girls multiplied by 25 pence per girl = £5-50p. Cost of box of choccys = £2-50p, a profit of £3-00!

We rehearsed Blue Suede Shoes today but during half term everyone had forgotten how to do the lifts and holds properly! It was crazy fast and we were all breathless by the end. Later, as we stood in the tea queue I watched Gabby examining her belly. She claimed she'd lost the equivalent of a jammy donut from her waistline! Life here would be quite dull without her.

Dulcie was caught by Hannah trying to sneak out the back entrance of the hall after tea. Hannah let out a blood curdling yell like a Red-Indian about to scalp a victim and in seconds the whole school had descended on her, grabbing her arms and legs and tossing her skyward thirteen times. Dulcie was a good sport and I admired her bravery. Afterwards she confessed to me that it was a hateful experience and by the fifth toss she'd nearly thrown-up, though I suspect Burt's pukey faggots and beans hadn't helped.

After tea I did my usual limbering practice. I was pleased to get the *whole way down* in both left and right front-leg splits, and flatten the outsides of my thighs on the floor in the flat-turned-out frog position. It still kills my legs.

I'd just started writing a letter to Alexandra telling her about rehearsals so far, and was able to tell her about my visit to the

Opera House to see Giselle. I knew she'd danced this role herself, so she might like to hear what I thought of it. I didn't mention about the similarities to our school ghost and the lake or she might have thought I was a ghost stalker.

THURSDAY 31ST MAY

We had a really dramatic day today. It all started at breakfast.

Burt was in an unbelievably narky mood, slopping milk everywhere and practically throwing our cereal bowls at us. A rumour was going around that Radish had had a massive argument with Nancy. Something about Nancy serving hot toast unbuttered so it didn't arrive cold and soggy. Nancy had thrown a wobbly, saying she'd been here all her life and wasn't going to be told what to do by an assistant half her age. She threatened to hang up her aprons and said it was her or Radish. Radish had walked! This was a disaster. Recently the food had been enjoyable because Radish had cooked most of our meals. We'd now lost our only ally and Burt the Spy was back in control. We were doomed.

Throughout today a petition was passed around the classrooms and dorms. By tea-time the whole school had gathered together in an organised protest outside the canteen. The students stacked tables at the main hall entrance and standing on the table tops chanted in loud voices "Bring back Radish!"

Before long Burt appeared in the dining-hall entrance to see what all the noise was about. Confronted with masses of yelling girls his face went from crimson to deep purple. His eyes flicked crazily around the room as he took in the army of protesting girls. He managed to choke out, "Well, I'll be damned! That's flippin' gratitude for you!" and with spittle streaked across his cheek he roared, "Right - that's it!"

In a fit of fury he grabbed his chef's hat, hurling it towards us like a missile. Enraged, he spun round and walked smack into the canteen door and everyone erupted into laughter. He stamped off cursing.

Immediately he left, Warrior Troll and her gang of heavies arrived. After some brutal arm-wrestling with the banners and the usual shoving and threatening, order was restored. Warrior Troll stood on a chair in the centre of the hall with her legs astride, fists clenched on her hips and shoulders rounded.

"Be warned!" she shrieked as her piggy eyes boggled at us and her head appeared to be sitting on top of her shoulders. "If any one of you pathetic dummies so much as sniffs, breathes, or attempts another stunt like this," she paused, "the whole school will be gated from the final Visiting Day. Got it?"

The whole school went silent, shrinking under her hypnotic stare. I'm convinced she's the leader of an alien invasion!

CHAPTER FORTY-SIX

FRIDAY 1ST JUNE

At breakfast today Burt was back in the canteen serving food as though yesterday had never happened. When I changed my mind from one to two Weetabix, he said, "Kippers and custard for you tomorrow, young lady," and gave me his toothless smile. He was wearing new glasses so he could see what he was doing. Nancy was there - looking very perky - in a new position standing beside Burt pouring out milk, bossing him around and clucking like a mother hen. Radish was at the far end of the canteen serving us proper tea and incredibly delicious *hot, unbuttered* toast served with individual butter portions. Everyone was calm. Maybe they'd had an overnight pay rise!

There was a new notice on the main board with rehearsal times for 'The Magical Toyshop'. Lists of names followed with my group at 5 p.m. I was curious what we'd be doing.

The day whizzed by. During double geography Mr Mainwaring hinted that IQ tests were starting next week. I had to talk to Janice about OPA before another prowler invasion happened. We must be prepared...

At 5 p.m. six of us waited outside the studio door, listening to loud thumping noises. Esme said it sounded like drumming and knowing Esme she was probably right. Finally Miss Olsen called us in and explained.

"This dance is about a fantasy world of toys, which come alive at midnight after the toymaker has shut his shop up. Just before dawn they must return to the shelves before they become toys again."

It sounded exciting and I prayed this would be my chance to shine. My hopes were dashed when she continued.

"The six of you are going to be porcelain figurines, dressed as elegant ladies and gentlemen of the 18th century. The figurines - you girls - will be positioned on the top of a musical box. Whenever the box is wound up, the music will begin and you'll rise up onto your tip-toes, turn, curtsy or bow," she demonstrated some of these moves, "then glide around on top of the musical box with your partner."

It was not what I had pictured.

First we had to listen to the music, which sounded exactly as I'd imagined. I could see us dressed in satin ball gowns whilst twirling like a merry-go-round on top of the musical box. The downside was three girls had to be boys and the fairest way to decide was by height. Uh-oh! Standing back-to-back Gloria, Tamsin and I were chosen to be boys and she partnered me with Kerri. We practised until 6-30 p.m. perfecting elegant bowing, curtsying and dainty turns. Apparently we'll be wearing heavy powdered wigs which mustn't fall off, and dancing at the back of the stage on a raked rostrum.

We had lots to think about and I was looking forward to the challenge.

Before lights out OPA gathered on Maddy's bed, discussing when Janice should conceal the jars in the undergrowth. I mentioned to Esme, "Mum said you can definitely come home with me this Vis Day."

I took this opportunity to say Dulcie was invited too but she didn't seem to mind.

SATURDAY 2ND JUNE

Things were really taking off with preparations for the summer show in July. Starting today, we no longer had to walk to the store on Saturday afternoons if we had rehearsals. After breakfast I checked the notice board for morning rehearsals, and was disappointed there were none, which meant that the shop trek was on.

Then I spotted that another notice had gone up which had two columns of names. I read each name closely and the blurb at the bottom, then my heart raced. A Masterclass was being held on the 14th June - my birthday - and the guest teacher was Alexandra Haydon! I could hardly believe my eyes and read it twice, but soon realised juniors weren't included. I was gutted. My heroine was teaching a Masterclass and if I couldn't join in I wouldn't meet her. Fate was cruel.

After breakfast I was gazing out of the dorm window feeling sorry for myself when I spotted Kerri's Dad's car drive past. I quickly raced over to the day girls' changing room to confide in my best friend. I poured out my tale of woe to Kerri. She suggested that I hung around outside the studio where the Masterclass was being taught so when Alexandra eventually emerged from teaching her class, I could stroll past and introduce myself. I didn't tell Kerri but I didn't have the confidence for this and felt miserable for the rest of the day. In the evening I was feeling particularly pathetic when Patsy appeared in the dorm. All sweaty from rehearsals, she stormed into the dorm like a tornado and belly-flopped on my bed. She made me feel better saying it was an advanced pointe work Masterclass, and produced two Walnut Whips from her pocket.

As we devoured our chocolate, I told Patsy about the dances I was in for the show. Patsy reassured me that when she was a junior she performed in one dance as one of twenty rats. We hooted with laughter when she showed me her 'rat' dance on her hands and knees!

I swore her to secrecy then revealed our OPA plan. She clapped saying it was audacious (I'd no idea what that was) but warned me to enlist some inside help - her friends - to avoid trouble with the prefects. She said she'd find out on the grapevine when the prowlers were most likely to make their next appearance. I didn't know how she intended to find out, all I knew was this. She was a gem.

TUESDAY 5TH JUNE

Lots of strangers visited school today and were given a tour around the school grounds by some students. Abbey said they were holding auditions this week for new girls. Mum had mentioned that assessors from the RAD might be visiting school anytime before end of term. From now on, if I spotted visitors being shown round and they came in to my ballet classes, I would have to do better than my best because they weren't going to advertise who they were. I couldn't imagine Miss Wanda saying "Girls, we have visitors from the Royal Academy, sent to consider whether you're still worth spending all this money on." The thought was unsettling. Dad said Miss Brookes was pleased with my progress, so I knew I was on the right track, but felt uneasy.

During last lesson today, Mr Mainwaring gave us a lecture about lateral thinking and then rambled on about logical thinking. It might have been my imagination, but when he said logical thinking he looked straight at me. Maybe I was getting paranoid.

Just before the school bell rang, he announced Prep form's time-rota for tomorrow's IQ tests. So that was what this 'logic' thing was about.

Mrs Balmaine was delighted during 'Blue Suede Shoes' rehearsal because we did our lifts perfectly. She told us she was going to choose a first and second cast, explaining that two casts gave everyone a chance to rest and to dance, like ballerinas having an understudy. It sounded a good idea until Esme told me first cast were better dancers, so on important nights they always performed. Mrs Balmaine said she'd try to be fair and we could cast swap for performances our parents had booked tickets for. This was followed by an awkward silence which Hannah broke.

"What about Press evening?"

"What about it, Hannah?" Mrs Balmaine looked irritated.

"Can we dance on Press night if we're in second cast?"

"This is not pick-and-mix! I was pointing out in difficult circumstances I'm prepared to compromise."

She read out two cast lists and I held my breath. Luckily I was in first cast with Kerri, Abbey, Mika, Maddy, Sanchia and Esme. Altogether there were sixteen.

Mrs Balmaine then announced eight girls from the first cast would have to double up as the second cast because there weren't enough girls. Gabby had been chosen for second cast alongside most of the younger girls. To make it seem worse all my friends were in both casts. Gabby looked crushed. With the casting performance over, everyone busied themselves practising.

Later we had some heated discussions. Unsurprisingly, Oracle had the last word.

"First cast has always danced on Wednesday, Thursday and Friday evening plus Saturday matinee and evening. There are six days of shows so the second cast gets to do two evenings"

"Sounds like second cast are just the rubbish cast" Gabby bleated.

"I don't make the rules. Generally it's Monday and Tuesday evening and Wednesday and Friday Matinee."

"So which day do Press attend?"

Hannah intervened. "They always watch Thursday evening and Miss Brookes uses our best dancers because the show gets national coverage".

Everyone then chimed in giving their opinions and I understood how strongly everyone felt.

After lights out I laid awake for some while, thinking about today and writing my thoughts in my journal to help me clear my head. My torch had new batteries and I hoped the light wouldn't attract Nanny's attention. I've realised that to be a successful dancer you needed to be thick skinned. Like Patsy said to me ages ago, it was a tough business and I'd got to toughen up to survive.

WEDNESDAY 6TH JUNE

Last night I dreamt I was demonstrating juggling oranges for the IQ Professor. I mentioned my dream to Janice who said it wasn't a co-ordination test.

Everyone was nervous at 9 a.m. when Shirley went in to be tested. Tiffany went in next and said it was good fun. It was hard to judge whether she was joking or not. I was dying to ask her questions and whispered under my breath, "What sort of questions did you get?"

"Easy, there was a problem-solving one, where there were lots of oranges..."

Oooh! I felt like there was a jinx on me. Or could Tiffany have overheard my conversation this morning with Janice?

I needn't have worried. The gentleman testing us stood up as soon as I walked in the room and, with a friendly smile, he leaned forward and shook my hand. His name was Professor Rytokoski. He asked me about my hobbies and when I'd relaxed, as though he'd read my mind, he explained the purpose of IQ testing and to enjoy the questions which were quite logical, so I imagined I was having a chat with Mr Mainwaring.

During the test, there was a question about bags of fruit; but when he mentioned oranges my brain went into meltdown. Seconds passed during which I sat rigidly in the chair with a frozen expression, feeling like an utter moron. He broke the agonising silence by repeating the question and on the word 'oranges' my brain froze again. DUH! Luckily for me he smiled kindly, moving quickly to the next question. Apart from a curious problem with questions involving oranges, I felt I'd answered the questions logically. Fingers crossed.

Not everyone felt the same way. Abbey came out in floods of tears, Kerri said the questions were confusing and Mika said she'd got so muddled the Professor had to repeat everything.

I felt better until Esme came out beaming, declaring the questions easy peasy. That evening as we waited in the tea queue, Kerri and I practised movements we'd learnt during 'Toyshop' rehearsal. I was enjoying being a boy. We got to travel around the rostrum doing 'manly gestures' like bowing and forming arches with our arms for the girls to duck underneath. We also had to twirl the girls around, either holding one of their hands above their head whilst spinning them around, or turning them whilst holding onto their waists with two hands. This hold gave us more leverage to propel our partners like spinning tops. Tamsin admitted she was relieved being a boy, because all that twirling would definitely make her faint.

CHAPTER FORTY-SEVEN

SATURDAY 9TH JUNE

At breakfast I received a big parcel from Mum. When I opened it Sydney spotted the contents, yelled, "come and look at her awesome legwarmers" and in seconds half the girls in the dining room had swarmed around me looking at the multi-coloured, sparkly leg warmers. Everybody wanted to buy a pair but I'd only got twelve sets. Luckily Patsy appeared, took control and said she'd organise selling them and who wanted to buy them. She whispered, "Hey kiddo - you're in business!"

After ballet Nanny told us to prepare for a dorm inspection, and made us empty everything from our lockers onto our beds. Warrior Troll arrived later with her cronies in tow and she sucked up to Nanny like a leech. As we stood beside our beds they rifled through our belongings for hidden tuck, and shook March Hare so violently it made me cringe. His stuffed legs went all floppy and I was about to rescue him when Nanny intervened.

"That's enough. Put that toy down!"

She snatched poor March Hare out of harm's way. Cimmie's nostrils flared and she snorted. Nanny got up close to her face and said, "Is there any further trouble you wish to cause?"

Nanny glared at Cimmie.

365

"Then it's clear you've no further business here. Kindly leave so my girls can tidy all this..." she made a sweeping gesture at our belongings, "wreckage you've made."

Cimmie stamped towards the door and eyeballed Hannah.

"This isn't finished!"

She stormed out followed by her cronies and we waited silently until the downstairs door slammed shut. Nanny smiled and heaved a sigh of relief.

"Well, I don't think that baggage will be back for some time. Let's try and tidy up before lunch bell goes."

I could have hugged her for standing up to Cimmie. She had real guts.

After lunch Hannah suggested we got Nanny flowers and volunteered to get them.

'Toyshop' rehearsals went well. Miss Olsen wanted to see the whole cast on stage to plan the opening scene. Gina was dancing the lead part as the princess from the fairy castle that wakes up first, then with her magic wand travels around the toyshop touching each of us in turn to wake us up. I could already imagine all the toys coming to life and dancing.

Unluckily for us, our group of six elegant ladies and gentlemen could only move round and round their little rostrum atop the music box. Miss Olsen said we'd have a spotlight on our group and no one else would be dancing when we danced. This sounded okay but Esme had been whinging ever since. I escaped to my bed to write my diary and avoid more ear bashing.

During church service today I thought over how I could manage avoiding the bumps on my birthday, but I've decided if Dulcie can brave it, then so can I.

Back in the dorm Hannah produced some beautiful roses she'd hidden under her blazer.

"Freshly cut for Nanny."

We all gasped.

"Where did you get them?" Esme demanded.

Hannah smirked.

"You didn't steal them, did you?" Gloria butted in.

"So what!" she snapped.

Tiffany cleared her throat.

"It doesn't matter. No one's going to grass on Hannah, right?"

Everyone agreed. We tied the roses using ribbon from Gabby's Italian christening blanket and left them on Nanny's bed with a notelet signed from us all, then went to main house for Sunday lunch. Radish had cooked pork with a separate tray of crackling cut into squares. Ear piercing screams of "Eggo" echoed around the hall as unwanted crackling was claimed. Who'd want to eat fat – it's so disgusting!

Patsy came to wait with me as we queued for seconds of pudding. She said eating fat was barbarian. Puddings were different, particularly seconds of shortbread with strawberry custard. As we neared the canteen, Patsy whispered, "How much d'you want for each pair of leg warmers?"

"£1-50 pence?"

"Peanuts! I've got thirty names and said prices start at £2".

"Wow. Will they pay that much?" I was doubtful.

"They're the latest fashion *and* they're unique." She winked at me, adding, "You have to create a demand. If you sell 'em cheap they'll think they're rubbish!"

Patsy said she'd collect their money that afternoon and collect the legwarmers from me at supper.

"Deal!" We shook hands.

This evening, Nanny came into the dorm and thanked us for the roses. She had tears in her eyes and said she was very proud of us. Weirdly, I suddenly felt like crying.

Patsy came round later in the evening before we had supper and we exchanged legwarmers for cash. I gave Patsy first choice of legwarmers and she chose the funky-striped ones. She wanted to pay me but I refused. Patsy shook my hand, saying 'Good job.'

When she'd gone I counted my money. I had £22-00. Excellent! I gave it to Nanny for safe keeping.

MONDAY 11TH JUNE

Today Miss Knox hinted that some decisions had been made about next term. So, the dreaded 'A' and 'B' streams had been decided. We tried to press Miss Knox for clues but she remained tight-lipped. It was *sooo* annoying.

'Toyshop' rehearsals were a shambles. Esme stepped on Tamsin's toe and Tamsin swore at her, which was such a shock we forgot our steps. Miss Olsen got lairy and said Esme was like a bull in a china shop and then Esme went into a proper royal strop. With Visiting Sunday soon and Dulcie coming home, it would be really embarrassing if Esme got stroppy. Perhaps her periods had started, which would explain her moods. It would be nice to have someone else in Junior Dorm who had monthlies. The elite club of mature girls currently consisted of Sydney, Tiffany and me.

WEDNESDAY 13TH JUNE

Time was really flying past. When not in the classroom, we spend our every waking moment rehearsing 'Blue Suede Shoes' and 'Toyshop'.

   After rehearsals, Kerri and I went to the kitchen to pick up my birthday cake sent by Mum and Dad. Burt emerged carrying a huge box. He said I must give it to Nanny until tomorrow. We peaked inside when Burt wasn't looking. It was amazing, covered in thick dark chocolate with silver stars sprinkled over it and a ballerina in a silver tutu standing in arabesque in the middle.

   I was sooo excited about tomorrow. My cake would feed the whole school. I received masses of post at tea and on the back of each envelope was 'OPEN 14th JUNE!'

   Just before lights out this evening, Janice called me to her bedside and showed me the huge collection of small stones she'd been secretly collecting to fill the bottoms of the coffee jars. We sneaked downstairs to where the jars were stored and put some stones into the jars - our first test run. They rattled beautifully when suspended by the string threaded through the holes in the lids. Now we had to put the plan into action.

CHAPTER FORTY-EIGHT

THURSDAY 14TH JUNE

This morning Gabby woke me singing Happy Birthday in my ear. Junior dorm gave me a massive card full of crazy drawings. I opened my family cards (everyone gave me money) and Aunty Phyllis's parcel marked 'Handle with Care'. On top of the present was a postcard of the Pyramids. Everyone watched me turn the card over and read aloud Aunty's message, "For my Great Niece on your Twelfth Birthday. No time to post card during trip to Egypt. The enclosed is a gift from Alexandria - it's reputed to ward off evil spirits. With fondest love, Aunty Phyllis xxx."

  Everyone gasped at the 'evil spirits' bit! Inside the box lay a glistening gold bracelet that snaked around a bright yellow-gold charm which looked like a very large golden eye. I held it up so everyone could see and a slip of paper fell from the box. Picking it up I read out 'The Eye of Horus. An Egyptian Sky God in the form of a Falcon'. I examined the glistening eye with curiosity and we agreed if any poltergeists were lurking from Sydney's séance, my Eye of Horus Falcon would send it packing.

During breakfast Patsy gave me a present, a book called *The Hound of the Baskervilles* by Arthur Conan Doyle. When I pulled a scary face Patsy said,

"It's a ghost story set on Dartmoor. With ancestors from Dartmoor and your fascination with ghosts, you'll love it."

"That's brilliant, thanks Patsy."

The rest of the day was great. Kerri bought me an amazing signed Marc Bolan poster and a photographic ballet book.

After school I was in the dorm waiting for ballet. Show rehearsals were postponed for the Masterclasses, so I lay on my bed looking at a photo of a male dancer. He was hovering in the air in a grand jeté and looked unbelievable. Nanny came over to my bed.

"I've got a message from Miss Brookes. She's requested you go to her studio immediately."

My heart leapt.

"What for?" I wondered what I'd done wrong.

"I have no idea. I just received an urgent message for you to visit her studio. She mentioned someone wanting to meet you."

It seemed the eyes of the dorm were on me and I started frantically brushing my hair until Nanny took my hand gently.

"I don't think she'll want to wait, run along now."

I raced down the dorm stairs and ran to Miss Brookes's studio with my heart banging like a drum. As I approached the door I could hear piano music, so I peered around the door and saw Miss Brookes sitting on her throne, surrounded by a halo of smoke. She spotted me, beckoned me over and I tiptoed so my Blakey's didn't clack. I could see Alexandra correcting a student's hand position, but felt everyone's eyes watching me as they practised. I curtsied to Miss Brookes when I reached her and felt myself shaking like a leaf. Leaning forward she grabbed my hand and drawing me towards her face said,

"Edgecombe. Alexandra has made a special request to meet you today."

"Yes, Miss Brookes. Thank you, Miss Brookes." Cringe. Why couldn't I just say, "Thank you. I'm so pleased to meet her because we've been writing to each other for ages."

I felt desperately awkward. The piano had stopped playing and when Alexandra approached me I wished I was in my dance kit with my hair in a bun, not dressed in uniform and clumpy lace-up shoes.

Everything went quiet when Alexandra stood in front of me. She was beautiful and flashed me the biggest smile with flawless teeth.

"Lara, how lovely to meet you at last," she said, leaning forward and giving me a peck on the cheek.

"I was disappointed you wouldn't be in my class, so I asked Miss Brookes if she'd arrange a meeting so we could at least say hello."

I managed to reply in a trembling voice.

"It's lovely to meet you, Alexandra. Thank you for seeing me."

Smiling, she gestured to the students, who were leaning against the barre gawping at me.

"I'd better get back to teaching before the girls get cold."

She reached underneath the grand piano then presented me with a parcel.

"A little bird told me it's your special day!"

I blushed but kept my eyes fixed on Alexandra, curtsied and said, "Thank you very much. It's been lovely meeting you."

She beamed. Miss Brookes waved her long red fingernails at Eunice then banged her glass down, slopping juice everywhere.

"Music, Eunice!"

Alexandra turned her attentions to teaching and I stood alone. Miss Brookes was watching me, so I bobbed into a curtsy, gave my biggest smile and bolted as fast as I could on skidding Blakey's.

The dorm was empty when I got back with everyone in ballet. I opened Alexandra's parcel and inside was a well-worn pointe shoe. Written on the sole was; 'Good Luck Lara 14-6-1973' and Alexandra's signature.

Nanny came in and I showed her my gift. She said I was lucky, and if I wanted to remain lucky I'd better get to ballet and explain why I was late. I hid my pointe shoe under my pillow, beside Horus for security.

I was very late because barre work was over. I approached Miss Wanda and started to explain, but she just got irritated saying she already knew. Teachers are so crabby.

During tea, conscious of the approaching torture I lost my nerve. Grabbing my tray I tried to slink outside, and almost made it when Hannah spotted me and a manic expression crossed her face. Bile rose in my throat as she screamed "HAPPY BIRTHDAY!" at the top of her lungs. In seconds hands were upon me. Resisting was pointless. As everyone hollered the Happy Birthday chorus, my mind glazed over and I underwent the human caber tossing ceremony.

I know. I'm a big baby, but it was truly terrifying. The ceiling came towards me and was sucked away as I hit the crowds thirteen miserable times (one for luck). I got poked in the eye twice, and I thought I'd lost my knickers. Someone tried to rip my leg off but I fought back. Finally I was plonked onto the hard floor to shrieks of "Hip-hip hurray". I lay comatose as they chanted, "For she's a jolly good fellow". Finally the crowds dispersed and a familiar face loomed over me.

"Hey kiddo. You're still alive!"

I moaned. It was Patsy and I was surprised to find that not only had I survived, but I could breathe, had both legs *and* my knickers. Back in the dorm I cut my cake under a bombardment of questions. Everyone wanted advice on what to write to a famous person. I was secretly chuffed I'd become a role model for advice about something unusual.

FRIDAY 15TH JUNE

Patsy heard on the school grapevine about a possible night time visit from prowlers. They might be coming to see girls living in the outbuildings near Junior Dorm tomorrow night. Apparently a fifth year called Cleo Harper had been encouraging them to visit her in the early hours while everyone slept! I called an emergency meeting with OPA to set our plans into action without delay. We only had one day to do this.

Before ballet I was battling with my minute laggy briefs when Millie collared me. She said Nanny had shrunk them all and hers were even smaller. I managed to get them on but they barely covered my bottom. I spotted Maddy lying face-up on her bed, struggling frantically to pull the briefs past her thighs. Gabby had us all creased up in stitches, parading down the middle of the dorm with them stuck around her knees, doing a model walk with her hips thrust forward.

During the elastic knicker drama, Millie revealed it would be a full moon that night. She said we'd stir up bad vibes with the Blue Lady if we messed around with prowler traps on the one night she reserved for her haunting. I'd clean forgotten about the full moon. I assured Millie I wouldn't go out after dusk as I fully respected the Blue Lady's time schedule and haunting grounds. I mentioned the only person disturbing the Blue Lady these days would be Mr Julius and Sultan. Unfortunately for the Blue lady, our Jesus look-alike had taken to patrolling the grounds on clear summer nights with trusty horse dog in tow.

I spent ballet class and 'Toyshop' rehearsals thinking of how to get our Maxwell House jar-traps set in position - all before dusk and supper. When rehearsals finished and just before we left the studio under our dorm, luck was with us. Nanny swept out of the building in a hurry reminding us we'd be late for tea. Our moment had arrived and it was well before dusk.

We watched Nanny hurry along the covered way and vanish. Then Janice, Esme, Kerri and I charged up to the dorm, grabbed torches, the bag of stones and string and carried out our mission. With Kerri on board we made quick work of filling the jars. We threaded the string through the holes in the tin lids and, making sure no one saw us, we crept through the dense undergrowth. Janice tied scraps of red wool to the dead branches laid strategically across the potholes - which were deep enough to engulf at least one man's leg! These shifty intruders wouldn't stand a chance. Getting the string to just the right tension was trickier. When the jars were all suspended and secure Janice acted out a stage fall, walking straight into the trip wire. It was very realistic. She did a manly walk towards the wire and in a split-second made contact with it and went down like a fly. We collapsed in hysterics. The willowy grass provided the perfect cover. I could barely contain myself. This was more exciting than watching Steve McGarrett and Danno in a car-chase episode of *Hawaii Five-O*. Eat you're heart out, Danno!

SATURDAY 16TH JUNE

Last night I lay propped up on my pillow until way past midnight, hoping the Blue Lady might grace the dorm with her presence, but not a dickie-bird. I wished our dear resident ghost appreciated that my unwavering belief in her existence was being severely tested due to her lack of appearances.

During our walk to the shop I was thinking about my Eye of Horus charm. This was only a maybe, but perhaps by banishing evil spirits Horus was actually keeping *all* the spirits at bay. No wonder the Blue Lady kept her distance. That must have been it – I'd thrown the spirit world into turmoil. My Eye of Horus would have to stay hidden during the nights of the full moon, particularly if we were ever to stand a chance of glimpsing the elusive Blue Lady.

Rehearsal music was now booming out twenty four hours a day. I could sometimes hear music after lights out. Everyone was involved in rehearsals, apart from those involved in dangerous liaisons - like Cleo Harper.

Patsy visited me before lights out, warning us to keep our heads down. We'd got to stay awake and be vigilant. Our school needed us!

CHAPTER FORTY-NINE

It happened! At 2 o'clock this morning the prowlers arrived. I was startled awake by a loud rattling noise, sat bolt upright and turned to see Janice sitting bolt upright too. Gabby crawled under Tamsin's bed to join us, and standing on my pillow I leant over the window sill and drew back the corner of the curtain. Opening the window a crack we heard men's voices. Janice crept across the dorm and woke up Mika, Esme and Maddy. We pinned our noses against the windows, hypnotised by the drama unfolding in our school grounds.

"Look," Maddy pointed at the shapes below, "It's Sultan and Max!"

The hairy hounds emerged from the darkness and came bounding across the undergrowth towards the men, howling like wolves. The men ran in the direction of the woods, but there was an almighty scream as one fell down a hole, followed by angry voices and swearing. Max and Sultan had separated and we could hear Mr Julius's voice shouting.

"See them off, Sultan!"

Sultan appeared and leapt through the undergrowth towards the men still standing, who turned tail and bolted for cover. Sultan followed in hot pursuit like the Hound of the

Baskervilles. It was like watching an adventure movie on telly. The man who'd fallen over stood up as Max approached him, head down in that wolf-about-to-pounce stalking position. The man grabbed a large stick, roared and waved it at Max. Max whined and scampered in the opposite direction! Then he limped into the undergrowth and escaped into the eerie woods.

We clutched each other wondering what might happen next, when the grounds were flooded with torch lights and mobs of prefects. With their dressing gowns billowing in the night breeze they brandished fire extinguishers and swung welly boots like weapons. Then we spotted Cimmie striding down the drive, wearing a black cape and skull cap and wielding her black umbrella above her head like a sword. Mika said she looked like a ninja warrior!

Then there was a sharp 'click' noise and our world of darkness was bathed in eye shrivelling light.

"Girls!" Nanny's voice was sharp. "What do you think you're doing, hanging out of the windows at two o'clock in the morning in your nightdresses?"

We muttered lame excuses. Nanny stomped over to my bed, slammed the window shut and stood back folding her arms. She looked oddly amused.

"Very well," her lips stretched into a tight smile, "you may find this prowler-chasing lark entertaining. However, *some of us* would like to get a decent night's sleep. I suggest you try the same thing. Get into your beds and goodnight." She marched out, flicking the light switch off.

I could hear her wedging the dorm door then her own door open. I couldn't sleep for ages afterwards but with the door open didn't dare talk. Our trap had actually worked.

At breakfast Patsy confirmed the police caught two prowlers loitering outside the school grounds and one had injuries!

After church today, I spotted Burt and Radish lugging ladders around outside our dorm. Curious, I asked Radish what they were doing. He said Mr Deluca had ordered security lights to be fitted on all out-buildings. Finally someone had done something sensible. I wondered how this might affect the Blue Lady's haunting pattern. She might alter her route if the grounds were too illuminated when she floated past. I mentioned this to Esme who looked exasperated and gave me her pitying look.

"For heaven's sakes, Lara, she's a ghost!"

"But when she floats past the security lights someone might see her shadow," I bleated.

Esme stuck her neck out and moved her mouth slowly and deliberately.

"She's i-n-v-i-s-i-b-l-e, you idiot, so it won't make any difference."

Sometimes Esme was difficult to like.

MONDAY 18TH JUNE

Kerri, Mika, Janice, Maddy and I had our costumes fitted today. The costume-making room was tiny, squeezed into the space under the roof rafters and was stifling. Two old ladies, Mrs Savage and Mrs Driscoll, were hard at work bent over their sewing machines. Mrs Savage looked like a man wearing a lady's wig and her glasses reflected the bare ceiling bulbs. I tried not to stare at her whilst she pinned the rock and roll costumes onto us. The material was snazzy and the dresses had puffed sleeves and full petticoats underneath satin skirts with matching knickers. My dress was orange, teamed with white

379

pumps, bobby socks and we have to wear wigs. Mrs Balmaine arrived at the fitting and said the wigs were perfect because they were thick. We could slip them on easily and the elastic would grip around the hairline. My wig was strawberry blonde and shoulder length with a cute fringe. We were given wig brushes and shown how to secure, brush and store them. I couldn't wait for my 'Toyshop' costume fitting.

WEDNESDAY 20TH JUNE

While everyone was at tea and there was still a bit of light left, Janice and Gabby finally rescued the jars. Yesterday evening team OPA had a secret meeting in the bathroom and agreed that with new security lights it was too risky after dark. Esme and I managed to Eggo six sausage rolls and smuggled them out under our cardigans which now reeked of pastry and pork. Back in the dorm, Gabby and Janice were soaked and muddy. Janice said a big boot was stuck inside one of the potholes. The jars were returned safely to their boxes.

Patsy came round before supper and demonstrated some of her show dances and I couldn't wait until I got to do all the stuff she did. I told her we'd got the jam-jars back and she said we shouldn't have bothered because we'd done the school a favour. I told her Nanny knew the jars were mine so I had to get rid of evidence at the crime scene. She laughed, promising to smuggle the jars outside to the dustbins immediately after she left the dorm. Patsy's my hero!

THURSDAY 21ST JUNE

This afternoon 'Toyshop' costumes were fitted. Mrs Savage fitted all three of us for men's suits. We wore grey high-waist trousers, a white shirt with ruffling at the chest and a long tailed jacket over the shirt. The white powdered wigs were like something from an 18th century film and we looked unrecognizable. Bending our knees to avoid the rafters we stood admiring our 'man' costumes in the long mirror. Gloria said she'd always been told she looked like a man, so her look was complete.

I was now resigned to the fact that with the wigs and stage make-up we'd be identical clones of each other. Mrs Driscoll drew around our feet for the leather shoes being specially made. Mrs Savage asked if we were renting or buying our costumes, and when she said it was twice the price to buy I chose renting.

SATURDAY 23RD JUNE

There were no rehearsals today and I took the opportunity to have a chat with Esme on the way to the shop. I bought a giant bottle of cream soda for us to share and two bags of Jelly Babies. When I gave her the bag of Jelly Babies I plucked up courage and asked her why she was behaving so moodily the whole time, adding quickly that it was just because she seemed to get so angry at everyone for no reason. I had touched a sore spot and she started crying, saying that her parents might have to move back to England for good. I felt sad for her because I knew how much she loved living in Kenya, so I quickly tried to think of all the good reasons why living in England could be better. I told her it wasn't so bad living here, that she could see all of us during the holidays and her parents on Vis Days AND never have to stay with her Aunt and Uncle again, but she was inconsolable. With tears pouring down her cheeks she clutched my hand and blew her nose hard on my Dad's hanky I had given her. She then sniffed and solemnly said, "If my family leave Kenya, three very bad things will happen"

"Like?"

"Well," she stifled a ragged sob, "First, we will have to leave our dog behind. Second, I will have to abandon my first and only true love – Stephan. And third, I will have to live in Wales, where it never rains but it pours." She took a deep breath and looked serious as she continued, "Lara, fate has intervened and dealt me a cruel blow. What will become of us all? My life as I know it is coming to an end!"

She was sooo dramatic. I understood her not wanting to leave her dog but I had to be brutally honest with her about Stephan. After all, every man might not be as long suffering as my dashing hero Rhett Butler. "Listen, I know I am not an expert on love," at this she raised an eyebrow so I battled on, "but if, as you claim, it really is true love, then true love always waits."

Her eyes widened like saucers and to my amazement she nodded in agreement. Boosted by this I felt confident enough to continue.

"And the Kenyan sunshine may be heaps better than Welsh rain, but in Wales you will always have water."

This was obviously not what she thought I was going to say but, miraculously, it made her laugh.

Later that evening I suggested we all got together and played a game of Monopoly. Esme's mood brightened even more at the mention of a game, and she even suggested us playing Scrabble as an alternative (she always won so there was no point). We ended up compromising by playing a fast moving card game of Rummy, followed by a game of Sevens. No prizes for guessing who won.

CHAPTER FIFTY

HOME FOR A DAY ~ WITH TWO FRIENDS

Dulcie, Esme and I were ready and waiting for Dad at 8-45 a.m.
this morning. I was so excited that my friends were coming
home and I hoped we would all have a brilliant day together.

When Dad arrived he got out of the car and gave each of us a
hug and said he and Mum had a big surprise for us.

Back home Lily had cooked us brunch. We were going out for
the day and Mum said we needed proper food to keep us
going.

It was hot and we sat outside in the back garden. Eight of us
squashed around two card tables under the shade of the trees.
As we ate, Esme kept everyone entertained with her impossibly
scary stories of LIFE IN THE KENYAN JUNGLE. She told
amazing tales of camping in tents at night out in the bush. She
said if you lay awake you could see the light from the camp
fires cast shadows of the lions on the canvas tent walls. She
added that it was rumoured a man had once been dragged
from his tent at night because he'd left meat inside the tent and
one thing led to another! Everyone gasped in astonishment.

Encouraged by her audience, Esme went the whole hog, telling stories of the bloodthirsty hyenas, man-eating snakes, and crocodiles dragging grown men to the bottom of the river and drowning them in a death roll. The most unsettling story was about the flying orange cockroaches. The mere thought of a kamikaze beetle was one step too far! Living in England had some advantages.

While everyone chatted I went to help Mum clear up the dishes in the kitchen.

Mum said she had two things to tell me while we were alone. For a minute I thought it was something awful and I was relieved when she said they had received the results from my IQ test. She told me they were very pleased because it indicated that I was rather intelligent. As a result I had been placed in the 'A' stream this coming autumn term. Yippee! I would be in Form 2A. I was about to get excited when Esme burst into the kitchen with more dirty plates. Mum changed the subject.

"Goodness, more washing up! I'll finish this lot on my own while you two go and get ready."

"Get ready for what, Mum?" I asked.

"Dad and I are looking after Mrs Montgomery's house out on the Ridge while she's visiting her son in India. She's kindly said that we are welcome to use her swimming pool when the weather is hot. I suggest you go upstairs and find yourselves some swimming costumes and we'll walk there in about ten minutes."

I was thrilled and told Esme how fantastic the Mongomery's pool and gardens were. Esme raced outside to tell Dulcie. I couldn't believe my luck - friends home *and* visiting the Montgomery's estate!

Lily and I found shorts and T-shirts so the girls could change out of their school uniform. Lily gave Dulcie her old swimming costume and I lent Esme my new polka-dot bikini, wearing my old costume which only just fitted. We walked to the Montgomery's house and Dulcie piggy backed Samuel all the way there with no shoes on. She was tough!

We entered the grounds through iron gates. On either side of the gates were stone pillars, on top of which were two large sitting dog statues. A gravel pathway led through a long, overhead archway of trailing bushes covered in tiny white flowers with a heady, sweet smell. Esme smiled and said it reminded her of the flowers around Lake Naivasha. When we emerged into the clearing the sun was dazzling. There, sparkling in the sunlight, was a large, kidney shaped pool with a diving board at one end. All around the pool area, stretching as far as the eye could see were green fields dotted with sheep and distant rolling hills.

The sun was scorching hot and we stayed in the pool for ages until my hands went white and soggy. Dulcie and Esme were both brilliant at diving. Dad took loads of photographs of the girls with my family to send to their parents abroad.

At half-past four Mum said we'd better get back home and have some tea because she didn't want us to be late back to school.

Dulcie and Esme walked ahead, giving Benjamin and Samuel piggy backs. I hung back so I could tell Mum and Dad about meeting Alexandra and her signed pointe shoe.

Back at home Mum gave me my box of supplies and included some extra bits to share with the girls. We had enough hairspray to see the whole school through a week's performances! Esme and Dulcie both said that their parents wanted me to come and stay with their families. Esme said it had better be soon or she might be living in Wales. I felt like we were one big family and wished that today could have gone on longer. Samuel started getting upset when the girls said goodbye and clung to Esme asking if Dulcie and her were staying with our family forever.

Back at school, I didn't get that stomach-churning feeling I got when I returned to school on my own. I was either growing up or had got used to living away from home.

Before lights out, everyone gathered on Mika's bed to swap Visiting Day stories.

Mika: Visited an animal park in the South Downs and got spat on by a Llama.

Maddy: Spent the day in a pub beer garden and got stung twice on the leg by the same wasp.

Sanchia: Spent the day with her godmother, who lives in Wittering. They had a picnic on the beach and her back got burned. It was redder than Radish's hair.

Gabby: Tried to disown her mother on Brighton beach but failed. She said her Mum stuck out like a sore thumb, dressed like the Mafia in scorching heat when everyone else was practically naked.

Millie: Has decided she'll train to become a marine biologist. Spending the day at Camber Sands looking at sand dunes reminded her how much she missed Tobago. It was her ambition to study turtles and their breeding grounds and it was time to choose between ballet and marine life before she got too old.

Esme: Told the girls she'd had the best day ever and we'd spent the whole day at a friend's private pool.

Dulcie: Said she had also had the best day ever - with me and Esme!

Janice: Her Dad took her to see a new Bond film called *Live and Let Die* at a cinema in Leicester Square. She described crazy speedboat chases and funerals where they played jazz music and sang and danced in the streets. She then told Millie that it was set on a Caribbean island which practised voodoo and had villains and drug barons living there. Millie folded her arms and said very crossly that it was nowhere near Tobago.

Me: Told the girls I'd had a fantastic Visiting Day with my friends and family. I looked up to see Hannah hovering in the doorway, miming sticking her fingers down her throat. Sometimes she was a bit too full of herself, and at that moment she was plain annoying.

CHAPTER FIFTY-ONE

DRESS REHEARSALS

MONDAY 25TH JUNE

My shoulders looked pink today but fortunately my back wasn't red. Mrs Balmaine was furious in rehearsals and has forbidden us to sit in the sun before the show. No wonder ballerinas looked pale and delicate - Giselle would look ridiculous as a sun-tanned ghost.

WEDNESDAY 27TH JUNE

Yesterday we rehearsed so late that tea was over. Burt threw a wobbly, gave us stale bread and sweaty cheese and said, "Make your own sandwiches."

Eventually we raced upstairs for our final costume fittings. Mrs Savage lived up to her name by yelling at everyone and threatened to cut my plaits off when my hair wouldn't fit inside my wig. Brandishing her crinkly sewing scissors she got in a right strop and forced my hair inside the rock and roll wig so it bulged and my head looked like Frankenstein. I blurted out, "I can't wear my wig like that!"

"You, Miss, will do exactly as you're told or I'll report you!"

I decided I'd have to work out my own way of scrunching my hair inside my wig without involving Savage's scissors. Silly old trout!

It seemed that at every meal there was some new notice pinned up, announcing dress rehearsals throughout the day and long into the evening. Normal dance timetables were suspended and classes after school replaced with non-syllabus dance classes.

Tomorrow's our first dress rehearsal for 'Toyshop' in the studio underneath Junior Dorm, just our 'musical box' gang, no make-up but full costume. It was sooo exciting.

THURSDAY 28TH JUNE

Dress rehearsal was a shambles. I sorted out my wig and looked almost dashing, but the girls' wigs were another story. Janice and Esme's wigs stuck together when they dropped their heads forward in their curtsying start position. I could see what was happening, but unfortunately had my arms held in the air in my opening position. Gloria tried to help, but Miss Olsen was in such a crabby mood she spotted the un-choreographed movement and yelled at the top of her voice.

"You boy!"

Disguised beneath wigs she hadn't a clue who was who.

"Arms into starting position, immediately. Stop horsing around and start behaving like professional dancers. People are paying to see you."

She marched up to our group and shrieked, "From the top!"

The music started but Miss Olsens' outburst hadn't rectified the head-locked wigs, and as we began the dance the girls attempted the impossible, moving their heads upwards producing more snorts. They looked like stags in combat!

Janice's and Esme's shoulders shook and I fought off hysterics. The 'men' gallantly shuffled around but were hampered by the wig-locked girls blocking the floorspace. Eventually the music stopped.

"What's going on?" Miss Olsen said, clutching her hands to her head.

The girls had removed their wigs which lay on the floor in a tangled heap of blonde ringlets.

Janice said, "Sorry Miss Olsen. The wigs stuck together so we couldn't separate our heads."

"Why didn't you say? You could have danced without wigs. Where are your brains?" She snatched the offending wigs from the floor. "Let's take it from the top."

After rehearsals we took the mangled wigs to psycho-Savage's attic. Savage was livid and grabbed the sewing scissors. The wigs weren't mine and I ran for it.

FRIDAY 29TH JUNE

The costumes and wigs looked fantastic during 'Blue Suede Shoes' rehearsals, which went on until late evening. I was exhausted, everything ached *and* I got kicked in the face this afternoon ending up with a heavy nosebleed. It was messy with blood everywhere. Once again I found myself the centre of attention for all the wrong reasons. Mrs Balmaine was so worried about blood dripping onto my costume that she held me in her arms like a baby and tilted my head backwards. I nearly choked so she made me lie on my back across three chair seats.

Then she made bad choice number one, making poor Kerri pinch the top of my nose. Kerri hated the sight of blood and turned a pasty grey, then passed out. Hannah and Tiffany, eager to be part of the unfolding drama rushed to the rescue and carried Kerri off by the arms and legs in the direction of sick bay. I watched helplessly.

Mrs Balmaine then made bad choice number two. She asked Tamsin to pinch my nose. Tamsin lasted for five seconds of nose pinching when the sight of fresh blood made her keel over too. Exasperated with another body limp on the floor, Mrs Balmaine snapped, "pinch your own nose!" After ten minutes I was sent back to the dorm to find Nanny.

SATURDAY 30TH JUNE

The notice board at breakfast displayed the morning and afternoon run-through held in the theatre. The show was called 'Let's Face the Music' (Stavely Brookes Company show production, 1973)

At the theatre it was chaos on the stage. Miss Wanda and Miss Olsen were measuring everyone's height and I nearly died when Cimmie - looking furious - was measured back-to-back with juniors. Luckily I was taller than her. Eventually the whole school was arranged in lines, tallest at the back with juniors kneeling on one knee.

Miss Wanda explained the school tradition of all dancers appearing on stage before the show in an overture called 'Le Rassemblement', (translated meaning 'The Gathering'), for which Mr Julius had composed avant-garde music. We would start in the wings, and then on set cues lines of girls would file onto stage until a pattern of lines fanned out from a central point to form a star-shape. The star's centre had an outer circle (taller girls) hiding an inner circle (shorter girls). On the final chords of the music there would be a total blackout, the girls forming the star's points would run offstage and leave the girls in the centre. As a bright spotlight illuminates them, the outer circle of dancer's bow to reveal the inner circle which then bow forwards. She said clever lighting provided wonderful drama to the eerie music.

After the lengthy explanation we were shunted round the stage by bossy students and I was placed near the front tip of the star facing downstage. Sadly the inner circle was reserved for shorter students, including Cimmie who'd ended up facing the backdrop.

Eventually we were sent back into the audience seats and Miss Wanda gave the go-ahead to start rehearsing 'Toyshop'. As we clambered back on stage, I noticed a curious raised block positioned at the back of the stage.

Esme grabbed my arm, "Is that our rostrum?"

I shrugged. It looked too small for six girls. Miss Olsen appeared from the wings and began placing everyone in starting positions on stage, whilst the musical box rostrum six stood gaping at the raised, circular platform intended for us. Positioned in the centre-back of the stage and slightly too close to the backdrop, it was ominously high and sloping. Gloria examined it.

"It's not even six-foot wide!"

"How can we all fit on it and move without someone falling off?" I exclaimed.

I was interrupted by Miss Olsen as she swept upstage towards our fretting group.

"Girls! The rostrum is - as you can see - a tad small. However, we'll have to work with what we've got, contain our movements and," she sprung like a gazelle onto the front of the rostrum which was at least two feet high, "practise leaning towards the backdrop because the stage," she wobbled as she attempted a few poses to demonstrate, "as you can clearly see, slopes downwards."

Leaning over, she pulled us up onto the precarious pint-sized platform. Once in our starting positions it didn't feel so bad. The stage was packed with groups of 'toys.'

The music started. Holding my position I found myself not only admiring Gina's dancing, but also watching the other toys come to life. Each group had its turn to perform. Abbey was a tin soldier, marching then lunging and aiming an imaginary rifle. I spotted Sydney and Tiffany as Punch and Judy, bobbing and ducking, throwing wild punches at each other. The Red Indians had the best dance moves with Mika performing leaps around the stage.

When our music started I tried to get into character. As we raised our arms up and down, bowing and pivoting, I felt a rush of excitement performing onstage, but it was difficult keeping upright due to the sloping platform. Several times Kerri tightened her grip on my hand as I twirled her round on the spot. I was relieved it wasn't just me finding it tricky staying upright. When our dance ended we had to turn back into toys, then Gina danced her finale and ran through the toyshop door into the wings. Miss Wanda jumped up from her seat in the audience and waved frantically.

"Light change, light change - it's all wrong!" she yelled.

Miss Olsen leaped onto stage and told us to sit down. Squinting at her clipboard she announced a list of corrections, including 'try to relax' and 'don't look so wooden'. I'm sure we'd look less wooden if we weren't trying so hard not to slide off the wretched rostrum.

The rest of rehearsals whizzed past. I spotted Patsy tap-dancing near the front in 'Putting on the Ritz'. Even among the other dancers my eyes were drawn towards her. Her magnetic personality and face lit up the stage.

I enjoyed watching the 'Surfin' dance. The girls had painted surf-boards and did cool surfer moves, like they were riding the waves. In the dance called 'Rolling' the girls had brought lassoes with them to practise with. A giant projected image on the backdrop pictured a real cattle drive. Miss Wanda got angry with the 'cowboys' and yelled at a girl who'd somehow got her lasso-rope looped around another girl's neck, causing a commotion.

The final dance in the first half was 'Flapper-mania', which got loads of laughs before we went back to school for lunch. I was famished.

In the queue we discussed which dance we liked most, agreeing 'Putting on the Ritz' was best so far. The dining hall was frenzied. Radish had cooked fish and chips on Burt's day off. I'd never heard so many ear-piercing cries of Eggo in my life. I Eggoed one extra meal and Kerri ate three.

After lunch the run-through was the same as the morning, only this time it was second cast and I got to dance again. Yay!

I couldn't wait to dance 'Blue Suede Shoes' in tomorrow's run-through.

CHAPTER FIFTY-TWO

SUNDAY 1ST JULY

I awoke way before rising bell this morning, watching the sunlight streaming through the curtains and studying Alexandra's signature on her pointe shoe. I thought about how I'd felt dancing on stage yesterday and prayed that when I was older I'd be given a chance to dance solo on stage. As I ended my prayer I felt a shadow pass over my closed eyes and quickly opened them. The curtains swayed slightly from the open window but everyone was sound asleep. I propped myself up on my pillow and looked around the dorm, expecting to see the Blue Lady floating across the beds on a tour of duty, but disappointingly saw nothing. I hugged March Hare tight when rising bell startled me, and seconds later Nanny and Hamish hurtled through the dorm door and I shot out of bed before the blankets were ripped off me.

At breakfast the canteen notice board displayed a notice instructing everyone to dress in correct uniform during school lessons, and forbidding girls crowding round studio windows watching rehearsals. It mentioned 'unexpected visitors' so I must be prepared.

After breakfast team BLAP were walking to the theatre when Mika said, "We've spent nearly a year trying to track down the Blue Lady and we're still no further forward."

"With girls to-ing and fro-ing past the lake and thumping music from the theatre," said Maddy, "we'll be lucky to get any more ghost sightings".

When we reached the theatre Esme showed us how to sneak in via the fire exits and bag the best front row seats for watching today's rehearsals. With the audience seats full Miss Wanda clapped her hands for silence. Clutching her clipboard against her chest she said, "Today's an opportunity to learn from yesterday's rehearsals, which were shambolic! Friday we'll have a technical run through then next weekend is the final dress-rehearsals before opening night the following Monday"

She then yelled for us to get into our starting positions. As I scrambled up onto stage I felt sick, then my stomach cramped. I was sure everyone could see my quivering hands as we stood frozen in our positions. There was an audible hiss and crackle from the speakers just before Elvis's voice launched into "Well it's a one for the money..." and we were off!

I danced my heart out, spinning, kicking, leaping and grasping my partner's sweaty hands. My eyes had to be everywhere. Bodies seemed to hurtle towards me like tornadoes as we flung each other around in lifts, twists and turns until the last guitar chords, and we all sank to the floor into our finishing positions shaking our jazz hands. A thunderous applause erupted from the audience and voices screamed 'More'! I felt a wave of emotion flood through me and a rush of appreciation coming from the girls cheering in the audience. Just as we staggered breathlessly to our feet, Mrs

Balmaine made a dramatic flying leap onto the front of the stage. Grinning, she clapped.

"Good job girls and great lifts! Now all you've got to do is m-o-v-e o-f-f..." she did an exaggerated walk around our huddled group..."your postage stamp."

She then charged around the perimeter of the stage shouting, "THIS IS THE REST OF THE FLOOR!"

I hoped we hadn't looked that daft.

"Spread yourselves out girls, and really use this stage!" Walking towards the audience she added, "Next week in dress rehearsals I want smiles, energy and -" she turned hollering, "ATTACK!" so loudly we jumped out of our skins.

Miss Wanda got up on stage and joined in.

"Next number. Hurry, we haven't got all day."

We raced back to our seats. This was so different to anything I'd been involved in before and I loved it. The rest of the morning passed in a blur. The contemporary dance, which won the choreographic competition, was straight after our rock and roll, and was more amazing than I remembered.

Next was a male dancer (on loan to Stavely Brookes) partnering a student in a Pas de Deux called 'Somewhere'. As they danced, the theatre went so quiet you could hear your own breathing. The girl was wearing the tutu we'd seen on the dummy in the sewing room. The male dancer lifted her like a feather and she was breathtaking. Their dance ended with him holding her in a lift, her body supported on his shoulder. She looked like she was flying and they got the biggest applause so far.

The remaining dances were good, especially the finale, which Oracle said was copied from the French Can-Can. Named 'Ooh-la-la' it was total madness. The audience clapped enthusiastically, encouraged by dancers who whooped, cart-wheeled and kicked their legs round their ears at breakneck-speed. They jumped high in the air and landed in splits without putting their hands on the ground! Bobbing up out of the splits like jack-in-the-boxes, their swirling colourful satin dresses and frothy petticoats were accompanied by frequent shrill screams. One girl hopped diagonally backwards with her leg held in a front split, holding her foot behind her head. A dramatic drum roll led to an energetic finale and thunderous applause.

Afternoon rehearsals were better, second cast having learned from this morning's mistakes. Mrs Balmaine said we'd over corrected and were now too far apart. There were several hair-raising moments when I nearly missed my cue of music and we practically raced to each position.

TUESDAY 3RD JULY

During ballet this afternoon a suspicious looking man in a suit was hanging around outside, carrying a clipboard and wearing dark glasses. At lunch time Mika said she'd spotted Mr Deluca's Ferrari parked outside main house at breakfast and a shady looking man getting out of the back. Now he was outside the studio with Mr Deluca and they just burst in, without warning, right in the middle of Adage. Mr Deluca spoke quietly with Miss Olsen and then both men sat watching us dance. Luckily they left before Grande Allegro. Weirdly, the stranger never removed his dark glasses, even when writing notes. Despite nerves I danced like a demon. No one was going to stop me being a dancer that easily.

At tea we all talked about The Man in Glasses. Maddy said he was watching me but then admitted the dark glasses had concealed his eyes. Honestly!

Last night I went to bed agonizing if the assessor was the man in dark glasses. If he was I wondered whether my scholarship would be continuing, and would my place even be secure here the following year. My whole future was hanging by a thread! The possibility of not coming back was unthinkable. Ages ago Dad asked me if this was what I really wanted to do. He said it was a bit like enlisting to go into the army; that you had to want to be in the army more than anything else. I told him from the moment I first visited Covent Garden and saw the ballet I knew without doubt I wanted to dance more than anything in the world!

A new notice at breakfast said we were needed today for final fittings.

Gloria, Tamsin and I visited Savage's lair after ballet and I tried on the men's leather shoes. Buttery-soft, they fitted like a glove.

Millie confided in me this evening. "Lara, I'm going to really miss team BLAP when I leave, but mostly I'll miss you. With so many rehearsals I forgot to remind you that next full moon's the day after we've gone home."

Without warning her eyes filled with tears, her nose went pink and she choked back a sob in her throat. I thought she might cry and then I might cry too, so I reassured her I'd write frequently and even take over responsibility of her role as 'Full Moon Monitor/Coordinator of BLAP'. I assured her once I'd sold enough legwarmers I'd be able to afford to visit her. We made a pact to visit each other often. I knew we'd be friends for life.

I'd really miss my Tobagan buddy, with her spooky sleep-walking, amazing stories of underwater sea-creatures, her photographs of Caribbean wildlife and outrageous ghost-busting charts.

CHAPTER FIFTY-THREE

FRIDAY 6ᵀᴴ JULY

At 9 a.m. we gathered in the big studio with armloads of costumes on hangers, wigs and costume shoes. Miss Wanda said she and Miss Olsen were in charge of the juniors this year. Any problems must go straight to her. We were instructed to go to the theatre where we queued outside the stage door for the first rehearsal for 'Le Rassemblement'. We protected our pointe shoes outside wearing plastic bags to keep them clean, and wore long-sleeved black leotards, pink tights and new pink soft-blocks ('softened' pointe shoes – what waste!). Our hair was scraped into a higher bun than usual and cemented with hairspray.

Finally, rehearsals got underway. Unfortunately for me, several unexpected things happened during dress rehearsal.

Firstly, a large jewel popped off my cummerbund. It fell noisily onto the rostrum stage as we waited in our starting positions for the musical box's opening chimes. When we moved Gloria stood on the wretched jewel, which made her foot roll. I watched her teeter sideways and as she tried to stop herself falling off the rostrum, her trousers split straight up the backside with a horrible ripping sound. Despite this disaster we carried on pretending nothing had happened. Then Kerri's

401

voluminous petticoat became attached to a nail sticking out from the rostrum floor, stopping us dead in our tracks. By the time we'd untangled her our section of music had been and gone.

When 'Toyshop' had finished and we came off-stage, Miss Wanda gave us a proper lecture, like it was our fault. Afterwards, Gloria said she'd like to see Miss Wanda carry on dancing with her backside exposed to the audience. Ha ha!

The rock and roll dance was great, apart from Hannah's plimsoll flying off her foot in a flick-kick and landing on someone's head in the front row. Miss Wanda went ballistic, telling Hannah her plimsole wasn't a football. Hannah defended herself until Miss Wanda threatened to remove her from first cast. How lairy was that!

Rehearsals finished at 9 p.m. but Miss Brookes stayed behind with Lance Gunn (The Only Man in the Show) and Talia, the beautiful student dancing with him. She was so graceful no wonder she was Miss Brookes' favourite.

Tonight's supper was iced buns. Burt had miscounted and masses were going spare. I Eggoed three, but had second thoughts remembering the tight cummerbund and popping jewel and handed them back before my head gave way to my stomach.

SATURDAY 7TH JULY

Rehearsals went well, with a trial make-up run before first dress rehearsal. Miss Wanda said they'd check our make-up was suitable for the theatre lighting.

With long queues in the studios, Miss Wanda and Miss Olsen were applying make-up and we soon morphed into identical egg-heads.

With eye-lids painted china-blue, black liner drawn round my eyes, lashes caked with mascara, rouge on my cheeks and carmine red lips I looked positively doll-like. With wigs we'd never be recognised on stage. This could be useful if you were in a dance you hated, though not great for parents hoping to recognise their daughter dancing her socks off in the annual show.

Whilst warming up in my rock and roll costume, Esme collared me and started moaning.

"Don't you think it's unhygienic, using the same make-up sponge for everyone?"

She did her infuriating stage whisper, "Some people have hideous spots which are infectious, full of germs and revolting bacteria which can be passed from person to person."

She glared accusingly at Gabby, who thankfully wasn't listening.

"Frankly, last year I couldn't have cared less. However, now I've got a boyfriend it's different. I can't return to Kenya covered in someone else's acne."

I told her to stop overreacting. This completely backfired on me as she spat out, "At least I have a boyfriend!"

I didn't believe Stephan actually existed and replied, "Don't think you're the only one with admirers!"

It was a big fat lie, but sometimes I couldn't help getting drawn into her silly games. I was seriously thinking of *not* having her to stay this holiday if she was going to carry on like this. Kerri overheard our exchange.

"She's really got it in for you."

I laughed it off and Kerri shrugged.

"Maybe she's starting her periods. I read in a women's magazine that before periods many women get mood swings."

"If it's not that, then I've just joined her hate list."

I can't believe there's only one day left until the show begins. I phoned home before breakfast and Mum and Dad both said 'break a leg' to me. Dad told me he'd bring Lily, Benjamin and Samuel to the show on Friday. Mum and Aunty Ellen are coming to the Saturday evening show and arriving for the garden party after the Matinee performance. I'll wear my lovely long dress Mum's made with my new wedges. I warned Dad they wouldn't recognise me on stage and made sure they knew my starting positions in both dances.

At breakfast there was a notice about the technical run through and a note from Miss Olsen, informing the juniors that after performing their final dance, they were permitted to sit quietly in the front rows of the auditorium. This was exciting news as we hadn't seen the show with full costumes, lighting and make-up. This would be our last chance before it opened to the public.

Today was like a real performance. 'Le Rassemblement' was very eerie, and as we filed onto the dimly lit stage I wondered whether the Blue Lady was watching over the theatre, pleased by the ghostly atmosphere. Everyone was deadly serious as they walked into their positions accompanied with dramatic music.

After 'Toyshop' we ran back to the studio, quickly changed into our dance kit and raced back to the theatre to watch the next six dances before half-time break.

There was yet another hitch in 'Rollin' when a lasso rope got hooked onto someone's belt. The culprit tried to detach the offending rope only to lose time with the music and forget all her steps! Miss Brookes shouted "Rubbish" from somewhere in the middle row. The victim freed herself but the dance looked messy. We clapped like crazy to make up for the blunder.

Worse was to come in 'Flapper-mania'. The girls looked fantastic in their brightly tasselled dresses and velvet chokers, clasping elegant cigarette holders. They had bobbed wigs with each girl wearing multiple strings of beads. As the dance progressed, a double-string of beads burst and beads flew in all directions across the stage! Chaos erupted with girls skidding on beads and falling over. Enraged, Miss Wanda hurtled down the aisle and leaping onto stage, ordered immediate removal of necklaces.

We missed watching the next dances because of costume changes for 'Blue Suede Shoes'. This felt really exciting when we performed it and Mrs Balmaine said we looked very together. We had to move really fast, and our lifts were so much better now we had the space on stage to throw our partners around.

When the curtain went down we raced to the studio to change.

I was desperate to see Lance and Talia's Pas de Deux. We returned just in time and slunk into our front row seats. There was such an air of mystery to their dancing. Lance, dark and brooding, stared intensely into Talia's eyes and I almost believed they were falling in love. I could hear them breathe and watched fascinated as their bodies entwined. The music ended and everyone leapt from their seats clapping.

I was fortunate to see the solo which followed. This was danced by a student, with three girls positioned at the back of the stage. Wearing black trousers and white shirts they sat on chairs, each holding an instrument, a trumpet, a trombone and a guitar, as they mimed playing them. The spotlight followed the tall soloist wearing an old-fashioned skirt and blouse. The dance was well acted; she simply flung herself around a wooden chair holding a cigarette in her hand. It was so impressive everyone yelled when she finished. Mr Julius and Mr Deluca both shouted "Bravo!"

All was running smoothly until the 'Space' dance, which used dry ice to create a thick mist on stage. The dancers, wearing spacesuits and round fishbowl helmets, walked on stage in slow motion and, placing their cylindrical guns on the floor, performed weird choreography to echoing music. On trying to retrieve their guns, which were invisible beneath the dry ice, they messed up their steps and bumped into each other. It was chaos. When the mist cleared space guns littered the floor.

Miss Brookes called the dancers back on stage. Everyone wore helmets so nobody could see anyone's expressions, just a line of fish bowls turning their heads from side to side. Suddenly, a Spaceman pulled off her helmet, and looking startled when everyone stared at her, burst into tears.

Sydney leaned towards me whispering, "Miss Brookes hates girls who cry."

Miss Brookes gave an exasperated huff.

"Oh *do* stop crying and pull yourself together!"

I committed this nugget of information to memory.

Following the finale, the 'Space' dancers stayed behind for further rehearsing. We've been handed timetables for practice classes next week, and instructions for first cast to be ready for the opening matinee at 2-30 p.m.

As we left the theatre I noticed Miss Brookes was kneading her temple. I won't let her down.

CHAPTER FIFTY-FOUR

MONDAY 9TH JULY

Everyone was talking about the matinee performance during our short school lesson this morning when Esme confided her periods had started, and apologised for getting ratty.

The matinee went well this afternoon without too many hitches. Being in front of a real audience was the most exciting thing I'd experienced at ballet school.

Before every performance, we have to take our 'Toyshop' costumes backstage ready for a quick change beside the wings. Each junior shares a student as their dresser (one between two).

I'd asked Patsy if she could dress Kerri and me, and when we rushed offstage there she was, beaming and taking charge. Hearing the final chords for 'Le Rassemblement' I'd had a fit of shakes, knowing we had to be ready in our costumes, shoes and wigs immediately after the girls on stage took their final bow. Patsy was quietly calming, instructing Kerri and me with "arms-up/head through/breathe in".

Amazingly we were ready just in time as the sound of clapping reached us in the wings. I felt butterflies in my stomach as students appeared through the wings and raced towards their dressing rooms. Patsy gave me a hug and

407

adjusted our wigs saying, "You'll do. Now get onto that rostrum and enjoy it!"

It was even more exciting dancing for a real audience than the dress rehearsals.

During 'Toyshop', no one fell off the incredibly sloping rostrum, but it did feel like we constantly leant in the opposite direction. The dance flew past in seconds, and it seemed like we'd only just begun when we'd finished. I felt huge appreciation from the enthusiastic applause as the curtain slowly descended.

The second half was better because we got to dance properly and had the whole stage to move around freely. My energy burst out like an explosion as we flew through our rock and roll routine.

We had a minor blip during 'Blue Suede Shoes' involving a large, spiky wig-brush. Somehow, the offending brush, used to smooth out tangles from our wigs, became attached to the back of Sydney's long, blonde wig as we went on stage. With the dance in full swing, flinging ourselves in every direction, satin skirts and frothy petticoats whirling, I became aware that every time Sydney got near me something was catching on my costume. After a few seconds I spotted the black wig-brush trapped in her wig. It wasn't long before the other dancers cottoned on to the unwelcome attachment, which was bouncing around like an airborne-missile between spins, lifts and drops. Anyone passing Sydney tried to craftily lunge towards her in an attempt to grab the spiky missile.

If I hadn't been concentrating so hard on performing I'd have wept with laughter, but the wig-brush continued to be flipped around forming a massive clump of blonde hair around it. The dance ended to humungous applause, hopefully for our dancing and not the acrobatic hairbrush!

After the last dance the whole school gathered backstage preparing for curtain calls. The loudest applause (except for the deafening ovation for Talia and Lance's Pas de Deux) was for our 'Blue Suede Shoes' dance!

Standing in the canteen later I felt on a high from today's performance. For some it was our first time performing in front of a paying audience. There seemed to be an overwhelming feeling of cheerfulness flooding through the very walls of the school and I felt lucky to be part of this. With all the love and laughter radiating, we spotted Rita...hugging Cimmie. Even Burt, normally short-tempered, was in summer show spirit, cooking everyone's favourite pizza for tea.

I received loads of Good Luck cards today. One from Mum and Dad (with drawings of stick dancers from Samuel and Benjamin and horseshoes from Lily), two from both Grandparents and one from great Aunty Phyllis with The Eye of Horus pictured on the front! I'd never received so much good luck.

We'd been told to walk to the theatre in groups after dark and protect our costumes. Thankfully it was hot and dry. Walking towards the theatre in darkness the lake looked larger and shimmered beneath the night sky, the old boat looked bigger and the undergrowth appeared wilder. The whole area just seemed spookier and I'm ashamed to say that all team BLAP actually ran! So much for ghostbusting.

The matinee went well this afternoon, but the evening show was nearly X-rated and it was all down to a simple thread that caused chaos.

It started off quite innocently. Beginning 'Toyshop', we struck our positions on top of the musical box. The music started, the curtain raised and the lights lit up the sleeping groups of toys. Gina skipped on and bourréd across the stage. As she woke up various groups of toys, our group - frozen in place on top of the rostrum - detected a long, glistening thread which caught our attention under the bright stage lights. It was dangling from Kerri's bodice. I assumed it was some random strand of wig hair.

The music started and as we began to move the dangling object took on a life of its own. As we pivoted and turned, I realised to my horror it wasn't a hair but an actual thread attached to Kerri's bodice which wound itself around our revolving group, unravelling more and more of Kerri's now loosening bodice. Our eyes were glued to the offending thread now forming a glistening web around our group. The unfortunate rostrum began to shake as we trembled, and by the time our music ended, Kerri's boobs were nearly popping over her bodice and the strain of keeping poker faces had left us as weak as kittens.

With the curtain down we fought to untangle ourselves. Back in the studio we presented Miss Olsen with the offending costume and she looked peeved.

"Really girls, we're not even half way through the week, do try to put on your costumes with more care."

"It wasn't my fault Miss Olsen, it's difficult getting all those laces done up in our quick change and..." Kerri was cut short by Miss Olsen thrusting the unravelled dress into her arms.

"Quick change or not, first thing tomorrow take it straight to Mrs Savage."

I promised to accompany her for moral support, but wasn't looking forward to it.

WEDNESDAY 11TH JULY

This morning we took Kerri's costume to Savage. Lucky for us she was already yelling at a student about her tutu, so continued her tirade whilst fitting the bodice onto Kerri. She stuck pins in randomly and told us to return by lunchtime to collect the mended garment.

With more rehearsals today it seemed crazy busy. This was because of a rumour that Press might attend the evening show. Esme said that Press night was officially on Thursday, but last year some larger European ballet companies had sent over scouts to view Wednesday and Friday evening shows, hoping to recruit new dancers for their companies.

THURSDAY 12TH JULY

Word was out that no journalists or talent scouts had appeared yesterday. With Press night looming, rehearsals were in full swing. I couldn't see why we needed to go over things again when they seemed perfect. Patsy told me that even in professional companies things went wrong during performances and shows should be practised to perfection. She said when you relaxed you made more mistakes. I couldn't imagine ever being too relaxed.

I suddenly thought about The Man in Dark Glasses who watched our class last week. Perhaps someone somewhere was making decisions about my future. The thought sent me into a cold sweat and made me recoil in horror at the very idea of not being here any more. I confided my fears to Patsy.

"Don't think about it another moment, honey" she clucked to me like a mother hen. "You're doing just fine. I've got a good feeling about you."

She slapped me reassuringly on the back which made me have a colossal coughing fit. I prayed she was right.

That evening, as we filed sombrely onto stage for the evening's opening performance of 'Le Rassemblement', I stood proud in my front-of-line position. I imagined Press reporters staring up at us from the audience. With my shoulders squared I set my gaze straight ahead. I thought about all the amazing things they could be writing about my school and the dancers they were about to watch performing. Then the penny dropped - suddenly I completely understood the importance of practising to perfection. Patsy was very wise.

FRIDAY 13TH JULY

Judging by the applause after last night's show, the Press had enjoyed it. Aunty Ellen would collect review cuttings and save them for me to keep with my ballet programmes.

Today everyone was talking about Talia. She'd been asked to join the Festival Ballet Company where Lance was a soloist.

Dad, Lily, Benjamin and Samuel were coming to see me tonight and with four shows left I didn't want it to end.

I hadn't spoken to Dad before the show, but I'd arranged for them to come to the stage door afterwards to see me. I wished I hadn't known where they were sitting. The thought was strangely distracting.

I forgot about everyone in the rock and roll number. The audience yelled like mad and someone wolf-whistled when we finished. Perhaps my brothers!

After the final curtain call I raced to the stage door, insisting Esme, Kerri and Dulcie came too, then Mika and Maddy joined us, followed by Gabby and Millie. When I reached the door team BLAP were all there to greet my family. Dad hugged me and said we were brilliant, and Lily asked Esme and me to teach her some rock and roll moves during the summer holidays.

Eventually Gina came round to the stage door and said Nanny would wonder where half of her dorm had got to. We watched as my family walked towards the car park, then we ran like loonies out of the theatre. As we skirted round the lakeside there was a whooshing sound, closely followed by a chill gust of wind. Millie looked wild-eyed and squealed "It's the lady of the lake - R-U-N!" and everyone scarpered. For a second I looked back and thought I saw the ghostly shape of a lady hovering over the upturned boat, then it was gone. I ran like fury until I reached the studio where the girls were already inside hanging up their costumes. Still out of breath I moved close to Kerri and grabbed her arm.

"Did you see her?" I gasped.

"Who?"

"The shadow - that shape hovering over the boat."

"What shadow? What shape?" Esme butted in as Kerri looked out of the window.

"My Dad's here, his car just drove past. See you tomorrow. Byeeee!" Kerri flew out the door and off towards her Dad's car.

The moment had gone. I tried to collar Millie. I wanted to tell her what I thought I'd seen, but for some reason not even Millie was interested any more. I felt like saying, "You can't give up the ghost!" It *was* suddenly like everyone in BLAP felt the Blue Lady no longer existed, or maybe the novelty had worn off and everyone had got fed up with watching and waiting. My Gran always said that things come to those who wait. And that was precisely it. We waited and finally, just when no-one expected it, she appeared. Except I was the only one who saw her.

CHAPTER FIFTY-FIVE

FINAL DAY OF THE SCHOOL YEAR

SATURDAY 15TH JULY

The whole school was bustling with preparations as today's audiences were family and friends.

I'd managed to pack my school things to take home after tonight's show. I felt sick at the thought of my scholarship not continuing, but remembered what Patsy said and pushed negative thoughts out of my mind.

The dorm was stacked with school trunks and my brown suitcase looked tiny next to them. With Gabby's help we'd dragged my tuck-box into the downstairs corridor, so when Mum came to pick up my cases she could drive up to the entrance and we wouldn't have far to carry it.

Kerri and I went to watch the Bedouin tent being set up on the front lawn. It resembled the Maharajah's palace without the desert. The sun was sweltering and I felt excited and jittery about our last performances.

I walked back to the day girls' changing room where Kerri showed me her long dress for open-day. Hers was cheesecloth and gorgeous. She confided that her parents had told her she'd be in the 'A' stream next term. I was so relieved and said I was too.

After lunch, having been transformed in make-up, I studied myself in the mirrors. I hardly recognised myself. Esme came up to the mirror, squashed up beside me whilst I was blending my blue eye-shadow and started winding me up.

"You can't imagine how hideous we look, in our long dresses and then *this*," she stabbed her finger at her face, "grotesque make-up ruins it all!"

"We'll look like pantomime dames!" I chortled, but immediately regretted being jokey because she got in a huff.

"It's no good being sarky, Lara. It was the same last year, with our elegant long dresses and our scary make-up. You wait - we'll look hideous."

She flounced around in a mock demonstration pulling a ridiculous face.

She did have a point and I giggled, imagining Cimmie close-up with her humungous false eyelashes and blackened eyes like Dracula's daughter.

The heat made conditions backstage stifling and the quick changes challenging. The sheer ballet tights worn for 'Le Rassemblement' refused to be pulled off. Worse still, the stretchy trousers I wore for 'Toyshop' got stuck half-way up my thighs because I was clammy. As Patsy fought courageously to pull the offending trousers over my hips, I remembered Gloria's trousers which had split up the backside. Despite the struggles I made it onstage seconds before the curtain went up. Late entrances were my worst nightmare.

The matinee went well and afterwards we tore back to the dorm to change into our long dresses. I dabbed on my Chanel then the whole dorm wanted some. Everyone looked so pretty apart from the unavoidable facial war paint and hair elastic ridges. Glammed up we hurried off in search of visiting parents.

While tottering on my wedges towards the main car park I heard my name being called. Turning I saw Mum and Aunty Ellen waving, and running towards them I nearly fell over my long dress. Mum and Aunty also wore elegant dresses, and Aunty kept saying how grown up I'd become.

Wandering towards the front lawn I noticed many Mums wore floppy hats and dark sunglasses. I recognised a few parents I'd seen on television.

Ladies in fashionable outfits produced parasols as the afternoon heat rose, and I caught glimpses of Mr Julius socialising with visitors. He looked very dashing in a long Indian shirt over white flares and Jesus sandals. Horse Dog was on a lead beside him, wearing an exotic embroidered doggy-coat around his middle - very cool!

It was so hot inside the tent it felt like an oven, so I queued for refreshments while Mum and Aunty rested on a shaded bench. Luckily I spotted Gabby ahead of me in the queue. She dropped back to join me, saying her Mum had also gone to find a seat. I asked if her Mum found the heat too much and Gabby replied, "Probably, but she's too large to stand for long."

I then noticed Cimmie at the head of the buffet queue, piling her tray with stacks of sandwiches. What a sight. She wore a violet, wet-look halterneck dress which made her boobs look gigantic!

Finally we reached the buffet and I grabbed some wilting sandwiches and fairy cakes for Mum and Aunty.

It was far too hot and queuing in the stuffy tent gave me a headache. It wasn't until I reached the bench that I realised I'd forgotten the drinks. Mum had a thermos of tea in the car, so after we'd eaten we could make our way back to the car park. We chatted for ages watching socialising crowds on the front lawn.

I told Mum and Aunty about my dances and some of the hitches we'd had. Aunty said these experiences were character building and a good grounding for a stage career. She mentioned outstanding reviews in the newspapers about our show, praising the standard and versatility of the students. I prayed with all my heart that I would still be here next year.

We returned to the car to escape the heat and have a nice cup of tea. We sat in the car for so long it steamed up, which was a blessing in disguise. Mum and Aunty needed to change into evening dresses before the evening performance. With nowhere to change they decided to undress in the car. This was hilarious because instead of getting in the back, they tackled the quick-change in the cramped front seats. I've never heard Mum or Aunty laugh so much. Mum even got out her hanky. Aunty got her dress sleeve stuck on the window handle and announced in an agitated voice "I'm stuck". I struggled to free her up but she became hot and bothered, "It's simply no good, dear. I'm stuck!" Then in a much more frantic voice, "And stop holding onto me!"

Mum said no one was holding her, and then I collapsed into giggles because the lace-material from her arm was completely twisted around the door-handle. Finally, we freed Aunty up, without damaging her sleeve. The windows had remained steamed up for the whole episode, so no one would have noticed the commotion inside. I sneaked out the back door when no one was around to prepare for the evening performance.

The Saturday evening performance had a different atmosphere. Everyone was high with excitement and big-night nerves. For students leaving it was their final school performance. The evening went quicker than usual without hitches, and when we danced 'Blue Suede Shoes' for the last time, I felt I never wanted it to end. The audience even clapped during our throws and lifts. Immediately we'd finished there was a deafening applause, and before running off stage I noticed that some of the audience were standing and shouting "Encore!" My whole body was tingling with exhilaration. I could hear cheering as we ran out of the stage doors and into the cool night. The freshness on my face and neck was welcoming.

As we waited in the studio, everyone jabbering about the holidays, I knew that underneath the brave faces we were all feeling sad that show week was ending. Kerri smuggled in a bag of Jelly Babies, and we sat under the costume rails scoffing one after another, waiting to be called back to the theatre for final curtain calls. I heard my name and looked up as Mika's head peered through the costumes. She beckoned for us to come over to the far end of the studio where the rest of team BLAP had gathered, sitting huddled against the mirrored wall having a final meeting before Millie left. Everyone was very emotional; Millie said she didn't want to cry and then tears brimmed over her eyes and flowed like train tracks down her cheeks.

Esme made an announcement to everyone that she was coming to stay with me for the last weeks of the summer holidays. I told Dulcie she was welcome to stay too.

Kerri promised me I could stay with her and then we could visit a great disco in her village hall.

Maddy told us she was spending the summer in Spain with Sanchia.

Then Gabby chipped in.

"Well, you'll all hear about me on the six-o'clock news."

"You never told us you were auditioning for a television part?" I teased her.

"That's because I'll be reported missing when my Mum notices I've gone."

Luckily for her, Mika saved the day and invited Gabby to stay with her for the summer holidays. Now everyone seemed happy.

As we chatted, Patsy ran into the studio.

"Come on girls, it's nearly time for curtain calls!"

She put her arm around me as we walked over to the theatre.

"Just wait until next term - you'll have the time of your life when you're a Tweenie." I grinned at the thought.

"I can't wait to move up to main house!"

My mind was whirling with mixed thoughts as we gathered into groups and shuffled into our positions backstage. The heat from the overhead lights made my skin clammy, and yet I was shivering. As I struggled with my feelings, I felt the hard pull of a hand on my shoulder. My arm was grabbed, and then I was being dragged along with everyone else as we ran through the wings and made our entrance to take our final bows. We reached the front of the stage holding hands each side above our heads, then brought our arms down to our sides and bent forwards into a bow. As we lifted our heads, straightening up, hands tightened their hold and we began fanning out backwards into a semi-circle as more dancers ran forward to take their bows.

I was stunned how many girls fitted onto the stage. Finally, Talia and Lance ran forward holding hands to an ear-splitting thunder of applause. It sounded like people were stamping their feet on the floor and I felt the stage juddering. The curtain came up and down seven times! Finally, the applause quietened and the weighted bottom of the curtain stayed down. After a split-second the area behind the curtain erupted like a volcano, releasing all its pent up energy to create a squealing, sobbing, laughing, boiling-over mass of very emotional schoolgirls.

Everyone was hugging each other and crying. Mascara ran down girls' faces in giant black streaks making them look like clowns. One girl had a false eyelash stuck on her cheek. I couldn't understand why so many girls were crying, but didn't get the opportunity to think about it too much because the juniors were abruptly gathered into a group by Miss Wanda. Like a flock of sheep we were herded together and given orders of where to return our costumes to, followed by more instructions ordering us to head straight back to the dorm where our parents were waiting. As we walked out of the stage door, I glanced back towards the theatre one last time and knew without a doubt that performing was now going to be a big part of my life.

Back in the dorm, Mum and Aunty were already waiting for me. There was a lot more hugging followed by more sobbing and then I wanted to get out of the dorm. I knew if I gave Millie one more hug I would start to blubber too. I didn't like crying because once I got going I couldn't stop.

Mum always knew how to get things moving. She took my arm to separate me from the wailing masses and as we walked towards the stairs we passed Nanny waiting outside her room.

I noticed that her eyes were brimming with tears and I felt a fresh wave of feelings rush up from my stomach. She put her hands softly either side of my shoulders, looked at my face for a second, then pulled me close to her big bosoms and gave me a giant hug.

"Thank you for everything, Nanny," I said, squeezing her tight.

Mum and I each took one side of my tuck box by the handles and, with Aunty carrying my suitcase, I left the entrance door of Junior Dorm, my home for the past year, for the last time.

As we loaded the car up with all my kit, I checked that March Hare and Alexandra's pointe shoes were safely packed up in the boot and rummaged inside my pocket to check my Horus charm was safe. As we got comfortable for the journey home, Mum leaned over to the back seat. Looking at me with her twinkly blue eyes and lovely smile she thrust a long envelope into my hand.

"Lara dear, I forgot to give this to you."

I turned the envelope over. It was addressed to my parents and the postmark was from London. Mum clicked the inner car light on so I could see.

I tore open the envelope and read the letter. It said congratulations and that I had been awarded the funding needed to continue training at ballet school until I reached 18 years of age!

My whole body was shaking. I couldn't believe it and I re-read it in shock, just to make sure. I thought I might actually burst. And I did, but first I laughed, then I screamed a loud WOW (making both Mum and Aunty jump) and only then did I *finally* burst into tears!

I cried with joy. But I also cried with relief. I gave Mum and Aunty a hug and told them I was the luckiest girl alive.

Eventually Mum started the car engine and drove slowly out of the school grounds. I wound down the window and breathed in deep gulps of the fresh night air. The car headlamps illuminated the school grounds and as we reached the final stretch of the long drive I had my last glimpse of the ageing willow tree, casting its ghostly shadows across the lake. I closed my eyes, rested my head against the back window and dreamed of what new excitement, mystery and adventures lay in store for me next year as a ballet boarder!

ACKNOWLEDGEMENTS

This book has been many years in the making (honestly, at times I thought it would never get finished!) and would not have been possible without the love and support of my amazing family. Heartfelt thanks to Natalie for the many hours editing my manuscript and for always sharing my enthusiasm for this story.

I'm incredibly grateful to Mike for his meticulous proof reading and for keeping me fuelled throughout the writing process with endless cups of tea and words of encouragement.

Thank you to everyone else who inspired Lara's journey.

About the author

The Edgecombe Diaries is Nell Young's first novel. It is loosely based on her early years of ballet training and her subsequent life-long love of dance.

LARA'S PLAYLIST

1. JEEPSTER BY T. REX
2. I'M INTO SOMETHING GOOD BY HERMAN'S HERMITS
3. CRAZY HORSES BY THE OSMONDS
4. RUN RUN RUN BY JO JO GUNNE
5. BREAKING UP IS HARD TO DO BY THE PARTRIDGE FAMILY
6. A HORSE WITH NO NAME BY AMERICA
7. TELEGRAM SAM BY T. REX
8. CROCODILE ROCK BY ELTON JOHN
9. PUPPY LOVE BY DONNY OSMOND
10. STRANGE KIND OF WOMAN BY DEEP PURPLE
11. TAKE IT EASY BY EAGLES
12. BURNING LOVE BY ELVIS PRESLEY
13. MAGGIE MAY BY ROD STEWART
14. HOW CAN I BE SURE BY DAVID CASSIDY
15. RESURRECTION SHUFFLE BY ASHTON, GARDNER & DYKE
16. BLUE IS THE COLOUR BY CHELSEA FOOTBALL CLUB
17. MAMA WEER ALL CRAZEE NOW BY SLADE
18. TINY DANCER BY ELTON JOHN
19. METAL GURU BY T. REX
20. STARMAN BY DAVID BOWIE
21. SCHOOL'S OUT BY ALICE COOPER
22. KEEP ON DANCING (LES MCKEOWN VERSION) BY BAY CITY ROLLERS

LISTEN TO THE PLAYLIST AT

WWW.THROWLEIGHPRESS.CO.UK

Printed in Great Britain
by Amazon